A Truly Magical Reso

More than a collection of recipes, *A Kitchen Witch's Cookbook* weds modern ingredients and utensils with potent traditional preparations for a truly magical resource! Be it in the sacred space of the hearthstone—or anywhere cooking takes you—your experience can be both creative and consuming as you sample the helpful hints, superb resources, and fascinating lore in *A Kitchen Witch's Cookbook*.

From food preparation to mealtime presentation ... measurement conversions to alternative ingredients ... seasonal celebrations to magical correspondences ... associations to atmosphere ... *A Kitchen Witch's Cookbook* provides step-by-step instruction for transforming meals into manifestations of your magical life!

- Gain new insight into how creative personal magic can be—not only at festivals, but in everyday life!
- Use the recipes for every-day cooking
- Attain a refreshing historical perspective on the rich diversity and "flavor" of magic
- Create totally new approaches to magic with little expense

❦§§❦

About the Author

Patricia Telesco is a trustee for the Universal Federation of Pagans and a professional member of the Wiccan-Pagan Press Alliance. Her hobbies include Celtic illumination, antique restoration, historical costuming, writing and singing folk music, sufi dancing, historical herbalism studies, carving wood and soapstone, writing poetry, and participating in the Society for Creative Anachronism (a historical re-creation group). Many of these activities have extended themselves into her small mail-order business called Hourglass Creations. Her articles and poems have appeared in journals such as *Circle*, *The Unicorn*, *Moonstone*, (England), *Demeter's Emerald*, *Silver Chalice*, and *Llewellyn's New Worlds of Mind and Spirit*. She welcomes the opportunity to do workshops and lectures. Patricia lives in Buffalo, New York, with her husband, son, daughter, dog, and four cats.

To Write to the Author

If you wish to contact the author or would like more information about this book, please write to the author in care of Llewellyn Worldwide, and we will forward your request. Both the author and the publisher appreciate hearing from you and learning of your enjoyment of this book and how it has helped you. Llewellyn Worldwide cannot guarantee that every letter written to the author can be answered, but all will be forwarded. Please write to:

Patricia Telesco
℅ Llewellyn Worldwide
2143 Wooddale Drive
Woodbury, MN 55125-2989
Please enclose a self-addressed, stamped envelope or $1.00 to cover costs.
If outside the U.S.A., enclose international postal reply coupon.

A Kitchen Witch's Cookbook

Patricia Telesco

Llewellyn Publications
Woodbury, Minnesota

FIRST EDITION
Seventeenth Printing, 2014

Cover art: Eris Klein
Cover design: Anne Marie Garrison
Recipe editor: Andrea Casselton
Book design and layout: Jessica Thoreson
Illustrations on pages 5, 18, 44, 139, 140, 142, 146, 307, 308, 309 by Anne Marie Garrison

Llewellyn is a registered trademark of Llewellyn Worldwide Ltd.

Library of Congress Cataloging-in-Publication Data
Telesco, Patricia, 1960–
        A kitchen witch's cookbook / Patricia Telesco — 1st ed.
            p.   cm.
        Includes bibliographical references and index.
        ISBN 13: 978-1-56718-707-6
        ISBN 1-56718-707-2
        1. Cookery.   2. Cookery, International.   3. Food—Folklore.
        4. Magic.   5. Paganism.   I. Title.
        TX714.T45   1994
        641.5—dc20   94-23403
                                                                              CIP

Note: These recipes have not been tested by the publisher. Some contain unusual ingredients. Personal sensitivities to ingredients should be researched before using.

Llewellyn Publications
A Division of Llewellyn Worldwide Ltd.
2143 Woodedale Drive
Woodbury, MN 55125-2989

www.llewellyn.com

Printed in the United States of America

Dedicated to

Gaia and Her providence
As we reap of Her blessings, so should we live.
As we take from Her bounty, so should we give.

In memory of

Scott Cunningham, who truly knew
the meaning of the phrase "food for thought"
and who was one of the greatest gifts given by the
Gods to this magical generation. Peace.

Other Books by the Author
  A Victorian Grimoire
  The Urban Pagan
  Llewellyn's 1994 Magical Almanac
  The Victorian Flower Oracle
  Folkways
  A Witch's Brew

Table of Contents

Acknowledgements

The new year (1993) has just begun, and with it my time for personal reflection. The last year has seen momentous changes for me, from being quietly in my broom closet to having a book published. Until something like this happens, you have no idea how it will change your life. I have to say, though, that this process has been the most growth-oriented event I can remember, and one which I would not trade for the world.

Most writers today don't have the opportunity to retreat and contemplate. They have jobs, families, and other responsibilities that have to be juggled around computer time. During this balancing act many friends and family members volunteer their time to help with one thing or another. It is because of this that I know, over the next year or so until this book is printed, there will be many more people to be remembered and thanked than appear on this page. To those individuals, please know you are not forgotten. I would not have had the chance to live my dreams without you.

First, I would like to thank a very special group of people who I consider to be part of my extended family, but with whom I can't always spend the kind of time I would like: Rosemarian, Daggonelle and Kiefron, Robert and Rosianna, Yoshi, Bruno, Bill and Diane, Rob and Sunshine, and Zak and the "gang." Second is another cluster of people who seem to have endless energy for writing letters that come to my door bringing smiles, good wishes, and just generally help keep me going: Laura, Ken, Dorothy, Linda, Tim, and Steven.

A warm greeting and hug goes to Lone Wolf Circles for his sensitive notes and lovely art, which has often arrived to bring joy just when I needed it most. Your vision for the Earth is inspirational, as is your friendship. An additional welcome goes to Tim, a refreshing new addition to our extended "family."

To Karen J., with her gentle wisdom and constant support, who has on numerous occasions kept me from going off the deep end—my sincere thanks for never balking at those panic-stricken, confused phone calls. For someone I have never met, you are indeed family.

Perhaps most importantly, thanks to the readers who have taken time to mail me comments and ideas. Your efforts are appreciated. Without those letters authors never truly know if they are meeting needs and touching lives, which is what magical books should be about. Thank you for sharing your experiences with me, and don't stop writing!

Introduction

The bookshop has a thousand books, all colors, hues and tinges
And every cover is a door that turns on magic hinges.
— Nancy B. Turner

Practicality, simplicity, creativity, beauty, love—this is the complete charge of kitchen magic, and it is one that can change our way of living. If these words were ordered by the points of a pentagram, love would be the pinnacle—motivated by spiritual perspectives, shaped by modest talent, inspired by spiritual insight, and completed with a garland of loveliness. Herein the home, and specifically hearthside, becomes a creative haven for our spiritual path.

The kitchen is a room filled with the scents and sounds of kinship, family, good meals, and laughter. This comfortable, home-cooked energy makes the kitchen a special place in the hearts of individuals who proudly deem themselves "kitchen witches." These people enjoy both the benefits and challenges of creating a personally significant spiritual path that begins in, and centers around, their own living space. From this foundation, "pantry magic" can add an extra dimension to life with little fuss.

Feasts at the end of a ceremony, welcoming a baby, blessing a new home, a simple picnic with close friends—there are many occasions when we might want to prepare meals that reflect our spiritual vision. You could hunt through several cookbooks at the library or your own pantry to try and find a recipe which suits

the circumstances, but the average cookbook doesn't include that all-illusive mystical flair. It was just such an occurrence in my life which lead me to think about a totally magical cookbook.

There is nothing more frustrating than getting ready to celebrate a wonderful Pagan festival, only to discover you don't have a clue as to what to cook besides the traditional wine and cakes. Before many of us chose a magical lifestyle we probably rarely, if ever, considered cooking a spiritual pursuit. If we change our perspective to consider culinary skills as a creative art, even simple wine and cakes can be jazzed up a bit to become more meaningful to the occasion.

It is this imaginative flair, with a bit of practicality, that this book tries to present. Additionally, the ideas introduced in these pages give you an opportunity to break one rule that your mother taught you. In this context it is good, and even recommended, to play with your food!

Many of these foods are traditional during certain festivals or times of the year. The power of heritage makes these recipes usable in a magical construct, about the only difference being the attitude you have during preparation.

For example, you might notice that most people, without thinking, stir their soups or stews clockwise in preparation. No one mentions this fact because, well, it just happens! A rural superstition from the Ozark Mountains tells us that clockwise, the direction the sun moves through the sky, is the best way to mix any food to insure success of the meal and the health of those eating it. Many early cultures, specifically the Celts, performed their ceremonies following the same solar motion.

Such folklore is a token of the ancient world, when light was the emblem of safety, warmth, and the time to hunt. This information became a natural part of the human code. This is also illustrated in prayers before meals. Prayers before eating acknowledge Nature's gift, and release a supplication for divine favor so disease will not be allowed to enter the body. It is not surprising to discover that prayer at mealtime is present in a variety of cultural groups and settings. These are but two illustrations of how the chronicle of culinary arts has been entwined with the more general history of humankind.

Using rudimentary implements and procedures, early humans devised the basis of an art which would be forever influential. Hunting and gathering defined the earliest spells, ceremony, and community roles. Thus, developments and changes in this area lead to an expansion of cooking techniques as well. Procedures which proved successful were taught meticulously to children so that a kind of familial rite was born, with symbolic significance in each ingredient and movement. In this way, food appropriate to peasants or kings were dictated by etiquette, social contrivance, and superstition. This ritualistic aspect, and the memorization and careful guarding of family recipes, gives kitchen magic tremendous potential for modern practice.

With each era, just as fashion evolved, so to did the discriminating palate. Thankfully, diligent scribes collected many recipes for us to try today. If a food has importance that influences its spiritual function and characteristics, it is noted in the recipe. This bit of historical information has an important magical bonus. If your patron goddess is Athena, what better way to honor her than by placing a Greek dish on her altar? This is one example of how creative cooking will enhance your magic and fill your home with personally significant (and tasty) foods. If you are interested in more information on this topic, turn to Appendix B, which lists some of the items attributed to different divinities.

The pages of this book are filled primarily with seasonal, magical cooking suggestions for your home and circle. Wherever possible I have also included information on the symbolic significance of a recipe's ingredients. For more specific ideas, look to Appendix C, the texts listed in the Bibliography, or a book on magical food/spices. Scott Cunningham's *The Magic in Food* is a great starter kit for any magical kitchen.

You will notice that a number of recipes list uncommon ingredients. Trying to assemble a book like this without repeating the efforts of past writers encouraged me to seek out new concoctions to try. A good case in point are the foods made with flowers.

These types of dishes open a whole new world of taste sensations from a vitamin- and mineral-rich source: blossoms. Some readers might find themselves hesitant to try such dishes, but don't let your initial reaction inhibit you. Flowers were readily eaten from the time of the ancient Greeks up through the turn of the century. Their flavor is similar to that of many common herbs or vegetables, and they also lend a wonderful fragrance to the finished dish. Be careful when cooking with flowers, however; many people have allergic reactions to common flowers. It is also important that the flowers are free of pesticides, dyes, and other contaminants. If you should have difficulty finding local suppliers for flowers or other unusual ingredients in the recipes, a pantry resource listing is given in Appendix G. There are also non-flower alternatives given for each of these recipes.

You will find blank pages provided for your use at the end of each recipe chapter. This is, after all, a cookbook, so use it the way families of old did—to keep your special favorites all in one spot. Such documentation allows you to create a legacy of spiritual foods that can be shared with your friends, family, and children. It also insures that the power of hearth-fashioned, love-filled magical traditions will be available for future generations to enjoy.

Part One

The Magical Pantry
Companion

*The hours we pass with happy prospects in view are
more pleasant than those crowned with fruition.
In the first case we cook the dish to our own appetite;
in the last, it is cooked for us.*

— Oliver Goldsmith

Chapter One

Culinary Wizardry

Cooking Made Magical

To have ideas is to gather flowers;
to think is to weave them into garlands.

— Madam Seutchine

By picking up this book you have expressed a yearning to embark on a transformational journey that takes a pragmatic, realistic look at contemporary living with one small difference. Magic is no longer just for Circle; it is no longer the occasional book read or spell performed—herein, magic becomes part of everyday experiences and expressions, specifically those involving food.

Something else walks hand in hand with magic, and that is sensibility. The Wise Craft had its beginnings with simple people who lived in harmony with the land. Our ancestors understood that in creation, and in themselves, were all the clues and patterns to understanding the vastness of the universe, or at least their corner of it.

Pantry enchantments encourage this same temperament within us as contemporary magical people—to use our wits, wisdom, and wizardry toward the betterment of body, mind, and soul; not just for ourselves, but for everyone whose lives we touch. Yet discovering ways to accomplish this goal is not always an easy task.

While one magical practitioner may be aware of how to blend in visualization or any number of other metaphysical approaches with his or her culinary efforts, another may not. For that matter, anyone may find him or herself at a loss when trying to find just the right components or unique symbols, appropriate to his or her magic, to employ. That is where this section comes in.

The purpose of this section is to help us move the opulent legacy of culinary arts into our homes with a magical embellishment. Here, in our niche, each person's Path can become as much an intimate part of the hearthside experience as it was for our ancestors. If spiritual ideals are an intricate part of daily activities, then allowing those concepts to extend to things which give us physical nourishment is natural.

Some of you must be thinking that the Twinkie last night and soda this afternoon hardly constitute nourishment. However, if that Twinkie was charmed to bring a little sweetness into your life, and that soda empowered with "effervescent" energy, these "junk foods" enter into a whole new category—sympathetic magic! Of course, these emblems are not recommended for people who are dieting or have poor eating habits in the first place. Even so, there is magical potential here which can be tapped in an inspired moment.

While you aren't actually combining the ingredients for your snack in this case, you are "stirring up" metaphysical components for a specific result. The extra time taken to bless or charge the food becomes part of the mystical "cooking" process. While you work, your attitude toward the item changes its function from one of simply filling a craving to internalizing vibrant magic.

Since we all have to prepare food at one time or another, why not make the best possible use of that time in the kitchen? More than once I have stood in my kitchen saying, "Okay, what do I have that will work for this spell, and how do I put it all together?" For cooking magic, the answer is limited only by your imagination and by what's available in your kitchen.

You not only have the opportunity to permeate your ingredients with magical energy, but also to choose ingredients according to their symbolic significance. In many cases you can find a standard recipe that includes ingredients that are already personally meaningful.

A simple illustration of this principle is baking an apple pie for your Samhain observances. Apples have been part of Halloween celebrations for hundreds of years, and have frequently been used in divination. This fruit is also traditional at fall harvests, making it the perfect choice for an October feast. The recipe doesn't really need any revisions since magical herbalism tells us that cinnamon is symbolic of purification, clove is for rapport and awareness, ginger is for health, and allspice is for healing and love.

It is your creative eye which has captured the difference in this dessert. Now instead of just baking a pie, bless your ingredients first. As you weave the top of the crust gently in your hands, so too is your spell being spun. For decoration, place a specially shaped bit of crust on the center to further enhance your magical goals. When it moves from the countertop to the oven, you are warming the energy of your magic to golden brown, then serving it up to kindred spirits.

A common misunderstanding that often occurs with kitchen witchery is that it is somehow less potent than other "high" magics. Nothing could be further from the truth. Simplicity does not imply weakness, nor do fancy rituals ensure dynamic magical results. Neither approach is better or more powerful, they are simply different means for different individuals or circumstances. What is important is that your personal approach to magic makes sense to you.

When we find ourselves caught by the modern misconception that magic has to be complicated to be effective, it is a good time to remember that an ancient name for witches was "Cunning Folk." Our ancestors did not have the advantage of the local superstore for ingredients or tools, yet their magic was no less potent or meaningful. It is this spirit of mystical enterprise and fortitude that we can reclaim today through any number of traditional or created magical approaches.

The difficult part about explaining kitchen witchery to others is that there is no one precise way in which to approach it. There are no spells or rituals carved in stone to follow. The best any book can offer is a variety of suggestions from which you can build your own version of pantry magic. Like working with an erector set, each person's magical foundation and edifice will be as unique as the individual. Each person's approach to every part of the cooking process will change to reflect this marvelous diversity.

Kitchen magic is unique among religious and philosophical viewpoints in that it can augment any Path. It is not restricted to magic circles or study groups, and can be added to almost any tradition, like sprinkles on ice cream! Spiritual living is (thankfully) not like a diet. You don't have to give up one good thing to have the other. Ideal cooking magic allows you to "blend" the beliefs from many positive sources into a harmonious, delectable sustenance for the soul.

Sometimes there is the misconception that kitchen magic is limited to the feminine domain. This does not have to be the case. While patriarchal societies may have labeled cooking "women's work," there is certainly no reason why men can't find it equally beneficial and enjoyable. Some of the world's greatest chefs are men; they have as much capacity to be inspired by "supernatural" cooking as women do.

Many of the gods of antiquity tended or ruled over fire. Vulcan, the Roman god of the forge, is one example. On the other hand, the fireplace or oven is the womb of flame, a creative source. So, kitchen magics present the perfect opportunity for men to relax a little in a setting that is less associated with masculinity and more known for inventiveness. Here they (and women) can begin to reconnect with the hearth god/dess in themselves.

The Sacred Kitchen

Real holiness has love for its essence, humility for its clothing,
and the good of others as its employment.
— Nathaniel Emmons

Most homes, as late as the turn of the century, used the kitchen for far more than food preparation. It was also the nursery (since it was the warmest room of the house), a classroom (for children who could not go to school due to chores at home), and the place where family traditions were shared.

History has shown us that even in ancient times the kitchen assumed a place of honor in the home. The area for maintaining fire was usually the first to be built in a new house to ensure that all the functions of the hearth could continue unhindered. In rural communities, household fires were rarely allowed to die out because of the feeling that if the flame was gone, love in the home would soon follow. In other words, the hearth was the heart of any house.

The wonderful part about contemporary metaphysical practices is that they are slowly regaining the charm reflected in folk beliefs. While many people today may not have spacious pantries, and even fewer have wood-burning stoves to attend, that doesn't mean that the sanctity of the kitchen has to be lost. It can still be a warm, vital area where you can meet mundane needs and magical goals.

In much the same way as you approach your cooking in a different manner for magical results, move into your kitchen with a distinct attitude, knowing it is about to become a sacred space. It is good idea not to work on a dish when you are tired, angry, ill, or otherwise out-of-sorts. In these states it is easy for even the best-trained person in the world to accidentally allow negative energy to spill over into the ingredients. Essentially, cooking enchantments are no different than any other spiritual pursuit, except that you have edible results when you are finished. This means that a little care taken with mental attitudes will help the final product fill both body and spirit.

The mood of the kitchen changes when you are using it as a sacred space. One simple way to begin setting this spiritual tone is to clean your kitchen before starting. If there are any bits of clutter, extra dishes, food boxes, etc., that might distract you, move them out of sight. Put out clean towels, some candles, a bit of fresh potpourri, incense or flowers, and open a window (if possible). Refresh the entire area so that you are free to focus on your magical goals.

Next, just as you would for your personal Circles, consider how best to create a protective spiritual sphere. Lighting a candle to signal the beginning of your magic is one simple way, as is sprinkling your kitchen with a little tap water (like asperging). You can add a favorite invocation at this point, call on your hearth god or goddess (see Appendix A), or give a brief blessing. Find a system that works well considering your spacial constraints and situation, then use it as inspiration dictates.

This type of system will help set culinary wizardry apart from your normal routine, which is important. It will not, however, take too much extra time, which is vital in a world in which every second of our days is in demand. You don't want to feel rushed or pressured during magic, and cooking for ritual can be a relaxing experience. For best results, don't ignore those fabulous spur-of-the-moment impulses, and try to pick a day when a few extra minutes spent in the kitchen won't disrupt your schedule.

Choosing a Holiday

When ancient opinions and rules of life are taken away,
the loss cannot possibly be estimated;
from that moment we have no compass to govern us.
— Edmund Burke

While writing *The Urban Pagan*, I read a wonderful book called *Every Day's a Holiday* (see Bibliography). The author of this text had done an amazing amount of research into celebrations around the world to illustrate a festival for every day of the year. How exciting it was to consider each day of living as something special to celebrate!

I think that, as magical people, we could learn much from this idea. Let's look at an ordinary calendar and pretend for a moment that it's President's Day. This is an excellent time to do magic for our leaders. With this in mind, a kitchen witch might consider preparing a special cornbread in honor of the occasion. In the United States, corn has been an emblem of providence and good judgement, something all leaders could use. As the bread bakes, it rises with pleasing smells that carry the magic to its destination. You can then share the bread with your family, along with a prayer at dinner for peace and wisdom among world rulers.

Or how about an observance unique to your location? You may discover traditions in your area that have tremendous potential for a magical holiday, too. The kitchen witch might translate a founder's day celebration into a special excursion for the whole family, appropriately accented with a feast of popular local foods. Other types of festivals to watch for include ice cream socials, farmer's market days, art festivals, etc. In all instances, there are plenty of ways to add specially prepared foods to these occasions. This extra effort will keep a continuity, an annual framework, of edible magical energy in and around your home.

A third alternative is food theme holidays. There are many examples where specific foods, because they are a major means of income for the region or are significant somehow to local history and religious rites, became the reason for a celebration. Here are just a few of the food festivals I discovered (more holiday ideas may be found in Appendix D).

- **Feast of St. Charlemagne's Breakfast** (France): Early January. Commemorates St. Charlemagne's understanding of his daughter when she smuggled a lover into the castle. Instead of getting angry, he asked who the lad was over breakfast the next day and began making wedding preparations. This story gives our contemporary notions of breakfast in bed by way of apology historical foundation.

- **Bean Throwing Day** (Japan): Usually February 3 or 4. A day to toss away your bad luck and welcome good fortune. Try making a bean salad, then plant at least one of the beans in the earth near your home for providence all year.

- **Tibetan Butter Festival:** Mid-February. Huge images of Buddhist gods (often of wealth) are carved from solid butter, then displayed. As night falls, after prayers have been said, the butter is given to the people to insure prosperity in their homes. It is interesting to note that divination by butter lamps is popular in Tibet. In the modern home, one might prepare butter cakes or cookies topped with green frosting to improve financial well-being.

- **Maple Syrup Festival** (Vermont): Observed in April. Commemorated with maple sugar on snow and a variety of syrup candies and foods. To me, this festival is perfect to represent the sweet things in life.

- **Lobster Festival** (Nova Scotia): Celebrated in late July. Marks the end of the fishing season. This is similar to a harvest celebration except that it is observed by eating a bounty of fish fare, with all due gratitude to the gods and goddesses of the sea.

- **Dividing of the Cheese** (Switzerland): September. On this day, the herdsmen who have kept their cheese in cooperative cellars all year claim their goods and spend the day sampling and sharing. As the herdsmen ride away from the cellars, they ring bells and yodel. This would be a good time to share with someone in need.

- **Carrot Sundays** (Scotland): September. Carrots are gathered, tied into bunches, then taken to a church for the night where prayers and spells are chanted over them. The Scots believed this gathering brought protection to the home. They considered forked carrots to be the best luck. The next day, the carrots were returned to the people for consumption. This holiday could be celebrated in our homes with any number of carrot dishes, including glazed carrots, carrot cake, carrot puffs, etc. Magically, you could use the traits of safety and fortune, attributed to the carrot by the Scots, as central to your observance, or you could consider the old wives' tale of carrots helping eyesight for improved spiritual vision.

Using these food holidays as a sample, you might think about any notable foods in your region. In Buffalo, we have beef on weck (a salty roll) and chicken wings. Based on this, it might be fun to have a celebration called "Weck and Wing Ding." Beef is an emblem of prosperity and wings symbolize freedom, so the observance could be magically focused on loosening any financial bonds in our lives.

Occasions such as birthdays, anniversaries, graduations, welcoming a new pet, reunions, or commemorating a new job are all moments of importance in our lives. Why not make them even more memorable by preparing meaningful, magical meals to go with them? In other words, make a holiday out of it!

Of course, you can use food to honor a particular god or goddess. Setting aside special days to remember their power is one way of keeping us in touch with something greater than, yet part of, ourselves.

While we don't see this type of communal exhibitions as much in Western society (except at Yule), Eastern lands have had holidays for their god/desses for thousands of years. One such holiday in China, the Feast of the Kitchen God, continues to be observed to this day. During this festival sweet cakes are offered and wondrous feasts prepared in tribute to this robust guardian of the home.

If you would like to do something similar for your patron god/dess, or perhaps your hearth god/dess, consider what he or she represents. In which country did the deity originate? What animals or plants are sacred to him or her? Check Appendix B for more information on this. Combined with your knowledge and insight, this should make a good basis for preparing a magical feast in honor of your chosen deity.

Choosing a Menu

A good dinner sharpens the wit while it softens the heart.
— John Doran

Once you have chosen the date and reason for your food festival, the next step is to decide what will be served. Any meal, no matter the menu, is a good opportunity to blend in a little magic for health or prosperity. If your home has been particularly tense, how about a creamed vegetable soup (smooth texture) for harmony and grounding? Such efforts may or may not fall on one of your planned holidays. Even so, your extra energy and thoughtfulness will definitely make the meal distinctive and memorable. This way, your menu scheme can reflect not only your special days, but also your immediate needs and those of friends and loved ones.

Next to appraise are motifs. Each season or celebration has a distinctive magical flavor to it. This ambience should be considered in choosing your menu, such as was discussed earlier in making an apple pie in the fall to commemorate the harvest season or Samhain. Here, the pie might be only one part of a harvest dinner, or it could act as a thematic accent to any fall meal.

Another aid in menu planning is astrology. The ancient Babylonians were one group of people who believed deeply in the positive and negative aspects that each moment in time could bring, depending on celestial influences. In their search to understand Fate's hand on their lives, they invented various systems to mark time and its boons or banes, which set the tone for thousands of years to come. In Appendix F you will find some astrological associations, gathered from a combination of omen and sign guidebooks, to use as a general reference. Also, the magical significance associated with a particular day, hour, or phase of the moon is easily discovered through magical almanacs, moon sign books, and astrological calendars, several of which are available through Llewellyn Publications.

A simple illustration of this approach is choosing to make a food for inspiration during a waxing moon, the time of growing awareness and creativity. Thus, your seasonal composition is further augmented by those characteristics presented in the day, hour, moon sign, or sun sign of preparation. Better yet, this timing may present a topic for magical menu arrangements in and of itself!

Diversity enhances kitchen magic. The more choices you have, the easier it becomes to find something meaningful, easy to prepare, and tasty. Start by looking at your favorite meals and their ingredients. It may be that one of the feasts you fix regularly already has all the magical components you need for your goals. If not, consider how you can change the menu slightly to enhance that objective.

Remember, the whole meal does not have to center around your magical aspiration or celebration, nor does a menu need to have many different courses. One item thoughtfully put together will be just as effective and powerful as a lot of fuss. It might prove to be even more productive because you won't feel rushed. Kitchen magic encourages simplicity as much as bountiful lavishness, depending on the circumstances involved. If you have the time and want to go "all out," great! If not, just whip up a small, purposeful side dish, appetizer, or snack, and internalize your magic just the same.

Ingredients

Each particle of matter is an immensity; each leaf, a world.

— John Lavater

Ingredients are the savory spell components of cooking magic. As you blend in each item, you are also mingling subtle energies into a perfect balance for your spiritual goals. But unless you are well versed in folklore and magical herbalism, how do you know what significance the individual ingredients of recipes have?

Hands-on experience from day-to-day living can change the connotations of any ingredient. It is this interpretation that should always be favored in kitchen enchantments because it comes out of the "ritual" of your own life. So, when you look at the list of ingredients for any dish, consider what they mean to you, then improvise accordingly.

First, look to Appendix C in this book. This is an abbreviated list of foods, ingredients, and magical associations. The Bibliography lists a number of books on magical herbalism. Books which deal with the astrological cycles will frequently have suggestions for holiday feasts as well. Additionally, a variety of foods appear in classical myths and legends of the world, making these stories another good resource for kitchen witches. Beyond this, an important consideration for pantry magic is personal vision.

I honestly don't care if twenty authorities have claimed a specific item should be used in a particular way. If that ingredient has a different meaning for you, and that connotation is strong enough, that is how it should be employed in your magical cooking efforts.

After discovering a recipe that has all the right components for your magical goals, you may wish to bless each of the ingredients according to their specific role in your spellcraft. For some people this sanctification is accomplished through a little prayer; others might set each ingredient on their altar for a few moments and invoke the favor of their chosen kitchen deity; others might visualize a light of an appropriate color filling the ingredient (red for love is one example). Whichever method you choose, whether one of these or one of your own, depends on what makes the most sense to you and/or what you are comfortable with.

Additives and Variations

Nothing is pleasant that is not spiced with variety.
— Francis Bacon

Perhaps the most important element in any kitchen witchery, and one which can not be stressed too much, is the personal creative flair. Cooking lends itself to this enterprising spirit, which all too often lies dormant within us. True, experimentation does not always produce the best results. Conversely, trial and error is a marvelous teacher. The more we allow ourselves a little inventive freedom, the easier it will become to devise truly original, meaningful dishes.

I am one of those people who is always tempted to tinker with a recipe. Yet no matter how enticing it might seem, the first time you try a recipe it is good to stick to the given directions. This familiarizes you with a tested procedure that should be successful. On the other hand, if immediacy is not a factor and you can try some alternatives, by all means do so!

There are a number of herbs and tinctures which can be safely added to recipes without changing their flavor. With baked goods, a small pinch of cinnamon, ginger, or orange or lemon rind will rarely be noticeable in the final product. Similarly, spices such as oregano, basil, thyme, and tarragon can be added to soups or casseroles in small portions without changing the taste, yet can maintain the congruity of meaning. It isn't important how much you change a recipe. What is essential is that the final product is still edible, and the alterations you make are sensible in terms of your magical goals.

By way of illustration, one recipe may call for allspice, which is normally associated with love, but for whatever reason you would like to prepare this item for health instead. In this case, you can easily substitute cinnamon and ginger for purification and healing. Cinnamon and ginger are commonly recommended as replacements for allspice in cooking, and they are far better representations of your magical desires. Here are two more examples:

- You are making a basting sauce which calls for wine, but do not want any alcohol to interfere with your magical perceptions. Apple juice or cider can replace the wine; magically, apples are favorably attuned to the wise use of power.

- A cake recipe calls for buttermilk, which is maternal in nature, but the dessert itself is being prepared for spirituality. A good option would be to substitute an equal amount of yogurt, which is noted for healthy, devout energy.

More information on substitutions can be found in the table at the end of this book.

Tinctures are good additions to recipes because they have already "watered down" the herbal flavor, and they will not detract from the success of your creation. The generally accepted recipe for a tincture is four ounces of herb to eight ounces of alcohol and four ounces of water. Let the mixture steep for at least two weeks. This mixture should be shaken daily, then strained at the end of the period for best results. The extra benefit of tinctures is that they can be set, secured, in sunlight or moonbeams to become more fully charged with magical energy that enhances your goals.

Here, if you were preparing spaghetti for love, you might make a tincture of basil in which to boil the noodles, empowering that tincture through a waxing moon so that love can grow similarly full. In this situation, sunlight could also be employed with the basil water for heating up passion in a relationship which has become slightly cold.

Aesthetics of the Serving Surface

Genius begins great works; labor alone finishes them.
— Joseph Joubert

During the cooking and serving of the meal, there are many ways to prepare or arrange foods for visual impact. Potatoes can be cut, engraved, or if mashed, formed into all sorts of magical images. Cakes, doughs, and even meat loaf can contain symbolism.

In the Middle Ages, a creative food presentation was called *sotelity*, and it was considered a highly valued art. Marzipan might be colored and sculpted into a perfect model of the king's castle, a notable guest, or a beast of whimsy. Alternatively, a chicken might be gilded. Edible flower petals, candy pieces, toast and carved bread, cookies, cakes, and hundreds of other foods were carefully shaped by the royal cooks for the amusement of the lords and their guests alike.

Sweets were most highly favored, since most times a sotelity was served after the main meal, and the Medieval people were well known for their love of confectioneries. As time wore on, disguising dishes became a kind of contest between cooks, especially during the Elizabethan era. The truest test of the subtlety was the element of surprise, since it outwardly looked like something other than it actually was. It is from this artistic flair that we get the rhyme of "four and twenty blackbirds, baked in a pie."

This bit of mastery is something I feel has tremendous potential for pantry magic. While the medieval subtlety could be very complicated, yours can be much simpler. For love, carve out gingerbread people embracing or holding hands and let them cook together. Cut dollar signs into your next baked potato for providence. Shape a highly spiced bread dough into the rune of protection when you feel the need for improved magical safety in your home. The possibilities here are endless.

If your food isn't one which lends itself well to creative carving or molding, how about arranging it in a symbolic pattern? For joy, make a smiling mouth out of strawberries, or for strength shape your spinach into an upward pointing arrow (the rune of the warrior). In other words, get inventive and have a little fun while your magic fills both your hunger and your life! In Appendix F of this book you will find a list and illustrations of simple symbols to try in either preparation or serving.

Finally, as you present your goodies to guests don't forget the finishing touches. The Japanese are careful to assure that their meals are not only delectable, but also attractively displayed. I know of no magical home that doesn't have a little extra room for beauty within. So, take a moment to add a sprig of parsley, shape a bed of red cabbage, or toss on a few rose petals or other colorful splash. Allow the finished product to be as splendid in visual appeal as it is in magical potency!

Chapter Two

From Cauldron to Table

*C*heerful looks make every dish a feast.

— Phillip Massinger

Ambiance: that wonderful French word that describes atmosphere with a romantic flair. Ambiance is an important part of magic because it can literally make or break the overall effect you were hoping to achieve. Take the illustration of a quiet, sentimental evening topped off with champagne and heart-shaped cheesecake for dessert. You wouldn't think of serving this meal under florescent light bulbs or having harsh music as accompaniment. In this atmosphere, even an innocent telephone call could disrupt the magic you have created, so why not avoid the problem altogether with a little forethought?

Once you have informed friends not to drop in unannounced, unplugged your phone, and planned your meal, you can then turn your attention to the room itself and possible decorations. For the purpose of the illustration I'm using here, I would suggest that the temperature in the room be comfortably warm, and that clutter is moved out of sight where you won't be distracted by it. Fresh flowers are always inspirational, especially if chosen for their magical significance. Candles, a special basket of herbs for romance, a pink or red doily here and there—before you know it, the entire eating area has been transformed into a reflection of your magical goals.

For gatherings, it is best to have centerpieces that don't impede eye contact among your guests. Consider using special china or glasses to mark the occasion, and share the significance of any of these pieces with your companions during conversation. Also, weigh the comfort of your guests when setting the table. Give each person enough personal space to aid relaxation and enjoyment. Comfort encourages the energy of pantry enchantments to move easily among you and your visitors, accenting each moment with positive magic.

Another pleasant decorating option is party favors. The favors can reflect the theme of your magical goals, and it's especially nice if the mementos are also edible. At Yule, you might consider making gingerbread (joy and protection) ornaments for each guest; for a wedding, candied nuts (fertility) in a pretty lace container are perfectly fitting. After a particularly spicy meal for cleansing, a terrific favor is a little cache of mints, whose taste accents the refreshing wizardry of spicy foods. Here is an easy pattern for a sachet favor which can be filled with anything you please.

Lay a minimum of four 8" strips of gauze or netting in the pattern show below, one over the other. Next, place a heaping tablespoon of your filling in the center. Gently gather together all the ends of the fabric, holding them in one hand. If the sachet looks empty, add a little more filling, then tie the bundle together with decorative ribbon. Make one or two for each guest so they can take extras home with them.

The best part about using favors is that people like to preserve them as mementos of a special occasion. Thus, your kitchen magic has become portable, and will continue to bless your guests even after they leave your home.

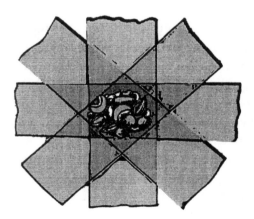

Other Embellishments

The beauty seen is partly in him who sees it.

— Christian Bovee

There are hundreds of ways to apply what are considered basic magical emblems to further enhance the significance of your meal. (Many of these are listed in greater detail with their general metaphysical associations in Appendix F.) This section is presented here just to give you a few extra ideas to work with when reading the recipes.

Colors

Through visualization or the color of the food itself, you can create the basis of a thematic meal. Since most menus include more than one dish, you can also use combinations of colors to imply magical energies. Red tomatoes served with a green spinach salad for growing fortitude, blue-tinted water and white potatoes with a touch of garlic for protection and health, and orange carrots with red bell peppers for empowered insight are all possible ideas.

Numbers

All recipes have measurements or yields that can be considered for symbolism, including the number of cups or teaspoons the recipe calls for, or even what size pan is suggested. You could also use symbolic numbers in deciding how many spoonfuls, slices, stalks, etc., to serve or eat. For instance, you might place 21 tablespoons of a favorite soup in each bowl to commemorate a loved one who recently went to Summerland, or eat five bites of carrot before embarking on a divinatory attempt to improve supernatural "sight." If these options don't seem possible with your recipe, you can always try to stir, test, or check the mixture a preset number of times for much the same results.

Aromatherapy

The tempting aromas of food, which often cause even the most reserved individuals to snitch a taste, can also become a vehicle for cooking magic. I remember the thrill of waking up to the smell of freshly baked bread whenever my grandmother would come to visit when I was a child. Unlike most days, I would not hesitate to rise or grumble about getting up, because of my tremendous expectation of the wonderful breakfast that awaited me.

The more savory and aromatic a magical meal is, the better (at least in my opinion). For individuals who have to be careful due to dietary restrictions, the best alternative I can offer is the idea of a simmering potpourri or incense of an appopriate scent.

In all cases, it is good to remember that fragrances are not just personal; the bouquets chosen will scent your home and excite the noses of your guests. One of the least disturbing and inconspicuous ways to consider including aromas as part of your enchanted atmosphere is also one of the most charming. A simple bouquet of flowers, leaves, and herbs, carefully chosen and placed somewhere in the room, brightens up the entire house. All the while, the petals spread their perfume on every breeze, and so too, your magic.

Chanting and Music

Spiritual canticles can help calm and center us as well as direct our energies. It is not hard to see where the verse about "Corn and grain ... all that falls shall rise again" in Starhawk's music could work wonders when you're baking bread. In this instance, the song not only encourages the bread to rise properly, but can instill growth-oriented power, too.

It should be noted that more "secular" songs can also be used in this context. On the radio, at the theater, and even in our cars, there are always the sounds of artists to fill our ears. Whether you want to sing it yourself or hum along with a recording, pieces such as "Just a Touch of Love" from *Sister Act* or "Gaston's Theme" from *Beauty and the Beast* have uplifting elements. The mantra-like quality evidenced also makes them perfect options for the kitchen witch. In the first instance, the music could be used to help the energy of a culinary effort stimulate caring feelings between two or more people; in the second, it might be used to bake up a more positive self-image and an improved sense of humor.

If you are uncomfortable with your voice, don't force yourself to sing; try humming instead. Just having these types of songs playing softly in the background while you prepare a dish can help the magical energy. Or, if you're alone and unfettered by an observant or critical eye, go ahead and sing anyway. Release the joy of music into your kitchen enchantments!

Visualization

Visualization for kitchen witches generally seems to fall into two categories: symbols and light. In the first, try to keep a token of your magical goals in your mind's eye throughout the preparation process. This token can be almost anything, but might be more effective if it were somehow related to your magical space. The list of pantry tools and their symbolism found in Appendix E might come in handy; here, you might envision a rolling pin with the word "consistency" on it for a magical crust to inspire improved control in your life.

For the second category, visualize a bright, clean light pouring from your hands and tools into whatever you bake. The color of this light can change to reflect your goals. Sometimes it helps to envision the light sparkling like glitter beneath a candle, or an ocean under a starry sky. Other people find it useful to see the light coming from above them like sunrays.

Kitchen Lore

The power of folklore lies in that it has been believed and followed by so many people for so long. It is this energy which gives superstitions at least some measure of truth, or possible applications for magic. To illustrate, the mother who always gave her children apples in the belief they "kept the doctor away" had sound judgement from practical medical standards. To take this notion one step further, apples, apple peels, apple flowers, or apple leaves and bark could all become useful components in cooking magic pertaining to health and wellbeing. The apple could be eaten to internalize its positive powers, dried apple peels could be placed in a pantry potpourri to encourage health, and the rest of the apple might be added to incense you create yourself. Here are some other examples:

- The saying "keep the home fires burning" comes from an English tradition in which the hearth fire symbolized the desire to cherish both family and friends. Today this can be accomplished through a long-burning candle (well protected or tended), or a light which is always left on to illuminate our love.

- Hearth fires were often used in divination. The housekeeper would watch what cinders jumped from the stove, then interpret their meanings according to common symbolism of the day. A contemporary version might be to inspect the cinders of a ritual fire for symbols that can be interpreted personally, or from the basis of a dream divination book.

- In parts of England, even as late as the turn of the century, a gift was often given to the threshold god before anyone entered the home. While the practice itself dates back to Rome where human sacrifices were made to preserve the household, a much less drastic version is to place a bit of wine or fresh egg on the entryway as an offering with a silent request to the household gods for their protection.

- In England, a hob is a type of house faerie who protects the kitchen. Leave a little offering of sweet milk and bread on your stove for the hobs to encourage their presence.

- The kitchen fires can not be lit so long as the sun's rays are touching the stove. This comes from the ancient belief that fire was stolen from the sun, and therefore cannot be ignited in its presence. Thus, when flame is not readily available, sunlight is an appropriate substitute for that active energy. One good application is in making sun tea for powerful discourse in relationships.

- It is not considered polite to poke or fuss around another person's hearth without asking permission. Such misconduct invokes the ire of the hearth god/dess present and brings ensuing trouble to the friendship.

- If you need a new broom for your kitchen, be sure not to buy one in May lest you "sweep the family away." This was the time of year in England when most broom salesmen would take their annual vacation. Brooms are still an emblem of cleansing and fertility for modern magicians.

- Bread, as one of the traditional staples of the world, should never be wasted. To do so tosses away your luck and prosperity with the garbage. Give your leftovers to the birds or make bread crumbs instead.

I also encourage you to think about your own family superstitions. These will have strong meanings for you because you probably follow them routinely without even thinking about it. Such oral traditions in any home should be cherished and shared with other family members, which enriches their power in the mystical realm.

Prayer Before Meals

Certain thoughts are prayers. There are moments when,
whatever be the attitude of the body, the soul is on its knees.

— Victor Hugo

The dictionary defines prayer as a devout supplication or earnest request. This means, at least in some form, that our meditations and invocations can also be considered prayers. With this perspective, it doesn't take long for the inventive kitchen witch to realize that praying over food or before meals is an appropriate addition to magical cuisine.

No matter how simple or fancy our words are, or to what divine presence we direct our expressions, this is an art which can, and should, find its way back into modern society. We have gotten so busy with our 9-to-5 world that sometimes we forget this small sign of gratitude. Here, we stop our rushing for a few moments to thank the Creator of the feast, the Originator of our world, and the Source of our magic.

Beyond thankfulness, there is the sanctification of our food. In metaphysical terms, this helps us to ingest only those ingredients that our bodies need, and release the rest. While this blessing does not excuse eating every sweet snack food we come across, I do feel it can transform the eating process from one of simply filling our hunger to an act of worship.

I have been gently reminded of the value of mealtime benedictions by my eight-year-old son, who insists we remember to pray before dinner. His phrases are few. "Goddess, thank you for this food 'cause I like it lots."

There is no lovelier accent to a metaphysically prepared feast than this final touch; the heartfelt words from a child to the Mother of us all, in joy for the goodness we have been given.

Putting It All Together

Life is not so short, but that there is always time for courtesy.

— Ralph Waldo Emerson

The Victorian lady felt that the true test of a loving, gracious home came into greatest focus when guests arrived. From the moment they entered the door to the time they left, their delight was the utmost priority. Joyful conversations, courteously served tea, a sideboard of scones or other finger foods, musical accom-

paniment, and a sumptuous meal would be balanced in harmony to provide pleasure and relaxation for all in attendance.

People have taken pride in their hospitality throughout history. In Arabia,
Bedouin guests would be welcome to stay for three days enjoying the full protection and lavishness of their hosts as long as they accepted the bond of salt
when they entered. This bond was a promise by host and guest that all were in
safe, considerate company.

Another example comes from Germany during the Middle Ages. If a trav-
eler came to a home, especially one of rank, and the family could not provide
adequate food or shelter for him or her, it was their social duty to escort the
guest elsewhere. Shelter could not always be found easily, and the patron of the
house might be searching for many hours before suitable shelter could be
obtained. Yet, such service was not done begrudgingly. It was simply their way
of offering a welcome which they perceived as being seemly for the guest.

Modern living does not always afford us the opportunity or funds to enter-
tain our guests (or ourselves) in the way we might like, but that doesn't mean
that the spirit of hospitality has to be lost to us. Cooking magic allows us to create a magical atmosphere around our homes that can be just as wonderful as
fancy, expensive preparations. Now the thoughtfulness of your efforts resonates
alongside the taste and aroma of good food.

Kitchen witches belong to the "keep it simple, it's the thought that counts"
school of magic. While you may not have much to share or feel a little awkward
with your cooking skills, pantry enchantments release a lot of the pressure to
perform great feats of culinary skill. Instead, they encourage you to be yourself,
get creative, and blend heaping amounts of magic into any dish, including instant
foods and package mixes. Even if dinner originated from Kraft, it is the love you
have placed in that macaroni and cheese which is really important.

Part Two

Blending the Magic:
The Recipes

*A dining room table with children's eager, hungry faces around it
ceases to be a mere dining room table and becomes an altar.*
— Simeon Strunsky

Chapter Three

Amuletic Appetizers and Snacks

$\mathcal{A}$ll who would win joy must share in it;
happiness was born a twin.

— Madam Seutchine

The original function of appetizers was to tempt the appetite for dinner. Today, however, appetizers can do far more. Besides being served before meals, they make good snacks or can be a first course by themselves. On the magical level, appetizers prepare the way for the spiritual theme that follows.

Bountiful Bagel Chips

The roundness of the bagel makes it a wonderful solar symbol (especially when baked), while the hole in the center is lunar, adding fruitfulness.

3 bagels (any flavor)	1 tablespoon ground sesame seeds
⅓ cup butter	1 tablespoon garlic powder

Preheat the oven to 350° F. Slice bagels into ¼-inch thick disks. In a small saucepan, melt the butter over low heat. Mix in the sesame seeds and garlic. Brush each bagel slice with the butter mixture. Place the slices on an ungreased cookie sheet. Bake for about 8 minutes; turn slices over and bake an additional 7 minutes until crunchy. Serve warm or cold. **Yield: About 6 dozen chips.**

Note: Buy day-old bagels from a local store or deli; they slice better and are usually cheaper. Choose your bagel type and spices according to magical goals, such as cinnamon bagels with ginger butter for prosperity.

Magical Associations: The Wheel of the Year, completion, fulfillment, fertility, potency.

Celebrations: New Year's, Solstice celebrations, graduation, the Great Rite.

Breadsticks of Abiding

⅓ cup parmesan cheese, grated	1 loaf frozen bread dough, thawed
⅓ cup romano cheese, grated	according to package directions
¼ teaspoon dried basil	1 egg, beaten

Preheat the oven to 400° F. Mix the cheeses and basil together in a small bowl. On a floured surface, roll or pat the bread dough into an 12-inch rectangle. Brush with egg. Sprinkle half the cheese mixture evenly over the dough. Fold the dough in half the long way; press the two halves firmly together. Brush with egg and sprinkle with the remaining cheese.

Cut bread dough into ½-inch strips. Pull the ends of each strip slightly to stretch. Braid the strips into hearts for love, an eternity sign for longevity, or any shape that suits your purpose. Place on a greased cookie sheet and bake for 15-20 minutes until golden brown. **Yield: 24 sticks.**

Variation: Consider the goals of your magic, then change the filling and shapes accordingly. For cleansing, use red pepper and garlic with dill; for harmony and health, brush with honey while baking.

Magical Associations: Enduring love or energy aimed toward a specific goal.

Celebrations: Being able to shape the bread allows you to make this into an appetizer for any occasion.

Toast Pieces for Canapés

10 slices bread, any flavor (if bread is hand-sliced, make slices ¼-inch thick)

Toast bread slices in a toaster set on medium darkness. If a toaster is unavailable; preheat the oven to 400° F. Place the bread slices on an ungreased cookie sheet; bake, turning occasionally, until lightly brown on both sides. Trim crist and cut toast into quarters. **Yield: 40 pieces; serves 10.**

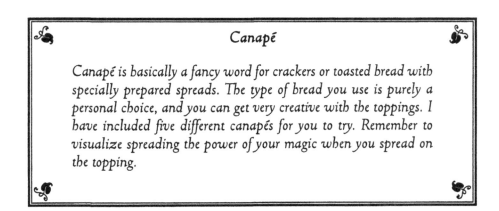

Canapé

Canapé is basically a fancy word for crackers or toasted bread with specially prepared spreads. The type of bread you use is purely a personal choice, and you can get very creative with the toppings. I have included five different canapés for you to try. Remember to visualize spreading the power of your magic when you spread on the topping.

Hot Cheese Canapé

Cheese has been prepared and eaten for at least 5,000 years; it was sometimes made into wedding cakes in ancient Greece. Curry is a spice of cleansing or for any fire-related festivals.

¼ lb. brie or other soft cheese, room temperature
¼ cup butter, room temperature
1 teaspoon oil

¼ cup sliced or chopped almonds
Dash of curry powder
Salt and pepper
Toast Pieces for Canapés (p. 29)

Using a fork, blend the brie, butter, and oil in a small mixing bowl until smooth. Mix in the almonds, curry powder, and salt and pepper. Spread over toast pieces. Garnish with a whole almond. **Yield: ¾ cup spread.**

Variation: For an extra-spicy flair, prepare the toast the same way you would prepare Bountiful Bagel Chips (page 28), substituting bread slices for bagel slices.

Magical Attributes: Earth and fire elements, goals, purification, energy, love.

Celebrations: Beltane, Summer Solstice, Valentine's Day.

Fish Canapé

Fish is associated with savior figures in several legends. It was the sacred food of divinities such as Poseidon, Inanna, and Venus. It is also connected with the astrological sign of Pisces and mystical sea creatures such as mermaids. The fiery aspects of this dish (horseradish or seafood sauce and pepper) give active energy to insightful magic, and lemon adds clarity.

1 cup crabmeat or other cooked, flaked fish
½ teaspoon horseradish or seafood sauce
Dash of lemon juice

Dash of pepper
1 tablespoon plain yogurt or salad dressing (approximately)
Toast Pieces for Canapés (p. 29)

In a small mixing bowl, mix together the crabmeat, horseradish, lemon juice, pepper, and just enough plain yogurt to make the mixture spreadable. Spread on toast pieces. **Yield: 1 cup spread.**

Magical Attributes: Plenty, guidance, endurance, awareness, fire and water elements, protection.

Celebrations: Candlemas, New Year's, Samhain, when the sun is in Pisces.

Olive Canapé

Olive oil was one of the main ingredients in most sacred anointing oils for both the body and hair. The biblical story of Noah indicates that the olive is a harbinger of hope. Green olives are a good color for growth and the triangle is a symbol of completion.

- 1 (8-oz.) package cream cheese, softened
- 1 tablespoon heavy cream
- 1 teaspoon minced onion

- 1 (8-oz.) jar green olives, drained and minced
- Dash of pepper
- Toast Pieces for Canapés (p. 29)

In a small bowl, using a fork, blend the cream cheese and heavy cream until smooth. Mix in the onion, olives, and pepper. Spread on toast pieces. Decorate with sliced olives in a triangular overlay. **Yield: 40 pieces.**

Variation: Substitute black olives to banish negativity. Use the extra-large size and stuff them with filling until they burst apart, symbolically breaking negative energy, then crush and spread them on crackers to "thin it out" even more.

Magical Attributes: Health, peace, spiritual goals, air element, protection.

Celebrations: Spring Equinox, birthdays, initiations.

Spinach Canapé

Picking spinach was one task for women living near feudal manor houses. In exchange, the family was granted a small plot on which to grow their own vegetables.

4 oz. processed soft cheese spread, any kind
1 cup sour cream
1 tablespoon mayonnaise
½ package dry vegetable soup mix
1 teaspoon onion powder
⅔ cup chopped, cooked, and drained spinach
Toast Pieces for Canapés (p. 29)

Place the cheese spread, sour cream, and mayonnaise in a medium-sized mixing bowl. Blend with a hand mixer at medium speed until smooth. Mix in the soup mix, onion powder, and spinach. Chill for 2 hours. Spread may be served hot or cold. To heat, place in a microwave on high for 2 minutes. Spread on toast pieces. This spread also makes a great vegetable dip. **Yield: 2¼ cups spread.**

Variation: Substituting raw or cooked broccoli for the spinach gives this spread a wonderful flavor.

Magical Attributes: Grounding, strength, congruity between diverse factions.

Celebrations: Earth Day, United Nations Day, as part of a forgiveness ritual.

Cucumber Canapé

English travelers in the early 1800s could expect to see street vendors selling cucumbers by the cartful. Cucumbers were a favorite treat among Scandinavian upper-class households, and were often served in brine.

1 cup plain yogurt
1 cup sour cream
½ package dry ranch dressing mix
¼ teaspoon dried dill weed
½ medium cucumber, peeled, seeded, and finely chopped
Toast Pieces for Canapés (p. 29)

Blend yogurt and sour cream in a medium-sized bowl until smooth. Mix in ranch dressing mix and dill; fold in cucumber. Chill for two hours. Spread on toast pieces. Decorate with a whole cucumber slice and a sprinkling of dried basil. Serve cold. **Yield: Enough dressing for 12 slices of bread (48 canapés).**

Variation: Try this using bean sprouts instead of the cucumber, and spring water sprouts as a garnish. This is for improved focus on health and the spiritual nature of self.

Magical Associations: Hindering lust, protection.

Celebrations: Royal Oak Day, Apple Blossom Day.

Crab-Bacon Bits

Some Asian cultures thought that the crab housed the reincarnated spirit of someone who had drowned. Crabs were raised in Crete as a food source; in Japan, crab shells were hung near the front entry of a house as a protective amulet.

- 12 oz. flaked crabmeat
- ⅓ cup seasoned bread crumbs
- ¼ teaspoon minced garlic
- 1 tablespoon fresh chives, or
  1 teaspoon dried chives
- 2 tablespoons white wine
- 1 teaspoon mustard
- 10 slices uncooked bacon,
  cut into thirds

Mix the crabmeat, bread crumbs, garlic, and chives in a medium-sized bowl. Mix the wine and mustard in a small bowl. Pour the wine mixture over the dry ingredients; stir until the mixture is slightly sticky. If the mixture is too dry, add more white wine. Chill for at least one hour.

Preheat the broiler after the crab mixture has been chilled. Form the mixture into 1-inch balls. Wrap each ball with a strip of bacon; secure the bacon with a toothpick. Place the balls on a broiler pan so that they do not touch. Place the broiler pan approximately 4 inches away from the heat element. Broil for about 15 minutes, turning occasionally, until the bacon is crispy and the crab-bacon bit has been thoroughly heated. **Yield: About 30 appetizers.**

Magical Associations: Protection from negative energy, health, improved magical insight, reincarnation, sea magic.

Celebrations: Festival of Brightness, Memorial Day, Old Dance, Ahes Festival, Samhain.

Egg Rolls (China, Japan)

Bean sprouts are found in many ancient Asian cookbooks. In China, over 150 forms of beans were developed as a quick-cooking, pleasant-textured food to help decrease fuel wood use.

2 tablespoons vegetable oil	½ cup minced chives
3 cups finely chopped chicken, fish, or beef	½ cup minced onion
3 cloves garlic, minced	¼ teaspoon ginger powder
½ lb. bean sprouts	1 package egg roll skins
1 cup water chestnuts, minced	1 egg, beaten
	Vegetable oil for frying

Heat the oil in a frying pan; add the chicken and garlic. Cook until the chicken turns white. Add the bean sprouts, water chestnuts, chives, onion, and ginger powder; stir-fry for 2 minutes or until the bean sprouts are tender. Remove from heat; drain any excess liquid from the pan.

Lay one egg roll skin on a flat surface; cover the remaining skins with a dampened towel to keep them from drying out. Place approximately ¼ cup of the mixture slightly below the center of the egg roll skin. Fold up the bottom corner so it covers the mixture; fold the left and right corners toward the center so that they overlap. Brush the top corner with egg and roll up the enclosed filling to seal. Repeat until you run out of filling.

Heat 2 inches of vegetable oil to 350° F. Deep fry 3 or 4 egg rolls at a time. Turn 2 or 3 times, until golden brown, about 3 or 4 minutes. Serve with mustard sauce, duck sauce, sweet 'n sour sauce, or soy sauce. **Yield: 12-14 eggrolls.**

Variation: Before preparing your egg rolls, marinate the meat or fish for a few hours. This can be done using ¼ cup soy sauce with a dash of ginger and garlic powder. Use ¼ cup red wine vinegar for a tangier taste. Remember to always marinate meat and fish in the refrigerator.

Magical Associations: Life, vitality, mystical awareness, conservation.

Celebrations: Birthday of Confucius, Russian Fair, Birthday of the Moon.

Fellowship Fruit Cup

Many philosophers of old thought that honey was useful for everything from aiding the natural healing process to helping in verbalizations! Fruit appears in hundreds of civilizations as an offering to the gods, or as an important element in local festivals. Yogurt's smooth consistency blends this energy together into a loving harmony. I like to serve fruit as an appetizer because it is light, refreshing, and a "happy" energy food. Add or delete fruits according to your personal preference.

2 ripe bananas, sliced
1 (8-oz.) can pineapple chunks
2 kiwi fruit, peeled and sliced
2 cups strawberries, sliced
2 ripe pears, peeled and sliced
2 navel oranges,
   peeled and sectioned
3 cups melon balls, any kind

1 (8-oz.) can mandarin oranges
2 apples, peeled and sliced
1 cup blueberries
2 cups grapes
¼ cup shredded coconut
16 oz. vanilla yogurt
3 tablespoons dark honey

Place the fruits together in a large bowl, blending in the yogurt and honey as you go. Allow to sit overnight in the fridge for fullest flavor. **Yield: 16 servings.**

Note: Fruits such as apples can be carved into shapes to reflect your magical goals.

Magical Associations: Spirituality, communication, friendship, health, pleasant gatherings, joyful occasions.

Celebrations: Spring Equinox, Aloha Week, Handsel Monday, Joan of Arc Day.

Fried Noodles (Siam)

Noodles, similar to rice, were a staple in many households, especially in the East where meats were scarce. In most cases, the meats in such dishes were only flavor accents, not the central ingredient.

1 lb. vermicelli	1 teaspoon soy sauce
2 cups olive oil	1½ teaspoons butter
1 clove garlic, minced	Dash of ginger
2 green onions, minced	Dash of pepper
1 lb. boned pork, cubed	Fresh chives for garnish
1 teaspoon lemon juice	

Cook the noodles in a large pan of boiling water for 15 minutes until tender. Drain; spread on paper towels on a flat surface. Warm oil in a deep skillet; add the garlic and green onions. Fry the noodles in small batches, making sure that they do not touch each other. Fry until lightly brown, turning twice; drain on fresh paper towels.

Pour off all but 4 tablespoons of the oil. Add the pork; cook for 5 minutes over medium heat. Add the lemon juice, soy sauce, butter, ginger, and pepper. Stir occasionally until the meat is thoroughly cooked. To serve, break up the noodles and spoon the meat mixture on top; sprinkle with chives.

Yield: 8 servings as an appetizer, 4 servings as a main dish.

Variation: For a richer flavor, reduce pork to ½ pound and add ¼ pound small salad shrimp and ¼ pound cubed chicken breast.

Magical Associations: Frugality, economy, conservation.

Celebrations: Monthly checkbook balancing, Earth Day, Asking Festival.

Stuffed Grape Leaves (Greek)

Any part of the grape plant is strongly associated with the "spirit" of wine, and thus with celebratory feelings. The Greeks call the cooked, stuffed leaves dolmas.

2	cups chicken stock	¼	cup currants
4	tablespoons butter	½	cup pine nuts
1	cup rice	¼	cup lemon juice
3	tablespoons olive oil	½	teaspoon paprika
1	clove garlic, minced	½	teaspoon allspice
2	lbs. lamb, finely chopped	½	teaspoon cinnamon
1½	cups minced onion	20-30	grape leaves, washed and dried

Preheat the oven to 350° F. Heat the chicken stock, butter, and rice to a boil in a medium-sized sauce pan over medium heat; stir occasionally. When boiling, cover and reduce heat. Simmer for 15 minutes. Remove from heat; fluff rice with a fork. Cover until needed.

Heat the olive oil and garlic in a large frying pan. Brown the lamb. Mix in the onions, currants, pine nuts, lemon juice, paprika, allspice, and cinnamon. Stir over medium heat for about 5 minutes. Add the rice.

Place about ¼ cup of the lamb mixture into each grape leaf. Vary the amount of the mixture according to the size of the grape leaf. Fold in the sides of the leaf and roll. Layer the stuffed leaves in a large, covered casserole dish. Bake for about 45 minutes. Serve hot. **Yield: 20-30 stuffed grape leaves.**

Magical Associations: Luxury, magic to honor Dionysus, prosperity, festivity.

Celebrations: April Fool's Day, Pardon of the Birds, Kermesse, Feast of Jupiter, before any magical brewing endeavors.

Muffin Munchies

Cheese, caraway, and pimento are all foods for adoration and fecundity. In some areas, caraway was valuable enough to be used as a form of currency.

1 package (6) english muffins	1 teaspoon salt
1 cup cottage cheese	2 tablespoons minced chives
2 tablespoons pimento, drained	12 slices cheese, any kind
3 tablespoons caraway seeds	

Preheat the oven to 450° F. Toast the muffins until golden brown. Mix the cottage cheese, pimento, caraway seeds, salt, and chives. Spread on the muffin halves. Place cheese slices on top of the muffins in a decorative or symbolic pattern. Place on an ungreased cookie sheet. Heat in the oven for about 8 minutes, until cheese is melted. **Yield: 12 servings.**

Magical Associations: Enjoyable sexual encounters, romance, love, prosperity.

Celebrations: The Great Rite, Valentine's or Sweetest Day, Coming of Age, anniversaries, handfastings, most spring observances.

Stuffed Mushrooms

Most often a food for the elite, mushrooms appear again and again in fanciful tales of fairy folk, making them a perfect edible when combined with thyme (a favorite wee folk home) for kinship with, or understanding of, the Fey.

- 2 tablespoons butter, divided
- 2 tablespoons diced green pepper
- ¼ cup chopped mushroom stems
- 2 tablespoons chopped onions
- ¾ cup bread crumbs
- 2 tablespoons cooked, crumbled bacon
- ¼ teaspoon dried thyme
- Salt
- Pepper
- ½ lb. large mushrooms, stems removed
- 12 small slices cheese (optional)

Preheat the oven to 350° F. Melt 1 tablespoon of the butter over low heat and sauté the mushroom stems, green pepper, and onions until tender. Mix in the bread crumbs, bacon, thyme, salt, and pepper. Spoon the mixture into the mushroom caps. Place the caps on a cookie sheet. Melt 1 tablespoon of the butter and drizzle over the stuffed caps. Top each with a cheese slice. Bake for 15 minutes. Serve hot. **Yield: About 1 dozen.**

Variation: Use large cherry tomatoes with the seeds scooped out instead of the mushroom caps. Substitute rosemary for thyme and add ⅓ cup grated cheddar cheese to the mixture before stuffing. This is for love.

Magical Associations: Strength, faerie magic, psychic ability.

Celebrations: May Day, Lammas, before divination efforts.

Nuts in Orange Glaze

Nuts were considered a food of the gods in Scandanavia, Greece, and Rome. The walnut's resemblance to the brain made it perfect for folk remedials dealing with the mind. Also, in Elizabethan times, sweet plates known as "comfits" were assembled. These often included nuts or nut pastes, such as marchpane (the medieval spelling of marzipan), to please the palate.

1 cup brown sugar	½ cup orange juice
¼ teaspoon grated orange peel	2 cups toasted pecans or walnuts

Heat the sugar, orange peel, and orange juice in a 2-quart saucepan over medium heat until the sugar is dissolved, stirring regularly. Stir in pecans and bring to a full boil. Reduce heat and simmer for 30 minutes until the nuts are coated and the liquid is evaporated. Spread the nuts on a greased cookie sheet to dry. **Yield: 2¼ cups.**

Magical Associations: Thought, concentration, mental productivity.

Celebrations: Graduations, Labor Day, St. Stephen Festival, Festival of Sarasvati.

Persian Pickles

Persians were fond of this simple method to pickle almost everything, including eggplants, onions, turnips, beets, and cucumbers. It was believed that pickles could help those suffering from obesity because of their sour taste. It was also in Persia that the idea of pickle cravings signalling a woman's pregnancy had its beginnings.

1 cup cauliflower, blanched	2 cloves garlic, minced
1 cup carrot sticks, blanched	2½ teaspoons salt
1 cup sliced celery	Dash of ginger
1½ cups cider vinegar	

Soak the vegetables in water overnight in the refrigerator; drain. Mix the vinegar, salt, garlic, and ginger in a small bowl. Place vegetables in a 2-quart jar; pour in the vinegar mix. Cover jar and marinate for 3 days in the refrigerator before serving. **Yield: 6 servings.**

Note: To blanch the vegetables, bring 2 quarts of water to a rapid boil. Immerse the vegetables and boil for 3 minutes. Remove from heat, drain, and cover with cold water.

Magical Associations: Weight loss, signs and warnings.

Celebrations: Spring, St. Swithin's Day, New Year's.

Rye Bread with Dill Dip

This is a personal favorite to make for any party or for dinner guests. It is light and full of flavor. The lettuce is a silent wish for providence for your guests. Rye bread is a food of friendship (as is breaking bread), and dill encourages the energy of kinship and love.

- 1 unsliced loaf dark rye bread
- 1 (8-oz.) package sour cream
- 1 pkg. dry ranch salad dressing mix
- 1 tablespoon dried dill weed
     Dash Worchestershire sauce
- 1½ teaspoon garlic powder
- 1 lettuce leaf (optional)
- 1½ teaspoon dried onion, or
- 1 tablespoon minced fresh onion

Blend the sour cream, mayonnaise, and Worcestershire sauce in a medium-sized bowl until smooth. Mix in the salad dressing mix, dill weed, garlic powder, and onion. Cover and chill at least one hour before serving; the flavor is best if refrigerated overnight.

To make the bread into a serving bowl for the dip, on the top of the loaf, cut in from the edge 1 inch all the way around the loaf. Remove the central portion by pulling out bite-size pieces until there is a hollow big enough to hold the dip. Fill the hollow with dip. (You may wish to line the hollow with a leaf of lettuce before adding the dip.) Eat by dipping the bread in the dip.

Yield: 4-6 servings.

Variation: Egg bread with a poppy-sesame seed dip may be used for fertility. To prepare the dip, substitute 1 tablespoon poppy seeds and 1 tablespoon sesame seeds for the dill weed.

Magical Associations: Kinship, peace, protection, prosperity, love.

Celebrations: This goes with just about any gathering!

Scones of Edinburgh (Scotland)

Scones are lightly sweet, bread-like treats which are good at almost any time of the day. Scones are a close relative to bannocks, a popular oat bread for ritual use, but unlike bannocks, which tend to be seasonal in appearance, scones are a major part of the Scottish diet. Treacle is a Scottish term for molasses.

1¾ cups self-rising flour	½ teaspoon ground ginger
3 teaspoons sugar (optional)	¼ cup butter
½ teaspoon cream of tartar	1 teaspoon treacle (molasses)
½ teaspoon cinnamon	¼ cup milk or buttermilk

Preheat the oven to 375° F. Mix together the flour, sugar, cream of tartar, cinnamon, and ginger. Cut in butter with a fork or pastry blender and combine the treacle with the milk. Stir in just enough milk to the flour mixture so that the dough leaves the sides of the bowl. Knead 10 times on a lightly floured board. Roll to ¾-inch thickness; cut in triangular shapes (or other configurations for different magical goals). Bake on a greased cookie sheet for about 10-13 minutes. **Yield: 1 dozen.**

Note: If you are not using self-rising flour, add ½ teaspoon salt and 2½ teaspoons baking soda to the flour mixture before adding the butter.

Variation: Try adding ½ cup fresh chopped strawberries and 2 teaspoons almond extract. To save time, beat into a cake-like batter (increase milk to 1 cup) and pour into a greased pie plate. Bake at 350° F for about 30 minutes until a test knife comes out clean and the top is golden brown. **Yield: 6-8 servings.**

Serving Suggestions: In the morning, add a little fresh jam. For lunch, add a slice of lunch meat. Enjoy them with tea in the afternoon, and at dinner use them for sopping up the last remnants of any sauce or gravy.

Magical Associations: Hearth and home energies, honoring Scottish deities.

Celebrations: Beltane, Hopi Winter Ceremony, Feast of the Kitchen God.

Spinach Pies (Mediterranean)

While the color and texture of spinach tend to relate to money, our contemporary character Popeye also gives us some symbolism to consider. Spinach was first eaten some time around the 1400s in Persia.

5 oz. frozen chopped spinach, thawed and drained	½ teaspoon dried basil
8 oz. feta cheese, crumbled	½ teaspoon dried oregano
1 medium tomato, diced	½ teaspoon minced garlic
1 medium onion, chopped and sautéed	6 turnover shells, cut in half
½ teaspoon dried dill weed	¼ cup butter, melted
	1 egg, beaten

Preheat oven according to turnover package directions. Mix the spinach, feta cheese, tomato, onion, dill weed, basil, oregano, and garlic in a medium-sized bowl. Beat the egg and butter in a small bowl. Brush the inside of each turnover shell with liberal amounts of the butter and egg mixture. Spoon the filling into the turnover shell; fold each corner so that they meet in the center, covering the filling. Brush the top of the turnover with butter. Bake according to the directions on the turnover package. **Yield: 1 dozen.**

Magical Associations: Strength, improving finances, love.

Celebrations: Feast of Banners, Old Dance, Labor Day, Feast of Jupiter, Feast of Mihr.

Sun Wheel Pickle Tray

In this recipe, the fiery spices and yellow food coloring combine with the layout to create the visual effect of sun energy radiating to your guests. Celery is associated with the element of fire and planetary aspect of Mercury. For an Elizabethan quality, add strawberries and rhubarb (fiery fruits) to the platter.

I small jar dill gherkins
I small jar pickled white onions
I (16-oz.) can large pitted
    black olives

I (8-oz.) bottle green olives
8 celery stalks

Cream Cheese Stuffing:
I (8-oz.) pkg. cream cheese, softened
2-3 drops yellow food coloring
¼ cup chopped fresh chives
½ teaspoon dried dill weed

½ teaspoon garlic powder
I teaspoon dried onion, or
    I tablespoon fresh minced onion

Blend together the cream cheese and the food coloring; the yellow food coloring will give it a slightly golden hue. Mix in the chives, dill weed, garlic powder, and onion. Stuff the celery stalks and black olives with the cream cheese mixture. Arrange the gherkins, white onions, olives, and celery on the tray as shown above. **Yield: 4-6 servings.**

Magical Associations: Fire magic, masculine attributes, increasing strength or leadership potential, conscious and logical thinking. Mild aphrodisiac qualities.

Celebrations: Summer Solstice, Candlemas, Beltane, Feast of Banners, Birthday of the Sun.

Super-Charged Snack Mix

Pretzels have been a popular food for fire festivals, and were often shaped specifically to honor the sun. Popcorn had its beginnings with the Native Americans, but corn itself is symbolic of divination, plenty, and vitality. Spices add protection and potency.

2 cups unsalted popped popcorn	⅓ cup butter
2 cups Chex cereal, any flavor	½ teaspoon salt
1 cup peanuts	1 teaspoon garlic powder
1 cup pretzel sticks	¼ teaspoon onion powder
1 cup small cheese crackers	¼ teaspoon Worcestershire sauce

Preheat the oven to 350° F. In a large bowl, mix the popcorn, cereal, peanuts, pretzels, and crackers; spread on a cookie sheet. In a small saucepan, melt the butter over low heat; stir in the salt, garlic powder, onion powder, and Worcestershire sauce. Pour over the dry ingredients until evenly coated. Bake 15 minutes. Cool. **Yield: About 7 cups.**

Magical Associations: Energy, protection, drastic change, stamina, devotion, prophecy.

Celebrations: Most spring festivals (especially Estore), Birthday of the Sun, Russian Fair.

Swedish Meatballs

The spices make this a fiery food, yet the sauce adds a certain balance for smooth transitions and personal transformation. Milk and cream are strongly associated with the Mother Goddess.

Meatballs:

1½ cups breadcrumbs
½ cup milk
1 lb. lean ground beef
3 eggs, beaten
1 medium onion, diced
1 teaspoon garlic powder
2 teaspoons salt
¼ teaspoon pepper
2 teaspoons nutmeg
1 teaspoon dry mustard
2-3 tablespoons butter

Sauce:

2 cups beef broth
2 tablespoons beef gravy
2 teaspoons tomato sauce
1½ cups sour cream
1 clove garlic, minced
Dash of Worcestershire sauce
Dash of soy sauce (optional)

Soak the breadcrumbs in the milk; mix with the ground beef. Add the eggs, onion, garlic powder, salt, pepper, nutmeg, and mustard; mix thoroughly. Shape into 40-50 bite size meatballs. Fry in the butter until browned on all sides.

Mix the beef broth, beef gravy, tomato sauce, sour cream, garlic, Worcestershire sauce, and soy sauce in a crockpot or 2-quart saucepan. Simmer until the sauce thickens. If necessary, add a little flour or cornstarch to give the sauce enough body to stick to the meatballs. Add cooked meatballs. Serve with toothpicks. **Yield: 40-50 meatballs.**

Note: For a lower fat alternative, bake the meat balls in the oven for about 20 minutes at 350° F instead of frying.

Variation: Vegetarian friends tell me that tofu can be ground and used in the same way as ground beef. In this form, the meatballs are aligned with moon magic, luck, and psychic insight.

Magical Associations: The meatballs can be shaped to suit any magical goal, but in round form they can be symbolic of cycles, movement, fertility, and masculine or solar energy.

Celebrations: Rites of succession, Feast of Banners, spring and summer festivals, fire festivals.

Turkey Temptation

Turkey was most probably made known to Europeans by the Spaniards on their journeys to Mexico around 1500. When this bird was brought back to Europe, it quickly became favored in Rome, and was known as the "wandering chicken."

1 lb. ground turkey	½ cup sour cream
1 teaspoon diced garlic	¼ cup minced chives
¼ cup chopped onions	Pepper
½ teaspoon lemon pepper	1 package small pitas
1 teaspoon lemon juice	1 cucumber, thinly sliced
2 crushed mint leaves	1 tomato, thinly sliced

Fry the ground turkey, garlic, onions, lemon pepper, lemon juice, and mint over low heat until the turkey is browned and the onions and garlic are tender. Drain fat; mix in sour cream, chives, and pepper. Cut the pitas in half; stuff with cucumber and tomato slices. Spoon in the meat mixture. **Yield: 6 servings.**

Variation: Chicken or any other lean meat may be substituted for the turkey in this recipe.

Magical Associations: Safe travel, adventure, weight loss.

Celebrations: Brendan's Voyage, before a vacation or new endeavor, Kermesse, many spring and summer rites.

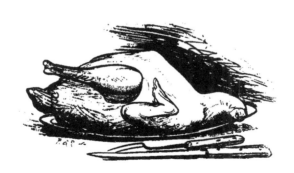

Vareneky (Russian)

This is a tasty type of dumpling that can be served as finger food. The filling can be changed to almost anything except processed fruit, which doesn't seem to cook as well. Potatoes have figured heavily in folk medicine, most specifically for banishing warts. As you prepare this dish, think of the dough as a protective coating for whatever magical goal you stuff inside, and heat to energize!

Dough:

2 cups flour	1 cup milk
¼ teaspoon salt	1 teaspoon oil
1 egg	

Filling:

½ lb. sharp cheese, shredded	¼ cup onion, sautéed
2 cups mashed potatoes	

Heat 3 quarts water and 1 tablespoon salt in a large pan. Mix flour, salt, egg, milk, and oil until it makes a slightly sticky dough. Roll out dough on a lightly floured board ¼" thick. Cut into circles using a floured cookie cutter or glass.

Combine cheese, mashed potatoes, and onion. Fill the center of the dough circles with 1-2 tablespoons of filling. Wet the edges of the dough; fold in half. Pinch the edges together so that the dough is completely sealed around the filling. Drop into the pot of simmering salted water; cook for 10 minutes. Remove and drain completely. Fry in butter until golden brown. Serve with side dishes of sour cream and melted butter for dipping. **Yield: 6-8 servings.**

Variation: Other good filling choices include cooked meats for prosperity, rice and mushrooms for patience and vision, or cabbage for protection. In Russia, sauerkraut and mushroom vareneki was a traditional Yule treat; in summer, fresh berries were used.

Magical Associations: Fertility, health, wish magic, empathy, protection.

Celebrations: Any spring observance, New Year's, Asking Festival.

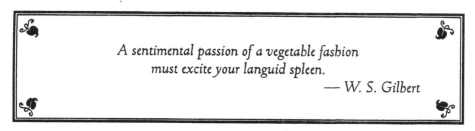

A sentimental passion of a vegetable fashion
must excite your languid spleen.

— W. S. Gilbert

Vegetable and Cracker Platter

A very easy appetizer is sometimes the most well received. Get as creative as you want with the basics suggested here, and serve after any magical gathering. Vegetables have the capacity to bring us back down to earth when flights of fancy threaten to carry us away. Cheese has a similar effect, so the combination used in this dish is an effective reinforcement of personal or spiritual groundwork.

Celery sticks	Cauliflower buds
Carrot sticks	Broccoli florets
Radishes	Mushrooms
Green pepper strips	Cheese slices
Chives	Whole wheat crackers

Dip:

1 (8-oz.) container sour cream	¼ teaspoon minced dry onion, or
1 cup mayonnaise	1 teaspoon minced fresh onion
¼ cup grated parmesan cheese	1 pkg. dry caesar salad dressing mix
¼ teaspoon garlic powder	

Blend the sour cream and mayonnaise in a medium-sized bowl until smooth. Stir in the parmesan cheese, garlic powder, onion, and salad dressing mix. Cover and chill for at least one hour. Arrange the vegetables on a tray either in a circle around the dip, or in any magical pattern with the dip on the side.

Yield: About 2 cups dip.

Magical Associations: Grounding, solid foundations, sensibility.

Celebrations: To ground the energy after any potent magical working, earth-related festivals, Labor Day.

Wings and Blue Cheese (Buffalo-style)

This recipe comes from Dynabara. I usually beg her to make chicken wings for me, so she graciously decided to give me the recipe so I would stop bugging her and make them myself! Chicken has long been considered a kind of healthy cure-all. Romans used to take chickens into battle with them to observe as harbingers of their fortune.

5 lbs. chicken wings	Oil for deep-fat frying

Dressing:

1 (8-oz.) container sour cream	2 tablespoons lemon juice
1 tablespoon Dijon mustard	½-1 cup crumbled blue cheese
1 cup mayonnaise	

Sauce:

1 tablespoon Tabasco sauce	2 teaspoons Worcestershire sauce
4 tablespoons butter	¼ teaspoon garlic powder
2 tablespoons tomato pureé	¼ teaspoon onion powder
2 teaspoons vinegar	

Blend the sour cream, mustard, mayonnaise, and lemon juice until smooth; stir in cheese. Cover and chill for at least one hour.

Heat at least 2 inches of oil to 365° F (hot but not smoking). Deep-fry the wings for 8-10 minutes until golden brown. Place in a large, heat-resistant bowl.

In a small saucepan, combine the Tabasco sauce, butter, tomato pureé, vinegar, Worcestershire sauce, garlic powder, and onion powder. Stir over low heat until sauce is hot but not boiling. Pour sauce over the wings, stirring to coat evenly. Do not let the wings soak in the sauce because they will get soggy. Remove and serve in another bowl. Have carrots and celery sticks on the side for munchies. The blue cheese dressing is a dip for both the veggies and wings. **Yield: 4 servings.**

Note: Instead of deep-fat frying the wings, bake them in an oven at 350° F for about 20 minutes; the exact time will depend on the size of the wings.

Variation: For vegetarians, instead of chicken wings, deep-fry cheese ravioli until golden brown and cover with sauce. Magically, this is for fiery love.

Magical Associations: Divination, fertility, protection, health.

Celebrations: Sealing the Frost, Samhain, Kamehameha Day, Sukkoth.

❦ Personal Recipes ❧

Personal Recipes

Chapter Four

Blessed Breadstuffs

If a soul be happily disposed, everthing
becomes capable of affording entertainment.

— Oliver Goldsmith

In observing my husband and friends who have a knack for creating luscious breads, I have noticed that their methods take the form of a painstakingly precise ritual. They will roll and sift, cuss a little if the dough is not "just right," check the oven several times before baking, and generally follow this procedure with every batch they make. I certainly can't blame them. In most instances the perfect recipe is something of a family heirloom, through which they invoke the power of lineage and history (knowingly or not).

Bread has been a source of life for many cultures, often marking the fine line between existence and death because of its inexpensive nature, and in certain forms, longevity (motzah, for example). It is estimated that ancient Egyptians had over 30 types of bread, and that they were the originators of leavening. Breads and grains in hundreds of forms have been offered to the gods, as shown by archeological remains in every area of the world. Even as recently as a century ago a couple may have been given a loaf of bread on their wedding day as a symbolic wish that they would never want for sustenance.

More important to the kitchen witch, however, is the idea of "breaking bread" with friends. This allows us to share what we have with those who are special to us. With this and the history of bread in mind, we begin to understand why it was considered so horrible to burn or throw away bread; emblematically, that meant destroying what we cherish most: health, kinship, and divine providence.

You will notice that many of these bread recipes do not have a country of origin. This is simply because bread is so universal that the origin of certain types can be difficult to trace.

Angelic Biscuits (From Fay's Kitchen)

1 envelope active dry yeast	4 teaspoons baking powder
½ cup warm water	2 teaspoons salt
(105° F-115° F)	¾ cup shortening
5 cups flour	1 teaspoon baking soda
3 tablespoons sugar	2 cups buttermilk

Dissolve the yeast in the warm water. Combine the flour, sugar, baking powder, and salt in a large bowl. Cut in shortening with a fork until the mixture resembles coarse meal. In a small bowl, mix the baking soda and buttermilk. Add the buttermilk and the yeast to the flour mixture; stir well. Chill dough, covered with a towel, in the refrigerator for 8 hours.

Knead dough 12 times on a lightly floured board; roll ½-inch thick. Cut into 2-inch rounds using a cookie cutter or a glass. Place on greased cookie sheets. Let rise in a warm spot for one hour. Preheat the oven to 400° F. Bake until golden, about 15 minutes. These biscuits are so light, they may float off your plate! **Yield: 24 biscuits.**

Variation: For love add 1 teaspoon anise, for a blessing add ¼ teaspoon cinnamon and ¼ teaspoon nutmeg, or for health and faithfulness add ¼ teaspoon orange extract.

Magical Attributes: Lifting cares, purity, beauty, divine love, safe travel, moon and Goddess magics.

Celebrations: Mother's Day, Candlemas, Pardon of the Birds, Feast of the Milky Way, Lammas.

Bannocks (Scotland)

Bannocks figured into the Celtic celebration of Beltane. Sometimes little charms were added when bannocks were prepared in cake form; each charm was symbolic of the recipient's good luck for the coming year.

2 cups hot milk	½ teaspoon baking soda
1½ cups instant oatmeal	1 tablespoon grated orange peel
1 egg	1 tablespoon chopped almonds

In a large bowl, pour the milk over the oatmeal; let sit for 10 minutes. Beat in the egg, baking soda, orange peel, and almonds. Consistency should be like a thick pancake batter. If the batter is too thin, add more oatmeal; if too thick, add a little milk. Heat griddle over a moderate flame; grease. Pour the batter onto the griddle; cook until bubbles form. Flip and cook the other side. Best served with butter and honey. **Yield: About 12 (2-inch) bannocks.**

Magical Attributes: Providence, good health, luck.

Celebrations: Beltane, harvest festivals, New Year's, Smell the Breeze Day, Thanksgiving Day breakfast, Fiesta of the Mother of Health.

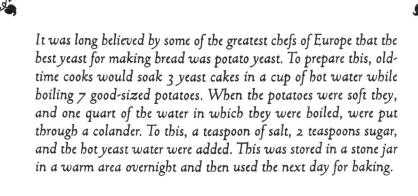

It was long believed by some of the greatest chefs of Europe that the best yeast for making bread was potato yeast. To prepare this, old-time cooks would soak 3 yeast cakes in a cup of hot water while boiling 7 good-sized potatoes. When the potatoes were soft they, and one quart of the water in which they were boiled, were put through a colander. To this, a teaspoon of salt, 2 teaspoons sugar, and the hot yeast water were added. This was stored in a stone jar in a warm area overnight and then used the next day for baking.

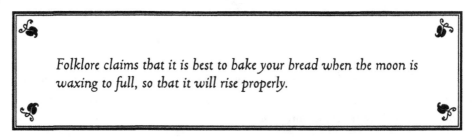

Folklore claims that it is best to bake your bread when the moon is waxing to full, so that it will rise properly.

Basic Bread Recipe (From Taka)

Many people feel that bread for ritual use should be broken by hand, not cut with a knife, to maintain the magical potency. In England, it was not until after 1440 that white bread was considered seemly for commoners. Before this time it was always a status symbol because the rich Romans would serve it to guests instead of darker breads.

6 cups all-purpose flour

2 envelopes active dry yeast

3 tablespoons sugar

1 tablespoon salt

2 tablespoons shortening

2 cups very warm water (120°F-130°F)

Mix 3 cups of the flour with the yeast, sugar, salt, and shortening in a large bowl; add the warm water. Beat with a mixer on low speed for 1 minute, scraping the sides regularly. Beat at medium speed for 1 minute. Mix in the remaining flour 1 cup at a time until the dough is easy to handle. Turn on to a lightly floured board; knead until dough is elastic, about 10 minutes. Place in a large greased bowl; turn over once. Cover bowl and leave in a warm place until the dough has doubled in size, about 45 minutes.

Divide dough in half; knead 5 or 6 times. Let the dough rest for 5 minutes. Shape into whatever form you have devised for your magical goal. Place in a greased loaf pan or on a cookie sheet. Brush lightly with butter. Allow to rise for 40 minutes.

Preheat the oven to 425° F. Bake for 25-30 minutes, until loaves are a deep golden brown and sound hollow when tapped. Baste with butter in the last five minutes of baking. Cool and enjoy. **Yield: 2 loaves.**

Magical Attributes: Life, providence, earth magic.

Celebrations: Lammas, harvest festivals, Binding of the Wreaths, Festival of Durga, Planting Feast.

Corn Bread with Honey

In the early days of the United States, these were often called journey cakes because they traveled well and provided good nourishment. For the portable form, however, the honey should be omitted.

1 ½ cups cornmeal
½ cup flour
2 teaspoons sugar
2 teaspoons baking powder
½ teaspoon baking soda
1 teaspoon salt

1 ½ cups buttermilk
¼ cup vegetable oil
2 eggs
2 tablespoons butter, melted
2 tablespoons honey
Dash of cinnamon (optional)

Preheat the oven to 425° F. Combine the cornmeal, flour, sugar, baking powder, baking soda, and salt in a medium-sized bowl. In a small bowl, beat the buttermilk, oil, and eggs. Add the buttermilk mixture to the dry ingredients; mix thoroughly. Pour the batter into a greased 8 x 8 x 2-inch baking dish. Bake for 25 minutes. While the cornbread bakes, blend the butter, honey, and cinnamon. Baste the top of the bread with the butter mixture during the final 5 minutes of baking. Serve hot or cold. **Yield: 12 good-sized pieces.**

Variation: I like to add ¼ teaspoon ginger and 1 teaspoon vanilla to this recipe for added flavor. Magically this is for success in love. In this instance, you may wish to bake the bread in small, heart-shaped pans often available at kitchen stores and serve the cakes for Valentine's Day.

Magical Attributes: Safe travel, abundance, cycles, reincarnation, divine blessing.

Celebrations: Ritual for the Dead, Festival of Brightness, Brendan's Voyage, St. Stephen's Festival, Thanksgiving.

Elder Flower Fritters (Medieval England)

It is bad luck to burn elder wood as the smoke draws evil intentions. It is believed that both the cross of Christ and hanging tree of Judas were made of elder. On a happier note, the French use elder flowers to pack apples. They claim this enhances the flavor.

1 egg	1 cup self-rising flour
1 teaspoon Rose Water (see below)	¼ teaspoon cinnamon
½ cup honey	2 cups elder flowers,
2 tablespoons brandy	freshly picked and cleaned

Mix the egg, rose water, honey, and brandy in a medium-sized bowl. Stir in the flour and cinnamon; the batter should resemble slightly thick pancake batter. If the batter is too thin, add a little more flour; if too thick, add a little more brandy. Fold in the elder flowers. Fry like pancakes or drop by the teaspoonful into a deep-fat-fryer until golden brown. Serve with a sprinkling of orange water and fresh lemon, or dip in fresh sweet cream. **Yield: about 2 dozen.**

Note: If you are not using self-rising flour, add 1 teaspoon baking powder and ½ teaspoon salt.

Variation: If you can't find elder flowers, substitute 1 cup finely diced apples and a hint of fresh mint for similar magical effects.

Magical Attributes: Protection from fairy folk, trust, beauty, energy for attraction, magical ambience.

Celebrations: May Day, Lammastide, Valentine's Day, Hallows.

Rose Water

Petals from two fresh roses

Place the petals and ¼-inch water in a small saucepan. Warm slowly until the petals turn translucent. Strain and use the liquid for cooking. Store in the refrigerator.

Variation: Any edible flower may be substituted for the rose petals.

Flat Bread (Italy)

Flat bread is another food that travels well. The symbolism of removing the air from this bread can be used as a magical process for removing negative energy from our lives.

3 cups flour	¼ cup olive oil
1 envelope active dry yeast	1 cup very warm water
2 teaspoons sugar	(120° F-130° F)
¼ teaspoon salt	3 tablespoons parmesan cheese

Mix one cup of the flour with the yeast, sugar, and salt in a medium-sized bowl; add the olive oil and water. Beat with a mixer on low speed for 1 minute, scraping the bowl frequently. Beat at medium speed for 1 minute. Stir in the remaining flour until the dough is easy to handle.

Turn dough onto a lightly floured surface; knead for 7 minutes. Place in a greased bowl; turn once. Let rise in a warm place for 1¼ hours.

Preheat the oven to 425° F. Punch down the dough and divide into the number of individual flat breads you desire. Form each portion into a ball; let rest 5 minutes. Roll each ball ½-inch thick. Place on greased cookie sheet. Cover and let rise for 15 minutes. Prick the surface with a fork; brush with olive oil and sprinkle with parmesan cheese. Bake until golden brown, about 13 minutes.
Yield: About 6 flat breads.

Variation: To further encourage protective energy, add red and yellow pepper slices, onions, and cheese over an olive oil, oregano, and garlic base (basically sauceless pizza).

Magical Attributes: Taking the "wind" out of gossip, decreasing undesired love, smoothing difficulties.

Celebrations: Forgiveness rituals, divorce, before court dates, Royal Oak Day, Yule, and for banishings.

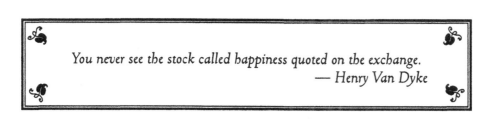

> *You never see the stock called happiness quoted on the exchange.*
> — Henry Van Dyke

Herb Bread with Cheese (From Morgana)

Morgana tells me this is her favorite bread to take along when visiting friends. Taking a small gift with you into a home helps appease the hearth God/dess and inspires hospitality.

1 teaspoon dried rosemary	1 teaspoon minced dry onion, or
½ teaspoon dried thyme	1 tablespoon minced fresh onion
½ teaspoon dried sage	1 cup shredded cheddar cheese
½ teaspoon dried parsley	Basic Bread recipe (p. 56)
½ teaspoon dried dill weed	

When preparing the Basic Bread recipe, add the rosemary, thyme, sage, parsley, dill weed, onion, and cheese to the dry ingredients. Complete the recipe as directed. Do not allow the dough to over-rise. Lower the baking temperature to 375° F, and bake for 35-40 minutes. **Yield: 2 loaves.**

Magical Attributes: This bread is perfect for people who want to become more closely attuned to herbal energies. It is also good for love, awareness, and general well-being.

Celebrations: Earth Day, Festival of Ishtar, Binding of the Wreaths, Festival of Durga, Planting Festival.

Marigold Buns (England, 1600s)

Marigolds were a favored flower of Margaret of Angouleme. These flowers, picked from her garden, were worn into battle by the Huguenot soldiers as a protective badge of honor. In Albertus Magnus' Boke of the Secrets (1560), he applauded this flower saying, "the vertue of this herbe is mervelous." According to Magnus, the flower is most potent for magic when gathered in August in the sign of Leo.

1 cup marigold petals	1 teaspoon baking powder
1 cup milk	¼ teaspoon salt
1 egg	6 tablespoon butter or lard
3½ cups flour	½ cup candied orange peel
½ cup sugar	1 cup raisins

Secure marigold petals in a small muslin or cheesecloth bag. In a small saucepan, heat the milk with the marigold "tea bag" over a low flame until very hot but not boiling. Cool. When milk is lukewarm, remove the marigold petals bag and beat in the egg.

Mix the flour, sugar, baking powder, and salt. Using a fork, cut in the butter. Stir in the orange peel and raisins. Add the milk to the flour mixture; beat for 10 minutes. Pour into a well-greased 12-cup muffin tin. Bake until golden brown, about 10 minutes. **Yield: 1 dozen.**

Variation: To replace the marigolds in this recipe, substitute a "sunny" fruit like dried pineapple or apricots for the raisins, and add ½ cup walnuts. These buns are very tasty with a trickle of honey over the top.

Magical Attributes: Sun magic, legal matters, psychic dreams, protection, integrity, abating jealousy.

Celebrations: Summer festivals, Memorial Day, Birthday of the Sun.

May Day Maple Hearth Bread

The maple used in this recipe commemorates the movement of sap through the trees, granting renewed life and vitality to every bough. Hazelnuts add improved productivity to this energy.

1 envelope active dry yeast	1 tablespoon baking powder
⅓ cup real maple syrup	½ teaspoon salt
¼ cup warm water (105°F-115°F)	1 cup coarsely ground hazelnuts
3 cups flour	¼ cup shortening
3 tablespoons packed brown sugar	

Dissolve the yeast and maple syrup in the water. Mix 1¼ cups of the flour with the brown sugar, baking powder, salt, and hazelnuts. Cut in shortening using a fork. Add the yeast mixture; stir. Slowly add the remaining flour until the dough is easy to handle. Turn onto a lightly floured surface; knead for 1 minute. Cover; let rise for 15 minutes. Form into a round or oval; place on a greased cookie sheet. Let rise for 30 minutes in a warm spot.

CONTINUED ON NEXT PAGE

Preheat the oven to 350° F. Slice the image of a heart or other appropriate symbol into the top of the bread. Bake for 30 minutes. The bread is done if the loaf sounds hollow when tapped. If desired, the loaf can be brushed with a little syrup and butter during the last 5 minutes of baking. This bread is very crusty. **Yield: 1 loaf.**

Variation: For an interesting flavor twist, add ½ teaspoon orange extract and 1 teaspoon grated orange rind. This encourages fidelity and health.

Magical Attributes: Health, money, love, joy, playful energy, fertility.

Celebrations: Beltane, most spring or fire festivals, April Fool's Day, any Friday.

Mercy Bread (Arabia)

The name for this bread comes from modern-day salesmen who take to the streets of Arabia with their golden baked flat bread as they shout "God is mericiful." Any scraps left afterward are given to animals and the poor, in thanks to Allah for his mercy. Sacred texts of the Arabic people claim that grain was sent by Allah from heaven, secured in seven handkerchiefs. In their language, bread literally translates to mean "life," and is honored as a Divine gift.

Basic Bread recipe (p. 56)

Preheat the oven to 475° F. Prepare the bread dough as instructed. Do not let dough rise. Divide into 12 pieces; form into balls. Roll on a lightly floured surface until ¼-thick. Place on well greased cookie sheets. Bake until slightly brown and raised, about 10 minutes. Brush the top of the finished bread with butter. Cover with a towel until cool. **Yield: 12 small loaves.**

Magical Attributes: Generosity, thankfulness, providence.

Celebrations: Any Arabic holiday, Thanksgiving, Asking Festival, any holiday that focuses on animals or community service.

Oat Apricot Muffins

In this recipe, the "earthy" oats give foundation to the gentle disposition of apricots for a dish to encourage the energy of reconciliation.

2 cups self-rising flour	¾ cup milk
2 cups oat bran	⅓ cup oil
1½ cups instant oatmeal	1 egg
½ cup sugar	½ cup chopped nuts
1 tablespoon baking powder	½ cup dried apricots

Preheat the oven to 400° F. Grease the bottom of 12 muffin cups. Mix the flour, oat bran, oatmeal, sugar, and baking powder in a medium-sized bowl. Beat milk, oil, and egg in a small bowl. Add the liquid ingredients to the flour mixture; stir until flour is moistened. Batter will be lumpy. Fill muffin cups about ¾ full. Bake until lightly browned, 15-20 minutes. Turn out to cool. **Yield: 12 muffins.**

Variation: In place of the apricots, substitute cheese for love, blueberries for joy, or apple bits for health.

Magical Attributes: Tranquility, peace, harmony, tolerance.

Celebrations: President's Day, Memorial Day, Sunning of Buddha, St. Joan of Arc Day, forgiveness rituals.

Picnic Loaf

Loaf Mass or Lammas was when the first ground grain was made into bread and offered to the gods in worship and thankfulness. The tomatoes in this dish also commemorate the harvest.

1 loaf unsliced Italian bread	¼ cup grated parmesan cheese
3-4 medium tomatoes, chopped and drained	1 tablespoon olive oil
¼ cup sliced black olives	¼ teaspoon basil
1 medium onion, finely chopped	¼ teaspoon thyme
½ green pepper, chopped	¼ teaspoon garlic
1 tablespoon minced chives	Dash of red wine vinegar
	Salt and pepper

Cut off one end of the bread. Carefully hollow out the loaf, tearing the bread out in small pieces. Mix the tomatoes, olives, onion, green pepper, chives, parmesan cheese, oil, basil, thyme, garlic, vinegar, salt, and pepper in a large bowl. Thoroughly mix in half the bread crumbs. If the mixture is soggy, add more bread crumbs. Spoon the mixture inside the hollowed-out loaf. Chill overnight. Slice to serve. The leftover crumbs can be retained for other baking needs or as a gift to the birds. **Yield: 4 servings.**

Variation: Substitute mozzarella cheese for parmesan and heat the loaf for a warm, stuffed pizza-like treat that is a food of peacefulness. For a more Greek flavor, substitute feta cheese for the parmesan and add ½ cup shredded lettuce and 1 cup cooked, marinated beef or lamb. Serve warm.

Magical Attributes: Kinship, awareness, festive spirits.

Celebrations: Any harvest or fire festival, especially Lammas.

Popovers of Prosperity

While the first major appearance of popovers came through a cookbook printed in 1910, there is evidence to suggest they had some form in the Middle Ages as well. In The Closet Opened, Sir Kenelm Digby describes making a "puff past" by blending a "gill of cold water, two egg whites, one egg yolk, a quart of flower; so rowl it up, but keep out of the Flower so much as will rowl it up" (1669).

Basic Popover:

2 eggs	1 cup milk
1 cup flour	½ teaspoon salt

Filling:

2 cups frozen chopped spinach, thawed	1 teaspoon minced fresh parsley
1 cup finely diced broccoli	1 tablespoon butter
	½ teaspoon salt

Preheat the oven to 450° F. Generously grease 6 custard dishes. Beat the eggs, flour, milk, and salt until smooth; do not overbeat. Fill the custard dishes half full. Bake 20 minutes. Decrease temperature to 350° F; bake an additional 20 minutes. Remove from custard dishes immediately.

While popovers are baking, prepare the filling. Place the spinach, broccoli, and parsley in a small saucepan with 1 inch of water. Cover; simmer for 3 minutes. Drain thoroughly. Add butter and salt. Split popovers. When filling each popover, visualize your pockets being likewise filled with cash! Serve immediately. **Yield: 6 popovers.**

Note: If you do not have custard cups, use muffin tins. The popovers will be smaller but just as good.

Variation: The best part about popovers is that you can change the fillings to reflect your magical goals. Use crushed raspberries for joy, apples for beauty, or honey butter for well-being.

Magical Attributes: Abundance, victory, success.

Celebrations: Birthdays, New Year's, weddings, many spring festivals.

Pretzels

The Roman name for pretzel translates into something closer to "bracelet." In Europe, pretzels are favored both for snacking or even as a breakfast treat with butter and other garnishes.

1 envelope dry yeast	2 teaspoons salt
1¼ cups warm water (105° F-115° F)	2 tablespoons melted butter
4 cups sifted flour	4 teaspoons baking soda
¼ teaspoon sugar	Coarse salt

Dissolve the yeast in the warm water; set aside for one hour. Mix the flour, sugar, and salt. Slowly mix in the yeast water until a stiff dough is formed. If the dough is too dry, add a little more water. Turn onto a lightly floured surface; knead for 10 minutes. Place in a large bowl; generously brush the dough with the melted butter. Let sit in a warm place until doubled in size, about 40 minutes.

Preheat the oven to 475° F. Bring 4 cups of water and the baking soda to a boil in a large pan. Cut off pieces of dough and form into whatever magical symbol you desire. Flatten the pretzel to half the desired finished thickness. Drop pretzels in the boiling water two at a time. Boil until they come to the surface, about 1 minute. Remove, drain, and place on a greased cookie sheet. Brush the top of the pretzels with melted butter and sprinkle with the coarse salt. Bake until golden brown, about 10 minutes. Thicker pretzels may require additional time. **Yield: 1 dozen large pretzels.**

Variation: Top the pretzels with powdered cheese for longevity or cinnamon sugar for energy. Both should be sprinkled on after applying the butter.

Magical Associations: Depends on how you shape it; especially good for cycles and connections.

Celebrations: Almost any!

Raspberry-Almond Coffee Cake

Almonds are commonly known today as wedding favors; in ancient times they were used abundantly in folk remedials, especially for sleep and headaches. The air-like qualities of this nut, when combined with the water element of raspberries, allows abundant love to sprinkle like rain, encourages health, and expresses joy.

¼ cup butter, softened
1 cup sugar
¼ cup butter, melted
1 egg
1 cup milk
2 teaspoons vanilla or
    almond extract

2 cups self-rising flour
½ cup brown sugar
4 oz. almond paste, chopped
⅓ cup slivered almonds
1 cup raspberries

Preheat the oven to 350° F and grease a 9 x 9 x 2-inch pan. In a medium-sized bowl, beat the softened butter, sugar, egg, milk, and extract at low speed until smooth. Add the flour; beat at low speed for 4 minutes. Spread half the batter in the baking dish. Mix the melted butter, brown sugar, almond paste, almonds, and raspberries. Sprinkle half the brown sugar mixture on top of the batter. Spread with the rest of the batter; top with the remaining brown sugar mixture. Bake until a knife inserted near the middle comes out clean, about 45 minutes. **Yield: 12 pieces.**

Note: If not using self-rising flour, add 3 teaspoons baking powder and 1 teaspoon salt.

Variation: Strawberries, blueberries, or cranberries may be substituted for the raspberries in this recipe. Cranberries may need additional sweetening.

Magical Attributes: Happiness, celebration, romance; well-being of body, mind, and spirit.

Celebrations: Handfasting or courtship rituals, Valentine's Day, Sweetest Day, anniversaries, May Day.

> *For the rose doth deserve the chiefest and most principall place among all flowers.*
>
> — John Gerald, The Herbal (1597)

Rose Pancakes (Arabia)

If a woman picked a rose on Midsummer's Eve and its color remained until the next month, she could be certain her lover was faithful. The scent of roses was once thought to cure insomnia and aid melancholy.

1 cup flour	1 egg
3 teaspoons baking powder	1 tablespoon honey
1 tablespoon sugar	1 tablespoon rose water (p. 58)
¼ teaspoon salt	2 tablespoons almond oil,
Dash of cinnamon (optional)	plus extra for the griddle

Mix the flour, baking powder, sugar, and salt in a medium-sized bowl. Beat the egg, honey, rose water, and oil in a small bowl. Stir egg mixture into the dry ingredients. Oil griddle; heat until a few drops of water bubble and dance on the surface. Fry until bubbles appear and the edges are dry; flip. Serve with butter and syrup, or strawberries and whipped cream. **Yield: 9 pancakes.**

Variations: For an international flair, try the following variations:

Belgian: Spoon applesauce in the center of the pancake, roll, and sprinkle with cinnamon.

Hungarian: Roll with chopped almonds and sweet cream in the center.

Irish: Add 1 cup mashed potatoes and 4 tablespoons corn syrup to the batter before frying.

Magical Attributes: Virtue, romance, faithfulness, improving spirits, aiding sleep.

Celebrations: Valentine's Day, handfastings or weddings, courtship ritual, Arabian holidays.

Rye Bread

Alignment with the planetary aspect of Venus and the element of Earth makes rye a carrier of strong energy for any loving pursuits. The cornmeal here serves to give foundation to the romance and caraway improves passion. Historically, rye bread was considered a peasant's food with origins near Rome.

3 envelopes active dry yeast	½ teaspoon salt
1½ cups warm water (105° F-115° F)	1 tablespoon caraway seeds
½ cup molasses	2 cups rye flour
2 tablespoon oil	¼ cup cornmeal
2½ cups white flour	1 egg white, beaten (optional)
¼ cup cocoa	

Dissolve the yeast in the warm water and molasses; let sit for 15 minutes. Add oil. Mix the white flour, cocoa, salt, and caraway seeds in a large bowl. Stir in the yeast water until moist. Mix in the rye flour a little at a time until the dough is easy to handle. Turn onto a surface lightly sprinkled with rye flour. Let sit for 20 minutes. Knead for 10 minutes. Place in a greased bowl; turn once. Let rise until doubled in size, about 1 hour.

Punch down; divide in half. Let rest 5 minutes; shape as desired. Place on a cookie sheet dusted with corn meal. Set loaves far enough apart so they will not touch after rising. Let rise for 45 minutes. Bake in a 375° F oven until loaves sound hollow when tapped, about 30 minutes. To give loaves a glossy finish, brush with the egg white during the last 10 minutes of baking. **Yield: 2 loaves.**

Note: For a great way to serve this bread to guests, try Rye Bread with Dill Dip (p. 41).

Magical Attributes: Protection, peace, kinship, money, love.

Celebrations: Handfasting, The Great Rite, reunions.

Soda Bread (Ireland)

Since this was commonly made on St. Patrick's Day, there is no reason not to invoke the "luck of the Irish" with this bread.

3½ cups unbleached flour	¼ cup butter
¼ cup sugar	1 cup currants
1 teaspoon salt	1½ cups buttermilk,
1 tablespoon baking powder	room temperature
1 teaspoon baking soda	1 egg
⅛ teaspoon cardamon	1 teaspoon grated lemon rind

Preheat the oven to 375° F. Mix the flour, sugar, salt, baking powder, baking soda, and cardamon in a large bowl. Cut in the butter using a fork or pastry cutter until fine crumbs are formed; stir in currants. In a small bowl beat the buttermilk, egg, and lemon rind. Stir the buttermilk mixture into the dry ingredients.

Knead the dough on a floured surface for 4 minutes. Divide into two pieces. Place in greased 8-inch pie pans; press dough until it reaches the edges. Cut an appropriate symbol in the top of the dough. Bake until golden brown, 35-40 minutes. Allow to cool for 5 hours before cutting. **Yield: 2 loaves.**

Magical Attributes: Love, happiness, simplicity, health, lunar magic (the lemon).

Celebrations: Most winter rituals, especially Candlemas, St. Patrick's Day, honoring Irish deities.

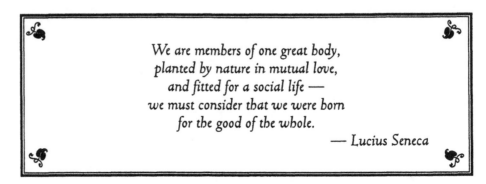

We are members of one great body,
planted by nature in mutual love,
and fitted for a social life —
we must consider that we were born
for the good of the whole.

— Lucius Seneca

Swedish Yule Bread

The beginning of the Christmas season in Sweden is named after a martyr who became the emblem of charity and kindness for the nation. Her name was Lucia, and she is claimed to have crossed icy lakes to bring food and beverage to the poor and bedridden. To this day, on December 13 a woman of each household is entrusted with the honor of taking these buns to family members in memory of Lucia's benevolence.

½ teaspoon saffron	1 egg
3 tablespoons hot water	4 cups sifted flour
2 envelopes active dry yeast	Combination of currants, candied
¼ cup warm water (105°F-115°F)	fruits, nuts, or raisins
¼ cup sugar, plus ¼ teaspoon	equaling 1½ cups
1 cup milk, scalded	2 tablespoons melted butter
⅓ cup butter	
1 teaspoon salt	

Soak the saffron in the hot water for 1½ hours. In a large bowl, dissolve the yeast and ¼ teaspoon sugar in the warm water. Mix the milk, remaining sugar, butter, and salt; cool. Add the egg, milk mixture, and saffron to the yeast; beat until smooth. Sprinkle the dried fruit with 2 teaspoons of the flour; mix until evenly coated. Mix the rest of the flour with the yeast mixture. Fold in the dried fruits. Turn onto a well floured surface; knead until smooth, about 12 minutes. Place in greased bowl, turn once. Let rise in warm place until doubled, about 1 hour.

Preheat the oven to 400° F. Knead dough twice. Divide into 24 pieces; form into small buns. Place on a greased cookie sheet. Cover; let rise until doubled, about 30 minutes. Bake for 10 minutes. Reduce heat to 350° F; bake for 10 minutes. Brush the tops of the buns with melted butter; bake an additional 5 minutes. **Yield: 2 dozen.**

Magical Attributes: Generosity, goodwill, empathy, service.

Celebrations: Thanksgiving, Asking Festival, Handsel Monday.

Tropical Bread

The banana is a sacred food to Hindus, and is often magically associated with male virility. This fruit was found by Magellan and his captains in the Phillipines, and was called a "long fig."

1½ cups sugar	½ teaspoon grated orange rind
½ cup butter, softened	2½ cups self-rising flour
2 eggs	⅔ cup chopped macadamia nuts
½ cup buttermilk	½ cup flaked coconut
3 large ripe bananas, mashed	½ cup crushed pineapple, drained
2 teaspoons vanilla extract	

Preheat the oven to 350° F. Grease a 9 x 5 x 3-inch loaf pan. Beat the sugar, butter, eggs, buttermilk, bananas, vanilla, and orange rind in a large bowl. Add the flour; stir until smooth. Fold in the nuts, coconut, and pineapple. Pour into the loaf pan. Bake until a knife inserted near the center comes out clean, about 60 minutes. Cool before serving. **Yield: 1 loaf.**

Note: If you are not using self-rising flour, add 3 teaspoons baking powder and 1 teaspoon salt.

Magical Attributes: Adding energy to any magical effort, joy, repose, safe travel, prosperity, and hospitality.

Celebrations: Brendan's Voyage, Aloha Week, during spiritual "retreats," traditional family holidays.

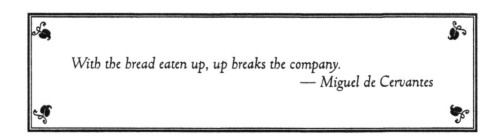

With the bread eaten up, up breaks the company.
— *Miguel de Cervantes*

Vasilopitta (Greek Bread of Fortune)

The 12 nuts on top of the bread symbolize the months of the year. Traditionally, coins would be wrapped in foil, then hidden inside this bread. The finders would be insured luck for the coming year, especially if the coin was carried as a talisman. If you try this, use a magical number of coins, such as three for symmetry. Please warn your guests about the tokens so no unexpected dental work is needed.

1 tablespoon ouzo (optional)	½ cup warm water (105° F-115° F)
½ teaspoon cinnamon	1 cup milk, hot
½ teaspoon anise seed	1 stick (½ cup) butter
¼ teaspoon ginger	7 cups unbleached flour
½ teaspoon grated orange peel	½ teaspoon salt
1 bay leaf	3 eggs
2 envelopes active dry yeast	12 whole nuts, any kind

Bring ½ cup water, ouzo, cinnamon, anise seed, ginger, orange peel, and bay leaf to a boil in a small saucepan; cool. Discard bay leaf. Dissolve the yeast in the warm water. Combine milk and butter in a medium-sized bowl; let sit until butter is melted. Add eggs, yeast, and spice water; beat until smooth. Mix flour, sugar, and salt in a large bowl. Slowly mix in liquid until dough is easy to handle. Turn onto a floured surface; knead for 20 minutes. Place in a greased bowl; turn once. Let rise for 5 hours.

Punch down dough; knead for 5 minutes. Let rest for 5 minutes. Shape into one large loaf or two smaller loaves; decorate with the nuts. Place on a greased cookie sheet. Cover; let rise for 2 hours. Preheat the oven to 350° F. Bake until loaf sounds hollow when tapped, about 60 minutes.

Yield: 1 large loaf or 2 small loaves.

Magical Attributes: Luck, prosperity.

Celebrations: New Year's, Chinese New Year, St. Patrick's Day, honoring Greek deities.

Zucchini-Cranberry Bread

Zucchini is associated with universal energies. This, combined with the safety provided by the cranberries (and their red color), makes this an excellent bread for personal warding, especially in the astral realms.

2 medium zucchini, shredded	3 cups whole wheat flour
2½ cups sugar	½ teaspoon baking powder
⅔ cup vegetable oil	2 teaspoons baking soda
¼ cup milk	1 teaspoon salt
4 eggs	1 cup cranberries, chopped
2 teaspoons vanilla	½ cup chopped nuts
2 teaspoons grated orange peel	½ cup raisins (optional)

Preheat the oven to 350° F. Grease the bottom of a 9 x 5 x 3-inch loaf pan. Beat the zucchini, sugar, oil, milk, eggs, vanilla, and orange peel in a large bowl using an electric mixer. Mix the flour, baking powder, baking soda, and salt in a small bowl. Stir the dry ingredients into the liquid. Fold in the cranberries, nuts, and raisins. Pour into the loaf pan. Bake until a knife inserted near the middle comes out clean, about 60 minutes. Cool before serving. **Yield: 1 loaf.**

Variation: On Samhain, substitute 1 (10 oz.) can pumpkin for the zucchini. For fresh, exciting love, replace both the zucchini and the cranberries with 3 cups finely chopped rhubarb.

Magical Attributes: Psychic and spiritual protection.

Celebrations: Any rite for the dead, Samhain, Festival of Brightness, Royal Oak Day, Riding the Marches.

❧ Personal Recipes ❧

Personal Recipes

Chapter Five

Brews from the Cauldron

W*ine is a noble, generous liquor, and we should be humbly thankful for it;*
but as I remember, water was made before it!

— John Eliot

Before the grand convenience of clean, home-delivered drinking water, people often drank a variety of hot or fermented beverages. Besides being a social contrivance and a sign of hospitality, the offering of wine at the table frequently was for health's sake. In the Middle Ages, various liquors were prepared specifically for their purported life-extending qualities.

The history of alcohol is as old as the discovery of fermentation. In Persia, there is a story of a king who found some odd-smelling grapes in a jar. This jar was stored away by the king, who thought it to be poison. Some time later, a distraught young servant happened on the bottle and thought to dispose of herself, so she ate the grapes, only to discover a change of attitude. When she reported her experience to the king, he decreed that jars of grapes were to be allowed to ferment for special guests.

Distillation was a whole other matter. While there is evidence to suggest that the Egyptians may have understood this process as early as AD 3, we don't see evidence of technological skills in brewing on the European continent until the mid 1600s, likely attributable to the Arabs. Homemade wines and meads were abundant, many of which were thought to have magical attributes depending on their ingredients. Indeed, wine and other beverages, like any valued food, were often offered as a gift to the gods.

In magic, there are many divine figures associated with "fruits of the vine," which may also apply to fruit juice, if you desire. These include Gestin (Sumerian), Osiris (Egypt), Dionysus (Greek), and Bacchus (Rome). Because many people in the Craft today prefer not to drink alcohol for a variety of reasons, I have also included a number of non-alcoholic beverages here. Remember, to make any wine or mead which is not fermented, eliminate the yeast and decrease the amount of honey or sugar to your personal taste. This will yield a spiced fruit juice which is pleasant cold or warm.

Non-alcoholic Beverages

Chamomile and Catmint (Catnip) Tea

While your cats may fight for a taste of this tea, both chamomile and catnip have been heralded by herbalists for their soothing qualities. The ancient Greeks called chamomile the apple of the earth. Herbal teas made from the spices on your kitchen shelves are one of the great gifts of pantry magic. Many spices have proven medicinal attributes which mystical energies can only enhance. Examples of this are chamomile-ginger tea to bring "peace" to the stomach, or anise-chamomile to calm a heated love.

- 1 teaspoon catmint leaves
- 1 teaspoon chamomile flower

Honey to taste

Mix catmint and chamomile. Place in a tea ball and steep in a cup of hot water until the desired strength is reached. If you do not have a tea ball, place the herbs in a cup and add hot water. Steep, then strain out the leaves. As you prepare the tea, envision pale blue light filling the cup with tranquility. **Yield: 1 cup.**

Magical Attributes: Calm during adversity, peacefulness, inner fortitude, sleep.

Celebrations: This is a good after-ritual tea to help encourage grounding. Healing rites, St. Joan of Arc Day, any Summerland ceremony.

Cherry Chill

Cherry trees were purportedly first found in the region of the Black Sea. As early as 8 BC, Assyrian herbalists regarded cherries as having some type of medicinal value with a pleasant aroma.

I (12-oz.) can frozen cherry juice
2 cups apricot nectar
I tablespoon sugar

½ teaspoon almond extract
Almonds and cherries (garnish)

Prepare the juice according to can directions. Mix the cherry juice, apricot nectar, sugar, and almond extract in a large bowl. Freeze until semi-solid. Transfer the mixture to a blender or food processor; mix until very smooth. Pour into glasses. Garnish with a whole almond and a cherry. **Yield: 6-8 servings.**

Variation: For the same energies, frozen strawberries, when thawed, yield a tasty juice which may be substituted for the cherry juice in this recipe.

Magical Attributes: Fertility, love magic, sexual balance, blending.

Celebrations: Spring festivals, Valentine's Day, rites for conception, Saturnalia.

Joy Juice

This was a special treat my mother used to make for me on hot summer days. It tastes terrific, and is healthy besides! The strawberry is sacred to Freya, and oranges were often used in Eastern lands as a symbol of felicity.

6 large strawberries
5 ice cubes, crushed
¼ navel orange, peeled

¼ cup orange juice
I teaspoon sugar

Place all the ingredients a blender; mix until smooth. Pour into a glass. Garnish with fresh berries. **Yield: I serving.**

Variation: Raspberries and blackberries are tasty substitutes for the strawberries.

Magical Attributes: Revitalization, health, happiness.

Celebrations: Good for summer observances, or any time you feel personal energies waning.

Love Potion #9

I recommend this juice as a reaffirmation or strengthening of love between two individuals who are already romantically involved. All the herbs and fruits of this recipe have been chosen for their long-standing association with love. The number of slices of each fruit is for various reasons. The lemon and orange represent the self in a partnership. The three berries are the trinity of you, your partner, and the togetherness as a couple. The total of six is for devotion.

2 cups apple juice	2 cups ginger ale
2 cups apricot nectar	6 raspberries
1 teaspoon vanilla	6 strawberries
⅛ teaspoon ginger	2 orange slices
⅛ teaspoon cinnamon	2 small slices lemon peel

Mix the apple juice, nectar, vanilla, ginger, and cinnamon. Slowly add the ginger ale; mix gently to retain the fizz. Pour into large glasses leaving at least one inch at the top. Add 3 raspberries, 3 strawberries, 1 orange slice, and 1 lemon slice. Interlock arms, look into each other's eyes, and drink to your love. **Yield: 2 servings.**

Variation: To bring harmony to a restless relationship, add 1 teaspoon lavender or violet water to your love potion before serving.

Magical Attributes: Vibrant romance, commitment, passion, understanding, wisdom.

Celebrations: Valentine's Day, handfastings, renewing vows, courtship rituals, the Great Rite.

Magic Melons

Melons were especially popular in Renaissance Europe, carefully carved for the feast table. The fruit was originally introduced from the East through Italy. In the Koran, one of the fruits which will be served to deserving Moslems on the day of judgment is melons.

4 cups diced, seeded watermelon	½ teaspoon vanilla
2 cups diced cantaloupe	6 ice cubes, crushed
2 cups diced honeydew melon	2 cups berry ginger ale
1 tablespoon sugar	

Mix the watermelon, cantaloupe, honeydew melon, sugar, vanilla, and ice in a blender or food processor until smooth, using the frappé setting. If that setting is unavailable, start at a slow speed and gradually increase. Just before serving, stir in the ginger ale. **Yield: Five 2-cup servings.**

Magical Attributes: Things coming into abundance, full moon magic, joy.

Celebrations: Birthday of the Moon, harvest festivals, Feast of the Milky Way.

Pineapple Mango Medley

Pineapples were brought to Europe by Columbus. They were originally called ananas *by natives; this fruit was quite rare due to its restricted growth areas.*

2 cups mango juice	½ medium banana
3 cups pineapple juice	Shredded coconut (garnish)
2 tablespoons brown sugar	

Mix the mango juice, pineapple juice, brown sugar, and banana in a blender on medium speed until smooth. Pour into tall glasses. Garnish with shredded coconut. **Yield: 4 servings.**

Magical Attributes: Welcome of old friends or loved ones, extending love.

Celebrations: Family or class reunions, almost any magical gathering with two or more people, Handsel Monday.

Pussy Willow Water (Persia)

In Persia, this water is used for making baklava. On Dingus Day, pussy willows may be used by maidens to try to secure a date and hopefully a husband. However, their application to the bottom of ill-behaved children also gives the pussy willow an air of authority.

2 cups pussy willow (musk of willow) flowers	¼ cup apple juice
4 cups tepid water	6 teaspoons sugar (approximately)

Soak flowers in the water until they become translucent and the water smells heavily of them (about 30 minutes). Strain; discard the flowers. Mix in the apple juice. Add sugar to taste. Chill. Serve over ice. **Yield: 4 servings.**

Variation: Any fruit with a feminine alignment may be substituted for the pussy willow. For wisdom in your corrections, decrease the apple juice to ¼ cup and add ¼ cup peach juice.

Magical Attributes: Young love, Goddess power, discipline, beauty.

Celebrations: May Day, Lady Day, Birthday of the Moon, Apple Blossom Day, Feast of Madonna, Festival of the Goddess of Mercy.

Rhubarb Punch (Early American)

Citrus fruits are excellent for protection because of their high acidic content, and aid health due to sizeable quantities of vitamin C.

4 cups chopped rhubarb	1 cup pineapple juice
1 stick cinnamon	¼ cup orange juice
¼ cup lemon juice	1½ cups sugar (approximately)

Simmer the rhubarb and cinnamon in 4 cups of water for 10 minutes. Strain; discard rhubarb and cinnamon stick. Mix in the lemon juice, pineapple juice, and orange juice. Add sugar to taste. Serve over crushed ice. **Yield: 4 servings.**

Magical Attributes: Protection, especially of health.

Celebrations: Smell the Breeze Day, Fiesta of the Mother of Health, New Year's.

Rose Geranium Punch (Arabia)

It is said that the prophet Mohammed brought this shrub-flower into existence when he threw his shirt over a mallow plant to dry. Under the rays of the sun, a marvelous transformation occurred to honor Mohammed; in the place of the mallow, a beautiful red flower bloomed. Yellow is for psychic insight while pink is for romance and health. Five is the number of awareness and mystical endeavors.

4 cups apple juice
1 cup sugar
6 rose geranium leaves
4 limes, sliced

5 drops yellow or pink food coloring
6 apple leaves (garnish)
Geranium petals (garnish)

Simmer the apple juice, sugar, and geranium leaves for 5 minutes. Add the limes; cool. Strain. Mix in food coloring. Serve over ice. Garnish with apple leaves and geranium petals. **Yield: 4 servings.**

Variation: Green food coloring may be used to encourage spiritual growth. If desired, 6 whole bay leaves or 3 peeled and diced citrons can be substituted for the geranium leaves.

Magical Attributes: Prophesy, well-being, insight, love, service to others.

Celebrations: Hallows, Sunning of Buddha, Sealing the Frost, Kamehameha Day, Handsel Monday, before initiation or any divination efforts.

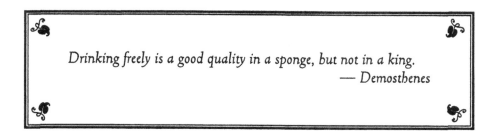

Drinking freely is a good quality in a sponge, but not in a king.
— *Demosthenes*

Soft Mead

For those who enjoy the taste of honey mead but prefer not to drink alcohol, this is a tasty solution. Honey wines have been known since the time of Hippocrates and were often used as a base for medicinal liquids to ease the bitterness of some folk remedies.

4 cups spring water	¼ teaspoon cinnamon
1 cup honey	1 lemon, sliced
½ teaspoon nutmeg	1 orange, sliced
½ teaspoon ginger	

Bring the water, honey, nutmeg, ginger, and cinnamon to a boil in a medium-sized saucepan. For the best flavor, use a stainless steel or non-metallic pan. Stir until honey is dissolved; the heaviness at the bottom of the pan should disappear. Use a wooden spoon to skim off the film that rises to the top until the surface is clear. Add the lemon and orange slices, squeezing as they are placed in the water. Cool completely; strain. Pour into a bottle. Store in the refrigerator.

Yield: About 4 cups.

Note: Some people find this recipe too sweet. Stir in the honey a little at a time until the mixture reaches the desired sweetness.

Variation: Substitute one cup of the following for the lemon: raspberries for happiness, strawberries to honor Freya, apple for health, peaches for long life, or pears for protection.

Magical Attributes: Pleasantries, revelry, health, love, prosperity.

Celebrations: Fall or spring festivals, weddings, an alternative to wine for children at Circles.

Switchel (Germany)

This was a favored drink for hayers and harvesters, helping to clear the nose and throat of pollen while quenching thirst.

8 cups water	½ cup white vinegar
1 cup real maple syrup	1 teaspoon ginger

Warm the water and maple syrup in a large saucepan over low heat; mix until fully blended. For the best flavor, use a stainless steel or non-metallic pan. The "heaviness" at the bottom of the pan should disappear. Pour into a glass pitcher. Add the vinegar and ginger; stir well. Chill. **Yield: About 9 cups.**

Variation: Honey or sugar may be substituted for the maple syrup. Sugar, however, is not the best choice if you are purifying your system.

Magical Attributes: Cleansing, purification, health, vital energies.

Celebrations: Before a ritual fast, Sukkoth, Birthday of Confucius, Ahes Festival, Beltane.

Tangerine Hospitality

In The Experienced English Housekeeper *(1769), instructions on the service of fruit were given with respect to each course of a meal. Tangerines and pineapple were both appropriate for desserts, if laid on china before one's guests.*

1 cup orange or vanilla yogurt	¼ cup tangerine juice concentrate
¼ cup water	1 tablespoon honey
¼ cup pineapple juice	Pineapple chunks (garnish)

Freeze the yogurt until firm. Break into small pieces. Process in a blender using the chop setting until smooth. Add the pineapple juice, concentrate, and honey; blend until smooth. Pour into tall glasses. Garnish with the pineapple pieces. **Yield: 2 servings.**

Magical Attributes: The spirit of hospitality, sociable courtesy.

Celebrations: Any time guests arrive, Aloha Week, New Year's.

Woodruff Cider (Germany)

Woodruff is a traditional May decoration, blooming abundantly at that time. In Germany it is called the master of the woods. It smells like a combination of biting cinnamon and vanilla. Woodruff has often been employed to protect against mischievous magic.

½ cup freshly picked
   woodruff flowers
4 cups warm apple cider
2 tablespoons sugar

½ cup water
4 orange slices (garnish)
4 cinnamon sticks (garnish)

Soak the woodruff in the cider for 30 minutes. Strain; discard the flowers. Mix in the sugar and water. Serve warm or cold. Garnish with an orange slice and a cinnamon stick. **Yield: 4 servings.**

Variation: To accentuate the energy of spring, substitute any other early-blooming, edible flower for the woodruff. One good choice is daisy petals. One vanilla bean can also be substituted for the woodruff flowers.

Magical Attributes: Victory, protection.

Celebrations: Any May observance, Royal Oak Day, Memorial Day, Patriot's Day, Old Dance Day.

Yogurt Bracer

1 cup fruit juice, any kind
1 (8 oz.) container
   plain or fruit yogurt

½ cup milk
Dash of nutmeg

Place all ingredients in a blender and mix well. Serve in tall glasses.
Yield: 2 servings.

Variation: Mix and match the fruit juice to the yogurt. Combine peach and apple for wisdom, or apricot and passion fruit for peace.

Magical Attributes: Stimulates personal and spiritual energy, excitement, inspiration.

Celebrations: Honoring any artistic ability, before initiation or meditation, preceding a special trip.

⋅§ *Alcoholic Beverages* §⋅

Broom Wine

Broom has a slightly almond-like flavor, and was originally used, bound to handles, for sweeping floors (as the name suggests). Pickled broom buds were served at the coronation of James II, and during the thirteenth century many people thought broom to be inhabited by a spirit who could divine how true love was. Be careful when using broom flowers; some are poisonous and can cause hallucinations.

1 package active dry yeast	2 oranges, sliced
¼ cup warm water (105° F-115° F)	6¾ cups sugar
1 lemon, sliced	1 gallon broom flowers

Dissolve the yeast in the warm water. Simmer the sugar, lemon, oranges, and 1 gallon of water in a large pan for 30 minutes. Cool to lukewarm. Place the broom flowers in a clean 2-gallon container. Pour the sugar mixture over the flowers. Stir in yeast. Cover; let sit in a warm space for three days. Strain; return liquid to the 2-gallon container. Cover; let sit for 10 days. Pour into sterilized bottles and cork. Age in a cool dark place for 6 months. **Yield: About 1 gallon.**

Variation: If broom flowers are not available, substitute 8 cups of crushed almonds.

Magical Attributes: Fertility, cleansing, neatness, humility.

Celebrations: May Day, Mother's Day, Feast of the Kitchen God, Handsel Monday, Sukkoth, Feast of the Madonna.

Daisy and Pansy Wine

The name "daisy" comes from two other words, "day's eye," because it opens its petals to greet the sun. The pansy is thought to be good for addled wits, and when consumed brings energy to encourage pleasant thoughts matched by consistent action. A wine similar to this one was popular in London in the nineteenth century.

1 gallon water, boiling	6¾ cups packed brown sugar
8 cups daisy blossoms	½ inch ginger root, bruised
8 cups pansy blossoms	½ package active dry yeast
1 lemon, sliced	¼ cup warm water (105° F-115° F)
2 oranges, sliced	

Pour the boiling water over the blossoms; let sit for 24 hours. Strain; discard the blossoms. Heat the remaining liquid, lemon, oranges, ginger root, and sugar in a large pan over a low flame. Stir occasionally until the sugar is completely dissolved. Cool to lukewarm. Dissolve the yeast in the warm water; let sit for 15 minutes. Pour yeast and sugar mixture into a 2 gallon container; mix. Do not cover. Let sit 3-4 days. Strain and pour into sterilized bottles. Loosely cork. Tighten corks after 2 months. Age 6 months to 1 year. When served, garnish with a few fresh flower petals. **Yield: About 1 gallon.**

Variation: Substitute dandelion blossoms for the pansy and daisy blossoms.

Magical Attributes: Innocence, love, divination, spring's refreshing energies, joy, simplicity, clear thoughts.

Celebrations: Coming of Age, Valentine's Day, May Day, any spring observance, courtship rituals.

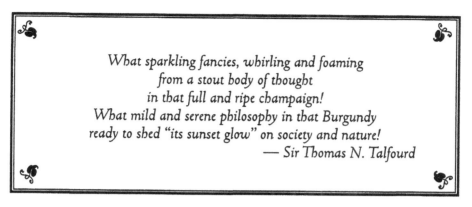

Kvass (Slavic)

Translated as meaning "leaven," this is a mild alcoholic drink traditionally made and shared at home. It is considered to be beneficial to one's health and is sometimes added to soup.

5 apples, sliced
2 cups honey
1 pound dark rye bread, sliced and toasted
1 pound barley or buckwheat meal
1 cup chopped meat
3 envelopes active dry yeast
¼ cup warm water (105° F-115° F)
1 cup raisins (approximately)

Bring 2 gallons water, the apples, and honey to a boil in a large pot. Remove from heat. Add the rye bread and barley meal. Let soak 3-4 hours. Strain; discard the fruit and bread. Pour liquid into a 3-gallon container. Dissolve the yeast in the warm water. Mix the yeast and chopped meat into the liquid. Cover with a clean cloth; let sit in a warm place for 6 hours. Strain. Drop 2-3 raisins at the bottom of each sterilized storage bottle. Pour liquid into bottles. Cork and store in a cool dry place. Age a minimum of 1-2 weeks. **Yield: About 2 gallons.**

Variation: Substitute 5 cups of raspberries for the apples. If you can not find barley or buckwheat meal, use another pound of rye bread.

Magical Attributes: Love, prosperity, peace, good will, energy of hearth and home, overcoming difficulty.

Celebrations: As a grain wine, Kvass is especially nice for harvest festivals (particularly Lammas).

Peach Pleasure

The peach comes to us from Persia. Peach wood and peach pits have been used for divination, protection, and longevity magic, especially in Eastern cultures.

2 cups chocolate milk	1 cup diced peaches
1 cup peach ice cream	2 tablespoon peach schnapps
1 teaspoon vanilla extract	1 teaspoon sugar (optional)

Place all ingredients in a blender; mix until smooth. **Yield: 2-3 servings.**

Variation: This beverage is just as tasty served without the alcohol. On a hot, sunny day serve over ice.

Magical Attributes: Wisdom, discernment, good judgement.

Celebrations: Birthday of Confuscious, Sunning of Buddha, Festival of Sarasvati, your birthday.

Raspberry-Tropical Rouser

All the fruits used in this drink are linked with the powers of change and the hand of fate in one's life. Brandy has been used in religious rites for offerings and as an incense component to carry prayers to deities.

1 liter brandy	1 cup crushed pineapple
1 cup orange sections	1 cup sugar
½ grapefruit, peeled and sectioned	1 teaspoon vanilla
2 cups raspberries	2 whole cloves
1 (12 oz.) can pears with juice	

Warm the brandy over low heat. Place oranges, grapefruit, raspberries, pears, pineapple, sugar, vanilla, and cloves in a large heat-resistant container. Mash lightly to release the fruit juices. Add brandy; make sure all fruit is submerged. Cover; let sit two weeks.

Strain through cheesecloth; gently squeeze fruit to release all the juices. Discard the fruit. Taste for sweetness. To sweeten, dissolve the desired amount of sugar in ¼ cup water and mix into brandy. To add tartness, mix in a little lemon or grapefruit juice. Cover; allow to age 2-3 months. **Yield: About 1 liter.**

Variation: Replace the brandy with rum for protection, or whiskey for health.

Magical Attributes: Mystical energy for transformation, luck.

Celebrations: New Year's, Samhain, graduations, Rites of Passage, Day of the Dryads, Feast of the Milky Way.

Restitution Refreshment (Russia)

Orange water is a symbol of fidelity and honest intention, while almond is for restorative energies. Cherry brandy, similar in form to this recipe, was used regularly by Empress Elizabeth Petrovna who adored it as much as love itself.

1 liter brandy	1½ cup almonds, crushed
1⅔ cup sugar	1½ teaspoon orange blossom water
2 cups cherry juice	(optional, see Rose Water, p. 58)
1 teaspoon cinnamon	1 teaspoon clove
¼ teaspoon lemon rind	

Mix all ingredients in a large non-metal container. Cover; let sit for 1 month. Strain. Pour into sterilized glass bottles. This may be served immediately but it is better when aged for 2 months. Prepare with your mind firmly focused on gentle restitution. **Yield: Over 2 liters.**

Variation: Substitute any other fruit juice that compliments the flavor of almonds for the cherry juice.

Magical Attributes: Healing or soothing any relationship.

Celebrations: Forgiveness rituals, renewing vows, Festival of Brightness, Feast of the Kitchen God, Handsel Monday.

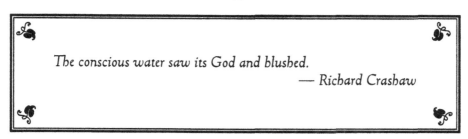

The conscious water saw its God and blushed.
— *Richard Crashaw*

Sima (Finland)

Raisins have often been eaten to try and provoke dream states. In this recipe, the citrus adds clarity and protection to your endeavor, while the yeast allows your vision to "rise."

¼ teaspoon yeast	1 cup white sugar
¼ cup warm water (105° F-115° F)	1 cup brown sugar
1 large lemon	6 quarts (24 cups) boiling water
2 medium oranges	1 cup raisins

Dissolve the yeast in the warm water. Peel the fruit; set aside the rind. Remove as much of the white membrane as possible from the fruit. Place the sliced fruit, fruit peels, white sugar, and brown sugar in a large heat-resistant container. Add the boiling water. Cool to lukewarm. Stir in the yeast mixture. Cover loosely; let sit overnight at room temperature to begin fermenting.

Strain; discard fruit and peels. Place 3 or 4 raisins in each sterilized storage bottle. Pour in liquid. Cap tightly. Leave at room temperature until the raisins float. After this, keep the sima cold until served. **Yield: About 1¾ gallons.**

Magical Attributes: Prophesy, visionary dreams, psychic awareness. Please note however, that since this is a fermented drink, only small portions should be consumed for their oracular effects.

Celebrations: Before a vision quest or other spiritual retreat, birthdays, Ahes Festival, Sealing the Frost, Kamehameha Day.

Wassail (England/Iceland)

Wassail, in old English and Icelandic, literally means a salute to good health and luck.

6 cups apple wine or dry red wine	2 teaspoons whole allspice
10 cups apple cider	2 large cinnamon sticks
½ cup packed brown sugar	2 oranges studded with
2 teaspoons whole cloves	whole cloves, sliced (garnish)

Place the wine, cider, sugar, cloves, allspice, and cinnamon in a large pan. Heat over a medium flame until it comes to a low boil. Cover; reduce heat and simmer for 20 minutes. Strain; discard spices. Serve in a punch bowl and garnish with slices of orange. **Yield: Sixteen 1-cup servings.**

Variation: For a non-alcoholic version, substitute apple cider for the red wine or use a different juice such as pineapple for protection and love.

Magical Attributes: Health, good fortune, fellowship, festivity, hospitality.

Celebrations: A traditional Yule and New Year's drink.

❧ For Goodness Sake ❧

The most popular use of medicinal elixirs was during the period of 1300-1500 when the Black Death, typhoid, and other sicknesses ravaged the people of Europe. During these years, alcoholic beverages such as brandy were used sparingly, and sold only for medicinal use. The warmth alcohol gave to the body was likened to life-giving energy. Such beverages, whether purposefully or by inference, also often carried magical symbolism that proved powerful to superstitious minds. Not all such cures had "spirits," but the role of distilled beverages in medicine is still remembered. While the romance of miracle cures has gone long out of style, we continue to find many cough syrups and other liquid elixirs which have an alcohol base because of its preservative, purifying quality. These recipes are offered, with some contemporary variations, to give you some ideas for beverages (with and without alcohol) which older books tout as being beneficial to health and general well-being. While such tonics honor history and in some cases have proven quite effective, they should never take the place of a visit to your physician or common sense. By the way, I have found several of them to be quite tasty for pleasure and ritual use as well.

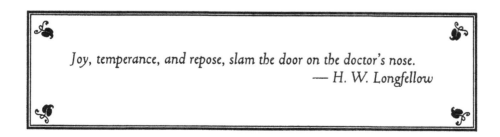

> *Joy, temperance, and repose, slam the door on the doctor's nose.*
> — *H. W. Longfellow*

Aqua Vitae (15th Century Germany)

Knights often drank this before battle, and it was frequently given to those thought dead in the hopes of reviving them. The basic idea here was that if this drink could not restore life, nothing short of divine intervention would. While the proportions of this recipe have been drastically reduced (the original recipe called for a base of 4 pounds or 2000 grams of brandy and equally large numbers of the other ingredients), the instructions are fairly simple.

¼ cup lavender
½ cup rose petals
1 teaspoon nutmeg
1 teaspoon cinnamon
1 teaspoon cloves
1 teaspoon sage
1 tablespoon ginger root, minced
1¾ cups sugar

2 cups raisins and figs
2 liters brandy
2 tablespoons molasses
2 tablespoons rose water (p. 58)
2 tablespoons elder flower water
(See Rose Water, p. 58)

Combine the lavender, rose petals, nutmeg, cinnamon, cloves, sage, ginger root, sugar, raisins, and figs in a 1-gallon non-metal container. Stir in the brandy, molasses, and flower waters. Cover; leave in the sun for 20 days. Strain; store in sterilized glass bottles. **Yield: About 2 liters.**

Variation: I have had reasonable success making an herbal water from this recipe by deleting the brandy and simmering the herbs for 2-3 hours over a low flame, then straining. This mixture should be refrigerated to keep it from fermenting.

Magical Attributes: Strength, vitality, recuperative powers, reincarnation, wits in spiritual battle.

Celebrations: Banishings, fire festivals, healing rites, Summerland rituals.

Cold and Flu Relief

The names of older liquors often reflected their expected medicinal or curative effects. This may have been called "stomach water" by a medieval healer, or "fitness tonic" by a turn of the century hawker.

2 pints (4 cups) brandy
1 cup honey
1 tablespoon orange rind
2 whole cloves
1 teaspoon cardamon
Juice of ½ lemon

1 tablespoon crushed
  peppermint leaf
1 teaspoon sage
2 teaspoons cinnamon
2-3 eucalyptus leaves

In a medium-sized saucepan, stir the brandy and honey over low heat until the honey is dissolved. Mix the orange rind, cloves, cardamon, lemon juice, peppermint leaf, sage, cinnamon, and eucalyptus leaves in a medium-sized container. Add the brandy. Cover; let sit for 2 weeks. Strain. Store in sterilized glass bottles. Take 1-2 teaspoons as needed. **Yield: 5 cups.**

Variation: For stomach problems, substitute chamomile for the eucalyptus leaves.

Magical Attributes: Improved finances, general emotional well-being.

Celebrations: Winter festivals during flu season for protection.

Psychic Physic

Each of the fruits and spices of this drink have been chosen for their psychic enhancement attributes. Additionally, peaches are for wisdom.

1 (12 oz.) can frozen non-alcoholic piña colada mix	¼ teaspoon anise extract
4½ cups cold water	¼ teaspoon peppermint extract
2 whole peaches, chopped	Rose petals (garnish)
¼ teaspoon cinnamon	Whole bay leaves (garnish)

Place the juice, water, peaches, cinnamon, and extract in a blender; mix until smooth. For a frostier drink, add 1 cup crushed ice. Garnish each glass with a rose petal and a bay leaf or serve over ice cubes with rose petals and bay leaves frozen inside. **Yield: About 8 cups.**

Magical Attributes: Awareness, psychic energy, divination, foresight, mystical insight, lunar energy.

Celebrations: Birthday of the Moon, Full Moon celebrations, before initiation or gaining a degree in a coven, Sunning of Buddha, Day of the Dryads.

Stomach Elixir (Scotland)

Beef tea and "hot toddy" are two drinks commonly offered to convalescents in Scotland, being both warm and soothing. Honey and whiskey have been used readily in folk medicine, and have been given both internally and externally.

4 oz. lean beef, shredded	1 shot whiskey
¼ teaspoon salt	1 teaspoon honey
1 cup water	

Slowly bring the beef, salt, and water to a boil in a small saucepan. Cover; simmer gently for 2 hours. Remove from heat; stir in the whisky and honey. Serve with plain hot toast. **Yield: 1 serving.**

Variation: For a plain beef tea, the whiskey and honey may be omitted in this recipe.

Magical Attributes: Rest, health, improved energy, fluency.

Celebrations: Old Dance, Pardon of the Birds, Birthday of Confucius, healing rites.

Transformation Tonic (Persia)

Fruit, usually a lemon, was sometimes used in the Middle Ages as a breath freshener and subtle hint for a kiss.

5 cups sugar	3 tablespoons dried mint
6 cups water	2-3 whole cloves
1 cup wine vinegar	2 lemons, sliced

In a large pan, bring the sugar and water to boil. Stir until the sugar is completely dissolved. Mix in the vinegar, mint, clove, and lemons. Simmer for 20 minutes. Strain and serve chilled. Garnish with a fresh mint leaf or a whole almond to encourage self-improving energies. **Yield: About 2 quarts.**

Variation: This will help settle the stomach if the vinegar is omitted.

Magical Attributes: Purification, health, joy, love, composed awareness, personal change.

Celebrations: Before any ritual for improved perception, initiations, marriage, and other drastic lifestyle changes.

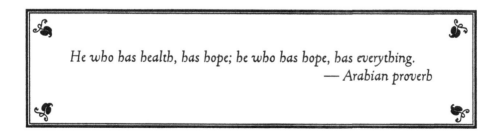

He who has health, has hope; he who has hope, has everything.
— Arabian proverb

Travel Drops (Medieval Spain)

The savory and vanilla in this drink is thought to lift the spirits of one who feels blue. Sage is the key ingredient to many early curatives, being considered a panacea.

- ¼ cup chamomile
- 2 sprigs fresh savory
- 2 whole cloves
- ¼ teaspoon nutmeg
- ¼ teaspoon marjoram
- ½ vanilla bean
- 1 liter brandy

- ¼ cup arnica
- 3 lemon balm leaves
- 3 teaspoon anise seed
- ¼ teaspoon cinnamon
- ¼ teaspoon sage
- 1 cup sugar

Combine all ingredients in ½-gallon non-metal container. Let sit in a sunny area for 40 days. Strain. Taste for sweetness and add sugar to taste. Store in sterilized glass bottles. **Yield: About 1 liter.**

Magical Attributes: Ridding melancholy, safe journeys, repose.

Celebrations: Any time you have cabin fever, Brendan's Voyage, before traveling to rituals, while on vacation.

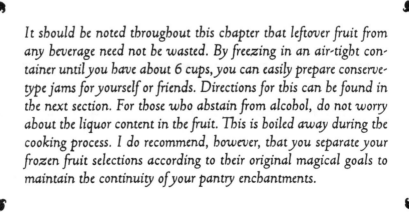

It should be noted throughout this chapter that leftover fruit from any beverage need not be wasted. By freezing in an air-tight container until you have about 6 cups, you can easily prepare conserve-type jams for yourself or friends. Directions for this can be found in the next section. For those who abstain from alcohol, do not worry about the liquor content in the fruit. This is boiled away during the cooking process. I do recommend, however, that you separate your frozen fruit selections according to their original magical goals to maintain the continuity of your pantry enchantments.

Personal Recipes

❧ Personal Recipes ❧

Chapter Six

Canning Comfort and Preserving the Peace

Let prudence always attend your pleasures; it is the way to enjoy the sweets of them, and not be afraid of the consequences.

— Jeremy Collier

The primary objective for canning and preserving has been, until recent years, as a means to supplement provisions during times of scarcity. Today, we preserve as a way of using extra food. For magical people this affords the wonderful option of "storing" our magically created foods, and their potency, for a rainy day! There will be creations such as "Mary's Strawberry Syrup for Love," "Aunt Jane's Protective Pickles" (heavy on the garlic), and "Sight Sauce" neatly lined up alongside other foods. The added bonus here is that your magical energy is already prepared and ready for any time you need it, with nothing extra to do but open the jar. These goodies also make lovely gift ideas. It is interesting to note that Hermes, the Greek God of communication, is attributed with teaching humanity about "hermetically" sealing items. He becomes an appropriate patron deity for kitchen witches during their magical canning and preserving efforts.

In order to make this section more useful to those of you less familiar with canning techniques, here are some helpful suggestions to get you started:

- Read the recipe thoroughly before attempting; make sure you have all the ingredients and utensils on hand.

- Use only unbruised fruit and vegetables at the peak of their ripeness.

- Use only lids, jars, and rings intended for canning. Do not reuse lids. Inspect all jars for cracks and chips on the rim. A chipped rim will interfere with a proper seal.

- A stainless steel or porcelain-coated pot is best for cooking because it will not give a metallic flavor to the fruits and vegetables.

- Use only the canning method recommended in the recipe. Using a different method may result in spoiled food and possible illness when the product is eaten.

- When straining fruit, use a jelly bag or line a colander with four layers of damp cheesecloth. Many recipes call for a long period when the juice is allowed to drip through the strainer. Squeezing the pulp will extract the maximum flavor but will leave jellies looking cloudy.

- Some recipes will refer to a "jell point." The jell point is the stage at which the jelly will set up correctly. Undercooked jelly will be runny and overcooked jelly will caramelize and lose color. If you have a thermometer, take the temperature of boiling water. The boiling point of water will change with altitude and atmospheric conditions. Cook the jelly to 8° F (9° F for jams) higher than the boiling point. If a thermometer is not handy, test by putting a spoon of the hot mixture on a cold plate. Place the plate in the freezer for a few minutes. If the jelly sets, it is ready to can. If the jelly is still runny, continue boiling. Remember to remove the jelly from the heat while you perform this test to avoid accidently overcooking it.

Canning Methods

The following two canning methods are used in this book. There is a third method involving the use of a pressure cooker. For safety, the pressure cooker method *must* be used when called for in a recipe found in a different cookbook.

Method 1

This method is also referred to as the "boiling water bath" method and can only be used for foods with a high acid content.

1. Wash the jars, lids, and rings in hot water. Keep the jars in hot water or a low oven (200° F) until ready to use. Scald the rings and lids according to manufacturer's directions.

2. Prepare the filling according to recipe directions.

3. Fill the jars using a wide-mouth funnel. Leave the amount of headspace, the space between the jar rim and the top of the filling, recommended in the recipe.

4. Wipe the jar rims with a clean damp cloth. Set a lid on each jar with the sealing compound in contact with the glass. Screw the rings on firmly but not tightly.

5. Place the filled jars on a rack or a folded cloth in a deep kettle filled with hot, but not boiling, water. Arrange the jars so they do not touch each other or the sides of the kettle. Add hot water until the jars are covered to a depth of 1-2 inches. Bring the water to a boil. Cover; boil for the time specified in the recipe. For altitudes above 3,000 feet, boil an additional 2 minutes for each 1,000 feet. Remove jars from the kettle using a jar lifter. Place on a folded towel or rack to cool. Set far enough apart to allow air to circulate between jars and keep free of drafts.

6. Test for a seal after 12 hours. If a seal has been formed, the center of the lid will stay down after being pressed with a finger. If the lid pops up, a seal was not formed and the contents should be refrigerated and used immediately.

Method 2

Only use this method for jellies. Jams must be processed using Method 1.

1. Wash the jars, lids, and rings. Sterilize jars by immersing in a pan of water and boiling for 15 minutes. Leave jars in the water or place in a low (200° F) oven. *Do not at any time touch the rim or inside of the jar with your hands.* Scald the lid and rings according to the manufacturer's directions.

2. Prepare the jelly according to recipe directions.

3. Immediately after the jelly has reached the jell point, fill the hot, sterilized jars using a wide-mouth funnel. Leave ½ inch of headspace (the space between the jar rim and the top of the filling).

4. Wipe the jar rims with a clean damp cloth. Set a lid on each jar with the sealing compound in contact with the glass. Screw the rings on firmly but not tightly.

5. Place on a folded towel or rack to cool. Set the jars far enough apart to allow air to circulate between them and keep free of drafts.

6. Test for a seal after 12 hours. If a seal has formed, the center of the lid will stay down after being pressed with a finger. If the lid pops up, a seal was not formed and the contents should be refrigerated and used immediately.

Chutney and Relish

Chutney and relish are similar. Both are made from a mixture of fruit and/or vegetables diced into small pieces, cooked with spices, then preserved. While chutney is enjoyed around the world, it had its origins in India. According to most Indian recipes, chutney is best when cooked slowly and aged at least two months. With proper preparation, chutney and relish have a shelf life of two years.

Cucumber and Tomato Reassurance Relish

4 cups finely chopped pickled cucumbers

1 teaspoon salt, divided

1 red pepper, seeded and finely chopped

6 medium ripe tomatoes, skinned and finely chopped

2 cups cider vinegar

2 large onions, finely chopped

1 cup brown sugar

1 teaspoon dry mustard

¼ teaspoon allspice

1 tablespoon pickling spice

Use Canning Method 1 (page 103). Place the pickled cucumbers in a large pan; sprinkle with ¼ teaspoon of the salt. Layer the tomatoes, red pepper, and onions on top of the pickled cucumber; sprinkle ¼ teaspoon salt between each layer. Cover; refrigerate overnight.

Drain off accumulated water. Mix in vinegar, brown sugar, dry mustard, allspice, and pickling spice. Bring to a boil. Boil until thick but moist, about 30 minutes.

Fill jars; leave ½-inch headspace. Process in a boiling-water bath for 10 minutes. This type of chutney is excellent with curry. **Yield: About 6 half-pints.**

Note: To skin tomatoes, dip into boiling water for 30 seconds and then dip into cold water. The skins should slip off easily.

Variation: To make a relish for growth, spring observances, and improved finances, substitute green tomatoes and peppers for red.

Magical Attributes: Peace, healing, protection, love.

Celebrations: Fire festivals, all rituals or holidays pertaining to protection. The colors of this relish make it a pretty side dish at Yule.

Fruit Chutney (India)

The word chutney comes from a Hindi word, catni, *which means "lick."*

- 3 cups white vinegar
- 2 fresh chili peppers, minced
- 1 tablespoon grated lemon peel
- ½ cup minced ginger root
- 1 clove garlic, minced

- 1 teaspoon salt
- 1½ cups packed brown sugar
- 3 lbs. raw mixed fruit (any kind), peeled and chopped
- 1½ cups blanched almonds

Use Canning Method 1 (page 103). Bring the vinegar to a low boil; add the chili peppers, lemon peel, ginger root, garlic, and salt. Cover; simmer for 10 minutes. Add the brown sugar, fruit, and almonds; stir. Cover. Simmer until a sticky, thick texture is achieved, about 1 hour; stir frequently.

Fill jars; leave ½-inch headspace. Process in a boiling-water bath for 15 minutes. **Yield: About 6 half-pints.**

Magical Attributes: Overcoming problems, creating accord through strength of actions.

Celebrations: Patriot's Day, Feast of Banners, Royal Oak Day, Birthday of the Sun.

Lemon Mustard Chutney

Mustard seed, in the form of a poultice, has had an important place in folk medicine of the world, especially for treating consumption. Because of the mustard seed's small size, it represents the power of faith.

3-4 lemons, seeded and chopped	2 tablespoons mustard seed
1 tablespoon salt	1 cup sugar
2 medium onions, chopped	1¼ cup cider vinegar
1 teaspoon allspice	⅓ cup raisins

Use Canning Method 1 (page 103). Place the lemons in a bowl; sprinkle with the salt. Cover; refrigerate overnight (12 hours). Pour lemons into a large saucepan; mix in the onions, allspice, mustard seed, sugar, cider vinegar, and raisins. Bring to a boil over medium heat. Reduce heat; simmer 1 hour. Test to be sure the lemons are soft.

Fill jars; leave ¼-inch headspace. Process in a boiling-water bath for 10 minutes. This chutney is especially good with chicken. **Yield: About 2 half-pints.**

Magical Attributes: Cleansing, purification, health, protection, strength, faith.

Celebrations: Before a ritual fast, Old Dance, St. Stephen Festival, Birthday of the Sun, Sukkoth.

Mint Chutney

Mint's bright green color makes it a perfect addition to prosperity theme meals. This herb has been used in hundreds of health-related remedies for everything from headaches to colds. This spicy chutney is one of the easiest to make because there is no cooking involved.

1 cup fresh mint leaf	1 tablespoon sugar
2 scallions, chopped	¼ teaspoon cayenne pepper
1 small onion, minced	¼ teaspoon curry
1½ teaspoons lemon juice	1 teaspoon salt

Place the mint, scallions, onion, and lemon juice in a blender; blend until the mint is completely minced. Add the sugar, cayenne pepper, curry, and salt; blend until smooth. Chill before serving. Store in the refrigerator. This chutney is especially good with lamb and game birds. **Yield: About ½ cup.**

Magical Attributes: Healing, safety, prosperity.

Celebrations: Smell the Breeze Day, Sealing the Frost, Ahes Festival, Fiesta of the Mother of Health.

New England Fruit Chutney for Lovers

In some form or another, each fruit and spice in this recipe can been used to woo and tempt love. The vinegar and salt add precision and extra energy to guide your magic toward its goal.

1 cup chopped onion	⅔ cup raisins
4 large apples, peeled and chopped	2 tablespoons minced ginger root
4-5 apricots, peeled and chopped	4 cloves garlic, minced
4 large pears, peeled and chopped	½ teaspoon nutmeg
2 medium peaches, peeled and chopped	½ teaspoon allspice
2 oranges, peeled, seeded, and chopped	1 tablespoon cinnamon
	1 teaspoon salt
Rind of 2 oranges, grated	2 cups cider vinegar plus ½ cup
2 tablespoons grated lemon rind	3 cups packed brown sugar

Use Canning Method 1 (page 105). Place the onions, apples, pears, apricots, peaches, oranges, orange rind, lemon rind, raisins, ginger root, garlic, nutmeg, allspice, cinnamon, salt, and 2 cups of the vinegar in a large pot. Bring to a boil; stir regularly. Reduce heat; simmer for 1½ hours. Make sure all the fruits are evenly cooked. Stir in the sugar and remaining vinegar; simmer 1 hour.

Fill jars; leave ½-inch headspace. Process in a boiling-water bath for 10 minutes. Age in a dark place for at least 8 weeks before serving. This chutney is very pleasing with cheese breads and baguettes. The bread can be cut into the shape of hearts before serving. **Yield: About 7 half-pints.**

Magical Attributes: The energy of romance, clarity of love, youthful vigor and idealism.

Celebrations: Valentine's Day, Wedding/Handfasting, Sweetest Day, most spring celebrations, Brendan's Journey, Kermesse.

Religious Corn Relish (Native American)

Corn represents the life of the land and was an important part of many Native American observances to honor the gods of providence. Tumeric adds protection against any baneful spirits trying to hinder your spiritual progress.

- 4½ cups cider vinegar
- 4¼ cups chopped cabbage
- 2 lbs. frozen baby corn kernels, thawed
- 2 green peppers, seeded and chopped
- 2 red peppers, seeded and chopped
- 1 large onion, chopped
- 1 teaspoon turmeric
- 1 cup sugar
- 1 teaspoon salt
- ¼ teaspoon ground clove

Use Canning Method 1 (page 103). Combine all ingredients in a large pan. Bring to a boil. Turn down heat; simmer for 1 hour. Stir often. Mixture should be thick. If it seems dry, add more vinegar.

Fill jars; leave ½-inch headspace. Process in a boiling-water bath for 15 minutes. To accentuate the idea of good fortune and plenty, serve with cornbread. This is an excellent addition to harvest tables. **Yield: About 7 half-pints.**

Magical Attributes: Understanding one's faith, getting closer to the land, sacred teachings and insight.

Celebrations: Earth Day, Planting Festival, Binding of the Wreaths, Joan of Arc Day, Feast of the Madonna, Sunning of Buddha.

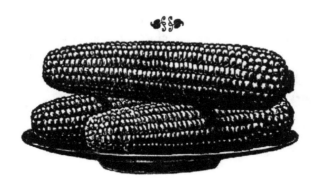

✌ *Fruit Syrups* ✌

Fruit syrups serve more than one purpose. The condensed versions can be used as a topping for ice cream, fruit, and other desserts, or they can be diluted to make refreshing, nutrient-filled drinks. Berries, which are high in vitamin C, generally make the best fruit syrups. The basic recipes given below can be easily applied to other peeled, fresh fruit and fruit mixtures.

Rose Syrup (Ancient Rome)

Roses are one of the most versatile cooking flowers known to humankind. In historical texts, they have been mentioned in everything from soups and desserts to healing salves.

12 cups water	2 cups fresh rose petals
8 cups rose hips, minced	4 cups sugar

Place the water and the rose hips in a large pan; bring to a boil. Cool for 15 minutes. Strain; discard the pulp. Return the liquid to the pan; add the rose petals. Bring to a boil. Strain; discard petals. This second boiling will give color to the syrup. Wash the pan before refilling with the liquid. Simmer until the liquid reduces to about 7 cups. Reduce heat to low; add sugar slowly, stirring continually until dissolved. Increase heat; simmer until thickened, about 5 minutes.

Fill jars; leave ¼-inch headspace. Process in a boiling-water bath for 10 minutes. Use small bottles. Once opened, the syrup stays good only about 2 weeks.

Yield: About 8 half-pints.

Variation: The various colors of the rose allow for a variety of magical application. Red might be used for passion and energy, yellow for creativity, or a combination of the two to help motivate romance. A little crushed pineapple may be added during the first boiling for protective zest. Love-related fruits such as peaches, plums, cherries, and apricots can be substituted for the rose hips and petals.

Magical Attributes: Various (see variation).

Celebrations: Flower festivals, spring and summer rites.

Tangy Black Currant Syrup (Greece)

The cleansing effect of lemon combines with the sweet, joyful nature of currants to help bring improved understanding, modesty, and sagacity.

5 cups water
8 cups black currants
¼ cup lemon juice

Rind of 1 lemon, quartered
3 cups sugar

Use Canning Method 1 (page 103). Place the water, currants, lemon juice, and lemon peel in a medium-sized saucepan; bring to a boil. Boil for 30 minutes; the water should be a deep reddish purple. Strain; discard the fruit. Wash the pan before refilling with the liquid. Simmer until liquid reduces to about half. Reduce heat to low; add sugar slowly, stirring continually until dissolved. Increase heat; simmer until thickened, about 5 minutes.

Fill jars; leave ¼-inch headspace. Process in a boiling-water bath for 10 minutes. **Yield: About 3 half-pints.**

Magical Attributes: Discretion, meekness, prudence, balance (especially in ego).

Celebrations: Many winter rituals, Asking Day, before a difficult confrontation.

✦ Marmalade, Jellies, and Jams ✦

Apricot-Almond Wine Conserve

Wine in any form is a symbol of festivity. It is still used in some churches for communion and has often been spilt as an offering to the God/desses. In Norse traditions, it is claimed that you must drink all the wine you have ever accidentally spilled before entering Valhalla. Finally, apricots bring peacefulness and almonds grant health.

3 cups finely chopped dried apricots
6 cups water
1 teaspoon lemon juice

6 cups sugar
⅓ cup blanched almonds, chopped
1¼ cups dry white wine

Use Canning Method 1 (page 103). Place the apricots and water in a medium-sized bowl. Cover; refrigerate overnight.

Transfer to a large saucepan; simmer 30 minutes. Stir in the lemon juice, sugar, almonds, and wine; simmer until the sugar is dissolved. Raise the heat and boil until the jell point is reached, about 15 minutes.

Fill jars; leave ½-inch headspace. Process in a boiling-water bath for 15 minutes. This conserve is excellent served on turnovers or pork.
Yield: About 8 half-pints.

Variation: Substitute currants for the apricots. This is traditionally served in Britain over mutton or roast.

Magical Attributes: Divine communion, rejoicing, sacred offerings, mindfulness, restful well-being.

Celebrations: The Great Rite, Drawing Down the Moon, harvest celebrations; to honor Osiris, Dionysus, or other figures to whom wine and fruit are sacred.

Circle Marmalade

So named because it has four representative elements, like the magical circle. This marmalade is to encourage fellowship and understanding in groups. Earth is quince and allspice, air is tangerine and almond, fire is pineapple and ginger, and water is pear and vanilla.

Rind from 3 tangerines	1 cup drained crushed pineapple
7 cups water	7 cups sugar
3 tangerines, peeled, seeded, and chopped	½ teaspoon almond extract
	½ teaspoon allspice
2 quinces, finely chopped	½ teaspoon ginger
2 pears, peeled and finely chopped	½ teaspoon vanilla

Slice the tangerine rind into very thin, short strips. Bring the rind and the water to a boil. Simmer for 2 hours. Mix in tangerines, quinces, pears, pineapple, sugar, extract, allspice, ginger, and vanilla. Cook over a low flame until the sugar dissolves. Increase heat; boil until the set point is reached, about 45-60 minutes. Skim off any foam that appears.

Fill jars; leave ½-inch headspace. Process in a boiling-water bath for 15 minutes.
Yield: About 8 half-pints.

Magical Attributes: Love, protection, longevity, bonding, discernment.

Celebrations: Serve at any magical gathering, during special meals for family and friends, weddings and handfastings.

Ginger Squash Jam

Both ginger and squash have been associated with a close perception of divine energy and direct communication with a higher power.

10 cups chopped raw summer squash, peeled and seeded	Rind of 3 lemons, chopped
Juice of 3 lemons	2 whole cloves
5 cups sugar	1 tablespoon chopped ginger root
	½ cup crystallized ginger, chopped

Use Canning Method 1 (page 103). Steam the squash until tender, about 20 minutes. Transfer to a large bowl; combine with the lemon juice and sugar. Secure the lemon peel, cloves, and ginger root in a small muslin or cheese cloth bag. Add the spice "tea bag" to the bowl. Cover; refrigerate for 24 hours.

Transfer to a large pan. Heat on low until the sugar dissolves. Stir in the crystallized ginger and ¼ cup water. Bring to a boil. Simmer until the squash is translucent and the syrup has thickened. Discard the muslin bag.

Fill jars; leave ¼-inch headspace. Process in a boiling-water bath for 15 minutes. **Yield: About 7 half-pints.**

Magical Attributes: Communication with God, spirituality, mystical energy, awareness.

Celebrations: Sunning of Buddha, St. Joan of Arc Day, Day of the Dryads, Ahes Festival.

Lavender Conserves (England 1600s)

In French, espic; in English, spikenard; lavender was used in Roman cookery and English hippocras, a spiced drink thought to be healthful. In the language of flowers, lavender means assent.

15 cups chopped apples, peeled   2½ cups fresh lavender petals
Sugar

Place the apples in a large pot; add enough water to cover completely. Bring to a boil. Reduce heat; simmer until fruit is pulpy, about 45 minutes. Mash the apples with a wooden spoon. Strain; let drip 12 hours. Reserve the juice.

Discard fruit; measure juice and pour into to a large pan. Add 2 cups of sugar for every 2½ cups of juice. Heat on low until the sugar has dissolved. Increase heat; boil until the jell point is reached.

Place ¼ cup fresh lavender petals in each hot jelly jar. Be sure to only use the petals or the flavor will be terrible. Fill jars; leave ½-inch headspace. Process in a boiling-water bath for 10 minutes. **Yield: About 10 half-pints.**

Variation: Replace the lavender flowers with 2 inches of fresh, crushed ginger for a magical conserve potent for wisdom and success.

Magical Attributes: Acknowledgement, recognition, answers, resolution.

Celebrations: Pardon of the Birds, St. Stephen's Festival, Festival of Brightness, forgiveness rituals, before magic for legal matters.

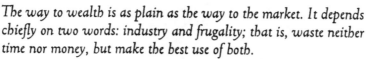

The way to wealth is as plain as the way to the market. It depends chiefly on two words: industry and frugality; that is, waste neither time nor money, but make the best use of both.
— *Benjamin Franklin*

Pear and Strawberry Brandy Conserves

Strawberries are the fruit of romance, whereas pears add longevity to these emotions.

- 5 cups sliced strawberries
- 2¼ cups chopped pears, peeled
- 6 tablespoons lemon juice

- 8 cups sugar
- 1 cup brandy

Use Canning Method 1 (page 103). Cook the strawberries, pears, and lemon juice in a large pan over low heat until softened. Stir in the sugar and brandy. When the sugar is dissolved, bring to a full boil. Boil until the jell point is reached.

Fill jars; leave ¼-inch headspace. Process in a boiling-water bath for 10 minutes. Serve at a romantic breakfast which includes apple fritters and orange-pineapple juice to further inspire love. **Yield: About 6 half-pints.**

Magical Attributes: Abiding love.

Celebrations: Before a handfasting or marriage, anniversary, any time you need to improve the love you show yourself, Valentine's Day, Sweetest Day.

Remembrance Jelly

Here apple is employed for youthful awareness, blackberry to stimulate ideas, and rosemary for remembrance.

- 10 cups chopped apples, peeled
- 8 cups blackberries
- 1¼ cups water

- 4 tablespoons rosemary leaves, divided
- 1 cup malt vinegar
  Sugar

Use Canning Method 2 (page 103). Bring the apples, blackberries, water, and 2 tablespoons of the rosemary to a boil. Reduce heat; simmer until the apple is pulpy, about 45 minutes. Mix in the vinegar; boil for 5 minutes. Strain; let drip for 12 hours. Save the liquid.

Discard the pulp; measure the liquid before pouring into a large pan. Add 2 cups sugar for every 2¼ cups liquid. Heat over a low flame until the sugar is dissolved, stirring frequently. Mix in the remaining 2 tablespoons of rosemary. Increase heat; boil until the jell point is reached, about 10 minutes. Skim off any foam.

Pour into hot sterilized jars and seal. This jelly is excellent with lamb.

Yield: About 5 half-pints.

Variation: A delightful substitute for rosemary is mint. In this case you will need 5 tablespoons of mint to replace the rosemary. Mint is considered a healing herb to help ease painful memories.

Magical Attributes: Insight, memory, recollection, honor, beauty, comfort.

Celebrations: Award ceremonies, Patriot's Day, Independence Day, Memorial Day, anniversary of a death, May Day, Apple Blossom Day.

✺ *Pickles* ✺

Pickles are different from chutney in that they do not have to be cooked for long periods of time. Most vegetables in pickling are soaked overnight in heavy salt-water solutions (brine) which improves crispness. Use sea salt and good quality vinegar to insure superior pickles.

Cured Olives (Greece)

The Bible says that the Hebrews discovered olives growing wild in Canaan. These quickly became so important that every home in Palestine was equipped with an olive press. In Greece, olives were considered the gift of Athena and were grown at the Acropolis to honor her.

½ gallon jar whole ripe olives, drained and rinsed	1½ cups sea salt
	¼ cup olive oil
2 cups apple cider vinegar	4 cloves garlic, minced

Dissolve the salt in the vinegar. Combine the olives and vinegar mixture. Place in a non-metallic container with the level of the olives and vinegar close to the rim. Cover with a weighted plate. The plate should keep the olives submerged in the vinegar. Let sit for 2 months.

Drain off the vinegar; rinse the olives. Place the olives back in their original jar. Mix the olive oil and garlic; pour over the olives. Cover; shake the jar until all olives are throughly coated. Let stand for at least 30 minutes before serving. Store in the refrigerator. **Yield: About 1¼ pints of olives.**

Magical Attributes: Peace (and preserving it), health, spirituality.

Celebrations: Earth Day, Memorial Day, forgiveness rituals.

Pickled Pride (Medieval Spain and England)

Known by the earlier name of gilliflowers, carnations were discovered in Spain at the time of Caesar. The word carnation comes from "coronation," because of this flower's close association with festivals and celebratory events. In the language of flowers, the carnation means dignity.

6 cups carnations	2 whole allspice
6 cups white wine vinegar	1 stick cinnamon
¼ cup packed brown sugar	2 blades mace
2 whole cloves	2 teaspoons rose water (p. 58)

Cut off the whites from the bottom of the carnations. Cover them with vinegar and spices in a large saucepan. Let sit for 15 minutes, then bring to a full boil, dissolving the sugar. Cool before bottling. To serve, mix with a little sugar and vinegar; especially good on lamb. **Yield: About 4 pounds.**

Variation: Try replacing the carnations with 6 cups olives. Magically this is for peace and harmony within.

Magical Attributes: Cheerfulness, calming the nerves, beauty, improving self-esteem.

Celebrations: Spring celebrations, any flower festivals, when feeling anxious, Hori, Old Dance.

Piccalilli

The crunchy, cool nature of piccalilli helps to balance flights of fancy and ground excess energy.

3 tablespoons pickling salt	2¼ cups vinegar
4 cups cold water	¼ cup sugar
3 lbs. mixed vegetables (cherry tomatoes, cucumbers, pearl onions, cauliflower, white cabbage), chopped into large pieces	½ teaspoon dry mustard
	½ teaspoon ginger
	2 cloves garlic, minced
	½ teaspoon turmeric

Use Canning Method 1 (page 103). Dissolve the salt in the cold water. Pour over the vegetables. Cover; let stand overnight.

Pour off the salt water; rinse vegetables. Bring the vinegar, sugar, dry mustard, ginger, garlic, and tumeric to a boil in a large saucepan. Boil 5 minutes. Add vegetables; simmer until vegetables are slightly tender, about 5 minutes.

Spoon vegetables into hot jars and completely cover with the boiling vinegar. Leave a ¾-inch headspace. Process in a boiling-water bath for 15 minutes. Serve chilled. This makes a nice side dish or garnish for meat and poultry.
Yield: 5 pints.

Variation: Make theme piccalilli. Use all white vegetable parts for protection and purification, all green (such as beans) for prosperity, or add red cabbage for safety and health.

Magical Attributes: Grounding, building foundations, protection, training.

Celebrations: Before initiation or magical study, after a powerful rite, graduations, before leaving for college.

Surety Dills

This is a pickle for garlic lovers. Elementally, the onion, vinegar, dill, garlic, horseradish, and bay all make this a very fiery snack full of active energy for protection or cleansing. Vampires beware!

12	cups cider vinegar	20	dill blossoms
6	quarts water	20	bay leaves
3	cups sea salt		Horseradish root, chopped
1	tablespoon mustard seed	20-30	cloves garlic
2	tablespoons dry minced onion	20	whole peppercorns
1	tablespoon garlic powder	100	small pickling cucumbers

Use Canning Method 1 (page 103). Bring the vinegar, water, salt, mustard seed, onion, and garlic powder to a boil.

At the bottom of each clean, hot, quart-sized jar place 2 dill blossoms, 2 bay leaves, 2-3 cloves garlic, a small piece of horseradish root, and 2 peppercorns. Pack in approximately 10 cucumbers. Cover completely with the boiling vinegar. Leave ½-inch headspace. Process in a boiling-water bath for 20 minutes. Let mature for at least two weeks before serving. **Yield: 10 quarts.**

Magical Attributes: Protection and purification.

Celebrations: Any fire festival, Hallows, Patriot's Day, Sealing the Frost, Royal Oak Day.

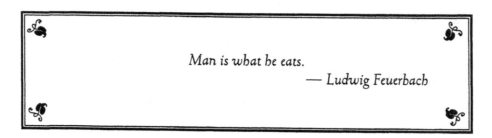

Man is what he eats.
— Ludwig Feuerbach

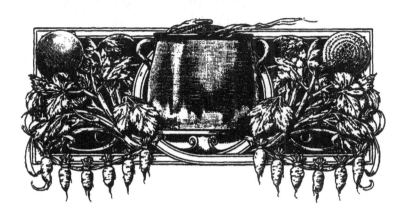

Sweet Pickles

Known also as bread and butter pickles, these might be used to sweeten someone's sour disposition ("butter them up"). The sugar in these pickles makes them especially helpful in smoothing tension in a romantic relationship.

5 medium pickling cucumbers, sliced	2 cups sugar
10 pearl onions, halved	1 red pepper, seeded and thickly sliced
1 green pepper, seeded and thickly sliced	1 teaspoon turmeric
2 cups malt vinegar	1 tablespoon mustard seed
	1 tablespoon celery seed

Use Canning Method 1 (page 103). Cover the cucumbers, onions, and peppers with ice water in a medium-sized bowl; let sit for three hours.

Drain. Bring vinegar, sugar, turmeric, mustard seed, and celery seed to a boil in a large pan; stir. After the sugar dissolves, add the vegetables. Cover; simmer until vegetables are just tender, about 5-7 minutes.

Spoon vegetables into hot jars and cover completely with boiling vinegar. Leave ½-inch headspace. Process in a boiling-water bath for 10 minutes.

Yield: About 5 pints.

Magical Attributes: Improving attitudes, cooling anger, positive perspectives.

Celebrations: During long winters, New Year's, birthdays, before job hunting, April Fool's Day, Kermesse.

⋇ Sauce, Catsup, and Condiments ⋙

Please note that this is just a brief section on condiment sauces. Those more directly related to use with pastas and main dishes are included in Chapter 10. As an interesting bit of history, the word ketchup is derived from the Malaysian *kepchop*, which translates to something like "salt water of pickled fish." Simple condiment sauces such as mint or horseradish are prepared by pouring hot malt vinegar over fresh grated, packed herbs and sealing in air-tight containers for later use.

Mustard Sauce of Valor

The mustard seed is small but potent; it makes itself known through robust, persistent flavor. Mustard poultices are excellent for colds and fever.

1 red pepper, seeded and chopped	1 tablespoon salt
2 green peppers, seeded and chopped	5 cups cold water
	2¼ cups wine vinegar
2 medium green tomatoes, chopped	1¼ cups packed brown sugar
1 small cucumber, chopped	2 tablespoons mustard seed
1 cup chopped pickled cucumbers	1 tablespoon flour
2 medium onions, chopped	¼ teaspoon turmeric

Use Canning Method 1 (page 103). Place red pepper, green pepper, green tomatoes, cucumber, pickled cucumber, and onions in a large bowl. Dissolve the salt in the cold water; pour over the vegetables. Let sit overnight.

Pour off the salt water; rinse the vegetables. Bring the vegetables, vinegar, sugar, and mustard seed to a boil. Make a paste from the flour, turmeric, and a little water. Stir gradually into the vinegar. Simmer uncovered until thickened, about 1 hour. Transfer to a blender; process until very finely chopped. Return to the pan and heat until boiling.

Fill jars; leave ½-inch headspace. Process in a boiling-water bath for 10 minutes. **Yield: About 4 half-pints.**

Magical Attributes: Courage, endurance, tenacity, tolerance, fortitude, faith, health.

Celebrations: Patriot's Day, Memorial Day, Independence Day, St. Joan of Arc Day, any rites for healing, fire festivals.

Mystical Mushroom Ketchup

Associated with fairy kind and having kin which cause hallucinations, the common mushroom has an interesting reputation for psychic insight. The spices here provide safety and potency.

15 cups chopped mushrooms
¼ cup salt
2 small onions, diced

2 cloves of garlic, crushed
2½ cups vinegar

Use Canning Method 1 (page 103). Sprinkle the salt over the mushrooms. Let sit for one day; stir every few hours.

Rinse. Place in a large saucepan with the onions, garlic, and vinegar. Bring to a boil. Reduce heat; simmer until the mushrooms are tender, about 5 minutes. Transfer to a blender, process until finely chopped. Return to the pan; boil for 5 minutes.

Fill jars; leave ¼-inch headspace. Process in a boiling-water bath for 10 minutes. **Yield: About 3 half-pints.**

Variation: Substitute 7½ cups chopped tomatoes for half the mushrooms and add 1 tablespoon dried basil for deep psychic connections between lovers.

Magical Attributes: Psychic protection and strength.

Celebrations: Samhain, Lammas, Day of the Dryads, Feast of the Milky Way, May Day.

Horseradish Onion Sauce

Both onions and horseradish have been used in protective spells because of their potent smell and taste. The former held a place of honor in certain ancient Egyptian homes. The latter is still sometimes ground and sprinkled around a home to keep evil and malin-tended magic at bay.

3 tablespoon butter	Salt
1 small onion, minced	Pepper
3 tablespoon flour	2 tablespoons prepared horseradish
1 cup milk	

Sauté the onion in the butter until tender. Slowly add the flour until a paste is formed. Gradually stir in the milk. Cook and stir until a smooth sauce is achieved. Using a fork, blend in the salt, pepper, and horseradish. Simmer for 5 minutes. Pour into a sterilized jar. Store in the refrigerator. **Yield: About 1 cup.**

Variation: To strengthen this mixture even more, add one or two cloves pulverized garlic.

Magical Attributes: Protection, purification, banishing negativity.

Celebrations: Before a ritual fast, New Year's, fire festivals (like the Hori), Royal Oak Day.

Sweet Almond Spread

Almonds are strongly aligned with the element of air, giving flight to our aspirations and movement where stagnation has been present. Honey is added to this recipe to encourage these winds to be gentle, bringing pleasing results.

1 cup butter, softened	½ teaspoon almond extract
2 tablespoons finely chopped almonds	2 tablespoons honey

Combine butter, almonds, extract, and honey in a small mixing bowl using a hand mixer set at low speed. Spoon into a sterile, large-mouthed jar. Store in the refrigerator. **Yield: About 1 cup.**

Note: Butters can be frozen to increase their life.

Variation: Dates, orange rind, and other fruits can be substituted for the almonds. Any flavor extract can be used. For a less sweet option, replace the almonds, extract, and honey with 2 tablespoons dried herbs like mustard, basil, or chives.

Magical Attributes: Pleasant dreams, smooth financial transitions, air magic.

Vinegar

Vinegar is essentially a by-product of brewing. In areas of the world where beer and ale were common, malt vinegar was produced. Wine turns to wine vinegar and apple cider to cider vinegar. Both the Bible and Hippocrates mention vinegar for medicinal use. To make some yourself, just retain the unused portion of dry wine at room temperature, covered lightly with a cloth until it turns. This is customarily true of cider, too. The general process for preparing herbed vinegars with a base of red, white, cider, or wine vinegar is the same, but here are three for you to try. Other favorite combinations include a mixture of any of the following herbs: tarragon, dill, dried onion, chives, sesame, and poppy.

Beet Vinegar (Jewish)

This is called Rosel and is used during the Jewish Passover to make a beet soup. It has a wine-like fragrance and comes out in a beautiful bright red color.

12 large beets, quartered   Water to cover

Place the cleaned beets in a crock; cover with cold water. Make sure no beets are above the surface of the water. Lay cheese cloth over the top and partially cover with a lid. Let this sit for about 4 weeks until sour. The mix should smell like vinegar. Skim off any scum. Strain; discard the beets. Store in an air-tight container. **Yield: About 5 pints.**

Magical Attributes: Inner beauty, depth of character, loving qualities, blood mysteries for women, trust in Divine guidance.

Celebrations: Girl's coming of age, Sukkoth, Passover, many summer rituals.

Sicilian Vinegar

The sunlight here not only serves to improve this vinegar's flavor, but also empower it with forceful energy for persuasion or similar solar goals. The Italian herbs add gusto!

- 4 cups red wine vinegar
- 2 large cloves garlic
- 2 tablespoons fresh basil
- 2 tablespoons fresh oregano
- 2 tablespoons fresh thyme
- 1 tablespoon fresh rosemary
- 2 bay leaves

Heat the vinegar until boiling. Place the herbs in a hot, sterilized, decorative bottle. Pour in boiling vinegar. Cap or cork immediately. Leave in a sunny window for 2 weeks before using. **Yield: 4 cups.**

Variation: For clarity in love, Greek style, use white vinegar and substitute ½ lemon (sliced), 1 tablespoon sliced ginger root and 1 clove garlic for the herbs.

Magical Attributes: Bargaining power, influential speech, self-assurance.

Celebrations: Before legal matters are decided, making presentations to the media or a group about the Craft, Feast of Banners, Birthday of the Sun, Sun Dance.

Spring Vinegar (Medieval Europe)

Daisy is the flower of innocence, rosemary is for happy memories, clover is for serendipity, elder provides protection, and dandelion gives golden spring color for fiery initiative.

- 4 cups white wine vinegar
- ¼ cup dandelion flowers
- ¼ cup elder flowers
- ¼ cup clover
- ¼ cup daisy petals
- ½ teaspoon rosemary
- 1 cinnamon stick (optional)
- 2-3 whole cloves (optional)
- 2-3 whole allspice (optional)

Bring the vinegar to a boil. Pack the dandelion, elder flowers, clover, daisy, rosemary, cinnamon, cloves, and allspice in a hot, sterile jar. Pour in vinegar. Cap immediately. Allow to sit for 1 week. Strain; discard flowers and spices. Use on spinach salads, flower salads, as a marinade, etc. **Yield: 4 cups.**

Variation: Substitute any favorite spices (1 teaspoon for each type of flower).

Magical Attributes: Joy, youthful exuberance, life, energy, freedom, rebirth.

Celebrations: All spring observances, Wiccanings, May Day, Independence Day, New Year's.

✌ Miscellaneous ☙

Spiced Tangerines (Arabia)

A common offering in Buddhist temples, the tangerine is considered a protective amulet in these lands. Since it is a member of the orange family it may likewise be associated with physical health and the well-being of relationships.

8-10	whole cloves	14-16	small tangerines
10-12	whole allspice	½	teaspoon baking soda
¼	vanilla bean	1¼	cups white wine vinegar
1	stick cinnamon	2¾	cups packed brown sugar
	½-inch ginger root		

Use Canning Method 1 (page 103). Secure the cloves, allspice, vanilla bean, cinnamon, and ginger root in a small muslin or cheesecloth bag. Wash the tangerines and pierce their skins with a fork. Place in a large pan; cover with water. Mix in baking soda. Bring to a boil; boil 15 minutes. Add the spice bag and vinegar; simmer 20 minutes. Remove the spice bag; stir in the sugar. Cover; boil for 20 minutes.

Place the tangerines in clean, hot jars. Continue to boil the liquid 10 more minutes. Pour over the tangerines. Leave ½-inch headroom. Process in a boiling-water bath for 15 minutes. Serve with pork or game meats.

Yield: About 4 quarts.

Magical Attributes: Protection of one's health, happiness in love.

Celebrations: Weddings/Handfastings, Valentine's Day, during cold and flu season, Old Dance, Ahes Festival, Birthday of Confucius.

Petaled Summer Honey (Lebanon)

Ancient people cooked with flowers for their beauty, aroma, and their purported magical effects. Flowered honeys are tasty and may be used like any honey.

⅓ cup rose petals, minced
⅓ cup violet petals, minced
⅓ cup lavender petals, minced
¼ teaspoon ground

1 cup honey
cinnamon (optional)
½ teaspoon minced
ginger root (optional)

Clean and thoroughly dry the flower petals. Combine all ingredients in a saucepan. Simmer over very low heat for 20 minutes. Watch that the mixture does not stick or burn. When the petals have turned translucent, remove from heat. Petals may either be strained out or left in. Pour into a hot, sterilized jar. **Yield: About 1¾ cups.**

Variation: For international flair, use tulip petals (a Turkish favorite for peace), peony blossoms from China for brightness of fortune, or marigold petals from France for solar energy. Another option includes omitting the flowers altogether and using common kitchen spices instead. These types of honeys make wonderful meat glazes.

Magical Attributes: Love, excellence, improved sense of humor, sweet summer energy, frolic.

Celebrations: April Fool's Day, any summer festivals, Russian Fair, Kermesse, Saturnallia, flower festivals.

Personal Recipes

Personal Recipes

Chapter Seven

Charmed Cheese and Enchanted Eggs

Peace is the golden wisp that binds the sheaf of blessing.
— Katherine Lee Bates

Together or apart, eggs and cheese have graced the tables of humankind for aeons. Magically speaking, the basic energies for any egg dish will be health, fertility, productivity, or hidden strength. Those for cheese dishes will be love, protection, change, and tenacity. So, in the interest of not being repetitive, I have focused extra attention on the other ingredients in these dishes which combine their attributes with either base for magical results.

⚜ Cheese ⚜

Legend has it that cheese was discovered by accident when an Arabian merchant set out on a long journey across the desert. He kept his milk supply in a bag made from a sheep's stomach. After many days, he noticed that the milk had separated. The liquid quenched his thirst and the curd satisfied his hunger.

From what we can tell, cheese was eaten at least 2,000 years before the birth of Christ. During the Middle Ages its preparation was left in the hands of monks. Italy was the most advanced cheesemaking center by AD 10.

Asparagus Rarebit (Wales and England)

Folklore claims that some peasants in Wales used to serve bread and melted cheese as a substitute for the prized rabbits of the huntsmen. Five is the number of flexibility. In Scotland they make this with eggs, bread, and anchovy butter. The Mexican version is called Ajoqueso and is prepared with garlic, onion, pepper, and sharp cheese.

¼ cup butter	¼ cup flour
1 cup milk	1½ cups grated cheese, any kind
½ teaspoon Worcestershire sauce	¾ cup white wine
½ teaspoon salt	15 spears cooked asparagus, hot
¼ teaspoon pepper	5 slices toast

Melt the butter in a small saucepan over low heat. Stir in Worcestershire sauce, salt, and pepper. Slowly add flour, stirring constantly until smooth. Mix in the milk gradually; slowly bring to a boil. Gradually add the cheese and wine until the cheese is melted and sauce is smooth. Lay five asparagus spears on each piece of toast and cover with sauce. **Yield: 5 servings.**

Magical Attributes: Versatility, adaptability, creative frugality, diversity.

Celebrations: Labor Day; any time when circumstances in your life are changing rapidly.

Blintzes

The blintz makes a protective sphere around several cheeses to create a potent symbol.

Filling:

1 cup crumbled farmer cheese	¼ teaspoon vanilla
½ cup well drained cottage cheese	⅛ teaspoon cinnamon
1 tablespoon sugar	⅛ teaspoon salt

Crepes:

1 cup milk	⅛ teaspoon baking powder
1 egg	⅛ teaspoon salt
⅛ teaspoon vanilla	Butter or oil for frying
½ cup flour (approximately)	Sour cream or cream
1 teaspoon sugar	

Prepare the filling by mixing the farmer cheese, cottage chesse, sugar, vanilla, cin-namon, and salt in a small bowl.

Make the crepe batter by beating the egg and milk in a separate bowl. Mix in the flour, sugar, baking powder, and salt; if necessary, add more flour to make a thin, pancake-like batter.

Melt butter in a frying pan over low heat. Pour in 3 tablespoons of the batter, rotating the pan so the batter spreads out. Flip over when golden brown and the edges are dry. Place 2 tablespoons of the filling in the center. Fold the edges over the filling to form a rectangular envelope. Add more butter to the pan; fry blintz until golden brown on all sides. Serve with a garnish of sour cream or cream. **Yield: 4-6 servings.**

Variation: Instead of the cheese filling, use 1 (16-oz.) can apple pie filling for sim-ilar magical results or to improve personal wisdom. Garnish with heavy cream.

Magical Associations: Protecting relationships.

Celebrations: Anniversaries, weddings, reunions, Valentine's Day.

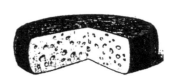

Bourrek (Greece)

Thirteen is the number of personal patience and conviction which is essential for any spiritual path to grow. Spinach, in a contemporary setting, is frequently associated with fortitude. Basil and oregano add to loving (and "green") energies for positive progress.

1½ cups crumbled feta cheese
1 cup cooked spinach, chopped
½ teaspoon pepper
1 teaspoon dried basil

½ teaspoon dried oregano (optional)
1 box phyllo pastry
1 egg yolk, beaten
Cream

Preheat the oven to 400° F. Mix the cheese, spinach, pepper, basil, and oregano in a small bowl. Roll out the phyllo pastry to ¼-inch thickness on a floured board. Work quickly because the dough tends to dry out. Cut into 3-inch squares. Place 1 tablespoon of the cheese mixture in the middle of each square. Wet the edges with a little water; fold over. Seal by pressing the edges together. Brush each pastry with egg yolk. Place on a greased cookie sheet. Bake for 13 minutes. Lower the heat to 350° F; bake for 20 minutes. Leftovers can be microwaved to warm up as snacks. **Yield: About 18 appetizers.**

Magical Attributes: Growing strength especially in love, personal development, progress of any "stalemate."

Celebrations: Before any life-changing activity such as marriage and graduation; your birthday.

Cheddar Cheese Proclamations

In ancient Athens, a petalism was a declaration of five-year banishment, delivered written on an olive leaf to insure peaceful reception. Here, the number 56 is used as representative of 8 times 7, the numbers of insight, authority, and energy.

1½ cups flour
¾ teaspoon salt
¼ teaspoon garlic powder
½ cup butter

3 cups shredded cheddar cheese
½ cup milk
56 olives with pimentos

Preheat the oven to 400° F. Mix the flour, salt, and garlic powder in a small bowl. Use a fork or pastry cutter to cut the butter into the flour mixture. Stir in the cheddar cheese. Mix in the milk to form a dough. Wrap each olive with dough. Place on a greased cookie sheet. Bake until golden brown, about 15 minutes.
Yield: 6-7 servings as an appetizer.

Variation: Try cherry tomatoes as a declaration of love or pearl onions for protection instead of the olives.

Magical Attributes: Positive communications, announcements, declarations.

Celebrations: Before any ritual involving personal statements of affirmation, Feast of St. Charlemagne's Breakfast, Festival of Sarasvati, St. Joan of Arc Day.

Cheese Fritters (Russia)

In general, dairy products are associated with the maternal and lunar aspect of the divine, milk especially (in sour cream form here) being a life-giving liquid from birth onward. It was also considered another appropriate libation to the Gods.

1 cup flour	5 egg yolks, beaten
½ teaspoon salt	6 cups crumbled farmer cheese
3 teaspoons sugar	Sour cream and chives (optional)

Mix the flour, salt, and sugar in a medium-sized bowl. Stir in the egg yolk. Add the cheese; mix until sticky. Form into logs 2-3 inches thick. If the mixture is too dry to form, add a little water; if too wet, add a little flour. Chill for 30 minutes. Cut into ½-inch slices. Melt butter in a frying pan. Fry until golden brown and heated all the way through. Serve with sour cream and chives.
Yield: About 12 servings.

Variation: In India, a similar fritter is made by substituting sliced celery for the cheese and adding 1 teaspoon curry. This would be appropriate for more solar-related magics. The French make fritters with orange flower water to encourage love. Fruit fritters historically have been made to honor visiting dignitaries. Apple and fig work especially well as a subsitute for the cheese; use sweet cream instead of sour cream.

Magical Attributes: Goddess energy, lunar magic, maternity and fertility, intuitive nature.

Chili Cheese Plate

The intense "fire" of the chili pepper makes it a food of protection, but its green color speaks of money, so combine the two (along with a little common sense) to help safeguard your assets when the economy is faltering.

1 cup fresh green chiles, chopped	4 eggs
4 cups shredded cheddar cheese	1 cup buttermilk baking mix
2 cups cream or buttermilk	

Preheat the oven to 425° F. Grease a 10-inch pie plate. Sprinkle the bottom of the pie plate with the chiles and cheese. Combine the cream, eggs, and baking mix with a hand mixer until smooth, about 30 seconds. Pour over the chiles and cheese. Bake until a knife insterted near the middle comes out clean, about 30 minutes. Let sit 5 minutes before serving. **Yield: 6-8 servings.**

Variation: Use red peppers instead of chiles to protect your personal vitality, or yellow peppers to encourage creativity.

Magical Attributes: Protection, especially of one's financial resources.

Celebrations: Borrowed Days, Feast of Banners, Royal Oak Day, Riding the Marches, Old Dance, Labor Day.

Fondue (Switzerland)

This dish is supposed to be so tasty that it will lure unexpected company to your home! Celery is for wise communications; broccoli is for friendship.

2 cups milk	½ cup cooked broccoli, finely chopped
1 lb. Gruyére cheese, grated	½ teaspoon celery seed
½ cup butter	Bread, fruit, or vegetables for dipping
4 eggs, beaten	

Pour the milk over the cheese in a small bowl; let sit 1 hour. Melt the butter in a large saucepan over low heat. Stir in the cheese mixture, eggs, broccoli, and celery seed. Beat with a whisk or fork until the cheese is melted and the sauce is

smooth. Serve warm as a dip for chunks of bread, fruit, or vegetables.
Yield: 8-10 servings as an appetizer.

Magical Attributes: Fellowship, messages, companionship.

Celebrations: Any place where two or more of a like mind are gathered, this dish is appropriate!

Mozzarella a la Romana (Rome, Persia)

Pliny the Elder believed that Zoroaster, the founder of the group which later became known as the Magi, lived for thirty years on cheese which was specially prepared to ward off the signs of age. Parsley adds the symbolism of serendipity and spring to this recipe, while the anchovies convey the attributes of deliverance through wonder and divine blessing.

12 slices bread	3 eggs
6 oz. mozzarella or goat cheese, sliced	4 tablespoons butter plus butter for frying
Salt and pepper	1 tablespoon lemon juice
1 cup cream	1 teaspoon minced anchovies (opt.)
½ cup flour	1 tablespoon minced parsley

Make 6 sandwiches from the bread, cheese, and salt and pepper. Cut into quarters. Beat the cream, flour and egg in a small bowl. Dip the sandwiches in the batter. Let any excess batter drip off. Melt butter in a frying pan over medium heat. Fry until the cheese is melted and the bread is golden brown. Melt 4 tablespoons of the butter in a small saucepan over low heat. Mix in the lemon juice, parsley, and anchovies. Pour over the sandwiches. **Yield: 24 squares.**

Variation: Add a slice of ham to each sandwich for a "theatrical" flair.

Magical Attributes: Miracles, youthful vigor, sustenance, longevity, luck.

Celebrations: New Year's, most winter and early spring rituals, April Fool's Day.

Ricotta Broccoli Pizza

The circular nature of pizza makes it the perfect representation of the Wheel of the Year, movement, and change.

1 package pizza dough	2 teaspoons basil
1 (8-oz.) container ricotta cheese, room temperature	2 teaspoons oregano
8 oz. mozzarella cheese, grated	1 teaspoon minced garlic
¼ cup grated parmesan cheese	2 tablespoons olive oil
1 cup cooked, diced broccoli	2 tablespoons butter

Optional toppings:

Tomatoes	Onions
Olives	Peppers

Preheat the oven to 350° F. Prepare the pizza dough according to the package directions. Spread on a well-greased pizza pan or cookie sheet. Mix the cheeses and the broccoli in a medium-sized bowl. Sauté the garlic, basil, and oregano in the olive oil and butter until the garlic is lightly browned. Spread the garlic mixture directly on the dough. Spread on the cheese mixture. Top with any additional items you desire. Bake for 15 minutes. Turn up the heat to 400° F; bake until the cheese and crust have small patches of golden brown, 7-10 minutes. **Yield: Serves 4-6 cheese lovers.**

Variation: Frozen bread dough also works for the pizza dough. If you feel creative, try shaping the dough like a heart for love or an eye for intuition. Various cheeses can be substituted for the mozzarella. Cheddar works very well with the broccoli.

Magical Attributes: Changing cycles; with broccoli for financial matters, tomatoes for love, peppers for personal awareness and olives to encourage peace.

Celebrations: During the major cycles of change: Spring and Fall Equinox, Summer and Winter Solstice; your birthday.

❧ Eggs ❧

It has been estimated that during the French Revolution, chefs in Paris knew at least 685 different ways to prepare eggs. This is not surprising, as the egg has had probably had as many uses off the dining table as upon it! Many early myths tell about the "cosmic egg" which birthed the universe. Beyond this, eggs have been used in divination, protection, and healing rites to enhance metaphysical dreams, improve fertility, and even banish "curses." It is perhaps this versatile nature of the egg and its rich symbolism which can inspire contemporary kitchen wizards to regard it with new reverence.

Candlemas Sunrise

When prepared correctly, the cooked egg looks like a golden sun rising out of the snow (egg whites). This is also a lovely breakfast for people who want to reinforce their commitment to each other, two being the number of harmony in relationships.

Dash of nutmeg	2 slices of toast, buttered
2 eggs, separated	2 slices cheese, any kind

Preheat the broiler. Combine the nutmeg and egg white; beat until stiff. Spread over the toast. Make a small indentation in the center; drop in the egg yolk. Sprinkle with salt. Cover the yolk with 1 slice of cheese. Broil until the egg is completely cooked and the cheese is melted, 3-5 minutes. **Yield: 2 servings.**

Variation: Use white cheese over the egg for a lunar effect to use in moon magic.

Magical Attributes: Renewal, increasing solar energy, peace and restfulness, partnership.

Celebrations: Candlemas, before handfastings, early spring and late winter rituals.

Deviled Eggs

The egg presented in this manner looks like a full noonday sun. The yellow color of the yolk grants energy for the mind and movement, while the number six portends completion. Eat with your mind firmly fixed on goals in your life which have seemed unattainable, then let the fiery energy burn away the barriers.

6 hard-boiled eggs, peeled	¼ teaspoon garlic powder
3 tablespoons mayonnaise	¼ teaspoon celery seed
½ teaspoon mustard	Salt and pepper

Slice the eggs in half lengthwise; remove the yolk. Blend the yolks, mayonnaise, mustard, garlic powder, celery seed, and salt and pepper until smooth. Place a spoonful of the filling in the hollow of each egg white. Garnish with a red pimento or pepper slice. **Yield: 6 servings.**

Magical Attributes: Fire energies, the Sun in splendor, mental abilities, active mind, illumination, finishing projects.

Celebrations: Most summer and fire festivals, Sunning of Buddha.

Earth Eggs

Burying an egg was sometimes used in folk medicine to "bury" an illness. The eggs in this dish look like they are surrounded by rich earth, making them perfect for any "organic" magical goals.

1 lb. lean ground beef	½ teaspoon onion powder
1 small onion, minced	6 hard-boiled eggs, peeled
⅔ cup seasoned bread crumbs	1 egg, beaten
¼ cup milk	Vegetable oil for frying
1 teaspoon salt	2 tablespoons Worcestershire sauce
½ teaspoon garlic powder	¼ cup ketchup

Mix the ground beef, onion, ⅓ cup of the bread crumbs, milk, salt, garlic powder, and onion powder. Divide into six equal portions. Form each portion over a hard-boiled egg so that the egg is completely covered. Dip in the beaten egg; roll

in the remaining bread crumbs. Fry the eggs in the oil over medium heat, turning frequently, until the meat is completely cooked and the crumbs are golden brown. Remove from the pan; slice in halves or thirds lengthwise. Pour off the remaining oil in the frying pan. Mix the Worcestershire sauce and ketchup in the frying pan; heat. Return the eggs to the frying pan for 2-3 minutes. Turn frequently until the eggs are well coated with sauce. **Yield: 6 servings.**

Magical Attributes: Health, grounding, connection to Nature, Earth magic.

Celebrations: Earth Day, Spring Equinox, Sealing the Frost, Binding of the Wreaths, Festival of Durga, Saturnalia, Planting Festival, Festival of Ishtar.

Egg Foo Yung (Asian)

Black mushrooms lend their color for banishing any negative psychic energies; carrots grant vision. The hot spices and runic character reinforce protection.

1 cup diced pork	2 cloves garlic, minced
2 tablespoons peanut oil	Salt and pepper
¼ cup black mushrooms	2 tablespoons soy sauce
1 cup scallions, chopped	6 eggs
¼ cup shredded carrot	¼ cup chicken broth
½ cup thinly sliced celery	½ cup bamboo shoots

Heat the peanut oil in a wok over a medium flame. Add the pork; cook until lightly browned. Add the mushrooms, scallions, carrot, celery, garlic, salt and pepper, and 1 tablespoon of the soy sauce. Stir frequently until the vegtables are tender. Reduce heat to low. Beat the eggs, broth, and remaining soy sauce. Pour

CONTINUED ON NEXT PAGE

over the vegetables; cover. When the eggs begin to set, arrange the bamboo shoots to form the rune of protection (see illustration) or a simple circle, which is also indicative of surety. When the bottom is brown, flip, and brown the other side to "cook in" the magic of the symbol. **Yield: 4 servings.**

Variation: Shrimp or chicken may be used in place of the pork. Shrimp will improve the powers of insight; chicken helps heal psychic wounds.

Magical Attributes: Awareness, psychic protection, clear sight, intuition.

Celebrations: Kamehameha Day, Lammas, Ahes Festival, Birthday of the Moon, Samhain.

Eggs and Lamb (India)

The lamb has often been a symbol of gentle forbearance. The number 12 adds to this energy with the symbolism of a full turning of the Wheel, durability, and fruitfulness from your abiding efforts.

4 medium onions plus 1 onion, minced	½ teaspoon ground chili pepper
4 cloves garlic, minced and divided	1 teaspoon ground cumin
1 cup butter, divided	½ teaspoon ground coriander
1½ lbs. ground lamb	¼ teaspoon dried parsley
⅓ cup bread crumbs	6 hard-boiled eggs, peeled and halved lengthwise
1 teaspoon minced ginger root	1 teaspoon curry powder
2 hot peppers, minced	Lime wedges

Sauté 4 of the onions and 2 cloves of the garlic in ¼ cup of the butter. Mix with the lamb, bread crumbs, ginger root, hot pepper, chili pepper, cumin, coriander, and parsley in a medium-sized bowl. Divide into 12 equal portions. Form around each egg half so that egg is completely covered. Sauté the remaining onion and garlic in ¼ cup butter; stir in the curry. Add the eggs and fry until the meat is completely cooked on all sides; about 10 minutes. Garnish with lime wedges. **Yield: 6 servings.**

Magical Attributes: Patience, tolerance, endurance, labors which bear results because of these attributes.

Celebrations: Most winter rituals, Hori, St. Joan of Arc Day, Sunning of Buddha, before accepting a training period in any esoteric mystery tradition.

Fried Bread and Eggs (Scotland)

Anchovies are traditional in this Scottish dish; Scots rave about its flavor. Anchovies are a magical symbol of the fisherman's "catch" which insured many seafaring towns of food and prosperity for a season.

⅓ cup butter	¼ cup minced anchovies (optional)
½ cup heavy cream	6 pieces fried or toasted bread,
7 egg yolks, beaten	any kind

Melt the butter in a medium-sized sauce pan over low heat. Beat in the cream, egg yolks, and anchovies. Stir until the mixture thickens and is creamy. Pour over the toast. Serve hot. **Yield: Serves 6 as an appetizer, 3 as a main dish.**

Variation: For those who do not enjoy the flavor of anchovies, try substituting ½ cup peas for the anchovies for financial improvements.

Magical Attributes: Abundance, especially in any matters of productivity.

Celebrations: Most spring observances, Ahes Festival.

Hot Egg Salad

The significance of this dish comes from the way it is laid out, sunward, with icons for all four directions/elements.

- 2 hard-boiled eggs, peeled and diced
- 2 tablespoons mayonnaise
- ¼ teaspoon mustard
- 2 tablespoons minced celery
- ¼ cup minced onion
- 2 slices toast
- 4 (½-inch wide) strips of cheese

Toppings:

- 2 pearl onions
- 2 pimentos
- 2 black olives
- 2 sprigs parsley or kelp

Preheat the oven to 350° F. Mix the eggs, mayonnaise, mustard, celery, and onion in a small bowl. Spread over the toast. Use 2 pieces of the cheese to form an X on each slice of toast (see illustration). Place a pearl onion in the east for air, a pimento in the south for fire, parsley in the west for water, and a black olive in the north for earth. Place on a cookie sheet. Bake until the cheese melts, about 5 minutes. Serve hot. **Yield: 1 serving.**

Note: The toast can be microwaved on high for about 1½ minutes instead of baked.

Magical Attributes: Elemental balance.

Celebrations: Samhain, New Year's, any midnight or noon rituals.

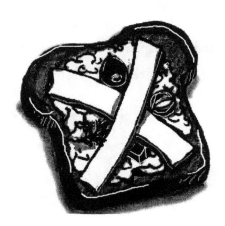

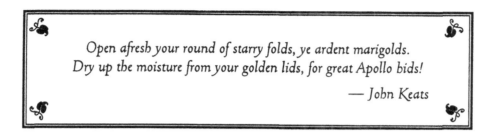

> *Open afresh your round of starry folds, ye ardent marigolds.*
> *Dry up the moisture from your golden lids, for great Apollo bids!*
>
> *— John Keats*

Marigold and Dandelion Eggs (Medieval France)

The marigold is said to be one of the flowers which gives forth small bursts of light, usually near twilight on clear days, like a beacon or flash of insight. In the language of flowers, dandelions are ancient oracles. They are also high in vitamin C. Make certain the dandelions you use are free of pesticides.

4 whole dandelion buds	¼ cup cream or milk
2 tablespoons butter	⅛ teaspoon salt
2 marigold blossoms, chopped	⅛ teaspoon pepper
4 eggs	⅛ teaspoon nutmeg

Pick the dandelion buds when they are just about to open. Melt the butter in a frying pan over low heat. Sauté the dandelions until they open wide. Beat the marigold, eggs, cream, salt, pepper, and nutmeg in a small bowl. Pour over the dandelions, which will poke through. Cover; cook over low heat until the egg is set and dry on top. Fold in half. **Yield: 2 servings.**

Variation: For the same magical results without the flowers, substitute 1 cup diced cashew nuts, ¼ teaspoon orange rind, and ¼ cup diced, peeled oranges.

Magical Attributes: Sun magic, positive outcomes in legal matters, prophesy, simple joys.

Celebrations: Spring and summer festivals, Birthday of the Sun, Samhain, Candlemas, Sun Dance.

Polish Eggs

Parsley or wild olive was used to crown heros in the games at Nemean in Ancient Greece. Four is the number of success.

- 4 hard-boiled eggs, unpeeled
- ¼ cup shredded cheese, any kind
- 3 tablespoons butter, softened
- 3 tablespoons sour cream
- 2 tablespoons minced fresh parsley
- ⅛ teaspoon salt
- 1 tablespoon bacon bits (optional)

Preheat the oven to 400° F. Using a sharp knife, slice the unpeeled eggs in half lengthwise. Try to keep the half eggshells in one piece. Scoop out the egg yolk and egg white. Chop; place in a small bowl. Blend with the cheese, butter, sour cream, parsley, salt, and bacon until smooth. Carefully spoon the mixture back into the eggshells. Bake for 10 minutes. **Yield: 4 servings.**

Magical Attributes: Victory, joy, heroic vigor.

Celebrations: Patriot's Day, Memorial Day, Independence Day, Royal Oak Day, founder's festivals, Old Dance.

Tea Eggs (Asia)

Sir Kenelm Digby, a medieval cookbook writer, believed that these eggs cured any weakness of the stomach and improved physical strength. The number of eggs here is also a number of energy and potency.

- 8 eggs, soaked in warm water
- 4 tablespoons prepared tea
- 4 tablespoons soy sauce
- 3 tablespoons salt
- 1 tablespoon pepper
- ⅔ teaspoon anise

In a large saucepan, bring enough water to cover the eggs to a boil. Gently transfer the eggs from the warm water to the boiling water with a spoon. Boil for 12 minutes. Remove the eggs from the pan. Allow to cool enough to handle. Carefully crack the shells all over; do not remove any part of the shell. Add the tea, soy sauce, salt, pepper, and anise to the hot water; bring to a boil. Add the eggs; simmer for 30 minutes. Run under cold water. Cool completely before peeling. Slice and serve on a bed of lettuce (for growth and peace) or red cabbage (for stamina and bravery). **Yield: 4 servings.**

Magical Attributes: Gentle strength, growing courage, healthful vitality.

Celebrations: Any healing rituals, Patriot's Day, Smell the Breeze Day, Feast of Banners, Birthday of the Sun.

Spanish Eggs

For commoners whose means were little, the eggs were images of plenty. As such, they were frequently offered to an image of the Holy Mother in hopefulness for divine providence. In this recipe, the five tomato bits represents strong psychic awareness.

- 1 lb. pork sausage
- ½ cup green onion, minced
- 1 green pepper, minced
- 1 cup salsa
- 1 medium tomato, diced
- ¾ cup shredded pepper cheese
- 4 eggs

Throughly cook the sausage, onion, and green pepper in a frying pan. Drain off the grease. Stir in the salsa; simmer 5 minutes. Divide meat into 4 portions inside the pan. Form each portion into a "nest." Make sure there is meat covering the bottom of the pan in the middle of the nest. Sprinkle a little bit of cheese and 5 tomato bits in the middle of the nest. Break an egg into the hollow. Cover; cook until the egg is firm, about 15 minutes. Sprinkle the remaining cheese on top. **Yield: 4 servings.**

Magical Attributes: Provision, insight, sagacity.

Celebrations: Asking Day, Thanksgiving, Sunning of Buddha, Birthday of Confucius, Fiesta of the Mother of Health.

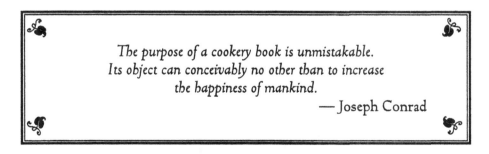

> *The purpose of a cookery book is unmistakable.*
> *Its object can conceivably no other than to increase*
> *the happiness of mankind.*
> — Joseph Conrad

Quarter Quiche

Quiche-like dishes were favored by the royal families of France; however, the famous Quiche Lorraine may have had its beginnings in Alsace, Germany, over 600 years ago. This dish is fast, easy, inexpensive, and can be made with whatever you have on hand.

4 eggs	1 9-inch pie crust
1½ cups cream	¼ cup cooked chopped spinach, well drained
½ cup grated parmesan cheese	
1 cup grated mozzarella cheese	⅛ cup bamboo shoots, drained
½ teaspoon salt	⅛ cup sliced black olives, drained
½ teaspoon pepper	⅛ cup shredded carrots
½ teaspoon dried thyme	⅛ cup minced onions
½ teaspoon dried oregano	⅛ cup chopped cauliflower
2 cloves garlic, minced	⅛ cup chopped broccoli
1 teaspoon soy sauce	

Preheat the oven to 375° F. Beat the eggs, cream, parmesan cheese, mozzarella cheese, salt, pepper, thyme, oregano, garlic, and soy sauce in a medium-sized bowl. Line a 9-inch pie pan with the crust. In the pie crust, arrange the spinach in the north (for earth), bamboo shoots and olives in the east (for air), carrots and onions in the south (for fire), and cauliflower and broccoli in the west (for water). Pour the egg mixture over the top. Bake until a fork inserted near the center comes out clean, about 45 minutes. Let stand 10 minutes before cutting.
Yield: 6 servings.

Magical Attributes: The Wheel of the Year, full cycles, succession of power.

Celebrations: Initiation, dedication, New Year's, major Esbats.

✦ Personal Recipes ✦

Personal Recipes

Chapter Eight

Divine Desserts

*G*o *to your banquet but use delight,*
so as to rise still with an appetite.

— Robert Herrick

Historically, desserts have not only been considered the crowing glory of a meal, but are used in celebrations, and even as expressions of love. Look at candies in piñatas for Mexican festivals, soul cakes on November 2, sweet bread on Good Friday, birthday feasts in your own home, and a wedding cake at a marriage, for example. In each instance the sweet food has a certain amount of symbolism.

The wedding cake has many folk associations. If it should crack during baking, it is best to make another lest the marriage likewise rend asunder. The bride should always cut the cake first and make a wish, and finally all guests who take cake home with them can place it beneath a pillow for sweet dreams, sometimes of future loves!

❧ Cakes ❧

God Cakes (England)

This recipe is a slightly altered version of cakes made by grandparents in certain districts of England. On New Year's, they were given out to bless the children.

2 tablespoons butter, softened	½ teaspoon nutmeg
3 tablespoons brown sugar	½ teaspoon cinnamon
¾ cup milk	½ teaspoon allspice
2 eggs	½ cup currants
2 cups flour	¼ cup candied orange and
3 teaspoon baking powder	lemon rind (p. 156)

Preheat the oven to 400° F. Grease and flour an 8 x 8 x 2-inch pan. Cream the butter and sugar. Add the milk, eggs, flour, baking powder, nutmeg, cinnamon, and allspice. Beat at low speed for 30 seconds; scrape the bowl frequently. Beat at high speed for 3 minutes. Fold in the currants and candied rinds. Pour into the pan. Bake until a wooden toothpick inserted in the center comes out clean, about 30-40 minutes. **Yield: 16 servings.**

Magical Attributes: Family bonds, the God aspect, honoring lineage.

Celebrations: Birthday of the Sun, solstices, Festival of Brightness, Feast of Banners, St. Stephen's Festival, New Year's, Father's Day.

Handfasting Cake (Scotland/England)

The tradition of multi-layered wedding cakes originates with grain and rice throwing of the Middle Ages, which was thought to insure the couple fertility. In Scotland, Drambuie is fondly referred to as the "nectar of the Gods." Marzipan was a favorite festival sweet in Medieval Europe having been brought back by Crusaders from Islamic lands.

1½ cups currants	2 teaspoons baking powder
1½ cups white raisins	1 teaspoon cinnamon
3 cups mixed candied fruit rinds (p. 156)	½ teaspoon nutmeg
4 cups flour	1 cup ground almonds
2⅔ cups butter	1 tablespoon powdered lemon rind
2 cups sugar	1 cup slivered almonds
½ cup Drambuie liqueur	5 cups marzipan
12 eggs	Icing, any kind, or powdered sugar

Preheat the oven to 325° F. Grease and line 2 or 3 (depending on size) spring-form pans with waxed paper. Mix the currants, raisins, candied fruit rind, and ¼ cup of the flour in a medium-sized bowl. Beat the butter, sugar, and Drambuie until creamy in a large mixing bowl. Beat in one egg at a time. Combine 3¾ cups of the flour, baking powder, cinnamon, and nutmeg in a medium-sized bowl. Mix the flour into the egg mixture a little at a time on low speed. Beat on high for 2 minutes, scraping the bowl constantly. Fold in the dried fruit, ground almonds, and powdered lemon rind. Sprinkle with slivered almonds. Pour into the pans. Bake until a wooden toothpick inserted in the middle comes out clean, 1½ - 2 hours. Cool. Spread each cake with marzipan. Stack the cakes on top of each other. Frost with the icing of your choice or sprinkle with powdered sugar..
Yield: 25 servings.

Magical Attributes: Love, joy, fidelity, patience, blessing.

Celebrations: Weddings/handfastings, vow renewals, engagements, Handsel Monday.

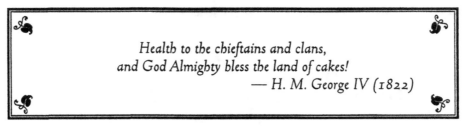

Health to the chieftains and clans,
and God Almighty bless the land of cakes!
— H. M. George IV (1822)

Honor Cake (France, England)

In England these were sometimes known as presentation cakes, and were often part of important palace gatherings for honored guests. The basic cake recipe is, however, from France. The 21 almonds reinforce energies for distinction.

6 eggs	2 tablespoons rum
1 cup sugar	⅔ cup finely chopped chestnuts
1 cup flour	½ cup heavy whipping
⅓ cup butter, melted	cream, whipped
1 teaspoon vanilla	21 whole almonds
¾ cup apricot preserves	¾ cup thin white icing (p. 163)

Preheat the oven to 350° F. Generously grease three 8-inch round pans. To make cake removal easier, also line with wax paper. Mix the eggs and sugar in a double boiler over low heat. Beat until tripled in size and slightly warm. Remove from heat. Mix in the flour, butter, and vanilla. Divide evenly among the pans. Bake until a wooden toothpick inserted in the middle comes out clean, about 20 minutes. Remove from the pans and cool.

Mix the apricot preserves with the rum. Fold the chestnuts into the whipped cream. Spread one of the cakes with half of the preserves; spread half the whipped cream on top of the preserves. Cover with another cake. Repeat. Spread the top cake with the remaining preserves and the icing. Decorate around the edge with 21 whole almonds. **Yield: 12 servings.**

Magical Attributes: Honor, respect, reverence, memories.

Celebrations: Patriot's Day, Memorial Day, Independence Day, any holiday which commemorates your patron deities, memorial services for loved ones.

Mothering Cakes

Sometimes called simnel, cakes similar to these were traditionally made by children for their mothers in England during mid-Lent. The favored frosting was butter cream. Almost all the ingredients are lunar in nature.

¾ cup butter	⅓ cup shredded coconut
1½ cups sugar	½ cup candied lemon rind,
4 eggs	minced (p. 156)
2 cups flour	2½ cups marzipan
1 teaspoon salt	2 tablespoons white wine
1 cup currants	

Preheat the oven to 350° F. Generously grease an 8-inch springform pan. Cream the butter and sugar; beat in the eggs one at a time. Gradually mix in the flour and salt. Beat on high speed for 2 minutes; scrape bowl frequently. Fold in the currants, coconut, and lemon rind. Pour half the batter into the pan. Mix the almond paste and wine until smooth. Spread over the cake batter. Pour in the remaining batter. Bake until the cake springs back when touched, about 60 minutes. **Yield: 12 servings.**

Variation: Replace one egg with ¼ cup plain yogurt for even stronger Goddess energies and a very moist cake. Also add 1 teaspoon rose water (p. 58), and this recipe becomes a serviceable "mooncake."

Magical Attributes: Maternal aspects, feminine power, consideration, moon magic, fertility.

Celebrations: Mother's Day, Birthday of the Moon, any Goddess-related holiday.

Potato Peanut Cake (1600s Spain)

Peanuts are aligned with Jupiter, a planet of prosperity and strong masculine traits. The potato is an earth plant, having healthful and protective qualities.

2 cups sugar	2 teaspoons baking powder
1 cup shortening	1 teaspoon cinnamon
1 cup mashed potatoes	½ teaspoon nutmeg
4 eggs, separated	½ cup peanuts, crushed
¾ cup milk	Crunchy peanut butter
2 cups flour	Thin white icing (p. 163)

Preheat the oven to 350° F. Grease and flour three 9-inch round pans. Cream the sugar and shortening. Mix in the potatoes, egg yolks, and milk. Combine the flour, baking powder, cinnamon, and nutmeg in a small bowl. Stir the flour into the wet mixture. Add the egg whites. Beat on high speed for 5 minutes; scrape the bowl frequently. Fold in the peanuts. Divide the batter among the pans. Bake until a wooden toothpick inserted in the middle comes out clean, about 20 minutes. Remove from the pans and cool. Spread crunchy peanut butter between each layer. Drizzle confectionery glaze on top. **Yield: 15 servings.**

Magical Attributes: Prosperity, Yin-Yang energy, fruitfulness, physical well-being, grounding.

Celebrations: Feast of Jupiter, Borrowed Days, Old Dance, Labor Day, Thanksgiving, Beltane.

❧ Candies ❧

After Dinner Wafers

Mint is naturally refreshing and was even praised in the New Testament. It is a calming herb which can strengthen nerves and ease digestive difficulty.

4 cups powdered sugar	2-3 drops green food coloring
⅔ cup sweetened condensed milk	½ teaspoon mint extract

Mix all ingredients until smooth. Form into 1-inch balls. Place on waxed paper. Flatten to ¼-inch thickness. Let sit until the top is dry, about 60 minutes. Turn over and dry the other side. Store in an air tight container. These are especially good after heavily spiced meals. **Yield: 8 dozen.**

Magical Attributes: Invigoration, rejuvenation, peaceful energy.

Celebrations: All spring holidays, Kermesse, Saturnalia, New Year's.

Apricot Delight (Turkey)

By the nineteenth century, Turkey had become widely recognized for its skill in creating candies. Many Turkish women believe this sweet treat enhances beauty, and it is regarded as a skill to know how to prepare this dish.

Powdered sugar	¾ cup cornstarch
3 envelopes unflavored gelatin	3 tablespoons rose water (p. 58)
⅓ cup lemon juice	1 cup chopped apricots
3 cups sugar	½ cup pistachios
¼ cup light corn syrup, scant	

Cover the bottom of an 8-inch square pan with powdered sugar. Mix the gelatin and lemon juice in a small bowl. Combine the sugar, corn syrup, and 1½ cups water in a medium-sized saucepan. Heat over a medium flame until the mixture reaches 240° F or until a small amount dropped into very cold water forms a ball that does not hold its shape. Mix in the cornstarch and ½ cup cold water; stir until thick. Remove from heat; mix in the dissolved gelatin and rose water. Fold in the apricots and pistachios. Pour into the pan and let set. Sprinkle the top with powdered sugar. Cut in 1-inch squares. Store in an airtight container.
Yield: About 60 pieces.

Magical Attributes: Perfection, faith, beauty, protecting personal information.

Celebrations: Apple Blossom Day, Summer Solstice, Sukkoth, Russian Fair.

Apple Sweets (Asia, Persia)

Persians believed the quince (apple) to be a kind of poison antidote, while the Greeks saw apples as an emblem of love. The Romans found other uses for apples, such as perfume, hair dye, and honeyed-wine syrup.

2½ cups peeled apples, sliced	1 teaspoon grated lemon rind
⅔ cup sugar	½ teaspoon cinnamon
⅓ cup finely chopped almonds	Powdered sugar

Steam apples until soft, about 30 minutes. Cool. Pureé in a food processor or blender. Pour into a medium saucepan. Stir in the sugar. Simmer over low heat until thickened, about 45 minutes. Remove from heat. Mix in the almonds, lemon rind, and cinnamon. Pour onto buttered a cookie sheet. Spread to ½-inch thickness. Chill. Cut into any shapes which enhance your spiritual goals and sprinkle with powdered sugar. Store separated by waxed paper.

Yield: About 20 1-inch cutouts.

Variation: Replace the almonds with walnuts for protection, hazelnuts for wisdom, or pistachios for romance.

Magical Attributes: Beauty, health, diversity, love.

Celebrations: Apple Blossom Day, Aloha Week, May Day, Valentine's Day, harvest festivals.

Candied Citrus Rinds

The word "candy" derives from an Arabic term, quandt. In Persia, flower waters may have been added to this recipe. By the time Queen Elizabeth I occupied the throne, candied citrus rinds were considered a wonderful and rather expensive treat.

Rind from 3 large oranges	1½ teaspoons ginger
Rind from 1 large grapefruit	½ teaspoon cinnamon
2 cups honey	Sugar

Scrape out the inside of the fruit rind to remove as much of the white pith as possible. Slice the rind into narrow, even sized strips. Bring to a boil in a large pan of water. Simmer for 5 minutes and drain. Repeat the boiling procedure 4

more times to remove the bitterness from the fruit rind. Combine the honey, ginger, cinnamon, and 1 cup water in a medium-sized saucepan. Stir until the honey is dissolved. The heavy feeling at the bottom of the pan will disappear. Add the rinds; cook over low heat until all the syrup is absorbed and the peels are soft, about 60 minutes. Spread on waxed paper; dust with sugar. Cover with cheesecloth; let sit until well dried. Store in an airtight jar. These will keep indefinitely. Candied citrus rinds make a nice garnish and refresh the breath.
Yield: About 8 cups.

Variation: If you enjoy a sweet-tart flavor, lemon and lime also work very well in this recipe. Any combination of citrus peels will work.

Magical Attributes: Sun energy, purification, health, lavishness.

Celebrations: Feast of Jupiter, Birthday of the Sun, Fire Festivals, Fiesta of the Mother of Health.

Lilac Crystals

Purple lilacs are symbolic of tenderness; the white ones mean happiness and youth.

- 1 oz. gum arabic
- 6 small bunches of lilac buds (about 3 cups)
- 1 tablespoon corn syrup
- 1 cup sugar

Dissolve the gum arabic in ½ cup hot water. Dip the lilac buds in the mixture and let dry. Heat the corn syrup, sugar, and ½ cup water until it reaches the soft ball (240° F) stage, when a small amount dropped into very cold water will form a ball but will not hold its shape. Dip the lilacs in the syrup. Lay on wax paper. Sprinkle with granulated sugar. Color the sugar blue for enhanced happiness or peace. Let sit until dry. **Yield: About 3 cups.**

Magical Attributes: Love, joy, youth, meticulousness.

Celebrations: Any flower festival.

Tenacious Taffy

The magical goal of your taffy can change with the flavoring you choose. For example, use cinnamon to "stretch" psychic awareness, ginger to help bring a dependable flow of money into your home, and mint for health.

1 cup sugar	1 teaspoon salt
1 tablespoon cornstarch	⅔ cup water
¾ cup light corn syrup	2 teaspoons extract, any flavor
2 tablespoons butter	Food coloring (optional)

Butter an 8 x 8 x 2-inch pan. Combine the sugar, cornstarch, corn syrup, butter, salt, and water in a medium-sized saucepan over medium heat. Bring to a full, rolling boil while stirring constantly. Continue cooking without stirring until the candy reaches the hard ball stage (256° F), when a small amount dropped into very cold water forms a ball and holds its shape until pressed. Remove from heat. Mix in the extract and food coloring. Pour into the pan until cool enough to handle. Butter your hands and begin pulling the taffy until satiny, light in color, and stiff. Cut into ½ x 1½-inch strips using greased scissors. Wrap individual pieces in waxed paper or plastic wrap. **Yield: 4 dozen pieces.**

Magical Attributes: Sea magic, determination, constancy.

Celebrations: Royal Oak Day, Ahes Festival, Labor Day.

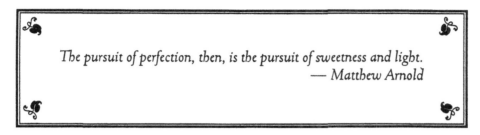

The pursuit of perfection, then, is the pursuit of sweetness and light.
— Matthew Arnold

❧ Cookies ❧

Kinship Cookies (Germany)

Small cookies similar to these were prepared by the early Pagans in Germany; the cookies were often shaped like animals. Very likely these treats are the roots of our modern animal crackers!

3 cups flour	2 cups sugar
½ teaspoon salt	2 teaspoons grated lemon rind
1 teaspoon baking powder	2 tablespoons grated orange rind
4 eggs	¼ cup anise seed

Combine the flour, salt, and baking powder in a small bowl. Beat the eggs until fluffy in a medium-sized mixing bowl. Continue beating and slowly add the sugar. When mixed properly this batter is pale and thick. Add a little milk if the batter is too dry. Stir in the lemon and orange rind. Mix in the dry ingredients a little at a time until the dough is smooth. Cover; chill for 1 hour.

Roll ⅓-inch thick on a flat, sugared surface. Cut into desired shapes. Place on greased cookie sheets. Sprinkle with anise seed. Cover; refrigerate for 24 hours. Preheat the oven to 325° F. Bake until lightly browned on the edges, about 20 minutes. Cool. Place in an airtight container and store for 10 days before eating. **Yield: About 5 dozen small cookies.**

Magical Attributes: Joy and love, especially among members of a magical group; animal kinship.

Celebrations: Almost any, but especially Yule and Winter Solstice. Also Feast of Madonna, Beltane, Sun Dance, Pardon of the Birds.

Serendipity Cookies

This is a wonderful Yule/New Year's cookie to share with family and friends, thus spreading a little good fortune with the gift. Coconut is one of nature's most versatile foods. Nutmeg is for awareness; vanilla is for love.

Crust:

½ cup butter	½ teaspoon vanilla
¼ cup white sugar	1¼ cups flour
1 egg	½ teaspoon salt

Topping:

2 eggs, beaten	2 tablespoons flour
1¼ cups packed brown sugar	½ teaspoon baking powder
½ cup shredded coconut	½ teaspoon nutmeg
1 cup chopped pecans	1 teaspoon vanilla

Powdered sugar

Preheat the oven to 350° F. Grease a 9 x 13-inch pan. Beat the butter, white sugar, egg, and vanilla in a medium-sized mixing bowl. Mix in the flour and salt. Pat the dough into the pan. Bake for 15 minutes.

To prepare the topping, mix the eggs, brown sugar, coconut, pecans, flour, baking powder, nutmeg, and vanilla in a medium-sized bowl. Spread on the hot crust. Bake 25 minutes. Cool. Dust with powdered sugar. **Yield: 32 bars.**

Variation: For a decadent change which will strongly attune this cookie to romance or prosperity, add 1 cup chocolate or carob chips to the topping.

Magical Attributes: Luck, love, joy, diversity, practicality.

Celebrations: May Day, Summer Solstice, Kamehameha Day, Aloha Week.

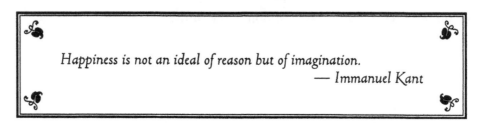

Happiness is not an ideal of reason but of imagination.
— *Immanuel Kant*

Threefold Laws

The triangle here is used to represent the unity of body, mind, and spirit with universal symmetry and purpose (goals). The eggs and cream impart Goddess energy, while the nuts balance with the God aspect.

½ cup butter, softened	2 cups flour
1 cup sugar	½ teaspoon salt
6 tablespoons whipping cream	½ cup finely chopped nuts
3 eggs	½ cup brown or white sugar

Cream the butter and 1 cup sugar in a medium-sized mixing bowl. Mix in the whipping cream and 2 of the eggs on medium speed for 1 minute. Stir in the flour and salt. Cover; chill for 24 hours.

Preheat the oven to 375° F. Roll to ¼-inch thickness on a flat, floured surface. Cut into triangular pieces. Place on a greased cookie sheet. Beat the last egg; brush on the triangles. Sprinkle with the nuts and ½ cup sugar. Bake until edges are light brown, 8-10 minutes. **Yield: 4 dozen cookies.**

Magical Attributes: Universal law, metaphysical studies, awareness of power.

Celebrations: Sunning of Buddha, before initiation, Day of the Dryads, Birthday of the Moon, Sukkoth.

Victorian Lace Cookies

Hazelnuts were part of Victorian divination techniques; in Scotland they are a symbol of fruitfulness. Lace is closely associated with knot magic for binding or loosing. This recipe might be used to open doors in your mind to aid mystical insight.

½ cup corn syrup	1 cup flour
½ cup margarine	1 cup chopped hazelnuts
⅔ cup packed brown sugar	

Preheat the oven to 375° F. Bring the corn syrup, margarine, and sugar to a full boil over medium heat in a medium-sized saucepan. Remove from heat. Stir in the flour and nuts. Keep the batter warm by suspending it over a double boiler

CONTINUED ON NEXT PAGE

or setting the pan in bowl of very hot water. Place spoonfuls of batter on a greased cookie sheet 3 inches apart. Bake for 5 minutes. **Yield: 4 dozen.**

Magical Attributes: Divination, knot magic, productivity, love.

Celebrations: Samhain, Valentine's or Sweetest Days, Riding the Marches.

ꙮ Frostings, Glazes, and Toppings ꙮ

You know the old saying, "everything else is just icing on the cake"? Your magic can be crowned with yet another sweet, enjoyable treat. Since these are meant to "top off" whatever magical cake or cookie you choose, I will not give suggested magical attributes or celebrations here.

Amaretto Whipped Cream

1 cup whipping cream, chilled	½ teaspoon vanilla
3 tablespoons sugar	2 tablespoons amaretto

Beat the cream, sugar, and vanilla in a medium-sized chilled bowl until stiff and peaked. Fold in the amaretto. Keep chilled until served. **Yield: 2⅓ cups.**

Citrus Frosting

1¾ cups powdered sugar	1 tablespoon grated lemon peel
3 tablespoons butter, softened	1 tablespoon orange juice
1 tablespoon grated orange peel	

Beat all the ingredients in a small mixing bowl until very smooth. Add a little orange juice or powdered sugar to obtain the desired consistency.
Yield: Covers 5 dozen cookies.

Chocolate Decadence Frosting

6 oz. semi-sweet chocolate
2 tablespoons butter
¼ teaspoon salt
2 cups powdered sugar

1 teaspoon vanilla
2 tablespoons milk
½ cup chocolate sprinkles
½ cup chocolate chips

Melt the chocolate and butter in a double boiler. Stir in the salt and powdered sugar. Mix in the vanilla. Stir in small amounts of the milk until the frosting is a good spreading consistency. Sprinkle the frosted cake with the sprinkles and chips. **Yield: Enough for a 9-inch cake.**

Honey and Cheese Glaze

4 oz. cream cheese, softened
1½ teaspoon apple juice

2-3 tablespoons honey

Beat the cream cheese with the apple juice until smooth. Slowly mix in the honey to taste. This glaze is excellent for zucchini or carrot cakes.
Yield: About ¾ cup.

Thin White Icing

⅓ cup butter
1½ teaspoons vanilla

2 cups powdered sugar
3 tablespoons hot water

Melt butter in a small saucepan over low heat. Add sugar and vanilla. Stir in water 1 tablespoon at a time until smooth. **Yield: 1½ cups.**

❧ Pies ❧

Dynahara's Nutty Apple Pie

Dynahara says this is a favorite for her and Rhenda (her sister-in-law). This dessert is a lazy cross between apple pie and apple crust. For the fun of it, toss the apple peel over your left shoulce to divine the first letter of the name of a future lover.

5-6	cups sliced apples, peeled	1½ cups flour
¾	teaspoon cinnamon	1¼ cup sugar
¾	teaspoon nutmeg	2 teaspoon brown sugar
½	cup butter, softened	1 cup chopped walnuts
2	eggs	

Preheat the oven to 350° F. Grease a 10-inch glass pie pan (metal pie pans will turn the apples black). Place the apples in the pan. Sprinkle with the cinnamon and nutmeg. Mix the butter, eggs, flour, sugar, and walnuts in a medium-sized bowl. The dough will be sticky. Spread evenly over the apples; sprinkle with additional cinnamon and nutmeg. Bake until the crust is golden brown and juices begin to bubble through cracks in the crust, about 45 minutes.
Yield: 8 servings.

Magical Attributes: Beauty, leisure, the spirit of America.

Celebrations: Independence Day, May Day, Apple Blossom Day, most spring festivals, family reunions, picnics.

Auntie Fay's Luscious Lemon Pie

To tempt their lords into staying home instead of going to battle, ladies of old might have baked a lemon pie. Lemon flower present in the bridal bouquet is thought to insure fidelity and joy to the couple.

Filling:

3 egg yolks	2 cups water
1 cup sugar, divided	2 tablespoons butter
6 tablespoons cornstarch	2 teaspoons grated lemon rind
¼ teaspoon salt	5 tablespoons lemon juice

Crust:

9-inch pie shell, baked

Meringue:

6 egg whites	¼ teaspoon vanilla
Dash of salt	

Preheat the oven to 325° F. Combine the egg yolks and ½ cup of the sugar in a small bowl. In a double boiler, mix ½ cup of the sugar, cornstarch, salt, and water. Cook over boiling water until thick; stir constantly. Cover. Bring mixture to a boil; boil 1 minute. Stir occasionally. Spoon a little of the hot mixture into the egg yolk, stir quickly. Beat the egg yolks into the hot mixture. Cook 2 minutes; stir constantly. Remove the pan from the water; stir in the butter, lemon rind, and juice. Pour into the pie shell.

Beat the egg whites and salt until foamy. Add the vanilla. Beat in the remaining sugar 1 tablespoon at a time; continue beating until stiff and shiny. Cover pie with the meringue. Make sure there are no gaps and the edges are sealed with the meringue. Bake until delicately browned, about 15 minutes. **Yield: 8 servings.**

Magical Attributes: Love, purification, cleansing, lifting burdens.

Celebrations: Valentine's Day, anniversaries, Candlemas, winter celebrations.

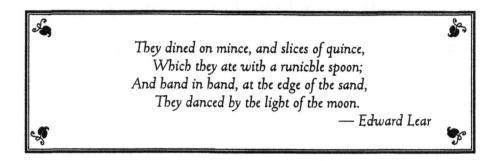

They dined on mince, and slices of quince,
Which they ate with a runicble spoon;
And hand in hand, at the edge of the sand,
They danced by the light of the moon.
— Edward Lear

Mince Pie

As many mince pies as you taste at Yule will equal the months of happiness to come next year. It is best never to cut mince pies, lest you cut your luck. If you get the first slice of mince pie, make a wish!

⅓ lb. beef, boiled
2 tablespoons suet
1 cup beef broth
⅔ cup brown sugar
½ teaspoon cinnamon
1 teaspoon clove
1 teaspoon nutmeg
¼ teaspoon salt

½ cup candied citrus rinds (p. 156)
1½ cup chopped apples, peeled
1 orange with rind, ground
½ lemon with rind, ground
½ cup raisins
⅓ cup currants
¼ cup cognac
¼ cup rum

Grind the beef with the suet. Place in a large saucepan. Stir in the beef broth, brown sugar, cinnamon, clove, nutmeg, salt, rinds, apples, orange, lemon, raisins, and currants. Simmer until the apples are soft, about 1 hour. Cool. Stir in the cognac and rum. Pour into a sterilized jar that has a lid. Cover and age a least 3 months in the refrigerator before using.

To bake, preheat the oven to 400° F. Pour the mincemeat into a 10-inch pie crust. A top crust will keep the pie moist but is optional. Bake for 30 minutes. **Yield: One 10-inch pie.**

Magical Attributes: Protection, passion, happiness, luck, wishes.

Celebrations: According to tradition, this pie was to be eaten between Yule and Twelfth Night. However, the passionate energies of this pie might also make it appropriate at the Great Rite or a Handfasting.

Pear Cashew Pie

Nutmeg was often used to cure rheumatism. Pear was used in China to treat fever, while the leaves were applied in poultice form for bruises. In the West Indies the natives recommend cashew nut liquor to aid stomach disorders. The juice of the nut applied to the skin is believed to create a youthful appearance.

Crust:

1⅓	cup flour	½	teaspoon nutmeg
⅓	cup sugar	⅔	cup butter
⅓	cup minced cashews		

Filling:

2⅔	cups pears, peeled and sliced	½	teaspoon orange rind
¼	cup brown sugar	½	teaspoon cinnamon
2	tablespoons flour	1	tablespoon butter, softened
1	teaspoon vanilla		

Preheat the oven to 375° F. To prepare the crust, mix the flour, sugar, cashews, and nutmeg in a small bowl. Cut in the butter using a fork or pastry cutter until the mixture resembles coarse meal. Press firmly against the bottom and sides of a 10-inch pie pan. Bake for 8 minutes.

To prepare the filling, mix the pears, brown sugar, flour, vanilla, orange rind, and cinnamon until the pears are well coated. Pour into the pie crust. Dot with the butter. Bake 20 minutes. **Yield: 8 servings.**

Magical Attributes: Health, beauty, freshness, air magic.

Celebrations: May Day, most Spring Rituals, Fiesta of the Mother of Health, Apple Blossom Day.

Romantic Raspberry-Guava Pie

The red color of the raspberry makes it a perfect "heart" fruit, filled with energy for your magical goals.

Pastry for a 10-inch 2-crust pie	½ cup flour
4 cups fresh raspberries	½ teaspoon ginger
4 cups chopped guava fruit	½ teaspoon allspice
1 cup brown sugar	2 tablespoons margarine, softened

Preheat the oven to 425° F. Mix the raspberries, guava fruit, brown sugar, flour, ginger, and allspice in a medium-sized bowl. Pour into a pastry lined 10-inch pie pan. Dot with the margarine. Cover with the top crust; seal edges. Make several slits in the top crust. Bake until the crust is brown and the juices have begun to bubble through the slits, 35-45 minutes. **Yield: 8 servings.**

Variation: To "heat" things up more, substitute passion fruit for the guava in this recipe. Strawberries or plums may replace either the raspberries or guava for similar magical goals.

Magical Attributes: Abundant love, increasing ardor, passion, fertility, refreshing relationships.

Celebrations: Valentine's Day, Sweetest Day, May Day, Summer Solstice, Festival of the Goddess of Mercy, Saturnalia, Festival of Mihr.

Puddings and Mousses

Creme du Mocha (France)

Luscious, rich desserts like this were common to French cookbooks during the 1800s, and were geared specifically to noble classes, as chocolate was not always an inexpensive, easily found commodity.

8 oz. semi-sweet chocolate	1 tablespoon vanilla extract
6 eggs, separated	2 tablespoons rum
¼ cup sugar	1 cup chilled whipping cream
1 tablespoon strong coffee	

Melt the chocolate over low heat in a medium-sized saucepan. Beat the egg yolks and sugar in a small bowl until thick. Stir the egg yolk, vanilla, rum, and coffee into the chocolate. Whip the egg whites until stiff and glossy; fold into the chocolate. Chill for 5-6 hours.

Beat the cream in a chilled medium-sized mixing bowl until stiff. Fold into the chocolate. Spoon into dessert dishes. Chill until served. **Yield: 8 servings.**

Magical Attributes: Dignity, elegance, wealth.

Celebrations: Borrowed Days, Feast of Jupiter, New Year's, Festival of Mihr.

Pumpkin Bread Pudding

It was considered very bad luck to throw bread away, so little leftover bits were sometimes made into a tasty treat such as this.

6 cups crumbled dry bread	1 teaspoon cinnamon
½ cup chopped nuts, any kind	2 cups milk
3 eggs, beaten	¼ cup butter, melted
1 (14 oz.) can condensed milk	1 teaspoon vanilla
1 cup cooked pumpkin	1 teaspoon rum extract
¼ teaspoon ginger	¼ cup rum
1 teaspoon nutmeg	

Preheat the oven to 350° F. Mix the bread crumbs and nuts. Place in the bottom of a lightly greased 9 x 9 x 2-inch pan. Beat the eggs, condensed milk, pumpkin, ginger, nutmeg, and cinnamon in a medium-sized mixing bowl. Stir in the milk, butter, vanilla, rum extract, and rum. Pour over the bread crumbs. Bake until a knife inserted in the center comes out clean, about 1 hour. A pan of water placed in the bottom of the oven will help keep the pumpkin moist. Top with Amaretto Whipped Cream (p. 162). **Yield: 16 squares.**

Magical Attributes: Luck, fellowship, sustenance through hard times, animal kinship.

Celebrations: Late fall and winter rituals, Sun Dance, Pardon of the Birds, Sukkoth.

Rose Mousse

In southern Greece, the Sabarites were said to be such light sleepers that a folded rose petal beneath their pillows would disturb them. In contrast, John Gerald felt that the scent of a rose aided sleep. Ancient Greeks ascribed the rose to the goddess of dawn and the god of silence, which may be why the rose appeared in many medieval banquet halls as a reminder of confidentiality.

6¾ cups sugar	6 egg whites
4 cups water	¼ cup rose brandy
Petals from 25 large red roses	½ teaspoon vanilla
1½ tablespoon lemon juice	

Dissolve the sugar in the water in a large saucepan. Stir in the petals and lemon juice. Bring to a boil; boil until the rose petals crystalize. Reserve 1 cup. Pour the rest into sterilized jars. Store in the refrigerator.

Beat the egg whites until stiff. Fold in the rose jam, brandy, and vanilla. Pour into a soufflé dish. Bake at 350° F for 5 minutes. Chill. Garnish with fresh rose buds. **Yield: 3 servings.**

Variation: Substitute any type of fruit jam and corresponding brandy for a magical pudding full of joy and energy. Suggestions include strawberry and peach.

Magical Attributes: Awareness of others feelings, enduring romance, trustworthiness, rest.

Celebrations: Renewing vows, forgiveness rituals, Festival of Brightness, Asking Festival, Handsel Monday.

❧ *Miscellaneous* ❧

Arabian Fritters

These fritters are usually eaten before the Ramadan, a time in Moslem tradition when no food may be eaten between dawn and dusk.

½ cup plain yogurt	1 teaspoon baking soda
1 tablespoon almond oil	3½ cups sugar
1 teaspoon rose water (p. 60)	3-4 tablespoons honey
2 cups cornstarch	Shortening for deep-fat frying

Mix the yogurt, almond oil, and rose water. Gradually mix in the cornstarch and baking soda; stir until smooth. Stir in ¼ cup water.

Bring the sugar and 2 cups water to a boil in a medium-sized saucepan; boil for 5 minutes. Stir in the honey; simmer for 4 minutes. Keep the syrup warm.

Melt enough shortening in a frying pan to obtain a 1-inch depth. Heat until hot but not smoking. Pour ⅓ cup of the batter into the shortening. Fry until golden, turning several times. Drain on a paper towel; dip in the warm syrup. Place on a rack to cool. Store in an airtight container. **Yield: About 8 fritters.**

Variation: If no rose water is available, substitute orange juice.

Magical Attributes: Religious observance, holy teachings and texts.

Celebrations: When working on your Book of Shadows, before a fast, when studying for initiation, Sukkoth, Russian Fair.

❧§❧

Kalioppe's Cinnamon Dessert Rolls

Kalioppe makes these rolls whenever there is tension in the home or the need for improved finances. She says the magic is aided if you work during a waxing to full Moon and on a day which is a multiple of 6. Specifically for prosperity, she adds a penny to the dough. Whoever finds the penny takes it with a portion of the pastry and buries it in a flower pot so money can "grow"!

Rolls:

¼ cup warm water (105°-115° F)

3 tablespoons plus ¼ cup sugar

2 envelopes active dry yeast

1¼ cup milk, scalded

1 teaspoon salt

2 tablespoons butter, melted

2 teaspoons cinnamon

¾ cup raisins (optional)

4 cups flour

3 tablespoons butter, softened

Icing:

2 cups powdered sugar

1 tablespoon evaporated milk

1 tablespoon butter, melted

½ cup chopped walnuts

½ cup chopped pecans

Dissolve the yeast and 1 tablespoon of the sugar in the warm water. Let sit for 5 minutes. Mix the yeast, milk, melted butter, salt, egg, and 2 tablespoons of the sugar in a large bowl. Mix in the flour a little at a time. Cover the bowl with a warm, wet towel; let sit for 15 minutes.

Turn the dough onto a flat, floured surface; knead for 10 minutes. Roll into a 15 x 9-inch rectangle. Spread with the softened butter. Mix the cinnamon and ¼ cup of the sugar; sprinkle evenly on the dough. Scatter raisins evenly.

Roll up lengthwise. Cut into 12 slices. Place in a greased 9 x 9-inch pan. Cover; let rise in a warm place 20 minutes.

Place in a cold oven. Set heat to 400° F. Bake until golden brown, 20-30 minutes. Brush tops with butter when removed from the oven. Mix the powdered sugar, evaporated milk, and butter. Drizzle over the top. Sprinkle with nuts. Serve warm if possible. **Yield: 12 rolls.**

Magical Attributes: Reestablishing harmony, prosperity.

Rosemary Sherbet (Tudor England)

Spanish lore tells us that rosemary was originally white until the Virgin Mary walked by, and tossed her robe over it. To honor her memory, it changed color to match her robe, forever.

2 tablespoons dried rosemary	½ cup cold water
2 cups hot water	1 tablespoon lemon juice
¼ cup sugar	½ cup orange juice

In a medium-sized bowl, soak the rosemary in the hot water for 10 minutes. Strain; discard the rosemary and return the water to the bowl. Bring the sugar and cold water to a boil over medium heat. Stir the sugar water, lemon juice, and orange juice into the rosemary water. Spoon into individual serving dishes, if desired. Freeze. **Yield: Six ½-cup servings.**

Variation: If you do not enjoy the robust flavor of rosemary, try substituting minced ginger root. The magical energy is similar.

Magical Attributes: Memory, health, love, felicity, success (especially in love).

Celebrations: Valentine's Day, Memorial Day, many spring rituals, Labor Day.

Snow Oranges (China, Japan)

When properly prepared, this dish looks like the sun rising off the snow. To increase the visual effect, try a pattern with the orange pieces (see illustration).

2 envelopes unflavored gelatin	2½ cups sugar
½ cup cold water	3 cups whipped cream
1 (12-oz.) can mandarin oranges, drained (reserve syrup)	

In a medium-sized bowl, dissolve the gelatin in the cold water. Add water to the mandarin orange syrup to make 2 cups. Combine the syrup and sugar in a medium-sized saucepan. Bring to a boil over medium heat; boil for 5 minutes. Add to the gelatin; stir until the gelatin is completely dissolved. Cool to lukewarm.

Slowly add the whipped cream to the gelatin. Pour into a chilled 9 x 9-inch pan. Garnish with the orange slices, pushing them down so that they are just visible through the surface. Chill. **Yield: 8 servings.**

Magical Attributes: Dawn, new beginnings, opportunity.

Celebrations: Candlemas, any sunrise ritual, before job interviews or the outset of new endeavors, initiation.

❧ Personal Recipes ❧

Personal Recipes

Chapter Nine

Mystical Meat,
Premonition Poultry,
and Sacred Seafood

*It is not the quality of the meat
but the cheerfulness of the guests which makes the feast.*

— Earl of Clarendon

As is the case with eggs and cheese, each meat has a basic association upon which the other ingredients of the following recipes build. In many instances, small portions of an animal were consumed to internalize the inherent ability of the creature, while other portions were offered up to the Creator in thankfulness. For instance, bear meat might be eaten to cure baldness, while fish was devoured to help fecundity. For an excellent resource on animal symbolism check any deck of Medicine cards or dream dictionaries.

❧ Mystical Meat ❧

Beef is associated with grounding, earth magic, agriculture, and maternal energy. Pork is given the attributes of success and rejuvenation. Ham is similar, except that it can be considered a dramatic ingredient.

The cow was sacred to Isis, who was sometimes portrayed with the head of this creature. In Scandinavia, the Mother Cow known as Audhumla gave birth to the gods by licking them out of ice. The bull and ox also have strong magical associations with the element of earth. In Egyptian mysteries, the ox was used to depict human nature and our dependence on the land and its creatures.

Apricot Fricassee (Rome)

Apricots, brought to Rome from Armenia, were used in Roman recipes nearly two centuries ago.

1 cup dried apricots	1 cup cooking wine
2 lbs. pork, boned and cubed	½ teaspoon dried mint
2 tablespoons olive oil	½ teaspoon dried dill weed
3 tablespoons butter	½ teaspoon pepper
1 medium onion, diced	2 teaspoons honey
1 tablespoon minced fresh chives	1 tablespoon vinegar
1 cup beef or chicken broth	1 tablespoon cornstarch

Cover the apricots with water in a small bowl. Soak for 1 hour; drain. Brown the pork in the olive oil and 2 tablespoons of the butter. Stir in the onion, chives, broth, and wine before the meat is fully cooked. Sauté for 5 minutes. Stir in the mint, dill weed, and pepper. Mix the honey and vinegar in a small bowl. Pour into the meat mixture. Add the apricots; stir. Simmer 2 hours. Add 1 tablespoon of the butter to the meat. Mix the cornstarch with 1 tablespoon of water until smooth. Slowly add the cornstarch to the meat; stir constantly. Simmer until thick. This is excellent over rice. **Yield: 5 servings.**

Variation: This is luscious with chicken, lamb, or beef. However, you may want to change your spices slightly to best compliment the kind of meat you use.

Magical Attributes: Personal development, maturity, improving the immediacy of magical energies.

Celebrations: Coming of Age, Croning, Elder rites, Initiation, Sukkoth.

Bavarian Pig

During the Roman Empire, young pigs were so much in demand for food that laws were passed to regulate their consumption. It was believed that eating the pig allowed individuals to incorporate its attributes into the body. This is a nice dish if you are having an outdoor gathering with a fire pit for roasting. The slow cooking improves flavor and tenderness.

1 whole pig (about 14 pounds)	¼ lb. bacon
Salt	1 pint dark beer
Rosemary	1 lemon (garnish)
Marjoram	1 tablespoon flour
½ cup butter (approximately)	½ cup sour cream

Preheat the oven to 350° F. Thoroughly rinse the pig in cold water. Truss the legs using wire or heavy cotton string. Pierce the skin with a fork. Rub the skin and stomach cavity with salt, rosemary, and marjoram. Slip pats of butter beneath the skin; rub the skin with butter. This will help keep the meat moist. Lay the bacon strips across the back; secure with toothpicks. This helps the basting. Place in an open roasting pan. Cover the ears with aluminum foil to prevent burning. Fill the pan with 1-inch of water. Roast for 7 hours. Baste once an hour. Add water to the pan during cooking if it becomes dry. During the last 10 minutes, baste with beer. Remove from the pan. To garnish, place a lemon in the mouth.

To make gravy, add enough water to the pan to make the desired amount of gravy. Place the pan on the stove. Bring to a boil while scraping the bottom of the pan. Dissolve the flour in 2 tablespoons water. Slowly stir into to the juices. Mix in the sour cream. Cook until the gravy thickens.

Yield: 10 generous servings.

Variation: In Cuba, they add the beer before cooking. In England, apples are used for the garnish. In South America, they stuff the pig with a corn bread mixture. In China, the pig is basted with honey, soy, fennel, and sweet-n-sour sauce.

Magical Attributes: Natural reciprocity, economy, temperance, victory.

Celebrations: Earth Day, Sun Dance, Festival of Durga, planting festivals.

Beef and Marigold (England 1700s)

Five here is used as the number of versatility, and the color yellow adds an inventive, intuitive flair.

2 tablespoons flour
1½ teaspoon dried rosemary
1½ teaspoon dried marjoram
1½ teaspoon dried thyme
1½ teaspoon onion powder
1 (5-lb.) beef roast
2 tablespoons butter

3 cups water
4 turnips, quartered
1½ teaspoons dried parsley
5 yellow marigold
  blossoms, chopped
2 cups pearl onions

Preheat the oven to 350° F. Mix the flour, rosemary, marjoram, thyme, and onion powder on a large plate. Coat the roast with the flour. Melt the butter in a frying pan; brown the roast on all sides. Transfer to a deep roasting pan. Add the water. Roast uncovered for 2½ hours. Baste every half hour.

Add the turnips, parsley, marigolds, and pearl onions. Add a little water if the pan is dry. Cover; cook until the turnips are tender, about 30 minutes. Baste occasionally. Use the drippings to make gravy. **Yield: 5 servings.**

Variation: Chicken can be substituted for beef in this recipe. The marigolds can be replaced with five pieces of yellow squash without affecting the magical energies.

Magical Attributes: The inalienable human spirit, diversity, personal creative power.

Celebrations: Aloha Week, New Year's, most spring festivals.

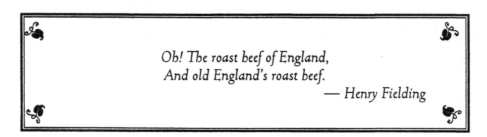

> *Oh! The roast beef of England,*
> *And old England's roast beef.*
> — *Henry Fielding*

Mapled Ham

- 1 boneless ham (about 3-4 pounds)
- 1 (8-oz.) can pineapple slices, drained; reserve syrup
- 10 whole cloves
- 1 cup real maple syrup
- ¼ cup brown sugar
- 2 tablespoons honey
- 2 tablespoons butter

Preheat the oven to 350° F. Prick the ham with a fork. Secure the pineapple slices on the ham with wooden toothpicks. Press the whole cloves into the ham. Place the ham in a medium-sized baking pan. Add 2 cups of water. Combine the syrup, sugar, honey, butter, and pineapple juice in a small saucepan. Stir over a low flame until warm. Pour half the juice over the top of the ham. Roast uncovered 1½-2 hours. Baste frequently with the remaining maple mixture.

Drain the drippings from the pan. Cook over medium heat until slightly thickened. Serve as a sauce. **Yield: 8 servings.**

Magical Attributes: Kinship, celebration, sweet things in life, family unity.

Celebrations: Yule, Thanksgiving, Maple Syrup Festival, Festival of Brightness, Riding the Marches, St. Stephen Festival, Hopi Winter Ceremony.

Pomegranate Beef (Persia)

In Persia, a red cow was sometimes used to personify the dawn, and it was considered great fortune to own one. Red is also the color of strength, vitality, and courage. In Persia, this dish is called Narsirk.

1 (4-lb.) bottom round roast	3 onions, quartered
2 teaspoons salt	3-4 whole fresh mint leaves
1¼ teaspoons ground coriander	2 pomegranates, halved
1¼ teaspoons cumin	¼ cup wine vinegar
2 teaspoons pepper	1 cup finely ground walnuts
1 teaspoon cinnamon	1 teaspoon rose water
1 teaspoon mastic	(optional, p. 58)

Place the roast and salt in a large pot; cover with water. Boil uncovered for 1 hour; turn occasionally. Skim off any fat which rises to the surface. Reduce heat to a simmer. Add the coriander, cumin, pepper, cinnamon, mastic, onions, and mint. Remove the pomegranate seeds; place in a small bowl. Press with a large spoon to extract the juice. Mix with the wine vinegar. Strain; discard the pulp. Pour over the roast. Mix the walnuts and rose water. Add to the roast. Simmer 1 hour. Use the drippings for gravy. **Yield: 8 servings.**

Variation: Substitute a leg of lamb for the roast. Potatoes are a nice addition to the pot as well; add after the spices.

Magical Attributes: The sun in splendor, dawn, fire, increasing energies.

Celebrations: Spring and summer rites, any fire festivals or sunrise observances, Hori.

Pork with Lily (Hawaii)

The use of the lily in Hawaii probably comes from the Asian population who are famil-iar with these lovely petals as part of soup, meat, and noodle dishes. It is common in China to rub the home stove with lily buds before making an offering to the hearth gods.

12 yellow lily buds	4 tablespoons soy sauce
1 cup sliced mushrooms	3 tablespoons sherry
¼ cup oil	2 tablespoons honey
2 cups diced pork	1 cup chicken broth
2 cloves garlic, crushed	1 tablespoon cornstarch

Sauté the lily buds and mushrooms in 1 tablespoon of the oil until the mush-rooms are tender. Transfer to a small bowl.

In the same frying pan, lightly brown the pork in 3 tablespoons of the oil. Add the garlic; cook 3 minutes. Combine the soy sauce, sherry, honey, and chicken broth in a small bowl. Stir into the pork. Cover; simmer for 30 minutes. Mix the cornstarch with 1 tablespoon water until smooth. Slowly add to pork; stir con-stantly. Simmer until sauce thickens. Serve over rice. **Yield: 4 servings.**

Variation: For a truly sunny meal, substitute one (8-oz.) can crushed pineapple (drained) for the lily buds. The flavor is slightly sweet-and-sour. The yellow color helps maintain the creative energy of the dish.

Magical Attributes: Pure creative insight, beauty, immortality, remembrance of hearth guardians.

Celebrations: Apple Blossom Day, spring rituals, Summerland rites, Wiccaning, Feast of the Kitchen God, Feast of the Madonna.

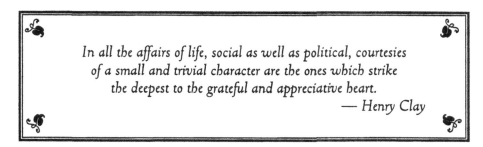

In all the affairs of life, social as well as political, courtesies of a small and trivial character are the ones which strike the deepest to the grateful and appreciative heart.
— Henry Clay

Sausage and Cheese, Italian Style

This is a recipe from Dynahara. Pork was often a part of ancient Celtic victory feasts and was considered the food of the Valkyries.

2 lbs. lean ground pork	1 tablespoon ground fennel
½ cup grated parmesan cheese	⅛ teaspoon red pepper
½ cup grated romano cheese	1 teaspoon pepper
¼ cup minced fresh parsley	1 teaspoon salt
4 cloves garlic, minced	4 tablespoons water
2 finely chopped bay leaves	

Combine all the ingredients and form into patties. Place waxed paper between each patty and wrap well. Freeze. Remove the number of patties needed at one time. Thaw in the refrigerator. Fry or grill. Great for unexpected company.
Yield: Eight ¼-pound patties.

Variation: For a leaner patty, substitute ground turkey for the ground pork.

Magical Attributes: Success, achievement, mastery.

Celebrations: Initiation, welcoming a new coven leader, before job hunting or entering any new endeavor.

Radical Honeyed Ribs

An old Chinese legend claims "barbecued" pork was discovered quite by chance when a pigsty burned down, which just goes to confirm that some of our greatest treats come from the time-honored tradition of accident!

¼ cup wine vinegar	1 teaspoon dried basil
2 tablespoons soy sauce	1 teaspoon dried rosemary
2 tablespoons Worcestershire sauce	1 teaspoon dried thyme
2 tablespoons plus	3 lbs. ribs, separated
1 teaspoon crushed garlic	1 cup barbecue sauce
2 teaspoons dried onion	½ cup honey
¼ teaspoon five-spice powder	

Combine the vinegar, soy sauce, Worcestershire sauce, 1 teaspoon of the garlic, onion, five-spice powder, basil, rosemary, and thyme in a large bowl. Place the ribs in the sauce. Cover; marinate in the refrigerator for at least 12 hours. Turn occasionally.

Pour off the marinade into a small saucepan. Bring to a boil; boil 5 minutes. Mix the barbecue sauce, honey, 2 tablespoons of the garlic, and 2 tablespoons of the marinade in a small bowl. Add more marinade for a heartier flavor. Broil or grill the ribs. Baste generously with the barbecue sauce. **Yield: 4 servings.**

Magical Attributes: Luck, fate, destiny, fortuity.

Celebrations: Most spring observances, picnics, New Year's.

Squashflower Pork (Mexico)

In Mexico, the squashflower is associated with the Aztec god Topiltzin Ce Acatl Quetzalcoatl. The use of three squashflowers in this recipe is to bring congruity and harmony.

2 green peppers	½ cup string beans
2 tomatoes	¼ cup fresh corn kernels
2 onions	3 squash blossoms, finely chopped
2 tablespoons oil	Salt
1 lb. pork, cooked and diced	Pepper
2 cups chicken stock	

Combine the peppers, onions, and tomatoes; grind. Heat the oil in a frying pan. Sauté the ground vegetables. Mix in the pork and chicken stock; simmer for 30 minutes. Add the beans, corn, squash blossoms, salt, and pepper. Simmer 1 hour. Serve with noodles or rice. **Yield: 2 servings.**

Variation: Beef may be used in place of pork. Squashflowers can be eliminated in favor of three hot peppers, which magically will create a dish that can provide cleansing before peaceful resolutions.

Magical Attributes: Energetic love, peace and joy, improving friendship or communication.

Celebrations: Handfasting, forgiveness rituals, spring rituals, Festival of Sarasvati.

❧ *Premonition Poultry* ❧

Chickens are honored as the mothers of eggs, which have many metaphysical applications. In certain mystery religions, the rooster is heralded as the greeter of the solar sphere, sacred to the sun and Apollo. It was also adopted as an emblem of Mars because of its qualities of watchfulness and defense. It may be this protective quality which gave chicken soup its healthful reputation.

Chrysanthemum Chicken (China)

In China, the chrysanthemum is the symbol of long life, ease, invigoration, health, and cool breezes. It has been cultivated there for over 2,000 years.

- 4 white chrysanthemum blossoms, chopped
- 1 onion, chopped
- ¼ cup butter
- 3 cups croutons
- 1 cup cooked long grain rice
- 1 cup cooked spinach, chopped
- ½ cup finely chopped cabbage
- 2 tablespoons soy sauce
- ½ teaspoon five-spice powder
- 1 (3-lb.) roasting chicken

Preheat the oven to 350°F. Sauté the chrysanthemums and onions in the butter until the onions are tender. Combine the croutons, rice, spinach, cabbage, five-spice powder, and soy sauce. Mix in the sautéed items, include the butter. If the stuffing is dry, add a little water. Stuff the chicken. Make a slit at the top of the bird and place a chunk of butter inside. Place the chicken in a roasting pan; add ¼-inch of water. Roast for 2 hours. Baste regularly. **Yield: 5 servings.**

Variation: Instead of chrysanthemums, substitute ¼ lemon (peeled and diced) or ¼ peach (peeled and diced) for similar results.

Magical Attributes: Vitality, well-being, foresight, leisure.

Celebrations: Any rite for Apollo, sunrise festivals, many spring and summer observances, dedication of a child.

Cornish Hen (Carthaginian)

An early version of cornish hen was known in Rome, and eventually adapted by Italian cooks for the Renaissance courts. The version we eat today began to develop around 1950. Six is the number of culmination.

3 Cornish game hens
(about 1¼ pounds each)

Sauce:

2 tablespoons butter
½ cup orange juice
1 tablespoon honey
1 tablespoon brown sugar

½ teaspoon salt
½ teaspoon sage
½ teaspoon rosemary
1 tablespoon cognac

Glazed Oranges:

4 large oranges
2 tablespoons butter
¼ cup brown sugar

1 tablespoon honey
¼ cup white wine

Preheat the oven to 350° F. Place the hens on a rack in a roasting pan, breast up. Rub with some of the butter. Roast uncovered 30 minutes.

Combine the remaining butter, orange juice, honey, brown sugar, salt, sage, rosemary, and cognac in a small saucepan. Heat over a low flame until the butter is melted. Use the sauce to baste the hens frequently. Continue to roast the hens until done, about 45 minutes.

Meanwhile, cut off the ends of the oranges. Slice each orange 8 times. Combine the butter, brown sugar, honey, and wine in a medium-sized saucepan. Add the orange slices; simmer until the oranges are glazed, about 25 minutes.

To serve, split each hen along the backbone using a kitchen scissors. Garnish each half with 6 slices of orange. **Yield: 6 servings.**

Magical Attributes: Relationships, fulfillment, completion of tasks, commitment.

Celebrations: Labor Day, marriages, initiation, before any intensive undertaking.

Lemon Chicken (Polynesia)

In Hindu lands, mangos are often used in love potions. Lemon adds clarity to romance, ginger adds a little liveliness, and lime adds zest.

2 lbs. chicken breast, cubed	2 tablespoons olive oil
1 tablespoon grated ginger root	1 cup chicken broth
½ teaspoon grated lime peel	1 tablespoon soy sauce
½ teaspoon grated orange peel	1 lemon, very thinly sliced
1 tablespoon lime juice	2 tablespoons cornstarch
1 tablespoon lemon juice	1 cup cubed mango
2 green onions, minced	½ teaspoon sugar
1 clove garlic, minced	¼ teaspoon cinnamon

Sauté the chicken, ginger root, lime peel, orange peel, lime juice, lemon juice, onions, and garlic in the olive oil until the chicken is white. Add the chicken broth, soy sauce, and lemon. Stir; simmer for 15 minutes. Mix the cornstarch with 3 tablespoons water until smooth. Add to the chicken a little bit at a time, stirring constantly. Mix in mango, cinnamon, and sugar. Simmer until the mango is warm and the sauce is thick. This is great on rice. **Yield: 4 servings.**

Variation: Reduce the mango to ½ cup and add ½ cup cubed papaya for passion.

Magical Attributes: Romantic love, dreams, happily-ever-after scenarios.

Celebrations: Engagements, vow renewals, Handsel Monday, handfastings, Valentine's and Sweetest Day, anniversaries.

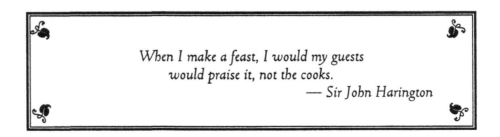

*When I make a feast, I would my guests
would praise it, not the cooks.*
— *Sir John Harington*

Mohammed's Praise (Pakistan)

A chicken appearing suddenly on your doorstep is a sign of company soon to follow. The followers of Mohammed believe that rose water was produced by the sweat of the prophet, which is why it is esteemed so highly.

1 (3-lb.) chicken, quartered	½ teaspoon cinnamon
1 teaspoon salt	¼ teaspoon cardamon
2 cups plain yogurt	½ teaspoon cumin
1 large onion, chopped	4 mint leaves
⅓ cup butter	3 bay leaves
4 cloves garlic, minced	1 cup long grain rice
3 chili peppers, diced	2 cups of water
3 whole cloves	Pinch of saffron
2 teaspoons minced ginger root	1 tablespoon rose water (p. 58)

Wash chicken thoroughly. Place the chicken in a large bowl. Sprinkle with salt. Cover with yogurt. Refrigerate for 30 minutes.

Sauté the onion in the butter for 5 minutes. Stir in the garlic, chili peppers, cloves, ginger root, cinnamon, cardamon, cumin, mint, and bay leaves. Mix in the chicken and yogurt. Cover; simmer for 30 minutes. Stir in the rice, water, and saffron. Cover; cook until the rice is tender, about 25 minutes. Stir in the rose water. Remove the bay leaves before serving. **Yield: 4 servings.**

Magical Attributes: Honored guests, hospitality, tradition, heritage.

Celebrations: St. Stephen Festival, Asking Festival, family gatherings.

Roman Duck

Ducks and their seasonal movements remind us of cycles and the instincts which humankind has often left by the wayside for logic. Ten turnips are to improve our sensitivity to our own "inner voice."

1	(4-lb.) duck	¼	teaspoon ground coriander
	Salt		Pepper
2	tablespoons butter	1½	cups sliced celery
½	cup cooking wine	1	carrot, sliced
1	cup beef broth	1	onion, diced
¼	teaspoon cumin	10	turnips, peeled and quartered

Preheat the oven to 400° F. Rinse the duck in cool water. Rub the skin and body cavity with salt. Place pats of butter in various places underneath the skin. Transfer to a roasting pan. Add any remaining butter to the pan. Roast uncovered for 30 minutes. Drain off the drippings. Mix the drippings, cooking wine, broth, cumin, coriander, and pepper; pour over the duck.

Place the celery, carrot, and onion in the roaster. Lower the temperature to 350° F. Roast, covered, for 45 minutes. Baste occasionally. Add the turnips. Roast, covered, until the turnips are tender and the duck is done, about 45 minutes. Use the drippings for gravy. Arrange the vegetables on a serving platter around the bird. **Yield: 4 servings.**

Variation: Rub the duck with honey inside and out; substitute rose wine for the cooking wine to bring perception in love.

Magical Attributes: Intuitive action, insightful talent, instinctive movement (especially pertaining to your own well-being).

Celebrations: Birthdays, New Year's, before a major decision or move to another location.

Turkey Toccata

The eight pieces of leek and the service for eight is to encourage fortitude. Leeks, part of the onion family, are generally considered protective vegetables, while the cheese sauce provides a gentler side for tender feelings.

1 (5-lb.) boneless turkey breast	2 tablespoons flour
¼ cup minced fresh basil	2 cups milk
1 clove garlic, minced	½ cup grated Swiss cheese
4 small leeks, halved lengthwise	¼ cup grated parmesan cheese
4 tablespoons butter, softened	

Preheat the oven to 425° F. Generously line a baking dish with aluminum foil. Lay the turkey breast skin side down in the center of the pan. Sprinkle with the basil, garlic, and leeks. Dot with 2 tablespoons of the butter. Wrap with aluminum foil. Bake 1 hour. Remove from the oven to baste. Bake until done, 30-45 minutes.

Melt 2 tablespoons of the butter in a small saucepan over low heat. Stir in the flour. Slowly add the milk; stir constantly until smooth. Mix in the cheeses a little at a time; stir constantly. Cook until all the cheese is melted and the sauce is smooth. Pour over the sliced turkey before serving. **Yield: 8 servings.**

Magical Attributes: Personal strength and change, protection (especially in love), power of persuasion, leadership qualities.

Celebrations: Birthdays, New Year's, forgiveness rituals, Feast of Banners, Birthday of the Sun.

Turkey with Syrian Stuffing
(Doreen's Wild and Weedy Kitchen)

This is a Italian-Lebanese dish taught to Doreen by her grandmother and aunt. It was a traditional component of Christmas dinner, alongside cheese ravioli.

1 lb. ground lamb	Salt
1 cup pine nuts	Pepper
½ cup butter	1 (12-15 lb.) turkey
3-4 cups cooked white or Basmati rice	1 apple
1 tablespoon cinnamon	

Preheat the oven to 325° F. Brown the lamb; drain off the fat. Transfer to a large mixing bowl. Melt the butter in the frying pan over medium heat. Add the pine nuts; roast until lightly brown. Mix the pine nuts, melted butter, rice, cinnamon, salt, and pepper with the lamb. Stuff the turkey with the pine nut mixture. Place the apple under the neck skin for garnish and flavor. Transfer to a large roasting pan. Roast, uncovered, 20 minutes per each pound of bird. After the turkey turns golden, cover loosely with a foil tent. **Yield: 20-30 servings.**

Variation: Doreen also recommends the stuffing as a main dish with a side of zucchini. Mix up the stuffing, place in a covered casserole dish, and bake at 350° F for 40 minutes.

Magical Attributes: Kinship, warmth, family traditions.

Celebrations: Yule, Thanksgiving, St. Stephen Festival, any family reunion.

❦ Sacred Seafood ❧

In Egyptian mythology, the constellation of the crab (Cancer) is related to the scarab, an important symbol of life. The Summer Solstice takes place when the sun was in Cancer, after which time the sun seems to walk backward (like the crab) through the zodiacal signs. In other traditions, the crab, being a water creature, is likened to the moon and generative abilities. The idea of eating fish on Friday may have originated with the Scandinavian Venus, Freya, whose name is given to that day. Fish is likewise sacred to the followers of Mohammed. In Hebrew, the word for fish also means growth and as such it is a food with pro-creative energy. This may well be why it took on such an important New Testament role, again being likened to self-generative power. The fish is one of the eight sacred symbols for the Buddha, a fish was the first incarnation of Vishnu in Hindu myths. Magically speaking, fish is most commonly ascribed to the areas of long life, fertility, miracles, and strengthening paradigm figures.

Fig Scallops (Greece)

The use of leaves in baking is very old. The large foliage provided protection and moisture to the food. Forty is the number of retreat to help provide safety for yourself, rejuvenate your spirit, and improve vision.

40 scallops	1 large onion, sliced
4 potatoes, sliced	and separated into rings
4 large fig leaves or 12 x 12-inch	1 tablespoon minced chives
aluminum foil pieces	¼ teaspoon thyme
4 figs, finely chopped	¼ teaspoon pepper
2 cloves garlic, minced	4 tablespoons butter, softened

Preheat the oven to 400° F. Divide the scallops and potatoes into four equal portions. Place in the center of the fig leaves. Mix the figs, garlic, onion rings, chives, thyme, and pepper. Sprinkle evenly over the scallops and potatoes. Dot each portion with 1 tablespoon of the butter. Fold the sides of the fig leaf over the filling. Fold down the top of the leaf and roll to seal in the filling. Place in a greased baking pan, seam side down. Bake until the scallops are white, about 20 minutes. **Yield: 4 servings.**

Variation: Follow the Malaysian tradition of cooking in banana leaves instead of fig leaves. This option is more appropriate for fostering long-term relationships.

Magical Attributes: Protection, hermitage, sanctuary.

Celebrations: During any time of personal solitude, Royal Oak Day, Birthday of Confucius, Sunning of Buddha.

Passion Fruit Seafood Supreme (Thailand)

Passion fruit is for romance, promoting friendships, and calming wrath.

4 passion fruit, peeled
and cut into strips

1 teaspoon lemon juice

2 tablespoons oil

2 lbs. mixed seafood
(shrimp, crab, whitefish, etc.)

2 sweet peppers, diced

1 tablespoon minced chives

2 cloves garlic, minced
Pepper

1 tablespoon soy sauce

1½ cups coconut milk

3 tablespoons crushed peanuts

Sprinkle the passion fruit with the lemon juice. Heat the oil in a wok or frying pan over a medium flame. Add the seafood and peppers; cook for 5 minutes. Stir in the chives, garlic, and pepper; cook until the seafood is golden brown. Stir in the soy sauce, coconut milk, and passion fruit. Simmer for 5 minutes. Sprinkle with chopped peanuts before serving. **Yield: 4 servings.**

Variation: If you do not like passion fruit, mangos, papaya, or even pineapple work well in this recipe for similar effects. (Use about 4 cups fruit.)

Magical Attributes: Peace between people, kinship, congeniality, reconciliation.

Celebrations: Forgiveness rituals, large group gatherings, Earth Day, Memorial Day, during any military uprisings.

Marian's Stuffed Salmon (Scotland)

In Scotland, the first fish caught on a fishing trip is traditionally returned to the sea for luck and in thankfulness. For this dish, the pink color of the fish combines with the number six to enrich one's outlook and provide devotion.

6 (⅓-inch thick) salmon steaks (½-¾ lb. each)	2 cups shredded mozzarella cheese
3 tablespoons lemon juice	1 onion, chopped
1½ cups seasoned croutons, crushed	2 cloves garlic, crushed
¼ teaspoon pepper	2 tablespoons butter
2 cups chopped, cooked spinach	3 eggs
1 cup diced, cooked broccoli	⅓ cup milk

Preheat the oven to 350° F. Cover the salmon steaks with lemon juice. Mix the pepper and crumbs. Coat the salmon steaks with the crumbs. Mix the remaining crumbs, spinach, broccoli, and cheese in a large bowl. Sauté the garlic and onions in the butter. Pour over the spinach mixture; mix well. Lay 3 of the salmon steaks in the bottom of a greased baking dish. Divide the stuffing into 3 portions; spoon on top of each steak. Place another steak on top, sandwich-style. Beat the eggs and milk in a small bowl. Pour ⅓ of the eggs over the fish. Bake for 15 minutes; pour on another ⅓ of the eggs. Repeat. Bake until the fish is flaky, about 15 minutes. (Total baking time should be about 45 minutes.)

Yield: 3 generous servings.

Variation: Orange roughy and halibut also taste great using this recipe.

Magical Attributes: Positive attitude, persistence, tenacity, improved perspectives, commitment.

Celebrations: Handfasting, before job hunting, for any project which has been delayed by procrastination.

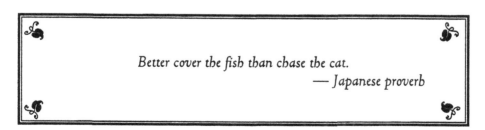

> *Better cover the fish than chase the cat.*
> — *Japanese proverb*

Prowess Oyster Patties (Japan)

In certain parts of Asia, fish are an emblem of unified, compatible living and are often given to newlyweds with wishes for a happy union.

1 teaspoon soy sauce	Salt
½ cup wine vinegar	Pepper
½ teaspoon Tabasco sauce	½ cup flour
1 pint oysters in juice	½ teaspoon baking soda
½ cup minced shallots	3 tablespoons almond oil
4 eggs, beaten	

Drain and chop the oysters; reserve the juice. Make a sauce by mixing the soy sauce, vinegar, and Tabasco sauce in a small bowl. Mix the oysters, shallots, eggs, salt, and pepper in a medium-sized bowl. Mix in the flour and baking soda; add enough oyster juice (⅓ - ½ cup) to make a pancake-like batter. Heat the oil in a frying pan. Pour in ¼ cup of batter; fry on both sides. Serve with the sauce. **Yield: 4 servings.**

Magical Attributes: Fertility, productivity, sexual energy, and sensitivity.

Celebrations: Spring festivals, conception rites, honeymoons, any time you need improved resourcefulness.

Spanish Halibut

In some lands, any fish found in a well was considered to represent the spirit of the water. Anise, clove, thyme, and lemon are all ruled by the element of water. This dish probably dates back to the Moorish settlement in Spain, when vinegared meats were common.

2 lbs. halibut	¼ teaspoon ginger
½ cup flour	⅛ teaspoon saffron
3 cloves garlic, minced	⅛ teaspoon anise
1 large onion, minced	⅛ teaspoon ground clove
1½ cups olive oil	½ teaspoon cumin
¼ cup vinegar	½ cup chives, chopped
2 tablespoons lemon juice	2 bay leaves, crushed
¾ cup water	1 lemon, sliced

Coat the halibut with the flour. Lightly sauté the garlic and onion in the oil. Spoon out the garlic and onion; place in a large, shallow pan. Reserve the oil. Mix the garlic and onions with the vinegar, lemon juice, water, ginger, saffron, anise, clove, and cumin. Reheat the oil; fry the fish on both sides until flaky and opaque. Lay the fish in the sauce. Let sit 5 minutes; turn. Sprinkle with the chives, bay leaves, and lemon. Cover; chill for 24 hours. May be served hot or cold. **Yield: 4 servings.**

Magical Attributes: Water magic, flow, movement, moon magic.

Celebrations: Ahes Festival, Birthday of the Moon, spring festivals.

Swordfish with Bay (Turkey)

The swordfish was so named because it looks so much like the weapon of antiquity. In the Middle Ages, the sword was not only a knight's means of self defense, but also an emblem of an honor-bound promise to defend all that was sacred.

¼ cup lemon juice	Pepper
½ cup oil	2 lbs. swordfish, cut in 1-inch cubes
2 tablespoons dry onion	4 tomatoes, wedged
2 cloves garlic, crushed	4 onions, quartered
¼ teaspoon dried basil	6 bay leaves, broken in large pieces
Salt	Bamboo skewers

Mix the lemon juice, oil, onion, garlic, basil, salt, and pepper in a large bowl. Add the swordfish. Cover; marinate in the refrigerator for at least 1 hour.

Pour off the marinade into a small saucepan. Bring to a boil; boil 5 minutes. Alternate the tomatoes, onions, pieces of bay leaf, and fish on the skewers. Brush with marinade. Broil or grill until browned on all sides, about 15-20 minutes. The marinade can also be served as a sauce, but only if it has been boiled for at least 5 minutes. **Yield: 4 servings.**

Magical Attributes: Honor, protection, defense of land or other beloved things.

Celebrations: Patriot's Day, Independence Day, Riding the Marches, Memorial Day, Sukkoth.

Whitefish Bouillon (Rome)

Stocks such as this were discussed in cookbooks dating to the early 1600s. It is said that the spices so precisely flavor the broth that no one knows it is a fish stock.

1 bay leaf	2-3 stalks of celery, chopped
2 sprigs parsley	1 large onion, diced
5 peppercorns	1 lb. whitefish trimmings
¼ teaspoon dried thyme	3 cups dry white wine
¼ teaspoon dried basil	1 teaspoon salt
1 small clove garlic	2 quarts water

Place the bay leaf, parsley, peppercorns, thyme, basil, and garlic in a tea ball or secure in a small cheesecloth bag. Combine the celery, onion, fish, wine, salt, water, and tea ball in a large pot. Bring to a boil; boil for 10 minutes. Reduce heat; simmer for 30 minutes. Strain through a sieve or cheesecloth. Reserve the liquid and discard the rest. Use as a soup and stew stock or as the liquid base for poaching fish. Freeze if not used immediately. **Yield: 2 quarts.**

Variation: This would also produce a marvelously flavored chicken broth which would aid in magic for alertness to deception.

Magical Attributes: Hidden matters, cunning, disguise.

Celebrations: Samhain, any time you feel too "visible."

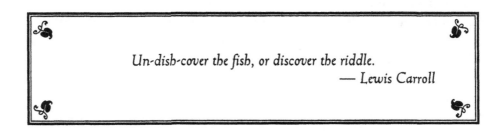

Un-dish-cover the fish, or discover the riddle.
— *Lewis Carroll*

❦ Personal Recipes ❧

✌ Personal Recipes ✌

Chapter Ten

Psychic Pasta
and Sigil Sauce

S tudy the past if you would divine the future.

— Confucius

One of the greatest food marriages ever made is between pasta and sauce. Pasta may have existed as early as the Etruscan period; tools resembling macaroni makers have been found in some tombs. The most documented roots for pasta, however, are in China and a region of the Roman empire known as Etruna, which produced fine wheats for making pasta. Depending on the type of noodles prepared, the magical significance changes. Wheat noodles, symbolic of fruitfulness and plenty, are sacred to many Earth or Mother Goddess figures, while spinach noodles, with their marvelous green color, are more appropriate to prosperity and growth.

Many sauces owe their perfection to France, where chefs garnished dishes with any number of rich, creamy toppings. By the fourteenth and fifteenth centuries, all well-regarded European chefs could prepare a variety of sauces to please the palate. The best sauces were those thought to entice the diner with smell and texture.

◦§ *Psychic Pasta* §◦

Allemande Noodles (France/Germany)

The French term allemande refers to food prepared by German techniques. No matter the country, however, the chefs who prepare this say the allemande enhances any meal. Three is the number of congruity.

3 cups diced veal or chicken	⅓ cup cream
3 mushrooms, sliced	1 tablespoon butter, melted
2 tablespoons oil	1 tablespoon flour
1 cup chicken broth	⅓ lemon, thinly sliced
¼ teaspoon nutmeg	12 oz. spinach noodles, cooked
3 egg yolks	

Brown the veal and mushrooms in the oil. Mix in the broth and nutmeg; simmer for 30 minutes. Beat the egg yolks and cream in a small bowl. Slowly stir into the veal mixture. Mix the butter and flour in a small bowl until smooth. Add a little of this mixture at a time to the veal mixture; stir constantly. Simmer until the sauce is thick. Remove from heat; add the lemon slices. Pour over the spinach noodles. Garnish with fresh mushrooms or lemon wedges. **Yield: 6 servings.**

Variation: Make the sauce without the meat and pour it over chicken or fish.

Magical Attributes: Amplification or reinforcement of balance or rationale.

Celebrations: Birthdays, before legal matters, Samhain, midnight or noonday observances, graduation.

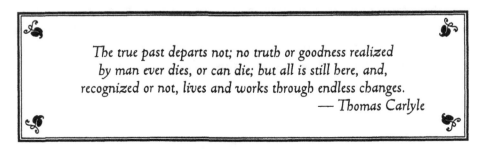

> *The true past departs not; no truth or goodness realized*
> *by man ever dies, or can die; but all is still here, and,*
> *recognized or not, lives and works through endless changes.*
> *— Thomas Carlyle*

Americana Noodles

While macaroni and cheese probably wasn't an American original, it certainly is a favorite. Here I have combined red peppers with white sauce and blue garnish for a truly all-American taste treat.

8 oz. macaroni, cooked
2 medium onions, chopped
3 cloves garlic, minced
3 tablespoons olive oil
2 tablespoons butter
1 tablespoon flour

1 cup milk
1 cup grated white cheddar cheese
1 cup grated parmesan cheese
1 sweet red pepper, diced
½ lb. bacon, cooked and crumbled

Keep the macaroni warm. Sauté the onions and garlic in the oil until the onions are soft. Drain; discard the excess oil. Melt the butter in a large saucepan over low heat. Mix in the flour to form a paste. Stir in the milk a little at a time. Add the cheeses. Continue stirring until the cheese is melted and the sauce is smooth. Add the macaroni, red pepper, and bacon; mix well. Garnish with anything blue. **Yield: 4 servings.**

Variation: Add some cooked broccoli for growth and prosperity, or cooked hamburger for grounding.

Magical Attributes: Patriotism, the spirit of freedom, liberty, confidence.

Celebrations: Patriot's Day, Memorial Day, Independence Day, when trying to overcome bad habits, divorce, separation.

Dien Hsing (China)

In both China and Japan, noodles are linked to long life and good fortune. The Chinese name of the dish translates as "heart toucher." The filling for Dien Hsing is very much like spring rolls, which were often part of spring and Chinese New Year celebrations.

Basic noodles:

4 eggs
¼ cup water
¼ teaspoon salt
4 cups flour

Marinade (optional):

½ cup soy sauce
1 teaspoon minced garlic
¼ teaspoon ground ginger
¼ teaspoon onion powder

Filling:

1½ cups finely chopped beef
1 tablespoon oil
1 tablespoon snipped chives
3 cloves garlic, minced
¼ teaspoon ground ginger
1 tablespoon soy sauce
½ teaspoon sugar
½ cup bamboo shoots, finely chopped
½ cup finely chopped chinese cabbage
½ cup bean sprouts

Beat the eggs, water, and salt in a small bowl. Place the flour in a deep bowl; make a well in the center. Pour the egg mixture into the well. Stir until the dough can be handled. Turn onto a flat, floured surface. Knead until elastic. Let stand 20 minutes. Divide dough into four equal portions. Roll out until paper thin. Slice into 3 x 3-inch squares. Lay on top of each other; refrigerate until needed.

Combine the marinade ingredients in a medium-sized bowl. Add the beef. Marinate in the refrigerator at least 12 hours.

Stir-fry the beef in the oil. Cool; shred or chop finely. Combine the chives, garlic, ginger, soy sauce, and sugar in a medium-sized bowl. Mix in the beef, water chestnuts, chinese cabbage, and bean sprouts.

Place 1 tablespoon of the filling into each wrapper. Dampen the edge of the wrapper with a little water. Fold each corner of the dough inward over the filling. Place seam-side down on a rack inside a wok; steam for 20-25 minutes. Otherwise, fry in hot oil until golden brown, 4-5 minutes. Serve with gingered soy sauce garnished with fresh chives, chinese mustard, and/or duck sauce.
Yield: 6 servings.

Variation: Chicken, pork and seafood are all tasty substitutions. Eat happily!

Magical Attributes: Adventure, safe journeys, curiosity, joyful discovery, success in love.

Celebrations: Chinese New Year, Feast of the Kitchen God, Brendan's Voyage, marriages and engagements, before any trip.

Hot Eggs and Noodles

8 oz. mezzani noodles, cooked

1 tablespoon plus
   ½ teaspoon fresh sage

1 tablespoon plus
   ½ teaspoon fresh parsley

3 tablespoons butter

12 hard-boiled eggs, peeled
   and halved lengthwise

¼ cup spiced vinegar

2 bay leaves

2 cloves garlic, sliced

1 teaspoon dry mustard

¼ teaspoon black pepper

¼ teaspoon cayenne pepper

½ cup beef stock

1 (16-oz.) can tomato sauce

¼ cup canned Italian-style
   tomatoes, drained

1 tablespoon Worcestershire
   sauce

Combine the noodles, ½ teaspoon of the sage, ½ teaspoon of the parsley and 1 tablespoon of the butter; spread in a shallow dish. Place the eggs on top of the noodles; sprinkle with the remaining sage and parsley. Mix the vinegar, bay leaves, garlic, mustard, black pepper, and cayenne pepper in a medium-sized saucepan. Simmer over low heat until the mixture is decreased by half. Strain; return the liquid to the pan. Mix in the beef stock, tomato sauce, tomatoes, Worchestershire sauce, and 2 tablespoons of the butter. Simmer for 10 minutes. Pour over the eggs and noodles. **Yield: 6 servings.**

Magical Attributes: Rebirth, cycles, cleansing by fire, renewal.

Celebrations: Spring festivals, fire festivals, New Year's, birthdays, renewing vows.

Hungarian Noodles with Barley

Carefully tend a sheaf of barley, and you likewise hold close the one you love. As you prepare this mixture, keep someone close to you in mind who needs extra support and direct your energy toward him or her. Maybe invite the person over for dinner!

2 eggs	¼ cup barley
2 tablespoon water	1 teaspoon paprika
1 teaspoon salt	Salt
2 cups flour	Pepper
¾ cup butter	½ lb. beef strips, cooked
Beef broth	

Beat the eggs, water, and salt in a small bowl. Place the flour in a medium-sized bowl; make a well in the center. Pour the egg mixture into the well. Stir until a soft dough is formed. Turn onto a flat, floured surface. Knead for 10 minutes. Cover with a damp cloth; let sit 20 minutes. Uncover; let sit for 30 minutes.

Preheat the oven to 150° F. Grate the dough over a lightly greased cookie sheet. Make sure the dough is evenly distributed on the cookie sheet. Bake until the dough is dry; turn occasionally. (Dried, the noodles can be stored indefinitely.)

Sauté the noodles in ½ cup of the butter until golden brown. Pour in enough beef broth to completely cover the noodles. Bring to a low boil. Add the barley, paprika, salt, and pepper. Simmer until both the noodles and barley are tender. Stir in the beef. Mix in ¼ cup of the butter just before serving. **Yield: 8 servings.**

Magical Attributes: Empathy, care toward others in need, love extended.

Celebrations: Binding of the Wreaths, Asking Festival, Handsel Monday, Valentine's Day.

Marc Anthony's Pasta Passionata

This recipe comes from the kitchen of Lisa Iris, who says, "this is an incredibly simple dish which becomes a pastoral love feast; a gift from the Mediterranean country still warmed by a touch of Aphrodite. First shared with me in New York, this meal is guaranteed to resolve any conflict between loved ones. Surrender to the fruits of the sea, sensuous pasta, and the glories of garlic!" This recipe requires intuition, passion and risk; it is never the same twice!

1 small can minced clams	Grated parmesan cheese
Fresh garlic	Salt
1 small can Italian tomatoes, drained; reserve juice	Pepper
Olive oil	Linguine or spaghetti for two people, cooked

Combine the clams, as much garlic as you can tolerate, and tomatoes in a small saucepan over low heat. Bring to a simmer. Stir in 1 or 2 tablespoons olive oil, just a bit of tomato juice (trust your instincts), parmesan cheese, salt, and pepper. Taste as you add spices for the perfect balance. Pour over the pasta. Serve with candlelight, Puccini, wine, and words of appreciation. Let love and garlic conquer all! **Yield: 2 servings.**

Variation: Substitute any other seafood for the clams, or eliminate the seafood and use spinach for prosperity.

Magical Attributes: Passion!

Celebrations: Most spring and fire festivals, Valentine's Day, at a handfasting or anniversary celebration.

Noodles in Fairy Butter (England 1700s)

This is a sweet side dish which, with its bright color and scent, inspires thoughts of spring frolic, abundant buttercups, and pranks by the Fey. People of the Middle Ages loved sweetened or spiced butter, especially honey or sage butter.

4 hard-boiled egg yolks	2 tablespoons orange flower water
½ cup sugar	(optional, see Rose Water, p. 58)
½ cup sweet butter, softened	1 lb. noodles (any kind), cooked
1 teaspoon dried thyme	1 orange, sliced (garnish)
1 teaspoon dried sweet basil	

Beat the egg yolks, sugar, butter, thyme, basil, and orange water in a small bowl until smooth. Mix enough of the butter with the hot noodles to coat the noodles with a golden-yellow color. Garnish with orange slices. **Yield: 8 servings.**

Variation: If available, buttercups and foxglove make an appropriate garnish for this dish.

Magical Attributes: Fairy kinship and magics, childlike energy, youth, light-hearted fun and friendship.

Celebrations: April Fool's Day, Lammas, spring festivals, May Day, Tibetan Butter Festival, Day of the Dryads, reunions, picnics.

Noodles with Scallions (Japan)

Buckwheat is generally associated with protection, especially in matters of financial security. However, since it is under the ruling of Venus, and these noodles are served cold, this dish is better prepared for shelter from unwanted affection or to calm sensuality.

1 lb. Japanese soba or	⅓ cup sake
buckwheat noodles	½ cup soy sauce
¼ teaspoon salt	1 tablespoon sugar
1 tablespoon seaweed	8 scallions with tops,
1 (½-inch) ginger root, halved	minced (garnish)

Bring the soba, salt, and 6 cups of water to a full boil. Drain; rinse in cold water. Cover and chill.

Place the seaweed in a tea ball or small cheesecloth bag. Combine the filled tea ball, ginger root, and 4 cups of water in a saucepan; warm over low heat for 15 minutes. Stir in the sake, soy sauce, and sugar. Heat until the sugar is dissolved. Remove ginger root and seaweed. Chill.

Arrange the cold noodles on small plates. Garnish with the scallions. The sauce is for dipping. Don't forget chop sticks!

Yield: 8 servings as an appetizer, 4 servings as a side dish.

Magical Attributes: Cooling romance or ill-timed physical excitement.

Celebrations: Valentine's Day, the peaceful ending of a relationship.

Pasta with Green Beans and Onions

2 medium onions, sliced and separated into rings
2 tablespoons butter
6 oz. noodles (any kind), cooked
1 (8-oz.) can french green beans, drained
1 (8-oz.) can cream of celery soup
½ teaspoon dry, crushed mint
¼ teaspoon salt
¼ teaspoon pepper
1 (8-oz.) can dried snack onions, crumbled

Preheat the oven to 300° F. Lightly fry the onions in the butter until tender. Combine the onions, noodles, green beans, soup, mint, salt and pepper. Transfer to a oven-proof pan. Sprinkle with the dried onions. Bake until bubbly. Garnish with fresh mint leaves. **Yield: 4 servings.**

Variation: Add some crisp bacon for wonderful flavor. Three cups cooked rice may be substituted for the noodles.

Magical Attributes: Cautious awareness, alertness to future dangers, easing grief or regret.

Celebrations: Patriot's Day, Summerland rites, forgiveness rituals, Feast of Banners, Riding the Marches, Bean Throwing Day.

Psychic Pasta

In Ireland, if you see a button mushroom it is considered best that you pick it, for after it has been seen it won't grow. Bay, celery seed, and thyme are all psychic enhancing herbs.

3 cups fresh mushrooms, sliced	1¼ cups heavy cream
1 cup chopped onion	1 teaspoon chopped bay leaf
3 tablespoons butter	1 teaspoon celery seed
½ teaspoon salt	1 teaspoon dried thyme
⅓ teaspoon pepper	6 oz. fettuccine, cooked
1 cup cooking wine	

Sauté the mushrooms and onions in the butter until tender. Add the salt, pepper, and wine; simmer over low heat until the mixture is reduced by half, about 5 minutes. Stir in the cream, bay leaf, celery seed, and thyme. Bring to a low boil. Pour over the pasta. Decorate the top of each dish with fresh, sliced mushrooms in the image of an eye or other psychic symbol. **Yield: 3 servings.**

Variation: Use Spinach and Carrot Fettucine (see below) for the pasta.

Magical Attributes: Psychic vision and awareness, intuition, deep understanding of astral matters.

Celebrations: Samhain, Ahes Festival, Birthday of the Moon, initiations, Feast of the Milky Way.

Spinach and Carrot Fettuccine (Italy)

Carrots were once thought to aid eyesight. This, combined with the green, flourishing energies of spinach, will help improve intuition.

5 oz. frozen spinach, cooked and drained	2 eggs
¾ cup sliced carrots, cooked and drained	1 tablespoon olive oil
	2 cups self-rising flour

Purée the spinach, carrots, eggs, and oil in a blender or food processor. Place the flour in a medium-sized bowl; make a well in the center. Pour the spinach mixture into the well. Stir until a stiff dough forms. If the dough is too sticky, add a little flour. Turn onto a flat, floured surface. Knead until elastic, about 5 minutes. Let sit for 10 minutes.

Divide into four equal portions. Roll each section into a paper thin rectangle on a generously floured surface. Cut into ¼-inch wide strips. Cover the dough not being rolled out. Place strips on a towel until completely dry, about 30 minutes. Store in an airtight container.

To cook, bring salted water to a boil. Add fettucine; boil until tender, about 5 minutes. **Yield: 8 servings.**

Note: If not using self-rising flour, add 2½ teaspoons baking powder and a pinch of salt.

Magical Attributes: The "Sight," inspiration, ability to consider "unseen" elements in a situation, growing awareness.

Celebrations: Carrot Sunday, many summer rituals, April Fool's Day, Sunning of Buddha, Ahes Festival, Birthday of the Moon.

Tortellini with Eggplant (Sicily)

Pasta is a sacred food in Sicily, and is identified with miracles and mysteries. Eggplant is aligned with Jupiter; the combination is especially good for financial turn-arounds.

1 medium eggplant, peeled	½ lb. tortellini, cooked
½ teaspoon salt	1 cup spaghetti sauce with meat
¾ cup herbed flour (see note)	½ lb. mozzarella cheese, grated
½ cup olive oil	1 medium tomato, sliced
2 cloves garlic, minced	¼ cup grated parmesan cheese

Preheat the oven to 350° F. Cut the eggplant into ½-inch slices. Soak in cold water with the salt for 15 minutes; drain. Cover each slice with the herbed flour. Heat the olive oil and garlic in a frying pan over medium heat. Fry the eggplant until golden brown and tender, about 10 minutes. Drain on paper towels.

Layer the ingredients in a greased 8 x 8-inch pan in the following order; tortellini, half the spaghetti sauce, half the tomato slices, all the eggplant, half the spaghetti sauce, half the tomato slices, mozzarella cheese, and parmesan cheese. Bake until heated all the way through and the cheese is browned, about 20 minutes. **Yield: 4 servings.**

Note: To make herbed flour, simply mix your favorite herbs and spices with ¾ cup flour. Suggested herbs include oregano, basil, rosemary, marjoram, thyme, salt, and pepper.

Magical Attributes: Monetary balance, blessings, "miraculous" change, universal riddles.

Celebrations: Feast of Jupiter, Russian Fair, Royal Oak Day.

Yin Yang Noodles (China)

The hot/cold combination here brings improved balance to the sexes. Sesame seeds and wine vinegar are for solar energy, while soy sauce and cucumber is lunar.

½ lb. egg noodles	1 teaspoon sugar
6 cups ice water	2 teaspoons minced ginger root
7 tablespoons sesame oil	3 teaspoons minced garlic
4 cups boiling water	1 teaspoon chili pepper
2 cups bean sprouts	1 teaspoon black pepper
½ cup chopped chives	1 cucumber, peeled and shredded
2 tablespoons sesame seeds	1 cup cooked, shredded
6 tablespoons soy sauce	chicken breast
1 tablespoon wine vinegar	2 tablespoons diced, salted cashews

Bring the noodles and 12 cups of water to a boil. Add ½ cup cold water just as the water comes to a boil. Reduce heat; simmer until tender. Drain. Soak the noodles in the ice water for 30 seconds. Drain. Mix the noodles with 3 tablespoons of the sesame oil. Cover and chill.

Pour boiling water over the bean sprouts; let stand 15 seconds. Rinse in cold water; drain. Combine with the noodles and chill.

Combine the chives, sesame seeds, soy sauce, vinegar, sugar, ginger root, garlic, chili pepper, black pepper, and 4 tablespoons of the sesame oil. Spoon evenly over the noodles. Sprinkle with the chicken, cucumber, and peanuts.
Yield: 6 servings.

Magical Attributes: Balance, harmony, symmetry, accord.

Celebrations: Sunning of Buddha, Earth Day, May Day, Handsel Monday.

❧ *Sigil Sauce* ☙

Bardic Muse (France)

It is said that this sauce was so famous in France that bards glorified it in song. The bread crumbs here serve to thicken the recipe in place of flour, as in the fourteenth century such thickening techniques were as yet undeveloped.

1 cup bread crumbs
⅓ cup white cooking wine
½ lb. frozen spinach,
    cooked and drained
½ cup cream
¼ teaspoon dried sage

¼ teaspoon ground ginger
½ teaspoon dried tarragon
½ teaspoon dried parsley
Salt
Pepper

Soak the bread in the wine in a medium-sized saucepan until thoroughly moistened. Stir over low heat until the bread turns into a paste. Transfer to a blender or food processor. Add the spinach and cream; mix on medium speed for about 1 minute. Pour back into the saucepan; heat over a low flame. Stir in the sage, ginger, tarragon, parsley, salt, and pepper. This is excellent on lamb.

Yield: About 1¼ cups.

Magical Attributes: Creativity, inspiration, the arts, the Fool card of the Tarot.

Celebrations: Birthday of the Moon, April Fool's Day, Ahes Festival, Aloha Week, Festival of Sarasvati, any celebrations to honor Apollo or Pan.

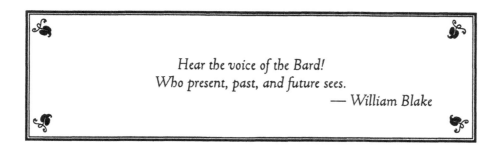

Hear the voice of the Bard!
Who present, past, and future sees.
— William Blake

Lobster Sauce (France)

3 tablespoons butter, melted
3 tablespoons flour
1½ cups milk
1 cup heavy cream
½ lb. lobster meat, shredded
1 clove garlic, minced
Salt
Pepper
½ cup butter

Combine the melted butter and flour in a medium-sized saucepan to make a paste. Stir in the milk and cream a little at a time to make a smooth sauce. Sauté the lobster, garlic, salt, and pepper in ½ cup butter until the lobster is thoroughly cooked. Add to the sauce. Serve over pasta. **Yield: About 3 cups.**

Variation: A similar sauce is made in Norway, the only change being the addition of 3 tablespoons of cognac. Magically, this is for fiery love.

Magical Attributes: Fire magic, solar energy, personal vitality, courage.

Celebrations: Lobster Festival, summer rituals, Birthday of the Sun, fire festivals.

Lychee Sweet 'n Sour (Asia)

Regarded as the hazelnut of China, the lychee has a natural sweet-sour taste, making it popular in jam and meat dishes. It is considered the fruit of love.

- 3-4 lychee fruit, peeled
- 1 tablespoon vinegar
- 1 teaspoon lemon juice
- ¼ cup dry white wine
- 1 teaspoon soy sauce
- ¼ teaspoon ground ginger
- 1 tablespoon cornstarch

Simmer the lychee fruit until soft. Drain and dice. In a small saucepan, bring the vinegar, lemon juice, wine, soy sauce, and ginger to a simmer over low heat. Add the lychee fruit; simmer for 15 minutes. Stir in the cornstarch a little at a time. Simmer until thickened. This can be applied to pasta, meats, barbecue dishes, gravy and stews. **Yield: About 2¼ cups.**

Magical Attributes: Any Chinese deity, romance, weather magic, balance.

Celebrations: Feast of the Kitchen God, Valentine's Day, Samhain, Feast of the Milky Way, Sealing the Frost.

Nasturtium Sauce

In the language of flowers, nasturtium means patriotism and commitment.

- 1 quart nasturtium flowers
- 1 quart vinegar
- 1 cup cooking wine
- 3 shallots, chopped
- 1 tablespoon minced chives
- 6 whole cloves
- 1 teaspoon salt
- 1 teaspoon pepper

Combine all the ingredients in a large saucepan. Bring to a boil; boil for 10 minutes. Pour into a sterilized jar; cover. Age at least 1 month. Strain before using. Use on lamb or pork. **Yield: 1 quart.**

Variation: In place of the nasturtiums use 6-8 whole peppercorns, 2 whole garlic cloves, and an orange (sliced and peeled). Follow the same directions. Magically this is for health and purification.

Magical Association: Dedication to a cause, devotion, personal convictions.

Celebrations: Patriot's Day, Memorial Day, Independence Day, anniversary, marriage, before acting on any matter of judgment.

Onion Sauce (Spain, France)

Onions are thought to be great protectors, especially against ghosts. In Egypt, they were the food of slaves, giving improved strength and fortitude.

1 medium onion, diced	2 cups beef broth
2 shallots, minced	2 tablespoons tomato purée
1 tablespoon olive oil	1 tablespoon minced parsley
2 tablespoons butter	Salt
2 tablespoons flour	Pepper
½ cup white wine	

Sauté the onion and shallots in the olive oil. Melt the butter in a medium-sized saucepan over low heat. Stir in the flour to form a paste. Add the wine a little at a time; stir until smooth. Mix in the onion, shallots, beef broth, tomato purée, parsley, salt, and pepper. Heat until sauce just begins to simmer.
Yield: About 3 cups.

Magical Attributes: Protecting personal freedom, safety from negative energies, endurance, tenacity.

Celebrations: Independence Day, President's Day, Royal Oak Day, job hunting, before starting new projects.

Pesto (India, Italy)

In India, basil is considered an herb of happiness. In Italy, it was so highly prized that is was harvested with a golden sickle.

2 cups fresh basil	5 cloves garlic
¾ cup grated parmesan cheese	2 tablespoons pine nuts
¾ cup olive oil	

Place all the ingredients in a blender. Mix on a low setting until smooth. This is excellent with any pasta or as the topping for pizza. **Yield: About 1¾ cups.**

Magical Attributes: Joy, individuality, protection of precious possessions.

Celebrations: Birthday, anniversary, Sealing the Frost.

Plum Sauce

The plum has been considered an aphrodisiac along with peaches and other fruits. The wood in fruit trees was sometimes cut and hung carefully around the lintels of a house to safeguard all within and maintain harmony.

½ clove garlic	⅓ cup plum jam
⅛ teaspoon salt	2 tablespoons vinegar
1 teaspoon dried basil	1 plum, skinned and diced
¼ teaspoon dried thyme	¼ cup water
1 teaspoon parsley, minced	

Mash the garlic with the salt in a small saucepan. The back of a wooden spoon works well. Mix with the basil, thyme, and parsley to form a paste. Stir in the jam; heat over a low flame. Mix in the vinegar, plum, and water. Cook until liquid has been reduced by ⅛ cup. Serve over black-eyed peas, beans, or as a glaze to ham and poultry. **Yield: About ¾ cup.**

Variation: A Russian version of this sauce is prepared with ¼ cup plum brandy instead of the water.

Magical Attributes: Protecting and encouraging love.

Celebrations: Weddings, anniversary, Valentine's Day, vow renewals.

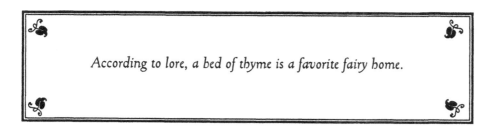

According to lore, a bed of thyme is a favorite fairy home.

Success Sauce (England, Scotland)

Saffron dye was used exclusively at one time to tint the robes of kings and other important officials. In the Old Testament it was called karcom.

2 medium onions, minced	½ cup water
3 cloves garlic, minced	2 teaspoons saffron
¼ cup olive oil	Salt
½ cup white wine	Pepper

Sauté the onions and garlic in the olive oil until tender. Stir in the white wine, water, saffron, salt, and pepper. Simmer for about 15 minutes. Excellent on fish and pasta. **Yield: 2 cups.**

Variation: If using the sauce for fish, add one (8-oz.) can Italian-style tomatoes. This is for loving guidance.

Magical Attributes: Wise leadership, prosperity, spiritual direction or guidance.

Celebrations: Eldership rites, investment of a new priest or priestess, many spring rituals.

Sigil Sauce (Merry Old England)

In a grimoire from the 1500s it says that to the Chaldeans, Latins, and English, the marigold was a flower of change because it turned its face to follow the sun each day.

1 egg	½ teaspoon grated lemon peel
1 cup butter, softened	1 cup marigold petals
1 cup sugar	¼ cup water
½ teaspoon lemon juice	

Cream the egg, butter, and sugar in a small saucepan. Heat over a low flame. Mix in the lemon juice, lemon peel, marigold petals, and water. Cook until thickened; stir frequently. This is a sweet-piquant sauce. **Yield: 2 cups.**

Variation: Replace the marigold petals with 8 whole cloves (the number of transformation). Follow the same directions, but remove the cloves before serving.

Magical Attributes: Sun and fire magic, good advice or council, clear sightedness, positive personal change.

Celebrations: Tibetan Butter Festival, Birthday of the Sun, any noonday or fire rituals, or perhaps during winter to help the sun in its journey.

Tarragon Sauce (France)

In French, tarragon means "little dragon." Allow the ancient powers of this mythical beast to be internalized with the sauce.

⅓ cup tarragon vinegar	⅛ teaspoon salt
2 shallots, minced	5 egg yolks
½ cup minced chives	⅛ teaspoon pepper
1½ teaspoons dried tarragon	1 cup butter

Combine the vinegar, shallots, chives, tarragon, and salt in a small saucepan. Simmer until the liquid is reduced by half. Remove from heat; add 1 tablespoon cold water, egg yolks, and pepper. Beat until thickened. Place over low heat. Mix in the butter a pat at a time. Best served with broiled chicken.
Yield: About 2 cups.

Magical Attributes: Ancient wisdom and knowledge, power of myth and legend.

Celebrations: Ahes Festival, Day of the Dryads, St. Stephen Festival, any festival which commemorates your path, May Day, Lammas.

Wine Sauce

When bordeaux wines first appeared in Europe, they were frequently not of a very good quality and quite bitter. To alleviate wastefulness and save money, the clever merchant or manor cook would make a heady sauce with the wine base and herbs.

1 clove garlic, minced	2 tablespoons lemon juice
2 green onions, minced	1 tablespoon butter
½ cup bordeaux wine	¼ teaspoon dried thyme
½ cup dry red wine	Salt
2 cups meat broth	Pepper
1 whole tomato, peeled and diced	

In a medium-sized saucepan, simmer the onions and garlic in the bordeaux over low heat until tender. Stir in the red wine, meat broth, tomato, and lemon juice. The broth should correspond to the meat with which the sauce will be used. Simmer until the tomatoes are very tender. Stir in the butter, thyme, salt, and pepper. Terrific with any cooked meat. **Yield: 3 cups.**

Magical Attributes: Thrift, economy, conservation, frugality, temperance.

Celebrations: Thanksgiving, Asking Festival, Borrowed Days.

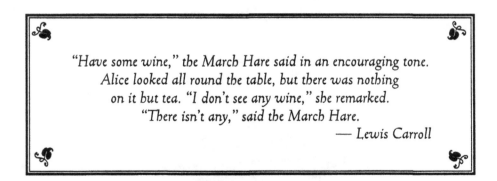

"Have some wine," the March Hare said in an encouraging tone. Alice looked all round the table, but there was nothing on it but tea. "I don't see any wine," she remarked. "There isn't any," said the March Hare.
— Lewis Carroll

Personal Recipes

Personal Recipes

Chapter Eleven

Quarter Quickies

O! for a muse of fire, that would ascend the brightest heaven of invention!
— William Shakespeare

The kitchen witch is often left in circumstances that try the very core of what it means to be creative. But waning finances or a demanding schedule don't have to mean the loss of tasty meals, or potent magic. Thus, this section is dedicated to meals that are either cost-effective or quick to prepare, and in some instances, both!

Chicken Bread-Pie (Russian)

The magical symbolism of this dish is based on the green coloring of the vegetables and the healthy nature of chicken. Additionally, broccoli is regarded as protective, and peas are a water-based vegetable for encouraging gentle, nurturing energies.

4 slices toast
⅓ cup butter
⅓ cup flour
⅓ cup milk
2 cups chicken broth
2 tablespoons dill
Salt
Pepper

3 cups cooked, diced chicken
5 oz. frozen peas, thawed
5 oz. frozen broccoli, thawed
1 onion, chopped
2 hard-boiled eggs, peeled and thinly sliced
4 slices bread

Preheat the oven to 400° F. Grease an 8 x 8-inch pan. Lay the toast on the bottom of the pan. Melt the butter in a medium-sized saucepan. Mix in the flour to form a paste. Add the milk a little at a time; stir until smooth. Stir in the broth, dill, salt, and pepper. Mix in the chicken, peas, broccoli, and onion. Lay half the egg slices on the toast. Pour on the creamed chicken. Top with the remaining egg slices. Cover with the bread slices. Bake until hot, about 20 minutes.
Yield: 4 servings.

Variation: Substitute veal or pork for the chicken. Veal pies were favored by the Normans during their conquest of the Saxons. Pork pies with sage are a favorite in Quebec. For harvest festivals, add ½ cup carrots and ½ cup corn.

Magical Attributes: Increasing health, growth, prosperity.

Celebrations: Before balancing your checkbook, initiation, cold and flu season, many spring rituals, Festival of Mihr.

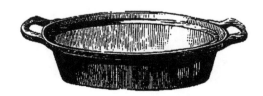

Corn Chowder

2 medium potatoes, diced
½ small zucchini, diced (optional)
2 stalks celery, chopped
2 carrots, sliced
1 large onion, minced
2 tablespoon butter

1-2 cloves garlic, minced
1 (16-oz.) can creamed corn
½ teaspoon onion powder
½ teaspoon garlic powder
¼ teaspoon pepper

Saute the potatoes, zucchini, celery, carrots, and onion in the butter in a medium-sized saucepan until tender. Mix in the creamed corn, onion powder, garlic powder, and pepper. Simmer for 15 minutes. Serve with bread.
Yield: 2 servings.

Variation: Add ½ cup broccoli, peas, cauliflower, or any other vegetable to this soup for grounding.

Magical Attributes: Harvest, reaping benefits from good actions, providence.

Celebrations: Lammas, Fall Equinox, Thanksgiving, Asking Festival, Planting Festival, Festival of Ishtar.

Creamy Bean Blend

Beans are unusual vegetables in that they are known to twine themselves counterclockwise (or widdershins) up a pole as they grow. They make marvelous foods for banishing.

1 (16-oz.) can green beans, drained
1 (16-oz.) can yellow beans, drained
1 (8-oz.) can lima beans or peas, drained
2 (8-oz.) cans cream soup, any kind

½ teaspoon celery seed (optional)
1 teaspoon garlic powder (optional)
1 teaspoon onion powder (optional)
3 tablespoons butter
2 cups bread crumbs

Preheat the oven to 350° F. Mix the beans, soup, celery seed, garlic powder, onion powder, and any other favorite spices in a small casserole dish. Melt the butter in a small saucepan. Add the bread crumbs; stir until well coated. Add more butter if needed. Sprinkle the bread crumbs over the top of the casserole. Bake until bubbly and bread crumbs are browned, 20-30 minutes.
Yield: 4 servings.

Magical Attributes: Reversals, change.

Celebrations: To break negative habits or turn malevolent energies away.

Curried Beef (India)

Curry is a natural purifier, and in many cultures was a highly prized and costly spice blend.

¾ cup sliced celery	1 (8-oz.) can beef soup
¾ cup sliced green pepper	1 cup cooked rice
2 cloves garlic, minced	¼ cup raisins
¼ teaspoon curry powder	1 medium apple, sliced
3 tablespoons butter	1 cup chopped peanuts

Combine the celery, green pepper, garlic, curry, and butter in a microwave safe 1-quart casserole dish. Microwave on high until tender, about 4 minutes. Mix in the soup, rice, and raisins. Microwave on high for 5 minutes; stop to stir once. Arrange the apple slices decoratively around the edge or into a magical symbol. Microwave on high for 3 minutes. Sprinkle with peanuts. **Yield: 4 servings.**

Celebrations: All fire festivals, specifically Beltane and Summer Solstice; any magic for conception, Hori.

Fennel Fish (Hawaii)

Hawaiian lore is filled with fish, mostly because it was the greatest source of food for the island dwellers. The fish hook is an emblem of good fortune, and this dish is traditionally prepared with mahi-mahi. Fennel is typically an herb of strength.

2 lbs. lean white fish	Pepper
3 tablespoons butter	1 sweet red pepper, thinly sliced
2 tablespoons olive oil	4 cups pea pods
3 tablespoons sesame seeds	½ cup chopped fennel bulb
Salt	½ cup chopped onion

Preheat the oven to 425° F. Lay the fish in an 9 x 9-inch baking dish. Combine the butter, olive oil, sesame seeds, salt, and pepper in a medium-sized saucepan. Stir over low heat until the butter is melted. Stir in the red pepper, pea pods, fennel, and onion. Pour over the fish. Bake until the fish is opaque and flaky, about 15 minutes. **Yield: 4 servings.**

Variation: If white fish is too expensive in your region, try this with white tuna.

Magical Attributes: Fortitude, spiritual sustenance, improved fortune, plenty.

Celebrations: Harvest festivals, Festival of Mihr, Initiation, Sunning of Buddha, Borrowed Days, Sukkoth, Aloha Week.

Friendship Stew (Aztec)

Turkey was one of the first meals the Aztecs offered the Spanish. Turkey remains an important part of Mexican observances, to the point where some grooms are required to provide one or more turkeys as part of the bride price.

6 lbs. turkey, cooked and sliced	2 tablespoons sesame seeds
2 tablespoons oil	3 cloves garlic, minced
1 onion, chopped	2 tablespoons chili powder
3 tomatoes, chopped	⅛ teaspoon ground cinnamon
1 green pepper, chopped	½ teaspoon anise seed
1½ oz. unsweetened dark chocolate, melted	⅛ teaspoon pepper
¼ cup roasted peanuts	1½ cups chicken stock

Preheat the oven to 225° F. Brown the turkey in the oil. Place in a large casserole dish. Combine the onion, tomatoes, green pepper, chocolate, peanuts, sesame seeds, garlic, chili powder, cinnamon, anise, and pepper in a blender or food processor. Mix at medium speed until a paste is formed. Transfer to a medium-sized saucepan; stir over low heat. Mix in the chicken stock a little at a time. Heat until the sauce just begins to simmer. Pour over the turkey. Bake until warmed all the way through, about 15 minutes. May be served by itself or with rice. **Yield: 6 servings.**

Magical Attributes: Kinship, trust, honoring promises.

Celebrations: Family bonding rituals, Initiation, Festival of Brightness, Handsel Monday, Chinese New Year, Thanksgiving, Yule.

Garbanzo Supreme (Middle East)

Mediterranean cultures are familiar with hummus, made from a base of garbanzo beans. In this part of the world, beans were often part of offerings to the Gods.

1 (15-oz.) can garbanzo beans, drained, reserve the juice
¼ cup sesame seeds
2 cloves garlic, halved
2 tablespoons lemon juice

1 loaf fresh bread, unsliced
2 tablespoons minced fresh cilantro
½ cup sliced green pepper
½ cup sliced cucumber
Alfalfa or bean sprouts

Place the garbanzo beans, sesame seeds, garlic, lemon juice, and ⅓ cup of the garbanzo bean juice in a blender or food processor. Mix on medium-high until smooth and easy to spread. Slice the loaf of bread in half lengthwise. Spread the bottom half with the bean mixture. Top with the cilantro, green pepper, cucumber, and sprouts. Cover with the top half of the bread. Slice and serve.
Yield: 4 servings.

Magical Attributes: Spirituality, offerings, water magic.

Celebrations: Ahes Festival, spring rituals, Birthday of the Moon.

Gypsy Casserole

Making leftovers into a feast was a gypsy talent which not only helped maintain supplies, but gave many people something warm and hearty to anticipate. Gypsies are vagabonds and adventurers whose love of freedom us almost religious, and whose awareness of magical arts is keen.

1 (18 oz.) can hearty beef or chicken soup
1 cup cooked noodles, any kind
1 cup peas, cooked

1 cup chopped onion
½ cup sour cream
¼ teaspoon dried dill weed

Combine all ingredients in a microwave-safe casserole dish. Microwave on high for 8 minutes; stop twice to stir. Or, heat for about 20 minutes at 350° F in a conventional oven. Garnish with cheese for change, parsley for protection and health, or tomatoes for love. **Yield: 4 servings.**

Magical Attributes: Clear thought, economy, conservation, safe travel, personal liberation.

Celebrations: Earth Day, Riding the Marches, Birthday of the Sun, Asking Festival, Chinese New Year, Independence Day.

Hot Pockets (Greece)

The seafood combines with the hot spices in the pocket to encourage fecundity.

10 oz. salad shrimp, cooked	2 cloves garlic, minced
2 cups chopped tomatoes	2 teaspoons hot peppers
¼ cup minced green onions	⅛ teaspoon black pepper
⅓ cup green pepper, diced	6 small pitas
1 tablespoon lemon juice	Lettuce
½ teaspoon olive oil	

Combine the shrimp, tomatoes, onions, and green pepper in a medium-sized bowl. Mix the lemon juice, oil, garlic, hot peppers, and black pepper in a small bowl. Pour over the shrimp and vegetables; stir. Slice the top off each pita. Place a leaf of lettuce inside. Fill with ½ cup of the shrimp mixture. **Yield: 6 servings.**

Variation: If shrimp is too expensive, use imitation crab meat instead for the same goals.

Magical Attributes: Fiery passions, intense productivity or fertility, clearly defined goals.

Celebrations: May Day, many spring rituals, Summer Solstice, conception rituals, Hori, Ahes Festival, Festival of Mihr.

Italian Sausage Rolls

Sausage was first created in Egypt. Almost any meat can be used in its preparation. The customs surrounding this dish, therefore, tend to vary from region to region depending on spices, time of year, and base meat.

- 1 loaf frozen bread dough, thawed
- 1 lb. garlic sausage
- 1 tablespoon minced garlic
- 2 beaten eggs
- ⅓ cup grated parmesan cheese
- ½ lb. mozzarella cheese, grated
- 1 lb. ricotta cheese
- 1 tablespoon snipped parsley
- Pepper

Preheat the oven according to the directions listed on the bread dough package. Brown the sausage with the garlic; drain off the fat. Beat the eggs, cheeses, parsley, and pepper in a medium-sized bowl. Stir in the sausage. Split the dough lengthwise. Press inside the cut to make an indentation. Pour in the filling. Seal by pinching the edges together. Bake per instructions on the bread dough package. Cut into 7 slices, the number of multiplicity. **Yield: 7 servings.**

Variation: Use American cheese or eliminate one of the cheeses in this recipe without harming the flavor.

Magical Attributes: Diversity and variety in harmony.

Celebrations: Aloha Festival, St. Joan of Arc Day, wind-related celebrations, Feast of Jupiter.

Piquant Black-eyed Peas and Ham (Southern U.S.)

In the southern United States, black-eyed peas are a traditional New Year's treat for luck. Hot pepper is ascribed to the element of fire and eliminating impurities.

- 1 cup black-eyed peas
- ½ cup diced ham or bacon
- ½ teaspoon dried hot red pepper, or
- 1 teaspoon minced fresh jalapeño
- 1 onion, chopped
- 1 teaspoon salt
- 3 cups cooked rice

Cover the black-eyed peas with water; soak for at least 8 hours.

Drain the black-eyed peas. Combine the ham, peppers, onion, and salt in a medium-sized saucepan. Cover with water; simmer for 5 minutes. Stir in the peas; add water to cover. Simmer until the peas are tender, about 45 minutes. Add water if necessary during cooking. Mix in the rice. **Yield: 5 servings.**

Magical Attributes: Cleansing, purification, good fortune.

Celebrations: Any fire festivals, rituals for health, Smell the Breeze Day.

Pizza Imposter

1 package refrigerator biscuits	1 teaspoon dried oregano
½ cup chopped tomatoes	2 tablespoons butter
½ cup chopped onion	1 cup spaghetti sauce
2 cloves garlic, minced	8 oz. mozzarella cheese, grated
1 teaspoon dried basil	

Preheat the oven per biscuit package directions. Lightly grease a pie tin. Press the biscuits on the bottom and sides of the pan so that there are no gaps between the biscuits. Use dampened fingers to seal biscuit edges together. Sauté the tomatoes, onion, garlic, basil, and oregano in the butter until the onions are tender. Stir in the spaghetti sauce. Spread over the biscuits. Top with the mozzarella cheese. Bake until golden brown, about 12 minutes. A nice side dish for this meal is antipasto and/or breadsticks. **Yield: 2-4 servings.**

Magical Attributes: Faerie glamour, shape-changing, gentle love, safety.

Celebrations: Halloween, April Fool's Day, Royal Oak Day.

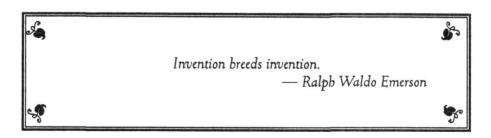

Invention breeds invention.
— *Ralph Waldo Emerson*

Pork Kabobs

For this dish I have tried to use the combination of meat, a grounding/earth energy food, with the various vegetables for fire, air, and water to bring renewed harmony during chaotic times. While you're outside preparing this, remember to breathe deeply and relax!

1 lb. boneless pork, cubed	3 tablespoons honey
3 tablespoons wine vinegar	3 tablespoons barbecue sauce
1 clove garlic, minced	Cherry tomatoes
1 tablespoon sesame seeds	Pearl onions
1 teaspoon onion powder	2 small yellow squash, cubed
½ teaspoon ground ginger	3 green peppers, cut into
½ teaspoon dried rosemary	1-inch pieces
½ teaspoon lemon pepper	Bamboo skewers

Combine the pork, vinegar, garlic, sesame seeds, onion powder, ginger, rosemary, and lemon pepper in a medium-sized bowl. Cover; marinate at least 12 hours in the refrigerator.

Pour marinade into a small saucepan. Bring to a boil over low heat; boil 5 minutes. Mix in the honey and barbecue sauce.

Alternate pieces of pork, tomatoes, onions, squash, and green peppers on the skewers. Grill 5-6 inches away from the coals or heat element until the pork is thoroughly cooked, about 20 minutes. Turn every 5 minutes to baste with the sauce. **Yield: 4 servings.**

Magical Attributes: Balancing energies, symmetry equilibrium, order.

Celebrations: Midday or midnight observances, before any legal matters, Spring Equinox, Samhain, New Year's.

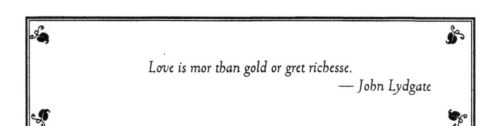

Love is mor than gold or gret richesse.
— *John Lydgate*

Potato-Hotdog Fry

Potatoes are a root vegetable, making them excellent grounding symbols. Hot dogs, by comparison, are a rather playful food, conjuring images of sunny days and leisure activities. Combined, they make a good meal to help return stability to a situation.

¼ cup vegetable oil
3 large potatoes, cut in ½-inch cubes
1 medium onion, sliced
3 hot dogs, sliced in ½-inch pieces
1 tablespoon butter

¼ cup sour cream
¼ cup dill relish
¼ teaspoon dried dill weed
Salt
Pepper

Heat the oil in a frying pan over medium heat. Add the potatoes and onion. Cook until the potatoes are tender. Stir in the hot dogs; cook until the hot dogs are thoroughly heated. Melt the butter in a small saucepan over low heat. Mix in the sour cream, relish, dill, salt and pepper. When hot, pour over the potatoes and serve immediately. **Yield: 3 servings.**

Variation: Any bits of leftover lunch meat or vegetables can be added to this dish for a wide variety of flavors and magical meanings.

Magical Attributes: Balance, steadiness, symmetry.

Celebrations: Samhain, New Year's, May Day.

Rosemary-Orange Beef (Medieval England)

The Countess of Hainault, whose daughter was Queen Philippa of England, believed that rosemary would bring cheer to any heart, keep away evil spirits, and help insure fidelity between people. At this time oranges were rare and were a symbol of affluence.

- 1 lb. beef, cubed
- 2 cups mixed cut vegetables, any kind
- 2 tablespoons butter
- 1 tablespoon cornstarch
- ¼ cup beef broth
- ¼ cup orange juice
- 2 tablespoons soy sauce
- 2 cloves garlic, minced
- ¼ teaspoon ground ginger
- ¼ teaspoon dried rosemary
- 1 orange, peeled and sliced
- 2 cups cooked rice

Fry the beef and vegetables in the butter until the beef is thoroughly cooked. Transfer the beef and vegetables to a bowl; leave the butter in the pan. Mix the cornstarch in the butter to make a paste. Slowly stir in the broth a little at a time until smooth. Heat over a low flame. Stir in the orange juice, soy sauce, garlic, ginger, and rosemary. Cook until a medium-thick sauce is formed; stir constantly. Mix in the beef, vegetables, and orange; cook for 5 minutes. Garnish with the orange peel. Serve over rice. **Yield: 4 servings.**

Magical Attributes: Easing melancholy, encouragement in abundance (especially in love), faithfulness, dependable financial means.

Celebrations: Any rites for Venus, Handsel Monday, Summerland rituals, handfasting, Labor Day, many winter rituals.

Seeds in a Shell (Tony's Kitchen)

Tony says this collection of seed vegetables and spices help bring stronger synergy with the male aspect of the divine. Prepare this dish on a bright, sunny day to accent this.

- 1 package soft tortilla shells
  Vegetable oil
- ½ cup fresh peas
- ¼ cup fresh corn
- ½ cup cooked pinto beans, or your favorite kind of bean
- 1 tablespoon sesame seeds
  Pepper

Preheat the oven to 375° F. Lightly coat half the tortilla shells with the vegetable oil. Arrange on the bottom of an oven-proof baking dish. Bake until crisp, about 20 minutes. Mix together the peas, corn, beans, sesame seeds, and pepper. Other more traditional taco fillings can also be added along with any other "seed" herbs and spices. Spread the filling over the crisp shells. Coat the rest of the tortilla shells with oil and place on top. Bake until the top shells are brown, 15-20 minutes. **Yield: 6 servings.**

Magical Attributes: Solar/God related magics.

Celebrations: Birthday of the Sun, Sunning of Buddha, many summer festivals.

Shepherd's Pie (Scotland)

In Scotland, wool continues to be one of the most important products of the country. This made the shepherd's job an honorable one. Even today in rural areas, sheep are allowed to wander somewhat freely, often using the roadway as a car might.

2 small onions, chopped	Pepper
2 tablespoons butter	1 lb. (3 cups) potatoes, boiled
1 lb. mincemeat (p. 166)	and sliced thin
1 cup beef stock	1 egg
Salt	2 tablespoons butter, melted

Preheat the oven to 300° F. Sauté the onion in butter until browned. Stir in the mincemeat, stock, salt, and pepper. Bring to a simmer. Pour into a pie pan. Layer the potatoes on top. Beat the egg and the melted butter. Pour over the potatoes. Bake until golden brown, about 15 minutes. **Yield: 4-6 servings.**

Variation: ¼ cup shredded cheese mixed in with the potatoes is a tasty addition.

Magical Attributes: Service, watchfulness, vigilance, observational skill, perspective, earth magic.

Celebrations: April Fool's Day, Handsel Monday, Festival of Durga, Sukkoth, Festival of Ishtar.

Shrimp with Garlic (from Dynahara)

½ cup olive oil
3 cloves garlic, minced
1 teaspoon Worcestershire sauce
1 teaspoon soy sauce
1 lb. shrimp, rinsed

Combine the oil, garlic, Worcestershire sauce, and soy sauce in a medium-sized bowl. Add the shrimp. Cover and refrigerate at least 1 hour.

Pour the marinade into a frying pan. Heat over a medium flame. When hot, add the shrimp. Fry until lightly golden. Serves as an appetizer, side dish, or as a topping for rice. **Yield: 2 servings.**

Variation: Try imitation crab meat for a more budget-minded alternative to the shrimp.

Magical Attributes: Spicy romance, zest and zeal.

Celebrations: Valentine's Day, anniversary, any time you need a "pick-me-up" emotionally or physically.

Stewed Scallops (1600s England)

White is a color sacred to the Lady, and this dish, when properly prepared, has almost a luminescent hue, similar to that of the lunar sphere.

1 lb. fresh scallops
Dash of nutmeg
3 tablespoons butter
½ cup heavy cream
Salt
Pepper
¼ orange
2 lemon slices (garnish)

Sauté the scallops and nutmeg in the butter until the scallops are white and the edges turn up. Stir in the cream, salt, and pepper. Squeeze the orange over the sauce; stir. Serve as is or over rice for a heartier dish. Garnish with lemon. **Yield: 2 servings.**

Magical Attributes: Moon and Goddess magic.

Celebrations: Birthday of the Moon, any holiday which honors a Goddess figure, full moon rituals.

Summer Turkey Surprise

Fruits are potent energy foods; both the orange and raspberry are aligned with love, and peaches are sacred in China as a symbol of immortality.

½ cup fresh raspberries
1 peach, peeled and sliced
1 orange, peeled, pitted, and sliced
3 tablespoons peach or raspberry brandy

2 tablespoons honey
¼ cup flour
1 lb. turkey, sliced
1 tablespoon vegetable oil

Place the fruit, brandy, and honey in a blender or food processor. Blend on medium speed for 2 minutes. Pour into a small saucepan; heat over a low flame. Cover the turkey slices with flour. Fry in the oil until done. Serve with the sauce. Garnish with fresh berries, orange slices, and a mint leaf. **Yield: 4 servings.**

Magical Attributes: Perpetual energy and happiness, especially in relationships.

Celebrations: All summer rituals, handfastings, when your spirits need a lift, anniversaries, birthdays.

Tansy Cakes (Ireland)

In Greek legend, Gannymede was given tansy in a cup, by Jupiter's order, to make him the immortal cup-bearer. In Italy, the tansy is indicative of distrust, so if you are having a heated argument with someone, crushing tansy can symbolize the end of dissention.

4 tablespoons flour	2 teaspoons chopped tansy blossoms
1 cup cream	½ teaspoon nutmeg
4 eggs	Butter for frying
¼ cup sugar	

Mix the flour and cream in a small bowl. Beat in the eggs. Add the sugar; beat until fluffy, about 15 minutes. Fold in the tansy and nutmeg. Melt butter in a frying pan; cook like pancakes. **Yield: 2 servings.**

Variation: For prosperity, 1 teaspoon cinnamon can be substituted for the tansy.

Magical Attributes: Water magic, hospitality, the intuitive mind.

Celebrations: Birthday of the Moon, Ahes Festival, any traditional holiday gathering, spring or seaside rituals, before brewing ritual wines.

Tuna Steaks

¼ cup butter	2 tablespoons soy sauce
1 tablespoon ground ginger	1 tablespoon cognac
¼ teaspoon lemon pepper	6 (½-lb.) tuna steaks

Combine the butter, ginger, lemon pepper, soy sauce, and cognac in a small saucepan. Heat over a low flame until the butter is melted. Brush sauce on the tuna steaks. Broil about 4 inches from the heat until the fish is opaque and flaky, about 8 or 9 minutes per side. **Yield: 6 servings.**

Variation: Add some white cheese to the top of the fish before it is finished broiling to encourage passionate love.

Magical Attributes: Quality, excellence, appreciation

Celebrations: Job anniversaries, retirement, Ahes Festival, Feast of the Madonna.

Turkey with Broccoli

Turkey white meat is perhaps the most coveted portion, being rich with juice and flavor. This savoriness combines with a green vegetable for prosperity and cream for smooth transitions.

1 (1¾-lb.) sliced turkey breast	1 cup milk
3 tablespoons butter	1 cup shredded cheese, any kind
2 tablespoons flour	2 cups diced, cooked broccoli

Preheat the oven to 350° F. Grease an oven-proof baking dish. Lay the turkey slices in the bottom of the pan. Sprinkle with spices of your choosing. (Suggestions include poultry seasoning, garlic powder, and salt and pepper.) Place pats of butter equaling 1 tablespoon on the turkey. Bake for 15 minutes; turn once.

Melt 2 tablespoons of the butter in a small saucepan over low heat. Stir in the flour to form a paste. Mix in the milk a little at a time until smooth. Add the cheese; continue stirring until a thick, creamy sauce is formed. Add the broccoli. Pour over the turkey breast. Bake for 10 minutes. **Yield: 3 servings.**

Magical Attributes: Prosperity, wealth, enrichment.

Celebrations: Feast of Jupiter, many spring festivals, Old Dance, New Year's.

Violet Soup

Violets were sacred to Venus, and favored by Mohammed. This flower was popularly used in cooking from the Middle Ages through the fifteenth century. Gerard in his herbal says the violet has a "comely grace" which makes it a delight for eye and soul.

1 (8-oz.) can chicken and rice soup	¼ teaspoon cinnamon
1 cup violet blossoms	

Prepare the soup according to can directions. Bring to a simmer. Add the violets; simmer 1 minute. Ladle into bowls; sprinkle with cinnamon. **Yield: 2 servings.**

Variation: A good alternative to the violets is one cup of peeled, diced apples. This makes a slightly sweet dessert-type soup which has similar magical energy.

Magical Attributes: Nature magic, garden magic, beauty, simplicity.

Celebrations: Earth Day, many spring and summer rituals, May Day, Candlemas, Saturnalia, Planting Festival.

Vita's Mashed Potato Pie

This recipe comes from my Italian mother-in-law who raised a son during financially trying times. It is inexpensive and delicious!

- 4 kinds of lunch meat, 2 slices each, chopped
- 2 cups shredded mozzarella cheese
- 1 cup bread crumbs
- 2 tablespoons olive oil
- 4 cups mashed potatoes
- 2 tablespoons melted butter

Preheat the oven to 350° F. Grease a 2-quart casserole dish. Mix the lunch meat, cheese, bread crumbs, oil, and spices of your choosing in a medium-sized bowl. Spread 1 cup of the potatoes on the bottom of the casserole dish; brush with melted butter. Cover with ⅓ of the lunch meat mixture. Repeat 2 more times. Top with the last of the mashed potatoes and butter. Bake until golden brown, about 15 minutes. **Yield: 4 servings.**

Magical Attributes: Providence, prudence, health.

Celebrations: Harvest festivals, any winter celebration.

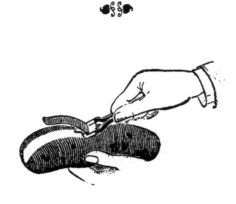

ᴇ§ Personal Recipes §ᴇ

Personal Recipes

Chapter Twelve

Spellbound Salads, Salad Dressings, and Soups

The bouillabaisse is a noble dish, a sort of soup, or broth, or stew.

— William M. Thackeray

In cold weather, soup and salad together are an unbeatable team. Alone, they make hearty, healthy main dishes, side dishes, and even snacks. Their marvelous variety tempts any culinary wizard into wondrous, magical feats to warm the stomach and please the soul.

⋅ᥩ Spellbound Salads ৡ⋅

In Latin, the word *sal* means salt. In Roman times greens would be eaten with a dressing made with salt, which at that time was highly prized. Italy and Greece further refined the art of salad making by adding olive oil and herbs, which quickly became popular. According to most chefs, the best way to prepare a green salad is with liberal amounts of good oil, a bit of vinegar, regulated portions of salt and spices, and a healthy amount of tossing.

Asparagus Salad

Asparagus was originally cultivated by the Greeks, and enjoyed by the Romans. In China it was often used as a meat substitute. Magically, both hazelnuts and asparagus are for sexual potency.

1½ lb. fresh asparagus tips	¼ cup sugar
¼ cup soy sauce	1 cup chopped hazelnuts
¼ cup wine vinegar	Salt
2 tablespoons salad oil	Pepper

Bring the asparagus to a simmer in a saucepan. Cook until tender. Drain. Combine the soy sauce, vinegar, oil, sugar, nuts, salt, and pepper in a medium-sized bowl. Stir in the asparagus. Serve warm or chilled. **Yield: 4 servings.**

Variation: If you are trying this as part of a fertility diet, I suggest replacing the hazelnuts with almonds, which have a stronger healing quality. For a Mexican version of this salad, add one (16-oz.) can of black beans. Medieval herbalists believed beans could enhance sexual urges.

Magical Attributes: Fertility, productivity, potency.

Celebrations: May Day, Summer Solstice, Mother's Day, Spring Equinox, Saturnalia, Festival of Mihr.

⋅ᥩৡ⋅

Karmic Potato Salad

The hot, cleansing nature of three mustards allows us to see our path more clearly. The potatoes encourage vision with strong foundations.

- 2 med. red potatoes, peeled
- 2 med. new potatoes, peeled
- 2 med. Idaho potatoes, peeled
- ¼ cup broth or water
- ⅓ cup white wine
- 2 tablespoons minced white onions
- 2 cloves garlic, minced

- 2 tablespoons wine vinegar
- 3 tablespoons olive oil
- 1 tablespoon Dijon mustard
- 1 tablespoon sweet-hot mustard
- 1 tablespoon mustard seed
- 1 teaspoon salt
- 1 teaspoon pepper

Boil the potatoes in salt water until tender. Drain. Cut into ¼-inch slices or cubes. Combine the broth, wine, onions, garlic and potatoes in a medium-sized bowl. Cover and refrigerate at least 12 hours.

Drain. Combine the vinegar, oil, Dijon mustard, sweet-hot mustard, mustard seeds, salt, and pepper in a small bowl. Pour over the potatoes; stir to coat thoroughly. **Yield: 4 servings.**

Magical Attributes: Karmic law and balance, threefold law, triune nature of God and humanity.

Celebrations: Initiation, birthdays, Wiccaning, Sunning of Buddha, Day of the Dryads.

Korean Spicy Salad

This is a customary part of almost every Korean meal, often prepared by the matron of the house whose culinary skill and discernment was most trusted.

1 cup sliced cucumbers	1⅓ cups water
½ cup chopped Chinese cabbage	5 scallions, chopped
1 cup chopped broccoli	3 cloves garlic, minced
1 cup chopped cauliflower	½ cup red peppers
1 cup sliced celery	¼ teaspoon chili pepper
1 cup sliced carrots	¼ teaspoon ground ginger
3 tablespoons salt, divided	

Combine the cucumbers, cabbage, broccoli, cauliflower, celery, and carrots in a large bowl. Rinse. Sprinkle with 4½ teaspoons of the salt. Let sit for 20 minutes. Rinse.

Combine 4½ teaspoons of the salt, water, scallions, red peppers, chili pepper, and ginger in a large bowl. Add the vegetables; stir. Cover and refrigerate 4 days before serving. Stir occasionally. **Yield: 6 servings.**

Magical Attributes: Acute awareness, clear sight and perspectives, pure motivations.

Celebrations: Candlemas, fire festivals, summer rituals, initiation or investment of a priest/ess, Ahes Festival.

Leek Salad (Wales)

In Wales, leeks are part of annual spring plowing festivals in which leek pottage is a chief dish, emblematic of community. The number of leeks symbolizes the traditional number of coven members.

13 leeks	1 tablespoon snipped parsley
3 tablespoons wine vinegar	½ teaspoon dried basil
¼ cup salad oil	½ teaspoon dried tarragon
3 scallions, chopped	3 hard-boiled eggs, peeled
2 cloves garlic, minced	

Simmer the leeks in water for 10 minutes. Drain. Cool and slice. Combine the vinegar, oil, scallions, garlic, parsley, basil, and tarragon in a medium-sized bowl. Add the leeks; toss. Garnish with the eggs. **Yield: 2 servings.**

Magical Attributes: Togetherness, unity against the odds, solidarity, fellowship.

Celebrations: Almost any gathering, but especially those which celebrate your coven/study group as a unified whole.

Macedonian Salad

During the Middle Ages, parsley was thought to aid circulation and improve spirits. Sometimes dishes with multiple vegetables were called macedoines—as rich in variety as the land itself!

½ cup chicken broth	½ cup sliced carrots, blanched
2 tablespoons wine vinegar	½ cup sliced red potatoes, cooked
6 tablespoons olive oil	½ cup yellow beans, blanched
2 cups mayonnaise	½ cup lima beans, cooked
½ cup fresh snipped parsley	½ cup peas, blanched
¼ teaspoon salt	½ cup crabmeat
¼ teaspoon pepper	Sliced mushrooms (garnish)

Mix the broth, vinegar, oil, mayonnaise, parsley, salt, and pepper in a large bowl. Stir in the cooled carrots, potatoes, yellow beans, lima beans, peas, and crabmeat. Garnish with mushroom slices. Chill before serving. **Yield: 6 servings.**

Note: To blanch the vegetables, bring 2 quarts of water to a rapid boil. Immerse the vegetables and boil for 3 minutes. Remove from heat, drain, and cover with cold water.

Magical Attributes: Blood mysteries, growing health, equality among people.

Celebrations: Coming of Age (women), Earth Day, May Day, Memorial Day, St. Joan of Arc Day.

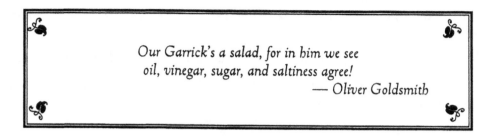

*Our Garrick's a salad, for in him we see
oil, vinegar, sugar, and saltiness agree!*
— Oliver Goldsmith

Mint Cucumber Salad (Persia, Egypt, India)

The cucumber is native to India, and was plentiful in areas of ancient Egypt. Today cucumbers are still popular in Persia, and are often served with yogurt and sweet basil.

¼ cup olive oil	¼ teaspoon pepper
1½ teaspoon lemon juice	3 cups sliced cucumbers with peels
1 clove garlic, minced	½ cup chopped scallions
2 teaspoons dried mint	1 cup springwater sprouts
½ teaspoon salt	

Mix the oil, lemon juice, mint, salt, and pepper in a medium-sized bowl. Stir in the cucumbers, scallions, and sprouts. Chill before serving. **Yield: 6 servings.**

Magical Attributes: Water magic, spiritual outpouring, fluidity, flexibility without losing strength.

Celebrations: Ahes Festival, spring rituals, Birthday of the Moon, full moon celebrations, before ritual baths.

Over the Rainbow

There are many myths about the rainbow, including a pot of gold, a bridge between worlds, and an Old Testament promise from God to humankind for future grace. This salad takes a little time to put together, but the results are beautiful and very tasty.

½ of a 3 oz. pkg. raspberry gelatin	1 (3-oz.) pkg. lime gelatin
2 cups sparkling cider, divided	1 cup lemon yogurt
1 cup raspberries	1 (3-oz.) pkg. blackberry gelatin
½ of a 3 oz. pkg. orange gelatin	1 cup blackberries
1 large orange, peeled and sliced	

Dissolve the raspberry gelatin in ½ cup boiling water. Stir in ½ cup of the cider and the raspberries. Pour into an 8 x 8 x 2-inch pan. Chill until firm.

Dissolve the orange gelatin in ½ cup boiling water. Stir in ½ cup of the cider and the orange slices. Pour on top of the raspberry layer. Chill until firm.

Dissolve the lime gelatin in 1 cup boiling water. Stir in the yogurt. Pour over the orange layer. Chill until firm.

Dissolve the blackberry gelatin in ½ cup boiling water. Stir in 1 cup of the cider and the blackberries. Pour over the lime layer. Chill until firm.

To remove the salad from the pan, dip the pan in hot water and loosen the edges with a knife. Cover with a chilled plate; invert. Cut into 2-inch squares.
Yield: 16 servings.

Magical Attributes: Dreams, wishes, ambitions, hope.

Celebrations: May Day, Smell the Breeze Day, Labor Day, Brendan's Voyage, birthdays, New Year's.

Passion Fruit Fantasy

All of the fruits in this recipe are magically associated with love. The cream lends sensitivity; the apple, peacefulness.

2 passion fruit, peeled and halved	¼ cup apple juice
1 papaya, peeled and diced	2 tablespoons sugar
1 mango, peeled and diced	¼ cup sweet cream
½ cup sliced strawberries	¼ cup shredded coconut
1 banana, sliced	

Scoop out the passion fruit seeds; place in a medium-sized bowl. Mix in the papaya, mango, strawberries, and banana. Beat the sweet cream, apple juice, and sugar in a small bowl. Pour over the fruit; mix until the fruit is well coated. Spoon into each half of the passion fruit. Sprinkle with coconut. A loving dish for two! **Yield: 2 servings.**

Magical Attributes: Sweet, gentle love.

Celebrations: Friendship festivals, anniversary, wedding, Valentine's or Sweetest Day, many spring observances.

Slouvaki Salad (Greece)

The bright colors of this salad look like flowers and grass peeking out from the first sprinkling of snow. This is one of my favorite salads to make at any time of the year.

2 cups beef, cooked and cut into ½-inch strips	½ cup olive oil
4 cups shredded lettuce	2 tablespoons wine vinegar
3 tomatoes, diced	1 clove garlic, minced
1 cucumber, diced	¼ teaspoon sugar
1 green pepper, sliced	½ teaspoon dried basil
¼ cup minced green onions	½ teaspoon dried oregano
12 ripe, pitted olives	Salt
1 cup crumbled feta cheese	Pepper

Combine the beef, lettuce, tomatoes, cucumber, green pepper, onions, olives and ¼ cup of the feta cheese in a large bowl. Mix the oil, vinegar, garlic, sugar, basil, oregano, salt, and pepper in a small bowl. Pour over the vegetables; toss. Sprinkle with the remaining feta cheese. Serve with pita bread. **Yield: 4 servings.**

Variation: This dish can be prepared without meat, if desired.

Magical Attributes: Slowed but consistent growth or maturity.

Celebrations: Late fall or early winter, Coming of Age, graduation.

Star Fruit Salad

Star fruit is grown in the tropics and is rich in vitamins. Unpeeled, they have a beautiful star shape, reminiscent of the magical pentagram, that can be used as an accent to any dish. Raw, their flavor is like jasmine or tart clover.

1 star fruit, sliced	1 cup sliced strawberries
1 orange, peeled and sectioned	3 pineapple slices
1 tangerine, peeled and sectioned	1 cup blueberries
2 kiwi fruit, peeled and sliced	1 teaspoon vanilla
1 banana, sliced	

Reserve 5 slices of the star fruit for decoration. Combine all other ingredients. Cover; chill at least 12 hours. Stir to coat with the juice that is formed. Place the reserved star fruit on top to form a pentagram. **Yield: 5 servings.**

Magical Attributes: Occult wisdom, celestial energies, astrology, health.

Celebrations: Initiation, appointment of a priest/ess, any lunar observances.

Tactful Tomato Salad

The abundance of red in this dish is employed as a gentle reminder to the cook. The idea is to watch our words so we don't end up as red in the face as this dish!

6 tomatoes, diced	1 cup Italian dressing
3 stalks celery, chopped	¼ teaspoon minced garlic
2 sweet red peppers, sliced	¼ teaspoon dried basil
2 cucumbers, sliced	¼ teaspoon dried oregano
2 med. purple onions, sliced	

Combine the tomatoes, celery, pepper, cucumbers, and onions in a medium-sized bowl. Mix the Italian dressing, garlic, basil, and oregano in a small bowl. Pour over the vegetables; toss. Cover; refrigerate at least 12 hours before serving. **Yield: 4 servings.**

Variation: For prosperity, eliminate the tomatoes and increase the red peppers to 3, add 1 cup peas, 1 cup green beans, and 1 cup green onions.

Magical Attributes: Diplomacy, digression, delicacy, consideration.

Celebrations: Picnics, reunions, public gatherings.

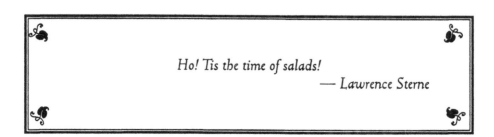

Ho! Tis the time of salads!
— *Lawrence Sterne*

❧ *Salad Dressings* ☙

Blue Moon Dressing

A blue moon is the second full moon in a month, a rare occurance. It is a potent time for any magic pertaining to insight, fertility, and creativity.

½ cup flaked blue cheese	1½ teaspoon lemon juice
1 cup mayonnaise	2 tablespoons chives, chopped
½ cup sour cream	⅛ teaspoon pepper
3 tablespoons wine vinegar	

Place all the ingredients in a blender or food processor. Mix on a medium setting until smooth. To mix by hand, beat with a wire whisk for 5 minutes. Store in the refrigerator. Shake before using. **Yield: 2 cups.**

Magical Attributes: Goddess and Moon energy, rare occurrences, serendipity.

Celebrations: Birthday of the Moon, full moon rituals, Lady Day, all goddess festivals.

Caesar Dressing

Julius Caesar has been heralded through the ages as a person of strong authority and administration.

⅓ cup grated parmesan cheese	2 cloves garlic, minced
½ cup plus 1 tablespoon olive oil	¼ teaspoon dry mustard
3 tablespoons wine vinegar	¼ teaspoon salt
3 tablespoons lemon juice	⅛ teaspoon pepper
1 teaspoon Worcestershire sauce	Croutons (garnish)

Place all the ingredients in a blender or food processor. Mix on a medium setting until smooth. To mix by hand, beat with a wire whisk for 5 minutes. Store in the refrigerator. Shake before using. **Yield: 1¾ cups.**

Magical Attributes: God/Solar energy, leadership qualities, strength.

Celebrations: Birthday of the Sun, Festival of Jupiter, Feast of the Banners, any fire festivals.

Cutting Dressing (France)

In France, this dressing is called "knife cutter" to honor its ability to penetrate the taste buds.

¼ cup sour pickles, chopped	2 cloves garlic, minced
2 white onions, chopped	2 teaspoons dry mustard
⅓ cup olive oil	¼ teaspoon dried tarragon
¼ cup white wine	¼ teaspoon dried basil
3 tablespoons wine vinegar	Salt
½ teaspoon lemon juice	Pepper

Place all the ingredients in a blender or food processor. Mix on a medium setting until smooth. To mix by hand, beat with a wire whisk for 5 minutes. Store in the refrigerator. Shake before using. **Yield: 1¼ cups.**

Magical Attributes: Breaking bonds, banishing, liberation, releasing fears.

Celebrations: Birthdays, New Year's, Independence Day, Riding the Marches.

Ginger Vinaigrette

Ginger tea is good for the stomach; in Eastern countries, ginger is still often used to entreat the Gods for favor.

½ cup olive oil	Salt
½ teaspoon ground ginger	Pepper
1 tablespoon wine vinegar	

Warm the oil and ginger in a small saucepan over low heat. Stir in the vinegar, salt, and pepper. Chill. This is especially good over cucumber slices.
Yield: ½ cup.

Variation: Eliminate the vinegar and decrease the oil to 2 tablespoons; add 2 tablespoons honey and 1 tablespoon lime juice for pleasing discourse.

Magical Attributes: Health, purification, prosperity, communion, love.

Celebrations: Any Chinese or Japanese observances, during cold and flu season, April 15th.

Open Sesame! (Middle East)

Sesame seeds are sacred to Hecate, the ancient wise Crone, while poppy is dedicated to Ceres and Demeter, and lends an earthy tone to this dressing.

⅓ cup olive oil	1 teaspoon sesame seeds
2 tablespoons lemon juice	1 teaspoon poppy seed
1 green onion, diced	⅛ teaspoon red pepper
2 cloves garlic, minced	½ teaspoon salt

Place all the ingredients in a blender or food processor. Mix on a medium setting until smooth. To mix by hand, beat with a wire whisk for 5 minutes. Store in the refrigerator. Shake before using. **Yield:** ¾ cup.

Magical Attributes: Ancient wisdoms with strong foundations, opening pathways, overcoming barriers, understanding universal truths.

Celebrations: Goddess-centered celebrations, Apple Blossom Day, Day of the Dryads, Feast of the Milky Way, Birthday of the Moon, Russian Fair.

Orange-Lemon Dressing

Both orange and lemon flowers have been carried by brides in times past as emblems of fidelity and fertility. The fruit of these trees is strongly associated with well-being and purification.

½ cup olive oil	2 tablespoons honey
¼ cup orange juice	2 tablespoons chopped nuts
1 lemon, peeled, seeded, and chopped	

Place all the ingredients in a blender or food processor. Mix on a medium setting until smooth. To mix by hand, beat with a wire whisk for 5 minutes. Store in the refrigerator. Shake before using. **Yield: 1 cup.**

Magical Attributes: Cleansing, health, sweet love.

Celebrations: Spring and summer rituals (note colors), May Day, Valentine's Day, handfasting or engagement, healing rituals.

Vivat!

Vivat is a medieval cheer often spoken after someone was recognized by the king for his or her contributions to a community/society.

1 cup olive oil	1 teaspoon dried oregano
½ cup wine vinegar	½ teaspoon dried rosemary
2 tablespoons minced green onion	¼ teaspoon dried thyme
3 cloves garlic, minced	⅛ teaspoon salt
1 teaspoon dried onion	⅛ teaspoon pepper
1 teaspoon dried mustard	1 teaspoon sugar
1 teaspoon dried basil	

Place all the ingredients in a blender or food processor. Mix on a medium setting until smooth. To mix by hand, beat with a wire whisk for 5 minutes. Store in the refrigerator. Shake before using. **Yield: 1¾ cups.**

Magical Attributes: Celebration, joy, acknowledgment of hard work or talent.

Celebrations: Retirement, birthday, Feast of the Madonna, Labor Day.

⛧ Soups ⛧

Soup, or soupe (in the medieval spelling), was originally a clear liquid for which herbs and meats were subtle garnishes. Pottages, by comparison, were heartier and thicker. In Italy, any broth with noodles or potatoes was called *minestra*, hence a popular contemporary soup, minestrone!

Chicken Soup (Greek-style)

Greeks adored lemons, using them for breath fresheners. This soup is excellent for convalescents.

4	cups chicken broth	1½	teaspoon dried dill
2	eggs, beaten	1½	teaspoon dried sage
1½	cups rice, cooked		Salt
¼	teaspoon lemon juice		Pepper

Bring the broth to a simmer in a medium-sized saucepan. Beat the eggs and 1 cup of the hot broth in a small bowl. Pour into the saucepan; beat until thoroughly mixed. Stir in the rice, lemon juice, dill, sage, salt, and pepper. Simmer 5 minutes. Garnish with a lemon slice. **Yield: 2 servings.**

Variation: In Scotland, a similar soup is prepared without the eggs, and with ½ cup chopped leeks. At Easter in Greece, this dish is prepared with lamb stock instead of chicken.

Magical Attributes: Health and well-being.

Celebrations: Many winter rituals, healing rituals, Fiesta of the Mother of Health, New Year's Day, Smell the Breeze Day.

Dandelion Soup

Oliver Wendell Homes likens the color of the dandelion to "sparks that have leapt from kindling sun's fire." In the language of flowers, it symbolizes prophesy. Thyme, celery, and bay are for psychic awareness.

2 tablespoons butter
2 tablespoons flour
2 cups milk
2 cups dandelion flowers
⅛ teaspoon celery seed

⅛ teaspoon thyme
1 bay leaf
1 hard-boiled egg, peeled and sliced (garnish)

Melt the butter in a medium-sized saucepan over low heat. Mix in the flour to form a paste. Stir in the milk a little at time until smooth. Mix in the dandelions, celery seed, thyme, and bay leaf. Simmer until the flowers are tender, 15-20 minutes. Remove the bay leaf before serving. Garnish with slices of hard-boiled egg. **Yield: 4 servings.**

Variation: Substitute 2 cups diced celery for the dandelions. Magically, the results are the same.

Magical Attributes: Divination, creativity, air magic.

Celebrations: Smell the Breeze Day and other spring rituals; Pardon of the Birds, New Year's Day.

French Bean Soup

Consider the matter for which you have prepared this soup as you eat. With each bean, draw the energy for positive conclusions into the center of your being.

2 medium onions, sliced
3 stalks celery, chopped
2 leeks, chopped
4 cloves garlic, minced
¼ cup olive oil
1⅓ cups cooked beans, any kind
½ lb. yellow beans
½ lb. french green beans

3 potatoes, diced
2 carrots, diced
3 tomatoes, peeled and diced
2 teaspoon basil
Salt
Pepper
4 oz. noodles, any kind, cooked
Grated cheese, any kind (garnish)

In a large pot, sauté the onions, celery, leeks, and garlic in the olive oil until tender. Add 6 cups of water, beans, potatoes, carrots, tomatoes, basil, salt, and pepper. Cover; simmer until the potatoes are tender. Stir in the noodles. Simmer 5 minutes. Garnish with grated cheese. **Yield: 6 servings.**

Magical Attributes: Fairness, equity, resolution.

Celebrations: Any arbitration, forgiveness rituals, Joan of Arc Day.

Green Abundance (France)

Green is the color of affluence, success, and wealth. The 12 Brussels sprouts add to this energy with the number of fruitfulness.

1 lb. lean pork, cooked and cubed
3 cups shredded green cabbage
4 potatoes, chopped
1 green pepper, chopped
2 cups chopped broccoli
12 whole Brussels sprouts
3 green onions with tops, diced

4 leeks, chopped
3 cloves garlic, minced
¼ teaspoon dried thyme
½ teaspoon dried basil
½ teaspoon dried oregano
½ cup red wine
2 quarts water

Place all the ingredients in a large pot. Simmer at least 2 hours. **Yield: 6 servings.**
Magical Attributes: Financial growth, prosperity.

Celebrations: Most spring rituals, Old Dance Day, Labor Day, Thanksgiving, Feast of Jupiter, Festival of Mihr.

Lentil Soup with Rice

Rice has been an important food in many countries, and was often used in offerings to the gods. Lentils were recommended by Pliny to help control temperament.

6 cups water or stock	2 teaspoons salt
1½ cups lentils, rinsed	¼ teaspoon pepper
½ cup long grain brown rice	3 tablespoons butter
½ teaspoon minced garlic	1 medium onion, diced

Place the water, lentils, rice, garlic, salt, and pepper in a large pot. Bring to a boil over low heat. Cover. Simmer until the lentils and rice are tender, about 40 minutes. Sauté the onions in the butter; stir into the soup just before serving. **Yield: 4 servings.**

Variation: Add sliced carrot, broccoli, cauliflower, kidney beans, and white beans for a three-bean soup which is hearty and magically attuned to divination.

Magical Attributes: Peacefulness, gentility, patience, especially in relationships.

Celebrations: Sweetest Day, Valentine's Day, any day you wish to improve communication in the home.

Nettle Soup (Saxon)

Nettles were often recommended for healthful drinks because of their high vitamin content. Next to chicken soup, this is one of the best for colds and flu.

1 cup chopped nettle	½ cup barley
2 lbs. beef, cooked and cubed	Salt
3 cups chicken stock	Pepper

Combine all the ingredients in a medium-sized pot. Cover. Simmer until the barley is fully cooked. **Yield: 4 servings.**

Variation: Onions, leeks, or scallions can replace the nettles in this dish. Magically these are more appropriate for cleansing energies.

Magical Attributes: Health, versatility, variety, adaptability.

Celebrations: Smell the Breeze Day, St. Joan of Arc Day, Earth Day, St. Stephen Festival, Aloha Week, New Year's Day.

Onion Soup

Onions and leeks were purported to have been worshipped by ancient Egyptians as divine figures. In my house, they are a sacred food served frequently to guests.

6 large spanish onions, sliced or ringed	6 beef bouillon cubes
2 stalks celery, minced	2 tablespoons Worcestershire sauce
2 cloves garlic, minced	¼ cup soy sauce
½ cup butter	2 tablespoons dried onion
6 cups water	1 bay leaf
	Pepper

In a large pot, sauté the onions, celery, and garlic in the butter until golden brown. (In this case, the browner you can get without burning, the better.) Add the water, bouillon, Worcestershire sauce, soy sauce, onion, bay leaf, and pepper. Simmer over medium heat until the soup has reduced by 1 cup, about 2 hours. Cover; refrigerate at least 12 hours. Warm; serve with croutons and melted cheese on top. **Yield: 4 servings.**

Magical Attributes: Connection with divine energy and vision, kinship with like-minded souls.

Celebrations: Any small group gathering, Beltane, Day of the Dryads, Feast of the Milky Way, The Great Rite, Drawing Down the Moon.

Passion Pottage

Many kinds of shellfish have been used to help warm the most difficult spirits. The cream version of this soup is more goddess-oriented (for instinctive love).

½ cup chopped lean bacon	2 cups diced potato
1 cup chopped onion	3 stalks celery, chopped
1 cup crabmeat (optional)	2 carrots, chopped
1 pint oysters, minced; reserve juice	½ teaspoon salt
1 (16-oz.) can minced clams, reserve juice	¼ teaspoon pepper
	2 cups milk

Cook the bacon and onions in a medium-sized saucepan until the bacon is crispy. Drain off the fat. Add the crabmeat, oysters, clams, potatoes, celery, carrots, salt, and pepper. Combine the clam and oyster juice; measure 1 cup, if less add water to equal 1 cup. Pour into the pot. Cover; simmer until the potatoes and carrots are tender. Stir in the milk; simmer 5 minutes. **Yield: 5 servings.**

Magical Attributes: Desire, fervor, affection, intense passion.

Celebrations: Honeymoon, conception rituals, couple retreats, spring rituals.

Roman Garlic Delight

The Romans often fed their soldiers garlic before battle to make them strong. In Europe, garlic was employed as a cure for baldness.

2 heads elephant ear garlic, pureéd	1 cup milk
6 cloves garlic, minced	1 cup water
2 stalks celery, minced	3 chicken bouillon cubes
4 tablespoons olive oil	2 cups grated mozzarella cheese
3 tablespoons butter	Grated parmesan cheese
3 tablespoons flour	French bread

Sauté the garlic and celery in the oil until the celery is tender. Melt the butter in a large pot over a low flame. Stir in the flour to form a paste. Stir in the milk and water a little at a time until smooth. Mix in the garlic, celery, bouillon, and mozzarella. Stir constantly until smooth and the cheese is fully melted. Garnish with grated parmesan and serve with French bread. **Yield: 4 servings.**

Magical Attributes: Protection.

Celebrations: Lammas, Samhain, whenever random spiritual activity seems high.

Yogurt Soup (Turkey)

A soup similar to this is a traditional part of Middle Eastern spring festivals, particularly those on May 1.

2 medium onions, sautéed	1 teaspoon dried mint
2 stalks celery, sautéed	¼ teaspoon dried basil
⅓ cup barley	Salt
4 cups chicken stock	Pepper
2 cups plain yogurt	Fresh mint leaves (garnish)

Place the onion, celery, barley, and stock in a large pot. Simmer for 1 hour. Stir in the yogurt, mint, basil, salt, and pepper. Simmer for 8 minutes. Serve with a fresh mint leaf floating on top. **Yield: 6 servings.**

Magical Attributes: Refreshment of ideas, subtle changes, rebirth.

Celebrations: May Day, Smell the Breeze Day, Wiccaning, Brendan's Voyage, Candlemas, birthdays, New Year's Day.

✦ Personal Recipes ✦

Personal Recipes

Chapter Thirteen

Temple Tofu, Rectory Rice, and Spiritual Sides

*K*nowledge is the eye of desire and can become the pilot for the soul.
— Will Durant

With more people concerned about nutrition and meat alternatives, tofu and rice have increased in popularity. While tofu was used primarily in Asia and rice was only a side dish before, now these foods have become primary sources of nourishment for vegetarians.

In China, tofu was considered a food of nobility and was often used in place of meat by those prohibited from eating animal flesh during certain religious observances.

❧ Temple Tofu ☙

Basic Homemade Tofu

Soybeans were sometimes thrown on floors or out the doors of homes on New Year's Day in China and Japan to help bring improved fortune.

1 cup cold water	2 cups boiling water
1 cup full-fat soy flour	6 tablespoons lemon juice

In a medium-sized saucepan, mix the water and flour to form a paste. Add the boiling water; stir until smooth. Simmer over low heat for 15 minutes. Mix in the lemon juice. Remove from heat. When the mixture sets, strain through a cheesecloth. Store the solid mass covered with water in an airtight container in the fridge. This makes very soft tofu. **Yield: 1 scant cup.**

Magical Attributes: Blessing, luck, psychic insight, spiritual service.

Celebrations: New Year's Day, birthdays, Handsel Monday, before a psychic reading or other effort to improve attitude.

Bok Choy Tofu (China)

Bok choy is a type of Asian chard, closely related to cabbage, which is thought to bring good luck.

4 tablespoons vegetable oil	1 clove garlic, minced
1 (12-oz.) package firm tofu, drained and cut into ¼-inch slices	¼ cup oyster juice
	1 tablespoon cornstarch
3 stalks bok choy, sliced ¼-inch thick	1 tablespoon cold water
4 green onions with tops, chopped	

Heat 2 tablespoons of the oil in a wok over medium heat. Lightly fry the tofu; remove from the wok. Stir-fry the bok choy, onions, and garlic in 2 tablespoons of the oil for 2 minutes. Add the oyster juice. Mix the cornstarch and cold water. Add to the wok; stir constantly. Simmer until the sauce thickens. Add the tofu. **Yield: 6 servings.**

Variation: You can also add fresh oysters to this recipe, cooking them with the garlic for even more passion.

Magical Attributes: Good fortune, especially with fertility or matters of affection.

Celebrations: Most spring festivals, Chinese New Year, Festival of Mihr.

Tofu Kabobs

Called dengaku *in Japan, these little treats were part of a traditional open-air festival on temple grounds.*

2 (8-oz.) cakes firm tofu	2 tablespoons saki
¾ cup miso paste	¼ teaspoon ground ginger
2 egg yolks	2 tablespoons sugar
2 tablespoons plum wine	Bamboo skewers

Drain the tofu for 1 hour; press out the excess water. Cut into ¾ x 2 x 1-inch cubes. Place on skewers. Beat the miso, egg yolks, plum wine, saki, ginger, and sugar in a small bowl. The result is a pleasing gold or pink color, depending on the kind of plum wine used. Brush the tofu with the sauce. Grill 3 minutes per side. **Yield: 4 servings.**

Variation: Replace the ginger with green tea powder for a green hue promoting prosperity and growth. Miso paste often comes in different colors as well.

Magical Attributes: Energy.

Celebrations: Any occasion which honors the arts.

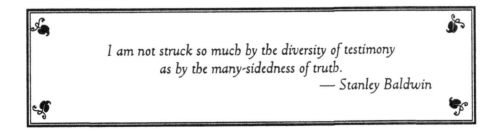

I am not struck so much by the diversity of testimony as by the many-sidedness of truth.
— *Stanley Baldwin*

Tofu Meatballs (Japan)

These little treats were often called "treasure balls" because they were rich in flavor, and could be used in soup or as a meal by themselves.

4 green onions, chopped	16 oz. soft tofu, drained and mashed
½ carrot, shredded	2 tablespoons sesame seeds
2-3 mushrooms, diced	2 teaspoons soy sauce
¼ teaspoon ground ginger	1 tablespoon cornstarch
1 tablespoon oil	Oil for deep-fat frying

Sauté the onions, carrot, mushrooms and ginger in the oil. Combine with the tofu in a small bowl. Mix in the sesame seeds, soy sauce, and cornstarch. Form teaspoonfuls into balls. Deep-fry until golden brown. Serve with mustard sauce. **Yield: 15 balls.**

Magical Attributes: Diversity, variety, creative applications.

Celebrations: New Year's Day, Feast of the Kitchen God, Saturnalia.

Tofu Meatloaf

Any time you feel too visible, hide your energy with the eggs in this dish. Or, to break an undesired stricture, eat the loaf to release new freedom.

16 oz. soft or medium tofu, drained and mashed	¼ cup baby peas
3 eggs, beaten	2 teaspoons ground ginger
2 tablespoons soy sauce	2 cloves garlic, minced
2 medium onions, minced	Salt
⅓ cup shredded carrot	Pepper
	Mushroom or tomato sauce

Preheat the oven to 350° F. Mix the tofu and eggs. Stir in the soy sauce, onions, carrot, peas, ginger, garlic, salt, and pepper. Press into a lightly greased loaf pan. Top with either mushroom or tomato sauce. Bake until lightly golden and a knife inserted in the center comes out clean, about 20 minutes. (Loaf will be moist.) **Yield: 6 servings.**

Note: Using a blender will make a smooth loaf.

Variation: Eliminate the carrot and form the mixture into patties. Grill as you might a hamburger, with a little melted cheese as garnish. Magically this is for tender love.

Magical Attributes: Overcoming personal restrictions, concealment.

Celebrations: Possibly divorce rituals.

Tofu Polynesian

The sweet-sour taste of this dish makes it an excellent conduit for magic pertaining to symmetry between people.

1 green pepper, sliced	1 (8-oz.) can pineapple with juice
1 sweet red pepper, sliced	2 tablespoons brown sugar
1 tablespoon peanut oil	(approximately)
1¼ cups cubed firm tofu	¼ cup tomato sauce
4½ teaspoons soy sauce	2 tablespoons wine vinegar

Sauté the peppers in the oil until tender. Add the tofu; fry until golden brown. Stir in the soy sauce, pineapple, pineapple juice, sugar, tomato sauce, and vinegar. Add more sugar if too tart. Simmer 5 minutes. Serve over rice.
Yield: 3 servings.

Magical Attributes: Balance of yin-yang energies.

Celebrations: May Day, Planting Festival, handfastings.

Tofu-Strawberry Splendor (Japan)

This dish is a part of the traditional Japanese Girls' Day celebrations held on March 3rd.

1 envelope unflavored gelatin	¼ cup kiwi purée
8 oz. soft tofu, drained	½ cup sugar
2 tablespoons lemon juice	¼ teaspoon vanilla extract
½ cup strawberry purée	¼ teaspoon almond extract
¼ cup peach purée	

Dissolve the gelatin in 1 cup boiling water. Cool to lukewarm. Combine all ingredients in a blender or food processor. Mix at medium speed until smooth. Pour into an 8 x 8-inch pan. Refrigerate until firm. Cut into floral designs. Garnish with whole mint leaves or berries. **Yield: 7 servings.**

Magical Attributes: Celebrating the Goddess.

Celebrations: Lady Day, Apple Blossom Day, all Goddess festivals, Mother's Day.

Rectory Rice

In Asia, rice holds the same importance as maize in Latin America. It is likely that the first rice crops came from India. It is said that Shiva, in an effort to win the heart of a goddess, promised to create the perfect food. When Shiva failed, he sought help from another divinity, who likewise faltered. During this process, the Goddess whom Shiva admired and an enchantress sought by his assistant both died. Yet from their tombs, the perfect food did finally sprout—rice.

Breakfast Rice (India)

This is a hearty Indian breakfast food, recommended only for people with a solid early day constitution.

1 large onion, chopped	1 teaspoon salt
2 cloves garlic, minced	Pepper
5 tablespoons clarified butter	1 cup lentils
½ teaspoon ground clove	1 cup rice
¼ teaspoon cardamon	4 cups water
¼ teaspoon ground ginger	2 hard-boiled eggs, peeled and sliced

In a medium-sized saucepan, sauté the garlic and onion in the butter until lightly browned. Add the clove, cardamon, ginger, salt, and pepper. Add the lentils and rice; stir until well coated with the spiced butter. Add the water. Bring to a boil. Cover; simmer until the rice and lentils are tender, about 30 minutes. Garnish with slices of egg. **Yield: 6 servings.**

Magical Attributes: Energy, fervency, hearty endurance.

Celebrations: Fire festivals, Hori, Birthday of the Sun, Summer Solstice.

Freedom Rice (Greek, Roman)

Borage, a small blue flower, tastes a bit like cucumber. It is thought to improve courage, sharpen one's wit, and hinder sadness. This dish is naturally red, white, and blue!

1¼ cups rice	1 red pepper, sliced
3 cups water	1 tablespoon oil
2 teaspoons dried borage	Fresh borage

Combine the rice, water, and dried borage in a medium-sized saucepan. Bring to a boil. Cover; simmer until the rice is done, about 20 minutes. Lightly sauté the red pepper in the oil. Top the rice with slices of pepper. Garnish with fresh borage. **Yield: 6 servings.**

Variation: Replace the borage with marjoram to encourage happiness.

Magical Attributes: Bravery, boldness, determination.

Celebrations: Feast of the Banners, Patriot's Day, Independence Day, Memorial Day, Riding the Marches.

Lotus Rice (China)

Lotus is an old, respected symbol of spirituality and life. In Egypt it was often given as an offering to the Gods.

2 cups diced pork, cooked	1 tablespoon soy sauce
3 cups cooked rice	2 tablespoons oil
¼ cup sliced mushrooms	6 lotus leaves, par-boiled
½ teaspoon sugar	

Sauté the pork, rice, mushrooms, sugar, and soy sauce in the oil. Place equal portions into each lotus leaf. Fold the leaf over the filling; tie together with cotton string. Place on a rack in a wok; steam for 10 minutes. (Please note that the leaf is not to be eaten, it simply adds a slightly tart flavor.) **Yield: 6 servings.**

Variation: Use a wrap of boiled cabbage leaves if lotus leaves are not available.

Magical Attributes: Time, purity, supernatural nature of the universe, longevity.

Celebrations: Day of the Dryads, Festival of the Milky Way, flower festivals.

Mango Rice

The Buddha meditated in a mango grove, and both Hindus and Huna regard mangos as having great power for prosperity and long-term joy.

2 cups chicken broth	1 mango, peeled, seeded, and diced
1 cup white wine	½ cup chopped macadamia nuts
1 tablespoon butter	2 tablespoons minced chives
2 tablespoons lime juice	Salt
½ teaspoon ground ginger	Pepper
1½ cups rice	

Combine the chicken broth, wine, butter, lime juice, ginger, and rice in a medium-sized saucepan. Bring to a boil. Reduce heat; cover. Simmer until rice is tender, about 20 minutes. Stir in the mango, macadamia nuts, chives, salt, and pepper. **Yield: 6 servings.**

Magical Attributes: Love in abundance, prosperity.

Celebrations: Festival of Mihr, May Day, Borrowed Days, Valentine's Day.

Plantain Rice (India)

On special occasions, gold and silver leaf are used to adorn this dish. For those who can not afford such luxury, slices of plantain can be substituted. The plaintain, a type of banana, is indigenous to Asia, and was cultivated in monasteries to give shade to holy men under the belief that the banana was actually the Tree of Paradise.

2-3 plantains, cut into ½-inch slices	1½ teaspoons ground ginger
¼ cup plus 1 tablespoon sugar	2-3 whole cloves
½ cup plus 1 tablespoon lemon juice	¼ teaspoon cardamon
1 lb. boneless chicken, cubed	¼ teaspoon cinnamon
1 medium onion, sliced	Pepper
1 green onion, minced	3 cups cooked rice
¼ cup butter	

Poach the plantains in ¼ cup of the sugar, ¼ cup of the lemon juice, and 1 cup of water for 20 minutes. Drain.

Sauté the chicken and onions in the butter until the chicken is white. Stir in the ginger, cloves, cardamon, cinnamon, pepper, and 1 cup water; bring to a simmer. Stir in 1 tablespoon of the sugar, 1 tablespoon of the lemon juice, and the rice. Simmer for 10 minutes. Garnish with the plantains. **Yield: 6 servings.**

Variation: In India, this dish is often prepared with lamb instead of chicken, and additional local spices such as coriander and cumin are added. If lamb is used, replace the lemon juice with lime juice.

Magical Attributes: Relief from the elements, religious solitude.

Celebrations: Weather rituals, Festival of Sarasvati, any Indian festivals.

Red Bean Rally (Cuba)

1 lb. red beans
½ lb. cooked, cubed pork
3 cloves garlic, minced
½ teaspoon dried thyme
½ teaspoon dried basil
1 bay leaf
Salt

Pepper
1 large onion, chopped
1 red pepper, diced
2 tablespoons olive oil
1 tomato, chopped
4½ teaspoons vinegar
3 cups cooked rice

Soak the beans in cold water for at least 12 hours. Drain.

Combine the beans, pork, garlic, thyme, basil, bay leaf, salt, pepper, and 5-6 cups water in a large pot. Simmer. Sauté the onion and pepper in the oil. Add to the beans with the tomato and vinegar. Simmer until the beans are tender, 20-30 minutes. Serve on a bed of rice with a garnish of hard-boiled eggs or lemon slices. **Yield: 6 servings.**

Magical Attributes: Strength, courage, vitality, fire magic.

Celebrations: Solar and fire festivals, Feast of Banners, Feast of Jupiter.

Rice Pilaf (Turkey, Spain, Italy)

Rice has often been used as a component in weather magic. It is also felt to protect the home from misfortune.

2 cups Italian sausage
2 med. onions, chopped
⅓ cup butter
2 cups beef broth
1 cup rice
2 cups shellfish (optional)

2 tomatoes, diced
1 cup baby peas
2 cloves garlic, minced
1 bay leaf
Salt
Pepper

In a large pot, sauté the onion and sausage in the butter until thoroughly cooked. Stir in the broth, rice, shellfish, tomatoes, peas, garlic, bay leaf, salt, and pepper. Bring to a boil. Cover; simmer until the rice is tender, about 20 minutes. **Yield: 4 servings.**

Variation: Nuts, chicken, and lamb are used for a similar dish in Persia; Indians add corn.

Magical Attributes: Weather magic.

Celebrations: Feast of St. Mark, Earth Day, Sealing the Frost, Sun Dance, Binding of the Wreaths, Pardon of the Birds, planting festivals.

Saffron Rice Royale

Creative chefs sometimes used saffron to create a yellow sauce to gild the main dish.

2 cups long grain rice	½ cup white wine
2 small onions, diced	3 cups cooked lobster
6 tablespoons butter	meat (optional)
8 threads saffron	¼ teaspoon dried thyme
4 cups chicken broth	

In a large saucepan, sauté the rice and onions in the butter until the onions are tender and the rice is glassy. Stir in the saffron, broth, and wine; bring to a boil. Reduce heat. Cover; simmer until the liquid is absorbed, about 20 minutes. Toss with the lobster meat and thyme. **Yield: 6 servings.**

Magical Attributes: Prosperity, abundance, success.

Celebrations: Festival of Mihr, Birthday of the Sun, Feast of Jupiter, Old Dance, Borrowed Days.

Venician Rice (Italy)

Sometimes this dish was used as a basis for a soup served on the Feast of St. Mark (April 25th) in Venice, the City of Lovers. The two bay leaves portend success.

1 cup brown rice	Salt
1 medium onion, diced	Pepper
½ cup butter	1 (10-oz.) pkg. frozen peas, thawed
2¾ cups chicken broth	½ cup grated parmesan cheese
2 bay leaves	½ cup grated romano cheese

In a medium-sized saucepan, sauté the rice and onion in the butter until the onion is tender and the rice turns slightly glossy. Stir in the broth, bay leaf, salt, and pepper. Bring to a boil. Reduce heat. Cover; simmer for 35 minutes. Stir in the peas. Cover; simmer for 10 minutes. Remove from heat. Keep covered and let sit for 10 minutes. Sprinkle with the cheeses before serving. **Yield: 4 servings.**

Magical Attributes: Courtship, the spirit of love.

Celebrations: Anniversaries, weddings, Valentine's Day, many spring festivals.

Vision Rice (China)

This dish is believed to inspire visionary dreams, and is appropriate for honoring Buddha. In France, the lily is a symbol of luck; in Mexico, an emblem of celebration; in China, a token of welcome.

1 cup chopped lychee fruit	1 teaspoon dried lotus flower
½ cup pitted cherries	¼ teaspoon cinnamon
½ cup dates, diced	1 teaspoon ground ginger
½ cup plums, diced	3 cups cooked rice
2 oranges, peeled and separated	1 tablespoon butter, softened
½ cup sugar	

Preheat the oven to 225° F. Combine the lychee, cherries, dates, plums, oranges, sugar, lotus flower, cinnamon, ginger, and 1 cup water in a medium-sized saucepan. Simmer over low heat until a syrup forms. Spread half of the rice in the bottom of an 8 x 8-inch greased pan; dot with half of the butter. Cover with half of the fruit mixture. Repeat. Bake until thoroughly heated; about 10 minutes. Serve hot. **Yield: 10 servings.**

Magical Attributes: Visions and dreams, prophesy.

Celebrations: Samhain, Sealing the Frost, Kamehameha Day, Birthday of the Moon, New Year's Day.

❧ Side Dishes ❧

Cranberry-Orange Sauce

This relish used to be prepared by my mother on Thanksgiving, adding a lovely color and taste to the traditional meal.

1 lb. fresh cranberries	4 cups sugar
1 orange with peel	1 teaspoon vanilla (optional)

Grind the cranberries and orange together with a food grinder or food processor. Retain the juice. Combine the fruit, juice, sugar, and vanilla in a medium-sized bowl. Cover; refrigerate at least 12 hours. Add more sugar if it is too tart. **Yield: 6 servings.**

Magical Attributes: Protection, especially for personal health; fire magic.

Celebrations: Colors are appropriate for both harvest and fire festivals.

Glazed Apple Bites (China)

Bees were considered the messengers of the gods; honey was a Divine gift. Apples mix well with this energy, adding sagacity.

½ cup honey
2 tablespoons water
¼ teaspoon cinnamon
¼ teaspoon nutmeg
2 egg whites

2 tablespoons flour
2 tablespoons cornstarch
3 red delicious apples, peeled
    and cut into ½-inch slices
    Oil for frying

Combine the honey, water, cinnamon, and nutmeg in a small saucepan. Heat over a low flame until the honey is dissolved. Keep warm.

Mix the egg whites, flour, and cornstarch in a small bowl to form a batter. Cover the apples with the batter. Fry in the oil over medium heat until golden brown

Arrange the apples on a platter in an appropriate magical symbol (see Appendix F). Drizzle with the honey glaze. This is an excellent accompaniment to pork dishes. **Yield: 6 servings.**

Magical Attributes: Wisdom, beauty, divine missives.

Celebrations: Apple Blossom Day, Festival of Sarasvati, spring observances.

Hyacinth and Figs

Hyacinth is thought to ease both the pain of childbirth and depression. In the language of flowers, it means constancy.

  1 lb. whole dates
15-20 almonds
  2 cups honey

2 teaspoons rose water (see p. 58)
Pinch of saffron
Hyacinth sugar (see note)

Place 1 almond in the center of each date. Bring the honey, rose water, and saffron to a boil over low heat. Add the dates; simmer for 1 hour. Remove the dates; drain and cool on a rack. Dust with the hyacinth sugar. Store in an airtight container. Serve as a side with other dishes used for dedication. **Yield: 3 servings.**

Note: To prepare hyacinth sugar, combine clean, dry hyacinth petals with 1 cup white sugar in a covered container. Shake occasionally. Petals should dry, not decay; remove any decaying petals. When the petals are completely dry, remove. Repeat this procedure until a strong scent of hyacinth is mingled with the sugar.

Variation: A substitute for hyacinth sugar is shredded coconut, which magically encourages chastity.

Magical Attributes: Devotion, fidelity, reliability, relieving physical or emotional pain.

Celebrations: Mother's Day, handfastings, any ritual where oaths are made.

Marian's Holiday Stuffing

1 cup diced celery	1 teaspoon dried thyme
1 large onion, diced	1 teaspoon celery seed
3-4 cloves garlic, minced	1 lb. herbed croutons
½ cup butter	8 oz. parmesan cheese, grated
1 tablespoon dried sage	1 lb. bacon, cooked and crumbled
1 teaspoon dried rosemary	

Lightly sauté the celery, onion, and garlic in the butter until tender. Stir in the sage, rosemary, thyme, and celery seed. Simmer for 5 minutes. Combine the croutons, cheese, and bacon in a large bowl. Add the butter-herb mixture and about ¼ cup water; stir until the croutons are lightly moistened. Use to stuff a bird or place in a covered dish and bake at 350° F for 20-30 minutes.
Yield: 8 servings.

Variation: For a fruity and energetic stuffing, omit the bacon, decrease the garlic, and add ½ cup Cranberry-Orange Sauce (p. 277). Sausage may be substituted for the bacon.

Magical Attributes: Compassion, benevolence, the spirit of true friendship, divine blessings.

Celebrations: Yule, Thanksgiving, Asking Day, any reunion.

Oracle at Delphi

Delphi was a prophetic center with ever-burning flames. The dandelion, a flower used in divination, is a perfect companion to the art of the sooth-sayer.

- 2 cups dandelion blossoms
- 1 egg, beaten
- 1 cup milk
- 1 cup flour
- ½ teaspoon salt
- ¼ teaspoon pepper
- Fat for frying

Pick the dandelions as close to the head as possible (the stems are very bitter). Rinse well; pat dry with paper towels. Beat the egg, milk, flour, salt, and pepper in a small bowl. Dip each flower into the batter. Deep-fat fry in oil that is hot (350° F–375° F) but not smoking, until golden brown. Drain on paper towels; sprinkle with salt. **Yield: 4 servings.**

Variation: Use 1-inch chunks of celery instead of dandelions. Add a pinch of celery seed to the batter to increase the flavor.

Magical Attributes: Vision, foresight, prophesy.

Celebrations: Samhain, Sealing the Frost, Kamehameha Day, Birthday of the Moon, New Year's Day.

Potato Stuffing (Ireland)

Potatoes were popular in folk medicine for curing rheumatism and warts.

5-6 cups mashed potatoes	Salt
2 large onions, chopped	Pepper
3 stalks of celery, chopped	4 oz. spiced croutons
3 tablespoons butter	1 cup chicken broth
1 tablespoon poultry seasoning	(approximately)
1 teaspoon garlic powder	

Place the potatoes in a large bowl. Sauté the onions and celery in the butter; stir in the poultry seasoning, garlic, salt, and pepper. Pour over the potatoes. Add the croutons and enough broth to moisten. Mix well. **Yield: About 8 cups stuffing.**

Magical Attributes: Grounding, sustenance, providence.

Celebrations: Harvest festivals, Thanksgiving, Asking Festival, Festival of Ishtar.

Prosperity Pudding (Scotland)

If a maiden picked nine pea pods and placed them on the lintel of her kitchen door, the next person to enter would bear the first name or initial of her future mate.

6 oz. split green peas	Salt
2 tablespoons butter	Pepper

Soak the peas in water overnight. Drain.

Place the peas on a muslin cloth. Tie up the corners to form a bag. Allow enough room for the peas to swell. Bring a large pot of water to a boil; add the bag. Simmer for 3 hours. Transfer the peas to a bowl. Beat in the butter, salt, and pepper until smooth. **Yield: 3 servings.**

Variation: For creativity, use yellow split peas.

Magical Attributes: Accomplishment, wealth, love divination.

Celebrations: Festival of Mihr, Labor Day, Borrowed Days, Spring Equinox.

Rhubarb Tart (Scotland)

Rhubarb is thought to insure fidelity in love.

Pastry for a 2-crust 9-inch pie	½ teaspoon ground ginger
2 lb. rhubarb, sliced	1-2 tablespoons milk
¾ cup sugar	

Preheat the oven to 425° F. Combine the rhubarb, ginger, and sugar. Spread in a pastry-lined 9-inch pie pan. Cover with top crust. Pinch edges together to seal; make slits in the top crust. Brush with the milk. Bake for 8 minutes. Reduce heat to 375° F; bake until juices bubble through the slits, 20-25 minutes. Serve warm, covered with sweet cream. **Yield: 8 servings.**

Magical Attributes: Rhubarb, ruled by Venus, is an excellent food for matters of love and beauty.

Celebrations: Spring and summer observances, love festivals.

Snapdragons

Magically, the snapdragon is thought to protect one from deception and negative magic.

1 cup large raisins	3 cups applesauce
1 cup brandy or cognac	¼ teaspoon cinnamon

Soak the raisins in the brandy until plump. Drain. Combine the raisins, applesauce, and cinnamon. Serve warm or cold. **Yield: 6 servings.**

Magical Attributes: Truthfulness, honesty, sincerity, surprises.

Celebrations: Forgiveness rituals, handfastings, any rituals which include an oath, surprise parties.

Personal Recipes

✤ Personal Recipes ✤

Chapter Fourteen

Visionary Vegetables

Charm is almost as poor a butter for parsnips as good intentions.
— Will Durant

Vegetables have been mentioned in mythology around the world. Beans were offered to the gods in Greece and Rome. Aztecs used hot peppers to exorcise malicious spirits. In Persia, leeks were worn over one ear to prevent drunkenness.

Vegetables can be found as part of early remedials. Romans ate mushrooms to improve strength. In renaissance Europe, potatoes were thought to cure impotency, and celery was used to help control weight. Today, one possible use for raw vegetables is to ground after energetic gatherings.

Flowers, which have been used in recipes throughout this book, are also a sort of vegetable. They can add variety and flavor to our dishes. It is important, however, to use flowers with care when cooking, as many common flowers can cause an allergic reaction or unpleasant side effects. Make certain that all flowers you use are free of dye, pesticides, and other contaminants. Never use an unfamiliar flower without researching it thoroughly.

Asparagus L'Orange (Italy)

Asparagus is aligned with the power of Mars and fire, while orange is associated with love, making this the perfect balance between heart and body.

⅓ cup cream
¼ cup chicken broth
½ teaspoon rose water (p. 58)
2 tablespoons orange juice
1 teaspoon grated orange peel

⅛ teaspoon nutmeg
⅛ teaspoon cinnamon
¼ teaspoon salt
1 lb. asparagus

Mix the cream, broth, rose water, and orange juice in a small saucepan over low heat. Stir in the orange peel, nutmeg, cinnamon, and salt. Simmer until the sauce is reduced by ⅓. Steam the asparagus until tender. Pour the sauce over the asparagus. **Yield: 4 servings.**

Magical Attributes: Romantic physical encounters.

Celebrations: Honeymoon, anniversaries, special liaisons, spring observances.

Benevolent Artichokes (Rome, Italy)

In ancient Greek and Rome, the artichoke was thought to have been created by a jealous god, who upon seeing the divine loveliness of a mortal, turned her into this rather unattractive vegetable.

3 large artichokes
6 tablespooons lemon juice
Olive oil
1 small onion, chopped
5-6 mushrooms, chopped
1 clove garlic, minced
3 tablespooons butter

1 tablespooon minced parsley
Salt
Pepper
2 tablespooons grated parmesan cheese
¼ cup bread crumbs
Grated white cheese

Remove the tough bottom row of leaves and any discolored leaves from the artichokes. Trim the stem close to the base so that the artichoke can stand on its own. Snip off the sharp tip of each leaf, about ¼-inch. Bring 3 quarts of water and the lemon juice to a boil. Do not use an aluminum or cast iron pan. Add the artichokes; simmer until the base is easily pierced with a fork, about 30 minutes. Rinse with cold water. Chop off the top of the artichoke. Spread the leaves until the hairy "choke" is revealed. Scoop out the choke with a spoon; make sure to get all the hairs. Brush with olive oil.

Preheat the oven to 375° F. Sauté the onion, mushrooms, and garlic in the butter until the onions are translucent. Stir in the parsley, salt, and pepper. Mix in the parmesan cheese and crumbs. Scoop into the center of each artichoke. Top with the white cheese. Place in an oiled baking pan, stuffing side up. Bake until golden brown, about 20 minutes. Garnish with parsley. **Yield: 3 servings.**

Magical Attributes: Overcoming jealousy or resentment, reestablishing trust.

Celebrations: Forgiveness rituals, separation or divorce, vow renewals.

Boston Baked Beans (Dynahara's Kitchen)

½ teaspoon baking soda
1 cup navy beans
1 tablespooon cider vinegar
6 tablespooons dark molasses
½ cup brown sugar

3 teaspoons dry mustard
Salt
Pepper
½ lb. bacon, chopped
1 large yellow onion, chopped

Dissolve the baking soda in 2 cups of water; add the beans. Soak overnight.

Preheat the oven to 300° F. Drain and rinse the beans. Mix the vinegar, molasses, sugar, dry mustard, salt, pepper, and 2 cups hot water in a medium-sized bowl. Place the bacon, onion, and beans in the bottom of a 2-quart casserole dish. Pour in the sauce. Cover. Bake for 4 hours; stir once per hour. If beans seem dry, add more water. Remove the lid; bake until desired thickness is reached, 1-2 hours. **Yield: 4 servings.**

Magical Attributes: The one obvious feature of beans is their abundance! Use them for magic pertaining to prosperity.

Celebration: Borrowed Days, Old Dance, Labor Day, Festival of Mihr.

Broccoli a la Romana

The people of ancient Rome claimed broccoli had many incredible qualities. Even so, it did not become a popular food item until well after 1920.

2 (10-oz.) packages frozen broccoli	¼ teaspoon dried basil
2 tablespooons herbed olive oil	¼ teaspoon dried oregano
2 chopped roma tomatoes	Salt
2 cloves garlic, minced	Pepper

Cook the broccoli according to package directions; drain. Heat the oil in a large frying pan; stir in the tomatoes, garlic, basil, oregano, salt, and pepper. Cook 2-3 minutes. Pour over the broccoli. **Yield: 4 servings.**

Magical Attributes: Extraordinary power, wondrous magic!

Celebrations: Festival of Jupiter, Day of the Dryads, Feast of the Milky Way, any time you feel your magic needs a "boost."

Brussels in Spice (Babylon)

Developed as a year-round cabbage, Brussels sprouts endure many temperature extremes without harm.

1 lb. fresh Brussels sprouts	1 clove garlic, minced
2 tablespooons oil	¼ teaspoon dried rosemary
2 tablespooons grainy mustard	¼ teaspoon dried basil
2 green onions, diced	

Bring 2 quarts of water to a boil. Add the Brussels sprouts; simmer until tender, about 10 minutes. Drain. Combine the oil, mustard, onions, garlic, rosemary, and basil in a small bowl. Pour over the sprouts; toss. **Yield: 4 servings.**

Magical Attributes: Withstanding severity, overcoming difficulties.

Celebrations: Winter festivals, when job hunting or facing other problems, Royal Oak Day, protection-related rituals.

Cabbage of Temperance (Egypt, Germany)

Egyptians believed that cabbage would hinder drunkenness, and early herbalists noted that if cabbage grows near grapes, the grapes often die.

- 1 large green apple, diced
- 1 onion, chopped
- 3 tablespooons butter
- 3 lb. red cabbage, shredded
- 4 tablespooons wine vinegar

- 1 tablespooon sugar
- Salt
- 1 raw potato, shredded
- ½ cup crumbled bacon

Sauté the apple and onion in the butter until lightly browned. Stir in the cabbage, vinegar, and sugar. Simmer for 10 minutes. Add the salt and 1½ cups water. Simmer until the cabbage is fully cooked, about 2 hours. Add the potato; simmer until thickened, about 15 minutes. Garnish with the bacon. **Yield: 6 servings.**

Magical Attributes: Moderation, prudence, self-control.

Celebrations: Before starting a diet, winter rituals, Sunning of Buddha, Thanksgiving, Asking Day.

Celery Pecan Casserole (Rome)

Some people believe that eating vegetables, especially celery, helps one obtain gentler affections and improved virility.

- 4 cups celery cut into ½-inch pieces
- 1 (8-oz.) can cream of celery soup
- 2 medium onions, sliced and separated (optional)
- ¼ teaspoon sesame seed

- ¼ teaspoon caraway seed
- ¾ cup chopped pecans
- ¾ cup bread crumbs
- 1 tablespooon melted butter

Preheat the oven to 375° F. Lay the celery in the bottom of a greased 8 x 8-inch baking dish. Mix the soup, onion, sesame seed, and caraway seed in a small bowl. Pour over the celery. Combine the pecans and bread crumbs. Sprinkle on top of the sauce. Drizzle with butter. Bake until the celery is tender, about 25 minutes. **Yield: 6 servings.**

Magical Attributes: Inspired passion.

Celebrations: Honeymoon, Valentine's Day, vow renewals, fertility and conception rituals.

Cheesy Potatoes
(Doreen's Wild and Weedy Kitchen)

Because of the fennel and anise, Doreen recommends this as a side dish for any meal which may cause indigestion. Magically speaking, both these herbs are potent for protection.

1 large onion, chopped	½ teaspoon dried oregano
¼ cup oil	¼ teaspoon dried tarragon
4-5 large potatoes, cubed	Salt
1 teaspoon whole fennel seed, crushed	Pepper
¼ teaspoon whole anise seed, crushed	½ cup grated cheddar cheese
	½ cup grated mozzarella cheese

Sauté the onions in the oil until softened. Add the potatoes, fennel, anise, oregano, tarragon, salt, and pepper. Stir until the potatoes are coated with oil. Cover; cook on low heat until the potatoes are nearly done. Remove the lid. Turn up the heat to medium and brown the potatoes until crisp. Sprinkle with the cheeses. Cover; remove from heat. Let sit until cheese is melted, 5-7 minutes. Serve as a side dish or the main course. **Yield: 4 servings.**

Variation: Chopped meat, especially ham, can be added in the last few minutes of cooking for a more filling dish.

Magical Attributes: Peaceful sleep, safety, protection from negative energies.

Celebrations: Any fire festival, Sealing the Frost, Riding the Marches, Royal Oak Day, Old Dance.

Clear-Sight Carrots

Cinnamon is for psychic awareness, while ginger produces clarity. Carrots, of course, have been regarded by mothers everywhere as giving good eyesight.

- 3 cups sliced carrots
- 3 tablespooons butter
- 1 teaspoon brown sugar (optional)
- ¼ teaspoon ginger
- ¼ teaspoon cinnamon

Boil or steam the carrots until tender. Drain. Add the butter, brown sugar, ginger, and cinnamon; stir until the carrots are well coated. **Yield: 6 servings.**

Variation: Garnish with a little coconut for diversity of psychic abilities.

Magical Attributes: Vision, psychic development, before any divination efforts.

Celebrations: Samhain, Day of the Dryads, Birthday of the Moon.

Creamed Nettles (Russia)

Nettles are a stinging plant, which gives them natural protection.

- 1 lb. nettle tops
- 4 tablespooons butter
- ¼ teaspoon salt
- ¼ teaspoon pepper
- ½ cup cream
- 1 medium onion, minced
- ¼ cup snipped chives
- 2 cloves garlic, minced

Place nettles in a medium-sized saucepan. Pour in just enough water to cover; add 2 tablespoons of the butter, salt, and pepper. Simmer until tender. Strain; discard the nettles and return the juice to the pan. Mix in the cream, onion, chives, garlic, and 2 tablespoons of the butter. Bring to a simmer over low heat. **Yield: 2 servings.**

Variation: Substitute leeks, which have a similar energy, for the nettles.

Magical Attributes: Protection, healing, passion.

Celebrations: Before a handfasting, Samhain, Beltane, fire-related festivals.

Fortuna Sweet Potatoes (Jewish)

This dish is sometimes made at Sukkoth, as the sweet potato is a symbol of the harvest.

¼ cup olive oil	Salt
½ cup honey	Pepper
½ teaspoon grated lemon rind	6 cups diced sweet potatoes
½ teaspoon grated orange rind	3 apples, peeled and diced

Preheat the oven to 350° F. Mix the oil, honey, lemon rind, orange rind, salt, and pepper in a large bowl. Stir in the sweet potatoes and apples. Place in a well oiled baking dish. Cover. Bake until the sweet potatoes are tender, about 35 minutes. Bake uncovered until golden brown, 5-10 minutes. **Yield: 6 servings.**

Variation: For Rosh Hashanah, substitute carrots. Magically this is for prosperity.

Magical Attributes: Bounty, benevolence, charity, compassion.

Celebrations: Asking Day, Thanksgiving, harvest festivals, Sukkoth.

Full Moon Cauliflower

This dish looks like the shining face of a full moon when cooked. The lunar energies are further enhanced by the cauliflower, milk, butter, and eggs.

¼ cup butter	¼ cup bread crumbs
2 tablespooons flour	1 cup grated parmesan cheese
1 cup milk	1 cup grated white cheese
3 eggs	1 head cauliflower, cut into
1 clove garlic, minced	florets and cooked

Preheat the oven to 400° F. Melt the butter in a small saucepan over low heat. Mix in the flour to form a paste. Slowly stir in the milk until smooth. Beat in the eggs. Stir in the garlic, bread crumbs, parmesan cheese, white cheese, and cauliflower. Pour into a greased baking dish. Bake for 30 minutes. Garnish with additional white cheese. **Yield: 4 servings.**

Magical Attributes: Moon magic, fruitfulness, insight.

Celebrations: Birthday of the Moon, rites for a patron Goddess, Ahes Festival.

Grilled Beets

It is believed that Aphrodite ate beets to maintain her loveliness. The deep red color of beets makes it a perfect food for matters of the heart.

8 medium beets, cut into ¼-inch slices	½ teaspoon lemon juice
3 tablespooons butter, melted	1 teaspoon orange juice
	¼ teaspoon dried dill weed

Divide the beets into 4 portions. Place each on a piece of aluminum foil. Mix the butter, lemon juice, orange juice, and dill weed. Pour over the beets. Wrap beets securely in the foil. Grill until the beets are tender, about 45 minutes. Turn frequently. **Yield: 4 servings.**

Magical Attributes: Long life, beauty, love.

Celebrations: Handfasting, Wiccaning, Coming of Age, summer festivals.

Holiday Peppers

The colors of this dish enhance almost any celebration.

- 1 large green pepper
- 1 large sweet red pepper
- 1 (8-oz.) package cream cheese, softened
- 1 tomato, diced
- 1 tablespooon chopped pimento
- 1 tablespooon minced garlic (optional)
- 1 tablespooon minced chives
- 1 tablespooon snipped parsley
- 1 tablespooon dried basil

Remove the tops of the peppers. Scoop out the seeds and pith. Mix the cream cheese, tomato, pimento, garlic, chives, parsley, and basil. Fill the peppers with the spiced cream. Slice into four equal pieces. Refrigerate for at least 2 hours before serving. **Yield: 4 servings.**

Variation: For a dish more magically aligned to creative gatherings and projects, use yellow peppers instead.

Magical Attributes: Celebration, rejoicing, kinship, merrymaking.

Celebrations: Any, especially Yule and summer festivals.

Italian Mushrooms

In some lands, the mushroom was thought to be the child of lightning, probably because so many seemed to spring up after storms.

- 1 lb. large mushrooms
- ¾ cup white wine
- ½ cup olive oil
- 1 teaspoon lemon juice
- 2 cloves garlic, minced
- ½ teaspoon dried tarragon
- ½ teaspoon dried rosemary
- 1 bay leaf, crushed
- Salt
- Pepper

Remove the stems from the mushrooms. Mince the stems. Combine the stems, white wine, oil, lemon juice, garlic, tarragon, rosemary, bay leaf, salt, and pepper in a small saucepan. Simmer until the mushrooms are tender. Spoon the mixture into the mushroom caps. Serve as is or bake. To bake, brush with butter and sprinkle with cheese. Bake at 225° F until hot and cheese is melted, about 10 minutes. Garnish with parsley. **Yield: 4 servings.**

Magical Attributes: Weather magic, enduring storms of an emotional nature.

Celebrations: Sealing the Frost, spells to help heal relationships/communication, rites which honor Thor or other sky/weather deities.

Leeks in Mustard Sauce

Leeks are thought to provide effective protection against natural fires. When eaten or rubbed on the skin, they are said to give improved strength.

3 medium leeks, thinly sliced	2 tablespoooons olive oil
½ cup shredded carrot	1 tablespoooon soy sauce
1 (8-oz.) can water chestnuts, drained and sliced	¼ cup prepared mustard
	2 teaspoons sugar
2 cloves garlic, minced	¾ teaspoon dried tarragon

Sauté the leeks, carrots, water chestnuts, and garlic in the oil until tender. Mix the oil, soy sauce, mustard, sugar, and tarragon in a small bowl. Pour over the vegetables; mix well. **Yield: 4 servings.**

Magical Attributes: Protection from fire, increasing potency and vitality.

Celebrations: Summer and fire festivals, Candlemas, Sun Dance, Birthday of the Sun, Fiesta of the Mother of Health, Hori.

Luck Limas

The green color of this dish is combined with the natural luck-attracting qualities of parsley for improved fortune.

3 lb. fresh lima beans
Salt
½ cup cream

2 tablespooons butter
Minced fresh parsley
Pepper

In a large pot, cover the lima beans with water; add salt. Bring to a boil; simmer until tender, about 25 minutes. Drain. Stir in the cream, butter, parsley, salt, and pepper. **Yield: 4 servings.**

Magical Attributes: Growth, good fortune.

Celebrations: Spring and summer festivals, birthdays, Wiccaning, Festival of Mihr, planting festivals.

Onion Ring-Arounds

The magical circle which has no beginning or end is a place of safety and learning. Here we gather our talents to bring spiritual renewal to ourselves and the Earth. Feel that warmth as you partake of these onion rings.

1¼ cups flour
1¼ cups beer
½ teaspoon minced garlic
½ teaspoon dried dill weed

4 spanish onions, cut into
¼-½ inch slices and separated
Oil for frying

Mix the flour, beer, garlic, and dill weed. Let sit at room temperature for at least 1 hour.

Thoroughly coat the onions with batter. Fry in hot oil until golden brown. **Yield: 4 servings.**

Magical Attributes: Cycles, eternity, completion, the indestructible spirit.

Celebrations: Summerland festivals, major seasonal observances, St. Stephen Festival, Feast of the Milky Way, Day of the Dryads, memorial rites.

Peas of Happiness (China)

Lemon, honey, and ginger are all associated with love and other pleasant things in life.

2 tablespoons soybean oil	1 lb. fresh snow peas
1½ teaspoon butter	2 tablespoons honey
1 teaspoon minced ginger root	½ teaspoon grated lemon rind

Heat the oil, butter, and ginger root in a wok over a high flame. Add the snow peas; stir-fry until tender but still crisp, 4-5 minutes. Remove from the wok. Drizzle with the honey and sprinkle with the lemon peel. **Yield: 4 servings.**

Magical Attributes: Love, joy, gaiety, any Goddess-related magic.

Celebrations: Any spring festival, Aloha Week.

Potato Cheese Patties

4 cups mashed potatoes	1 cup finely shredded
2 tablespoons butter, melted	cheddar cheese
Salt	1 clove of garlic, sliced (optional)
Pepper	Oil for frying

Mix the potatoes, butter, salt, and pepper in a medium-sized bowl. Sprinkle with a little of the cheese; stir. Repeat until all the cheese is added. Heat oil in a frying pan over a low flame; add the garlic. Cook until the garlic is golden brown; remove the garlic from the oil. This provides a slightly richer flavor to the oil but does not overwhelm the potatoes. Form ¼ cup portions of the potatoes into patties. Cook until golden brown on both sides. **Yield: 4 servings.**

Variation: These are marvelous with ¼ cup minced onion, ¼ cup diced ham, and swiss cheese instead of cheddar cheese. This makes a tasty breakfast entreé.

Magical Attributes: Providence, meeting the needs of your household.

Celebrations: Harvest festivals.

Pumpkin Plenty

The orange sphere of the pumpkin is not only the face of protection in the fall, but also an emblem of the rich earth, when the harvest has been kind and all have what they need.

1 pumpkin (about 3 lbs.)	⅛ teaspoon nutmeg
2 onions, chopped	⅛ teaspoon ground ginger
4 tablespooons butter	1 tablespooon fresh snipped chives
1 cup heavy cream	

Scoop out the seeds and fibers from the interior of the pumpkin. Scoop out all but about ½ inch of the meat. Save the pumpkin shell and lid to use as your serving bowl. Mince the pumpkin meat.

Sauté the onions in the butter. Stir in the pumpkin meat. Add 4 cups water; simmer for 25 minutes. Pureé the mixture in a blender or food processor. Return to the pan. Stir in the cream, nutmeg, and ginger. Bring to a simmer. Pour into the pumpkin shell to serve. Garnish with the chives. **Yield: 6 servings.**

Variation: Use acorn squash instead of pumpkin.

Magical Attributes: Bounty, abundance, providence.

Celebrations: Harvest festivals, Samhain, Thanksgiving, Hopi Winter Ceremony, any ritual which honors the Mother aspect of the Goddess.

Roman Medley

In the early days of Rome, vegetables were often eaten as desserts! Even after this went out of style, Italians continued with vegetable antipastos before, during, or after main dishes.

3 tablespooons herbed olive oil	Celery sticks
⅔ cup butter	Cucumbers, sliced
4 cloves garlic, minced	Red peppers, sliced
4 green onions, minced	Green peppers, sliced
Carrot sticks	Radishes

Combine the oil and butter in a small saucepan over low heat. When the butter is melted, add the garlic and the white part of the green onions. Heat for 5 minutes. Garnish with the tops of the green onions. Serve warm. Use as a dip for the vegetables. **Yield: 1 cup dip.**

Magical Attributes: Diversity, the cauldron of Cerridwen, change.

Celebrations: Aloha Week, Apple Blossom Day, Earth God/dess festivals.

Saints Be Praised (Buddhist)

Strict Buddhists are vegetarians and make marvelous vegetable dishes. This one is both comely and tasty.

5 tablespooons cooking oil	¼ cup water chestnuts
1 clove garlic, minced	½ cup onion, diced
2 pieces lotus root (optional)	¼ cup soy sauce
½ cup chopped chinese cabbage	1 tablespooon saki
½ cup snow peas	1 tablespooon cornstarch
½ cup bean sprouts	¼ teaspoon sugar

Heat the oil and garlic in the wok. Stir-fry the lotus root, chinese cabbage, snow peas, bean sprouts, water chestnuts, and onion for 5 minutes. Mix the soy sauce, saki, and 2 cups of water. Pour over the vegetables. Bring to a boil; reduce heat and simmer until the vegetables are tender, 10-15 minutes. Mix the cornstarch, sugar, and 2 tablespoons of water. Slowly add to the vegetables; stir constantly. Simmer until thickened. Serve over rice. **Yield: 4 servings.**

Variation: Mushrooms, zucchini, and even melon pieces can be added to this mixture in ¼ cup amounts. Magically, this is for variety.

Magical Attributes: Morality, goodness, excellence.

Celebrations: Any saint's day, Apple Blossom Day, Feast of the Madonna, Rites of Passage, Feast of the Kitchen God.

Solstice Carrots

The bright orange color of carrots is reminiscent of fire and solar energy.

5 cups diced carrot	¼ teaspoon garlic powder
¼ teaspoon pepper	¼ teaspoon salt
¼ cup heavy cream	Sour cream
¼ cup butter, melted	2 cups baby carrots

Cook the diced carrot until tender; drain. Place in a blender or food processor. Add the cream, butter, garlic, and salt. Purée until smooth. In the center of a serving platter, form the carrots into a mound. Place a little sour cream in the center. Arrange the baby carrots around it to form the solar disk.
Yield: 8 servings.

Variation: Substitute parsnips for creativity, turnips for balance, or beets for love.

Magical Attributes: Sun magic, especially pertaining to increased strength and improved mental faculties.

Celebrations: Birthday of the Sun, Sun Dance, Summer Solstice, before exams or studies.

Succotash

We owe thanks to the Native Americans for teaching settlers how to make this wonderful mixed vegetable dish. The name of this recipe is a creative combination of several Native American words.

3 slices bacon, chopped	3 cups corn
2 tomatoes, sliced	1 cup cubed squash
1 medium onion, chopped	3 lbs. fresh lima beans
2 cloves garlic, minced	½ cup cream
1 tablespooon paprika	Salt
1 tablespooon minced parsley	Pepper

Fry the bacon, tomatoes, onion, and garlic until lightly brown in a large saucepan. Mix in the paprika and parsley; cook for 1 minute. Stir in the corn, squash, and lima beans until thoroughly coated with the spices. Add just enough water to cover. Simmer, covered, until the beans are tender and the water is reduced by half, about 30 minutes. Stir in the cream, salt, and pepper. Bring to a simmer. **Yield: 8 servings.**

Magical Attributes: Variety, flexibility, adaptability.

Celebrations: Harvest festivals, Thanksgiving, Fourth of July.

Turkish Eggplant

The first person to taste this recipe was supposedly a sultan who loved it so much, he fainted with pleasure.

2 medium eggplants	¼ teaspoon dried basil
3 large spanish onions, diced	¼ teaspoon dried oregano
2 cloves garlic, minced	Salt
½ cup herbed oil	Pepper
1 tablespoon tomato pureé	3 large tomatoes, diced
1 tablespoon butter	½ cup bread crumbs
¼ teaspoon dried dill weed	

Boil the eggplants in salt water for 15 minutes. Soak in cold water until cool. Cut in half lengthwise. Scoop out the pulp; leave the skin intact. Brush the skins with oil. Lay on a baking tray, open side up. Dice the pulp.

Preheat the oven to 350° F. Sauté the onions and garlic in the herbed oil until soft. Mix in the tomato pureé, butter, dill weed, basil, oregano, salt, and pepper. Add the tomatoes and eggplant pulp. Simmer for about 15 minutes. Mix in the bread crumbs. Scoop half the filling into each eggplant skin. Garnish with parsley. Bake for 15-20 minutes. **Yield: 4 servings.**

Magical Attributes: Joy, entertainment, satisfaction, delight.

Celebrations: Most spring and summer rituals, reunions, family gatherings, Kermesse, Russian Fair.

Zesty Zucchini

All the spices used in this recipe are chosen for their fiery aspects, combined with the inherent psychic attributes of the zucchini.

- 2 medium zucchini
- 1 tablespoon olive oil
- 1 small hot pepper, chopped
- 2 cloves garlic, minced
- ¼ teaspoon ground ginger
- ⅛ teaspoon cumin
- ½ teaspoon curry powder

- ½ teaspoon salt
- 1 spaghetti squash, peeled and finely chopped
- ¼ cup red wine (optional)
- ¼ cup raisins
- White wine

Preheat the oven to 350° F. Cut the zucchini in half lengthwise. Scoop out the meat and leave the skin intact. Finely chop the zucchini meat.

Heat the olive oil, hot pepper, garlic, ginger, cumin, curry powder and salt in a large frying pan. Stir in the zucchini, squash, and wine. Cook 5 minutes. Stir in the raisins. Scoop into the zucchini shells. Sprinkle with white wine. Cover with aluminum foil. Bake until tender, about 30 minutes. **Yield: 4 servings.**

Magical Attributes: Spiritual energy in abundance, protection, cleansing and purification.

Celebrations: Hori, fire festivals, Samhain, summer rituals, Birthday of the Sun, Beltane, Sun Dance.

✑ *Personal Recipes* ❧

Personal Recipes

Chapter Fifteen

Witch's Dishes

A clever cook can make a good meal of a whetstone.
— Desiderius Erasmus

What one person considers a "gourmet food" or "delicacy," another won't touch. This is plainly evidenced in ancient cookery books for royal tables and rich householders. Items such as Eskimo seal blubber, Arabic sheep eyes, Elizabethan lark tongues, and Scottish haggis were all considered tasty treats.

The foods attributed to witches were no less unique or questionable in their contrivances. All we need do is turn to Macbeth's witches to see them around a cauldron stirring in a number of rather "halloweenish" ingredients.

Thus, this chapter is presented to you with the help of Mr. William Shakespeare and my friend Morgana. In a recent conversation, we were thinking it might be fun to have magical parties, especially at Samhain, where the foods were creatively titled from Shakespeare's Macbeth. I think you can have a lot of fun considering these, or finding recipes of your own to disguise with magical names.

Glazed Parsnips and Carrots

Shakespearian: Adder's Fork

2¼ cups sliced carrots
2¼ cups sliced parsnips
1 tablespoon vinegar

¼ cup butter, melted
¼ cup packed brown sugar

Preheat the oven to 350° F. Bring the carrots, parsnips, vinegar, and 1 quart of water to a boil. Simmer until tender, about 25 minutes. Drain. Transfer to a baking dish. Mix the butter and brown sugar. Pour over the carrots. Bake until the glaze is thickened, about 15 minutes. **Yield: 4 servings.**

Variation: Honey may be substituted for the brown sugar.

Magical Attributes: Change, transformation, growth, the eternal spirit.

Celebrations: Spring observances, graduation rituals, Summerland rites, initiations, Carrot Sunday.

Watermelon Boat

Magical: Athena's Ferry
Himalayan: Durga's Tribute

Melons, round and high in water content, are excellent lunar foods which improve intuition, creativity, and resourcefulness. Athena is often pictured on a ferry with her owl at one shoulder, moving through the heavens. Durga is the Himalayan Earth Goddess.

1 large whole watermelon
1 lb. strawberries, hulled
1 pint blueberries

1 (8-oz.) can mandarin oranges
1 cup shredded coconut
1 lb. seedless green grapes

Carefully cut the watermelon so that a basket is formed (see illustration). Further embellishing can be done using a small knife. Hollow out the melon using a melon baller; remove as many seeds as possible.

Combine the melon balls, strawberries, blueberries, oranges (include the juice), coconut, and grapes in a large bowl. Spoon into the watermelon basket for a lovely edible party accent. **Yield: 20 servings.**

Magical Attributes: Can be changed by altering the carving and/or the fruits. Generally for joy.

Celebrations: Housewarmings, baby showers, picnics, receptions.

Tomato Soup

Shakespearian: Baboon's Blood
Greek: Vulcan's Delight
Magical: Solstice Fire

According to the Chinese calendars, the Year of the Monkey is one filled with mischief, adventure, and the unexpected. In Greek mythology, Vulcan was the god of the fire and the forge, making this an excellent choice for summer observances.

2 onions, diced
½ cup shredded cabbage
4 cups beef or chicken broth
1 tablespoon butter
6 ripe tomatoes, diced
1 teaspoon sugar
1 clove garlic, minced
¼ teaspoon dried thyme
1 teaspoon dried basil
2 teaspoons salt
2 teaspoons pepper
¼ cup flour
1 cup sour cream

Simmer the onion, cabbage, broth, and butter for 1 hour in a large saucepan. Stir in the tomatoes, sugar, garlic, thyme, basil, salt, and pepper. Simmer for 45 minutes. Transfer to a blender or food processor; purée. Return to the saucepan. Mix the flour and sour cream and stir into the tomato mixture a little at a time. Simmer until thickened. **Yield: 4 servings.**

Variation: Substitute carrots for the cabbage to encourage startling psychic insights or unexpected, passionate encounters.

Magical Attributes: Gambles, surprising results, abundantly playful energy.

Celebrations: April Fool's Day, fire festivals, children's rituals.

Spaghetti with Lemon Pepper Sauce (India, Greece)

Shakespearian: Blind Worm's Sting
Magical: Web of Life
Greek: Lachetis Tangle

What child, at one time or another, hasn't compared spaghetti to worms? The sting in this recipe is the zesty sauce. In Greece, Lachetis was one of the three Goddesses who wove, measured, and cut the strands of life. You can create a central serving platter with some of the noodles decoratively laid out on top in the form of a web (see illustration).

1 onion, diced	2 tablespoons olive oil
1 clove garlic, minced	3 tablespoons lemon juice
⅛ teaspoon dried thyme	½ cup wine vinegar
⅛ teaspoon dried basil	½ cup broth, any kind
1 bay leaf, crushed	2 tablespoons butter
1 teaspoon pepper	1 teaspoon cornstarch
Salt	1 lb. spaghetti, cooked

Sauté the onion, garlic, thyme, basil, bay leaf, pepper, and salt in the olive oil until the onion is tender. Stir in the lemon juice, vinegar, broth and butter. Cook for 5 minutes. Mix in the cornstarch; simmer until the sauce thickens. Pour over the spaghetti. **Yield: 6 servings.**

Magical Attributes: Healing magic, refreshing energy, alertness, protection.

Celebrations: Spring and summer, Ahes Festival, any observance with fish in the menu, solar rituals, any celebrations which focus on the senses.

Stir Fry with Celery, Bamboo, and Mushrooms

Magical: Broom Sticks and Black Cats, Samhain Sampler

Brooms were used in the Craft as emblems of fertility, especially during harvest festivals. They were also considered an indispensable household item, which moved luck into a home, and ill-fortune out! This dish looks quite a bit like a broom if you lay some uncooked sprouts on top of the serving dish as shown below. Black cats have the honorable position of being one of the most widely known of witch's familiars.

2 tablespoons sesame oil	2 cloves garlic, minced
4-5 stalks celery, chopped	2 tablespoons soy sauce
1 (8 oz.) can bamboo shoots, drained	1 teaspoon celery seed
	2 cups alfalfa or bean sprouts
1 cup sliced wood ear mushrooms	2 cups cooked rice

Heat the oil in a wok or frying pan. Stir-fry the celery, bamboo shoots, mushrooms, and garlic until tender but crisp, 5-7 minutes. Mix in the soy sauce and celery seed. Add the sprouts; cook until the sprouts are warm, 1-2 minutes. Serve over the rice. **Yield: 4 servings.**

Magical Attributes: Study of Wicca, Craft workings, the magic circle, honoring magical history.

Celebrations: Samhain, initiation, study group formations.

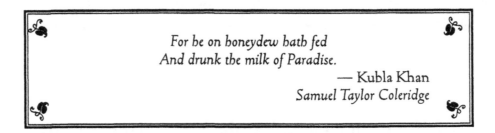

> For he on honeydew hath fed
> And drunk the milk of Paradise.
>
> — Kubla Khan
> Samuel Taylor Coleridge

Divinity Candy

Shakespearian: Bubble, Bubble, Toil, and Trouble
Magical: Candlemas Snow

I have no idea how divinity got its name, but I can hazard a guess; it is because of its divine taste which is so light, it's likely to float away!

- 1 cup water
- 1 cup light corn syrup or honey
- 4 cups sugar
- ½ teaspoon salt
- 4 egg whites
- 1 teaspoon flavoring, any kind

Combine the water and corn syrup in a large saucepan; bring to a boil. Remove from the heat; mix in the sugar and salt. Return to the stove. Stir constantly over low heat until the sugar is dissolved. Continue to cook without stirring until a candy thermometer reads 260° F or a small amount dropped into very cold water forms a ball that holds its shape but is pliable. Beat the egg whites until very stiff. Very slowly pour the hot mixture into the egg whites while beating constantly. Add the flavoring; beat until the mixture holds its shape and is slightly dull. Quickly drop from a buttered teaspoon onto wax paper. Let sit until firm. Store in an airtight container. **Yield: 8 dozen candies.**

Variation: For other times of the year, change the flavoring and add a little food coloring, such as mint and green for bountiful spring energy.

Magical Attributes: Lifting burdens, carefree days, effortless liberation.

Celebrations: Late winter observances, spring rituals, New Year's, Candlemas.

Sweet Mint Black-Eyed Peas

Shakespearian: Eye of Newt
Magical: Eyes of the Spirit
Egyptian: Osiris' Pleasure

The "eye" of this bean makes it the perfect medium for edible magics towards improved discernment. Mint adds vitality to this culinary wizardry.

10 oz. black-eyed peas	Butter
1 teaspoon crushed, dried mint	Salt
1 teaspoon sugar	Pepper

Cover peas with water; soak overnight.

Drain. Combine the beans, sugar, mint and 2½ cups water in a saucepan. Cover; simmer until tender. Serve with butter, salt, and pepper. Garnish with a fresh mint leaf. **Yield: 4 servings.**

Magical Attributes: Vision, insight, rejuvenation, centering.

Celebrations: Birthdays, New Year's, Spring Equinox, Sunning of Buddha, waxing to full moon rituals, Bean Throwing Day.

Granola Honey Cookies

Shakespearian: Honeyed Locusts
Magical: Pleasing Providence
Egyptian: Min's Munchies

While we know that locusts were sometimes portrayed as the agents of divine fury, they were also often part of stories which centered around individuals who later became oracles. Somehow the extreme transformations this insect brings also clear the way for broader spiritual vision. In Egypt, the Goddess Min was given offerings of honey or honey cakes.

1¼ cups flour	2 eggs
½ teaspoon salt	1 teaspoon vanilla
½ teaspoon baking soda	½ teaspoon grated orange rind
¼ cup oil	1 cup granola
¼ cup honey	½ cup raisins

Preheat the oven to 325° F. Combine the flour, salt, and baking soda in a small bowl. Beat the oil, honey, eggs, vanilla, and orange rind in a medium-sized bowl. Mix the dry ingredients into the egg mixture. Stir in the granola and raisins. Drop by the teaspoon onto a greased cookie sheet. Bake for 10 minutes.
Yield: 2-3 dozen cookies.

Magical Attributes: Drastic change, hermitage, quests, prophetic gifts.

Celebrations: Winter rituals, Birthday of the Moon, Kamehameha Day, New Year's, Yule, Samhain.

Fried Honeycakes

Magical: Fairy Folk Fritters
Druidic: Dryad's Delight

These small cakes are not unlike those made on the night before Beltane by women around the turn of the century. These cakes were left in the garden to please fairy visitors.

½ cup sweet white wine	2 tablespoons sugar
1 egg	1 cup honey
⅔ cup flour	⅛ teaspoon nutmeg
⅛ teaspoon cinnamon	Oil for frying
⅛ teaspoon salt	

Beat the wine and egg in a medium bowl. Combine the flour, cinnamon, salt and sugar in a small bowl. Stir into the egg mixture. Let stand 30 minutes.
Combine the honey and nutmeg in a small bowl. Heat ½-inch of the oil in a frying pan until hot but not smoking. Drop the batter into the oil 1 tablespoonful at a time; fry until golden brown. Drain on paper towels. Dip into the honey.
Yield: 1½ dozen.

Magical Attributes: Kinship with the Devic and Faery world.

Celebrations: May Day, Lammas, Day of the Dryads.

Fish Cakes (Scotland)

Shakespearian: Lizard Tail
Magical: Aspiration Patties
Breton: Ahes Gift

In the Hopi tradition, the lizard reminds us to pay attention to symbolic lessons and messages. Additionally, thyme and bay are thought to improve psychic awareness. In Breton, Ahes was a triple form of the sea goddess.

1 lb. cooked, flaked fish	2-3 drops green food coloring
1½ lb. mashed potatoes	1 cup bread crumbs
Salt	1 bay leaf, crushed
Pepper	¼ teaspoon dried thyme
1 egg	

Preheat the oven to 325° F. Combine the fish, potatoes, salt and pepper. Beat the egg and food coloring in a small bowl. Mix into the potatoes. Stir in the bread crumbs, bay leaf, and thyme. Form ¼ cup portions into the shape of a lizard tail or any other symbol appropriate to your goal. Add a little milk if the mixture is too dry to hold together. Bake until golden brown, about 30 minutes.
Yield: 6 servings.

Note: If you prefer, these can be fried in 2 tablespoons oil instead of baking.

Magical Attributes: Dream shadow magic, metaphorical visions and missives.

Celebrations: Any twilight or night time observances, vision quests, Birthday of the Moon, Ahes Festival.

Turkey Triangles with Peas and Sauce

Magical: Triple Aspects

The turkey is a bird which represents sharing selflessly with others.

1 tablespoon butter	10 oz. frozen baby peas, thawed
1 tablespoon flour	2 tablespoons oil
1 cup milk	4 turkey breast slices
1 cup chicken bouillon	

Melt the butter in a saucepan over a low flame. Stir in the flour to form a paste. Slowly add the milk, stirring constantly until smooth. Stir in the broth and peas. Simmer until a thick, smooth sauce is formed. Fry the turkey breasts in the oil until done. Cover with sauce. **Yield: 4 servings.**

Magical Attributes: Charity, kindness, mindfulness of others needs.

Celebrations: Asking Festival, Thanksgiving, Yule, Sukkoth, Tibetan Butter Festival, many harvest observances.

Artichoke Soup (Israel, Italy)

Shakespearian: Scale of Dragon
Magical: Spring Prosperity Broth

The legendary dragons are long-lived beasts who guard the secrets of their magic tenaciously. To this day in Scotland it is believed that at least one dragon lives to watch over the standing stone circles throughout the world.

1 lb. artichoke hearts	2 cups broth, any kind
2½ cups milk	1 clove garlic, minced
2 tablespoons butter	Salt
2 tablespoons flour	Pepper

Steam the artichoke hearts until tender. Cool; remove any tough leaves. Place in a blender or food processor with 1¼ cups of the milk; purée.

Melt the butter in a medium-sized saucepan. Stir in the flour to form a paste. Slowly add the remaining milk, stirring constantly until smooth. Stir in the broth, garlic, salt, and pepper. Simmer until thickened. Mix in the artichokes. Cook for 5 minutes. Garnish each bowl with grated cheese and a whole artichoke scale (for the dragon). **Yield: 6 servings.**

Magical Attributes: Ancient wisdom, protection, growth, prosperity.

Celebrations: Initiation, investment of a new priest/ess, Drawing Down the Moon, Russian Fair, Festival of Sarasvati, Birthday of Confucius.

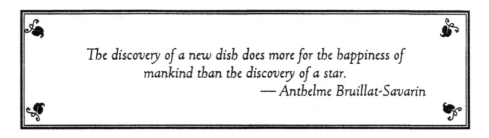

> *The discovery of a new dish does more for the happiness of*
> *mankind than the discovery of a star.*
> — *Anthelme Bruillat-Savarin*

Sweltering Stew

Magical: Solstice Stew
Roman: Penates Pride
Hindi: Agni's Allocation

The Penates were a type of Roman hearth and pantry god, and Agni is the Hindu god of fire. The colors and spices are chosen here for their association with fiery energy.

2 lb. meat, cubed (any kind)	3 carrots, sliced
2 tablespoons oil	8 oz. pearl onions, peeled
1 cup dried red beans	1 cup tomato sauce
1 (8-oz.) can yellow beans	4 cups water
1 tablespoon Tabasco sauce	3 freshly grated peppercorns
1 large sweet red pepper, chopped	4 bouillon cubes, same type
2 small hot peppers, chopped	as the meat
3 large tomatoes, diced	2 teaspoons minced garlic
1 medium yellow squash,	2 bay leaves
peeled and diced	2 tablespoons dried oregano

In a large pot, brown the meat in the oil. Add the rest of the ingredients. Cover. Simmer for 4 hours. Stir regularly. **Yield: 8 servings.**

Magical Attributes: Sun and fire magic, purification, abundant energy.

Celebrations: Sun Dance, Birthday of the Sun, many spring and summer festivals, any celebrations which honor solar or fire deities.

Sunflower Seeds with Sage Butter

Shakespearian: Tooth of Wolf
Magical: Sundrops

In many lands the sunflower is associated with solar deities. This combines well with the image of the wolf, who in Shamanistic traditions is a teacher and pathfinder.

  2 tablespoons butter
  1 tablespoon Worcestershire sauce
  2 teaspoons dried sage

  1 lb. hulled raw sunflower seeds
  Garlic salt

Preheat the oven to 300° F. Combine the butter, Worcestershire sauce, and sage in a medium pan over low heat. When the butter is melted, add the sunflower seeds. Stir until the seeds are evenly coated. Spread on a greased cookie sheet. Sprinkle with garlic salt. Bake until lightly browned, 10-15 minutes. Stir occasionally. **Yield: 4 servings.**

Magical Attributes: Wisdom, learning, study, marking new spiritual paths.

Celebrations: Honoring an elder or teacher, graduations, Coming of Age, Sunning of Buddha, Festival of Sarasvati, Saturnalia, planting festivals.

✦ *Final Notes* ✦

This book has been a challenge and joy to write — and I must admit a little fattening, too! I know that through the writing process my pantry has changed to be more reflective of my magical lifestyle. I have cleaned, reorganized, redecorated, and had more fun in my kitchen than I did before. Each meal can become a magical escapade, brimming with innovation, insight, and intuition. It is this spirit of variety that this book has tried to celebrate. With this in mind, I hope you enjoy the adventures your own kitchen presents.

Well, I had better go make dinner ... what enchantments shall we devour tonight? To find out, meet me at the dining room table with menus of your own. I'm eating promptly at 6:00!

Blessings in Light,
TRISH

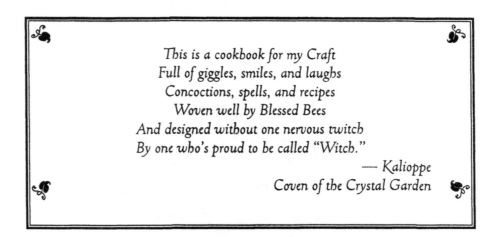

This is a cookbook for my Craft
Full of giggles, smiles, and laughs
Concoctions, spells, and recipes
Woven well by Blessed Bees
And designed without one nervous twitch
By one who's proud to be called "Witch."

— *Kalioppe*
Coven of the Crystal Garden

Personal Recipes

Personal Recipes

Part Three

Tables and Appendices

*Correspondences are like large clothes before the invention
of suspenders: it is impossible to keep them up.*

— Sydney Smith

Appendix A

Kitchen Gods, Goddesses, and Representations

An old mystic says somewhere, "God is an unutterable sigh in the innermost depths of the soul."

— Theodore Christlieb

Cooking magic has been closely related to hearth gods and goddessess. Some lands, such as China, even have a special day to pay their respects to these divine figures by leaving small offerings and preparing elegant feasts.

In considering whom your kitchen will honor, you can approach the decision in several ways. You can either choose a god or goddess who is appropriate to your celebration, or select a permanent divine figure to honor who is reflective of your Path. You can also combine these two options by having one god/dess symbolically abiding full-time, then calling on other suitable images for more specific purposes.

To illustrate, someone studying Celtic traditions might have Cerridwen as a hearth goddess, but invoke the blessings of Apollo on their foods for creativity (see associations to follow). Alternatively, a home with many guests might choose to distinguish Ganymede, the Greek cup-bearer. In many cultures, like the Japanese and ancient Norse, cups are a symbol of welcome and hospitality.

Which images of the divine you honor is a purely personal choice. This is your kitchen and your sacred hearth, and it should mirror your visions and hopes. How you feel about your hallowed pantry, and how comfortable you are in that space, will influence the outcome of your magic. Here are a few possible gods and goddesses to consider, along with their country of origin, for your reference:

Possible Hearth Gods

Agathadaimon: Egyptian god of fortune.

Agni: Hindu fire god.

Asclepius: Greek god of health.

Ataksak: Eskimo god of joy.

Baldur: Scandinavian god of goodness and wisdom.

Bannik: Slavonic god of the household and prophesy.

Cupid: Roman god of love.

Diancecht: Irish god of healing.

Ea: Babylonian god of wisdom and magic.

Esmon: Phoenician god of vitality.

Ganymede: Greek cupbearer.

Gengenver: Egyptian goose god who laid the cosmic egg.

Gibil: Babylonian god of fire and arbitration.

Gucumatz: Mayan god of farming and domestic life.

Hastsehogan: Navajo god of the home.

Hermes: Greek god of communication.

Hotei: Japanese god of happiness.

Hymen: Greek god of marriage.

Inari: Japanese god of prosperity.

Kama: Hindu god of love.

Nusku: Babylonian god of fire, lamps, and justice.

Okitsu-Hiko: Japanese kitchen god.

Omacatl: Aztec god of delight and celebration.

Shou-hsing: Chinese god of long life.

Tamon: Japanese god of the north and luck.

Tien Kuan: Chinese god of happiness and well-being.

Tsao-wang: Chinese hearth god.

Untunktahe: Dakota god of magical mastery.

Veveteotl: Aztec god of fire and creativity.

Vulcan: Roman god of fire and the forge.

Xochipilli: Aztec corn god.

Yabune: Ancient Japanese house god.

Possible Hearth Goddesses

Aeons: Gnostic aspect of feminine potency.

Agnayi: Hindu goddess of fire.

Albina: Greek goddess of barley.

Anat: Canaanite goddess of love and fertility.

Anna Perenna: Roman goddess of the year and providence.

Aradia: Italian witch goddess.

Ashnan: Babylonian goddess of grain.

Belit-ilanit: Chaldean goddess of love.

Benten: Japanese goddess of love, luck, and good fortune.

Berchta: Teutonic goddess of marriage.

Brid: Irish goddess of creativity.

Buddhi: Hindu goddess of prosperity.

Ceres: Roman corn goddess.

Cerridwen: Celtic Mother figure and grain goddess.

Chicomecoatz: Aztec maize goddess of rural abundance.

Concordia: Roman goddess of peace and harmony.

Dugnai: Slavonic house and bread goddess.

Ekadzati: Tibetan goddess of wisdom and the mystical.

Erce: Old English goddess of blessings.

Fornax: Roman goddess of ovens.

Fuchi: Japanese fire goddess.

Hebe: Greek cupbearer.

Hera: Greek goddess of marriage.

Hestia: Greek goddess of home and hearth.

Hehsui-no-kami: Japanese kitchen goddess.

Huixtocihuatl: Aztec salt goddess.

Hygeia: Greek goddess of health.

Ida: Hindu goddess of fire and devotion.

Ivenopae: Indonesian mother of rice.

Isani: Hindu goddess of abundance.

Kamrusepas: Hittite goddess of health and magic.

Kedesh: Syrian goddess of health and life.

Lakshmi: Hindu goddess of good fortune and plenty.

Li: Chinese goddess of nourishing fires.

Mama Occlo: Inca goddess of domestic arts.

Namagiri: Hindu goddess of inspiration.

Nikkal: Canaanite goddess of first fruits.

Ogetsu-hime-no-kami: Japanese goddess of food.

Okitsu-hime: Japanese kitchen goddess.

Pax: Roman goddess of peace.

Pirua: Peruvian maize mother.

Pukkeenegak: Eskimo provider of food and clothing.

Samkhat: Babylonian goddess of joy.

Vasudhara: Hindu goddess of abundance.

Vesta: Roman goddess of domestic fires.

Appendix B

Food of the Gods

For this is wisdom: to love, to live, to take what Fate or the Gods may give.
— Lawrence Hope

Early humans prayed to divine figures for nourishment. When it came, at least part of that bounty was returned to the altar to thank the Great Powers for listening and responding to the people's needs. Even when food wasn't abundant, offerings were made to try and appease angry spirits, and perhaps change the course of fate.

While our knowledge and vantage point of cause and effect has changed, we do not have to lose this legacy. The link between food and the god/desses has been firmly established by our ancestors. Listed below are many foods which you may want to use in kitchen magic. If you are preparing thematic meals by country or deity, this list will be helpful. Similarly, in consecrating or blessing your ingredients for spiritual sustenance, you may wish to call on a god or goddess image who is associated with those items for improved results.

Food	Associated God/dess	Country
Ale	Shoney	Scotland
Almonds	Artemis	Greece
	Nana	Phrygia
	Ptah	Egypt
Alphabet soup	Evander	Rome
	Nabu	Middle East
Apple	Hapy	Egypt
	Hera, Zeus, Melanion	Greece
Bamboo shoots	Hina	Polynesia
Banana	Kanaloa	Hawaii
Barley	Indra	India
	Demeter, Albina	Greece
	Ninkasi	Sumer
	Isani, Ishwara	Middle East
	Ilmarinen	Finland
	Taliesin	Wales
Basil	Vishnu	Middle East
	Erzulie	Haiti
Bay	Eros, Adonis, Apollo	Greece
	Ceres, Faunus	Rome
Beans	Demeter	Greece
	Carnea, Apollo	Rome
Beef	Audhumla	Scandanavia/Germany
	Dakshina	Middle East
	Hathor	Egypt
	Heitsi, Eibib	Africa
Beer	Isis, Hathor	Egypt
Beet	Aphrodite	Greece
Beverages	Feket	Egypt
	Ganymede	Greece
Blackberry	Brigit	Ireland
Bread	Isis	Egypt
Broccoli	Jupiter	Rome
Broom flowers	Blodeuwedd	Wales
Butter	Ea, Shamash	Mesopotamia
Cheese	Apollo, Aristaeus	Greece
Chicken	Upulero	Indonesia
	Huntin	Africa

Food	Associated God/dess	Country
Cinnamon	Dionysus, Aphrodite	Greece
	Venus	Rome
Citron	Ge	Egypt
	Zeus, Hera	Greece
Coconut	Hina, Kane	Hawaii
	Athena, Ganymede	Greece
	Tamaa	Polynesia
Corn	Corn Mother, Sheu	America
	Quetzalcoatl	Aztec
	Cerridwen, Gwion	Wales
	Marinette	Haiti
Crab	Apollo	Greek
Daisy	Freya	Scandanavia/Germany
	Artemis	Greece
	Thor	Scandanavia/Germany
Dandelion	Hecate, Theseus	Greece
Dates	Anu, Ea, Marduk	Babylonia
	Apollo, Artemis	Greece
Dill	Horus, Amsety	Egypt
Egg	Shiva, Vinata, Brahma	Middle East
	Eostra	Scandanavia/Germany
	Venus	Rome
Fennel	Prometheus, Dionysus	Greece
Fig	Amun Ra, Thoth, Isis	Egypt
	Dionysius, Juno	Greece
Fish	Ra, Isis	Egypt
	Poseidon, Neptune	Rome
	Nanshe	Chaldea
	Episu	Japan
	Gwion	Wales
	Maui	Polynesia
Fruit	Gaia	Greece
	Nikkal	Canaan
Fruit juice	Hebe, Themis, Ganymede	Greece
Game meat	Sati	Egypt
	Diana	Rome
	Artemis	Greece
	Agloolik	America/Asia

Food	Associated God/dess	Country
Garlic	Hecate	Greece
Grain	Ashnan, Enlil	Sumer
	AkaKanet	Chile
Grapes	Dionysus, Aristaeus	Greece
	Bacchus	Rome
Hazelnuts	Thor	Scandinavia/Germany
	Artemis	Greece
	Chandra	Middle East
Honey	Ra, Min	Egypt
	Demeter, Artemis	Greece
	Persephone	Phoenicia
	Hannahannas	Middle East
Lettuce	Min	Egypt
Lily	Venus, Juno	Rome
	Kuan Yin	China
Liquor	Varuni	Middle East
	Patecatl	Aztec
Lobster	Apep	Egypt
	Ares	Greece
Mace	Hermes	Greece
Mango	Buddha	China
Marjoram	Venus	Rome
	Aphrodite	Greece
Mead	Gunnloed	Scandanavia/Germany
Milk	Hathor, Isis, Min	Egypt
	Amalthea	Crete
	Ilmarinen	Finland
Mint	Pluto	Rome
	Hecate	Greece
Mulberry	Minerva, Diana	Rome
Mustard	Aesculapius	Greece
Nettle	Thor	Scandanavia/Germany
	Agni	Middle East
Olive	Aten, Ra	Egypt
	Minerva, Apollo, Juno	Rome
	Athena, Aristaeus	Greece
	Brahma	Middle East
Parsley	Persephone	Phoenicia

Food	Associated God/dess	Country
Peach	Hsi Wang Ma	China
Pears	Athena	Greece
Pepper	Ares	Greece
Peppermint	Pluto	Rome
Pheasant	Li	China
Pomegranate	Zeus, Dionysus	Greece
	Persephone	Phoenicia
	Ceres	Rome
Poppy seed	Demeter	Greece
	Ceres	Rome
Pork	Carnea	Rome
	Goleuddydd	Wales
	Qat	Australia
Quince	Venus	Rome
Rabbit	Cerridwen, Gwion	Wales
Rice	Gauri	Middle East
	Inari	Japan
	Ineno Pae, Omonga	Indonesia
	Saning Sari	East Indies
Rose	Venus	Rome
Saffron	Ashtoreth	Phoenicia
	Eos	Greece
	Amun Ra	Egypt
	Brahma	Hindu
Sage	Zeus	Greece
	Jupiter	Rome
Salmon	Murigen	Ireland
Salt	Set, Osiris	Egypt
	Poseidon, Neptune	Rome
	Tiamat	Sumer
	Ukko	Finland
Sesame	Hecate	Greece
	Ganesha	Middle East
Soup	Cerridwen	Wales
Soy beans	Ebisu, Daikotu	Japan
Spring water	Adsullatu	Wales
	Nanshe	Chaldea
	Agassou	Haiti

Food	Associated God/dess	Country
Strawberry	Freya	Scandanavia/Germany
Sugar	Kane	Hawaii
Sunflower	Demeter, Apollo, Helios	Greece
	LuYu	China
Violet	Athena	Greece
Water	Ahurani	Persia
	Apsu	Babylon
	Egeria	Rome
	Ea	Chaldea
	Mimir	Scandinavia
Watermelon	Set	Egypt
Wheat	Sul	British Isles
	Ceres	Rome
	Demeter	Greece
	Ishtar	Babylon
Wine	Gestin	Sumer
	Ishtar	Mesopotamia
	Osiris, Horus, Isis	Egypt
	Dionysus, Hebe, Themis	Greece
	Bacchus, Liber	Rome

Appendix C

Magical Correlations of Ingredients

*V*_{ariety is the mother of enjoyment.}

— Benjamin Disraeli

The purpose of this list is to give you a broader range of options for cooking magic. Here, you can consider choosing and combining singular foods/additives for spiritual goals.

Take the example of sparkling water. Water as an element is very healing and nurturing. The bubbles are fun, and help to lift burdens. So, when you are feeling emotionally out-of-sorts, sparkling water can become a perfectly viable medium to internalize your personal magic.

Item	Magical Associations
Alfalfa sprouts	Providence, sustenance
Allspice	Luck, health
Apple	Peace, love, health, earth magic
Apricot	Romance
Artichoke	Growth, safety
Avocado	Beauty
Baking soda/powder	Raising energy or expectations
Banana	Heroic energy, male sexuality
Barley	Love, controlling pain of any nature
Bay	Psychic powers, strength and health
Beans	Divination, prosperity, decision-making
Beef	Prosperity, grounding
Beets	Passion, love, beauty
Blueberry	Peace, calm
Bread	Kinship, sustenance
Broccoli	Strength, leadership, physical improvements
Brussels sprouts	Endurance, tenacity, stability
Butter	Tenacity, smoothing relationships
Cake	Celebration, joyous occasions, hospitality
Caraway	Protection from theft and negativity, trust
Cardamon	Increase the strength of unions/partnerships
Carnation	Pride, beauty
Carrot	Vision, masculine energies
Catnip	Rest, joy, cat magic
Cauliflower	Lunar/water-related magics
Celery	Passion, grounding, peace
Cheese	Joy, health, things coming to fruition
Cherry	Love, female sexuality
Chicken	Health, well-being, sunrise magic
Chives	Protection, breaking bad habits
Chocolate	Lifting emotions, love
Chrysanthemum	Longevity, ease, vigor
Clove	Stolen kisses, fun love, protection, piercing illusions
Clover	Triple god/dess
Coconut	Diversity, flexibility, spirituality
Coffee	Energy, alertness, mental awareness
Cookies	Maternal instincts, nurturing love
Coriander	Love, well-being, intelligence

Item	Magical Associations
Corn	Life of the land, cycles, eternity
Corn syrup	Solidifying plans or ideas
Cowslip	Faerie magic, grace
Cranberry	Energy for security and protection
Daisy	Innocence, fidelity, dawn, new beginnings
Dandelion	Divination, foresight, oracles
Date	Resurrection, eternity, spirit
Deer	Elegance, grace, refinement
Dill	Protecting children
Eggs	Fertility, mysticism, ancient questions
Elder flower	Protection from Fey, blessing, wishes
Flour	Revealing hidden matters, consistency
Garlic	Hex breaking, banishings, protection
Ginger	Health, cleansing, vibrant energy, zeal
Grape	Dreams, visions, fertility
Grapefruit	Purification, health
Gravy	Smooth transitions, consistency, uniformity
Guava	Romance, fantasy, relieving sorrow
Ham	Theatrical flair, dramatic energy
Hazel	Wishes, good fortune
Hazelnut	Wisdom, fertility
Honey	Sweet things in life, happiness
Horseradish	Protection, fiery energy
Hyacinth	Reliability, constancy
Jelly	Joy, energy, pleasantness (see also fruit, by type)
Juice	Rejuvenation, vitality, energy
Lamb	Sensitivity, kindness, warmth
Lavender	Spiritual vision, acknowledgement, comfort
Lemon	Longevity, purification, marriage, joy, faithfulness
Lettuce	Financial magics, peace, relaxation
Lilac	Love, youth, joy, fastidiousness
Lime	Cleansing
Marigold	Cares, burdens, change, luck in love
Milk	Goddess energy, maternal instinct, nurturing
Mustard	Faith, mental alertness
Oats	Life of the land, prosperity, sustenance
Olive	Peace, spiritual pursuits
Orange	Health, fidelity, love

Item	Magical Associations
Orange flower	Purity, faithfulness, fruitfulness
Pansy	Glee, fancy, fondness, fairy folk
Parsley	Luck, protection from accidents
Passion fruit	Promoting kinship and love
Peanut	Earth magic, male energy
Pear	Longevity, luck
Peas	Goddess magic, love
Pepper, black	Cleansing, purification, protection, banishing
Pepper, green	Growth, prosperity
Pepper, red	Energy, vitality, strength
Pepper, yellow	Empowered creativity.
Pineapple	Healing, protection, prosperity
Pomegranate	Fruitfulness, hospitality, wishes
Popcorn	Lifting burdens, recreational activities
Pork	Fertility, profuseness
Potato	Folk medicine, health, grounding, earth magic
Quince	Happiness
Raspberry	Vigor, stamina, love
Relish	Protection (dill), enhanced passion (sweet)
Rice	Abundant blessings, fertility
Rose	Love, faithfulness, friendship
Saffron	Bounty, leadership, prosperity
Salt	Cleansing, purification, grounding
Sausage	Zest, variety, god magic
Soup	Steady change and improved communication
Strawberry	Zest, intensity, romance
Sweet potato	Well founded, gentle love
Syrup	Tree magic, amiable meetings
Tea	Divination, insight, meditation, restfulness
Tomato	Attracting love
Tulip	Declaration of love
Turkey	Colorful displays, holiday feasts, family gatherings
Violet	Grace, modesty, excellence, expression
Waffles	Gathering or reserving amiable feelings, accommodation
Walnut	Mental faculties
Wine	Celebration, joy, honoring positive actions
Yogurt	Health, spirituality, Goddess magic

Appendix D

Celebrations

*M*inute events are the hinges on which magnificent results turn.

— John Cumming

Holidays and the hearth have always been closely linked. What child (or adult, for that matter) doesn't think of cookies come Yule, braided breads at spring celebrations, and unusual delectables for New Year's? Now, however, we take all these things and sprinkle in a little magic.

I have listed some ancient, modern, and international holidays to inspire ideas of your own. The cultural origins of these festivals are noted for people who wish to focus on a particular path for their magical goals. The variety in this list reinforces the notion that every day of living, if approached magically, is a time to celebrate.

Culinary enchantments give us another opportunity to reconnect with the Gaia spirit and our own creative powers by paying closer attention to the seasons and their magical significance. With this awareness in hand, we can then blend those symbols and ideas into our regular cooking even as our ancestors did. Thus we not only celebrate the beauty of creation, but the bounty of the creator in all our efforts.

New Year's Day: January 1. Any traditional food for luck, health, and prosperity is welcome at this celebration. Try at least one completely new food.

Handsel Monday (Scotland): First Monday in January. A time to commemorate those who serve and to renew promises. Have a feast with your partner or dear friend, and send off some cookies to a favorite person just to say thanks.

Festival of Sarasvati (Hindu): January 12. Power of wisdom, music, and the written word. Try making alphabet or runic potato slices and writing a poem.

Feast of the Kitchen God (China): January 20. Here, the virtue of the home is venerated. Cleanse and bless your sacred hearth, and give the divine presence there the night off. Eat out.

Planting Festival (Rome): January 27. This holiday honored both Ceres, the earth mother, and Tellus, a land god. If you plan to have a garden, now is the time to consecrate your seed. Buy new spices for your magical pantry.

Candlemas: February 2. A quiet but lovely holiday full of lights; the idea here is to help the sun on its journey. Therefore, prepare yellow, red, and orange foods, visualizing this color reaching the heavens.

Valentine's Day: February 14. The spirit of romance with a flourish. Try a strawberry guava pie for your true love, and anything chocolate.

Festival of Mihr (Armenia): February 26. A time for magic of prosperity and fertility. Think in terms of greens and golds.

Festival of Ishtar (Babylonia): March 8. Another image of the Earth goddess. Try foods which grow near to the soil such as potatoes, mushrooms, spinach, any root vegetable, peanuts, etc.

Hori (India): March 16. Spring fire festival dedicated to celebrating the passing of winter and good fortune. Anything with curry, tons of garlic, or traditional Indian spices is fitting.

Spring Equinox: About March 23. Food for joy, life, harmony, and productivity; the rebirth of the Earth. All egg dishes are welcome.

Smell the Breeze Day (Japan): March 27. A festival of luck, health, vitality, the air element, and simple pleasures. A good day to consider your first spring outing and picnic.

Borrowed Days (Scotland): March 31. Time to focus on internalizing magic for prosperity and providence, and pay your debts. Anything green and leafy is a good choice for eating, accented with a side dish of dilled rice.

April Fool's Day: April 1. Fun, frivolity, and regaining a sense of humor/perspective. Eat joyfully; try finger foods!

Sunning of Buddha (Tibet): April 5. Give offerings of foods to your patron god; work toward insight and the energy of tranquility with cucumber and celery salad topped with wine vinegar and oregano.

Festival of Brightness (China): April 7. Honoring the dead, meals with family. Inspire feelings of kinship with a passion fruit pie or wine.

Sealing the Frost (Guatemala): April 12. Protection from evil, any weather magic, divination foods, blessing crops. As an after dinner drink, try mint, cinnamon, and nutmeg tea.

Patriot's Day (New England): April 18. Protection of your own city or village, warnings; make bravery-focused baked goods with yeast to rise in our hearts.

Apple Blossom Day (Virginia): April 24. Apple treats for beauty, health, and any trait you want to flourish in your life.

Beltane, May Day: May 1. Magical holiday of love, fertility, weaving of masculine and feminine energy. Enjoy oat cakes, spring wines, and the ever-fruitful egg!

Feast of Banners (Japan): May 5. Masculine attributes, bravery, courage, overcoming difficulties. Sun empowered or "hot" foods are recommended.

St. Joan of Arc Day (France): Second Sunday in May. Feminine power, divine guidance, religious tolerance. Smooth, white foods (yogurt, potatoes) are one choice.

Brendan's Voyage (Ireland): May 16. Safe travel, idealism, the energy of adventure. Try a new recipe!

Feast of Madonna (Italy): May 23. Honoring the goddess; blessing animals, tools, and occupations. Cleanse and consecrate your kitchen utensils; prepare foods with goddess ingredients such as apples, eggs, tomatoes, or mushrooms.

Royal Oak Day (England): May 29. Protection, safety, triumph over difficult odds, druidic energy. Use foods fresh from the garden or a natural cooperative.

Memorial Day: Last Monday in May. Foods for peace, wisdom and to honor those who have died in battle (including magical people killed as heretics). Anything prepared with olive oil, peaches, or honey.

Kamehameha Day (Hawaii): June 7. Prophecy, protection of children, wisdom, and leadership attributes. For spices look to basil, garlic, dill, oregano, bay, chives, and ginger.

Riding the Marches (Scotland): June 12. Protection of natural resources (the land), sweet things in life. Give yourself some freedom and go out to eat!

Summer Solstice: About June 22. The longest day of the year is dedicated to fire festivals, love, beauty, passion, and energy! Cook spicy main dishes and fresh fruit desserts.

Sun Dance (Assinibone): July 3. Life and health of animals (cook something special for your pets), fire-related foods, the energy of victory.

Independence Day: July 4. Red tomatoes and peppers, white cabbage, rice, or potatoes, and blue table accents to encourage the power of freedom.

Old Dance Day (Tibet): July 12. Triumph over evil, improved finances, health. Eat uplifting foods and have a basket of apples as a center piece.

Binding of the Wreaths (Lithuania): July 20. Love, connection to nature, blessings. A good day to make an herb wreath with basil, bay, cinnamon sticks, dill sprays, rosemary, and thyme for your sacred pantry.

Pardon of the Birds (British Isles): July 29. A holiday to honor lyrical arts and animal kinship; make bread cookies in the form of musical notes, then feed the birds!

Lammas: August 1. Also known as Loaf Mass; the first harvest and a druidical feast of first fruits. Any homemade bread or things brought from your own garden are appropriate.

Day of the Dryads (Macedonia): August 2. A time to honor elemental spirits and connect with supernatural energy; make sweet cakes for the Fey, and eat sparingly before meditation.

Feast of the Milky Way (China): August 7. Celebrate astrology, celestial powers, and fair weather with star fruit and white, fluffy potatoes.

St. Stephen Festival (Hungary): August 20. A time of prayer, recounting history, and joy in heritage; make one of your favorite inherited dishes.

Ahes Festival (British Isles): August 26. A festival for the sea goddess of ancient times, focused on healing and intuition; eat fish and kelp at a table decorated with shells and driftwood.

Labor Day: First Monday in September. Be thankful for your job, take your boss out for lunch, or make some sweet bread as a special treat to go with morning coffee.

Festival of Durga (Himalayan Mountains): September 7. A celebration of the Earth goddess; perhaps abstain from meat or other food from the land and its creatures to honor Her.

Birthday of the Moon (China): September 15. Any lunar magics are great on this day. Consider foods such as cabbage, coconut, eggs, lemon, mushrooms, potatoes, watermelon, or any other moon-related food.

Birthday of the Sun (Incan): September 20. A good time to honor fire. Include marigolds, oranges, pineapple, and sunflower seeds as part of your meal.

Fall Equinox: About September 21. A harvest festival where corn, squash, and wheat bread might become part of your meals.

Birthday of Confucius (China): September 28. A day to ponder. Consider your dietary and spiritual needs and how to meet them with kitchen magic.

Kermesse (Germany): October 7. A time to honor patron gods, dance the dance of life, and revive your humor.

Sukkoth (Jewish): Mid-October. Protection of animals and fields, improving one's faith, good deeds, and focus on holy teachings. Stick to simple foods and clear liquids to allow for clear thoughts.

Festival of the Goddess of Mercy (China): October 22. A time which focuses gentle energy on married women. Look to the foods of love; peas, anise, rosemary, tomato, raspberry, oranges, and milkshakes.

Samhain: October 31. The Celtic New Year and a time when all worlds and dimensions are close. Psychic abilities are best honed with bay, celery, fish, and fruit juice. Other seasonal favorites include turnips, carrots, and cider.

Aloha Week (Hawaii): November 7. Encourages the spirit of welcome, rejoicing in folk customs, and diversity. Serve homemade wine to guests, then give them the recipe to try.

Feast of Jupiter (Rome): November 13. This feast actually honored Juno and Minerva as well. Foods normally aligned with Jupiter are also expensive, rich dishes and desserts which likewise encourage prosperity.

Asking Festival (Eskimo): November 14. Sharing with those who are less fortunate comes into focus here, the essence of charity. Make or buy some foods for a local organization that feeds the needy and homeless.

Thanksgiving: Last Thursday in November. A type of harvest festival, we remind ourselves to be grateful for our bounty.

Russian Fair (Old Russia): December 5. Day of sports, the mysteries, and dance. Consider having a pot luck dinner.

Fiesta of the Mother of Health (Mexico): December 8. Gives tribute to the healing goddess. Look to foods commonly connected with wellness including garlic, sage, apple, lemon, cucumbers, and olives.

Saturnalia (Rome): December 13. A time to sow seed, rejoice, and frolic. Any seed or grain foods are a good choice.

Hopi Winter Ceremony: December 14. A festival which celebrates the home and remaining crops.

Yule: December 21. The longest night of the year. Make gingerbread cookies both for yourself and for your tree spirits to encourage the return of the sun.

Kitchen Tools as Magical Implements

*P*hilosophy is, indeed, a goddess whose head is
in the heavens, but whose feet are upon earth.

— John Cumming

To appraise a common kitchen utensil in spiritual terms we have to look at not only how it is used in a variety of settings, but how those applications can relate to other traditional magical tools.

Let's use a spoon as an illustration. The serving spoon, when blessed and charged for kinship, becomes a good choice for meting out the portions of a magical dish. The mixing spoon might be used in place of a wand to stir the energy of a circle into proper balance. Straining spoons can be hung at the perimeter of a sacred space (including around the home) to filter out negative influences, and finally, a decorated spoon can become the token of the chosen hearth god/dess.

Other common cooking utensils or kitchen objects, with some suggested symbolism for your enchantments, are given below. This is an abbreviated list to which you could add hundreds of items simply by looking around your kitchen with an imaginative, magical eye.

If a choice is available, decide among different tools according to your magical goals. If you have the option of either a whisk or a fork for mixing, the decision can reflect the meaning of the creation itself. Whisks are more for energy and prosperity while the fork is for penetrating hidden matters. Consider everything in your kitchen as having the potential to help your magical efforts progress smoothly along their intended path.

Item	Magical Associations
Blender	Mingling with others, stirring up energy
Cookbook	Book of Shadows, excellence, virtue
Cookie tin	Sweet things in life, pleasure
Crisper	Invigoration and restoration
Cupboards	Savings, supplies, providence
Dish towel	Stricture, determined precision
Dishwasher	Leisure, the water element, convenience
Drain	Troubles, burdens, bad habits
Drawers	Hidden matters, material goods
Food wrap	Prudence, conservation, control, secrets
Fork	Piercing, penetrating, perception
Funnel	Flow, unhindered order, coaxing energy along
Knife	Cutting away, sharpness of mind, separation
Measuring cup	Evaluation, allotment, caution
Microwave	Acceleration, legal expedition
Oven	Passion, fertility, fire element
Oven burners	The four directions/elements
Oven fan	The air element, movement, clearing vision
Pitcher	Abundance, invigoration, refreshment
Refrigerator	Cooling temper, preservation, protection
Rolling pin	Discipline, moderation, control
Sifter	Sorting out confusion, organization, filtering negativity.
Spatula	Sensibility, recycling, changing directions
Steamer	Slow processes, even temperament
Tea kettle	Divination, alertness, kinship, health
Thermometer	Observational skills, analysis
Whisk	Excitement, increasing bounty
Windows	Winds of change, refreshment, vital energy

Appendix F

Common Associations

*Philosophy is, indeed, a goddess whose head is
in the heavens, but whose feet are upon earth.*

— John Cumming

Aromatic Correspondences

Apple	Wise choices, health, insight
Basil	Harmony, agreement
Rosemary	Conscious mind, health, love
Cloves	Protection, romance
Vanilla	Awareness, love, improved energy
Pine	Purification, refreshment
Rose	Devotion, health, peace
Nutmeg	Psychic perception

Astrological Correspondences

Moon	Intuitive nature, water element, creativity, nurturing, Goddess energy
Waxing Moon	Growth, fullness, fertility, positive energy
Waning Moon	Reduction, slowing, reversals, banishing negative energy
Blue Moon	The second Full Moon of a sign; time for miracles
Moon in Aries	Cleansing and personal development of talents or crafts; breaking down barriers, rebirth or beginnings
Moon in Taurus	Productivity and abundance, stubborn tenacity
Moon in Gemini	Communication, wit, study, changeability
Moon in Cancer	Sesitivity, creativity, insight; home and hearth are strong influences now
Moon in Leo	Strength, pride, showmanship, generosity, vitality, power
Moon in Virgo	Financial improvements, victory, health; details and intellectual matters
Moon in Libra	Balance, development of discernment; art and color are enhanced, as are partnerships
Moon in Scorpio	Scrutiny, intense energy, heightened sensitivity; secrets and criticism
Moon in Sagittarius	Philosophy, higher thinking, spirituality, self-mastery
Moon in Capricorn	Frugality, concern with material, ambition
Moon in Aquarius	Eclecticism, new and different energy, humane and rational actions
Moon in Pisces	Spirituality, sensitivity, lack of clarity; a time for divination and fantasy
Sun	God energy, leadership qualities, strength, the fire element, cleansing, change

Color Correspondences

Red	Strength, courage, vitality, fire
Orange	Energy, harvest, warmth, compassion
Yellow	Mind, divination, creativity, air, movement
Green	Growth, prosperity, faith, health
Blue	Water, peace, healing, joy, contemplation
Purple	Spirituality, devotion, sensitivity
White	Protection, purification, innocence
Black	Banishing, the void, rest

| Brown | Earth, nature, foundations, new endeavors |
| Pink | Kinship, relaxation, leisure, positive attitude |

Monthly Correspondences

January	Weave magic for safety and protection
February	Contemplate foods which focus on motivations, forgiveness, and healing
March	Enhancement of success magic
April	Meals which encourage openings, opportunity, and a little good luck are especially powerful
May	Growth, development, and maturity
June	An excellent time to prepare dishes for love and commitment
July	Consider what you can prepare to bring the skills of authority and self-regulation into your life
August	The Roman month of peace; prepare foods that encourage accord and symmetry in your life
September	Spiritual development and growth
October	Transformation and change
November	Empathy and a deeper understanding of universal truths
December	The spirit of the law, not the letter, is accented

Number Correspondences

1	Unity, birth, accord, sun magic
2	Balance, blessing, partnership
3	Symmetry, purpose, body-mind-spirit
4	Elements, time, goals, victory
5	Versatility, awareness, psychic endeavors
6	Protection, devotion, finishing projects
7	Insight, diversity, moon magic
8	Energy, personal change, authority
9	Universal law, service to others
10	Follow-through, inner voice of reason
12	Fruitfulness, durability, a full year
13	Devotion, patience, convictions
21	Honor, memory, distinction
40	Hermitage, retreat, refilling inner wells

Weekday Correspondences

Monday: Originally known as Moon's day. Cooking on Monday will improve magics for creativity, insight, maternal nature, and goddess-related efforts.

Tuesday: Tiw was a God of athletics, combat, and law. Consider meals to improve physical well-being, encourage justice, or increase strength and strategy.

Wednesday: Odin (Woden) was a god of the mystical, poetry, and resourcefulness. Meals prepared today can accent magics for improved focus on your spiritual path, artistic ability, or imagination.

Thursday: Thor, the god of strength and commitment, ruled over this day. Consider dishes prepared to enhance vigor, stamina, devotion and dedication.

Friday: From Frigg, the goddess of relationships and fertility. A good day to create foods for any lunar magics, love-related spells, and improved productivity.

Saturday: Saturn was a God of harvests and planting. A good weekday to consider combining with harvest theme meals, or to sow any seeds to bring positive traits into your life.

Sunday: The Sun is the ruler of this day. Any solar magic, god-related foods, and foods for leadership, logic, study, etc. are enhanced when prepared on this day.

Symbolic Correspondences

Health	Flow
Protection	Light, joy
Psychic ability	Gate, path
Completion	Harmony
Prosperity	Goddess, fertility
Spirituality	New beginnings
Weight loss	Grounding
Strength	Movement, air
Growth	Maternity
Safe travel	Innovation
Life	Balance
Love	Moon energy
Communication	Cup, womb
Retreat	Fire, god energy
Openings	Luck

Appendix G

Pantry Resource Listing

He was a bold man who first ate an oyster.

— Charles Dickens

Sometimes it is difficult to find "gourmet" ingredients at the local supermarket. If you are having trouble locating something specific, try calling nearby natural food stores, herb shops, cooperatives, delicatessens (according to culture), and/or a "super store." When these avenues fail, try mail order.

When corresponding with these companies, it is recommended that you include a SASE (self-addressed stampled envelope) for a speedier response. Please note that many of the food markets have a much more diverse international selection than might seem from this listing, so do not hesitate to ask for help in finding unique items.

Utensils and Small Appliances

Kitchen Aid
Hobart Corp.
Troy, OH 45374

Magic Mill
235 West 2nd Street
Salt Lake City, UT 84101

Moulinex
1 Montgomery St.
Belleville, NJ 07109

Nutone Scoville
Madison & Red Banks Rd.
Cincinnati, OH 45227

Bazar de la Cuisine
160 E. 55th St.
New York, NY 10022

Ronson Corporation
1 Ronson Rd.
Ogletown, DE 19702

Bridge Company
212 E. 52nd Street
New York, NY 10022

Zabar's
2245 Broadway
New York, NY 10024

Imported and Foreign Foods

General Items, Including Spices

European Imports
23 N. Bemiston Ave.
St. Louis, MO 63105

Roffman's House of Delicacies
2500 Haney St.
Omaha, NB 68131

B. Altman's
5th Ave. at 34th St.
New York, NY 10016

Bloomingdale's Delicacies
340 Madison Ave.
New York, NY 10017

SS Pierce
33 Brookline Ave.
Boston, MA 02215

J. Goldsmith & Sons
123 S. Main St.
Memphis, TN 38103

German

Bremen House
218 E. 86th St.
New York, NY 10028

French

D'Artagnan
St. Paul Ave.
Jersy City, NJ 07306
800-DARTAGN

Italian

Manganaro Brothers
488 E. 9th Avenue
New York, NY 10018
212-563-5331

Balduccis
Mail Order Division 11-02
Queens Plaza South
Long Island City, NY 11101
800-822-1144

Todaro Brothers
555 2nd Avenue
New York, NY 10016
212-679-7766

Greek

Istanbul
247 3rd Street
San Francisco, CA 94103

Grecian Market
3244 S. Dixie Highway (US 1)
W. Palm Beach, FL 33405

Helenic Store
5510 W. Harrison Ave.
Boston, MA 02116

Acropolis
8441 Joy Rd.
Detroit, MI 48204

Indian

American Tea, Coffee & Spice
1511 Champa St.
Denver, CO 80202

Delmar & Co.
501 Monroe Ave.
Detroit, MI 48226

Java India Co.
442 Hudson
New York, NY 10014

Kalustyan Orient Export
123 Lexington Ave.
New York, NY 10016

Indonesian

House of Rice
4112 University Way NE
Seattle, WA 98105

Scandinavian

Nyborg & Nelson
937 Second Ave.
New York, NY 10022

Hungarian

Paprikas Weiss
1546 2nd Ave.
New York, NY 10028
212-288-6117

Kosher

Katz's Deli
205 E. Houston St.
New York, NY 10009
212-254-2246

Japanese

House of Hanna
1468 T. Street NW
Washington, DC 20009

Pacific Mercantile Co.
1946 Larimer St.
Denver, CO 80202

Diamond Trading Co.
1108 N. Clark St.
Chicago IL, 60650

Oriental Trading Co.
115 Farnam St.
Omaha, NB 68102

Oriental Food Shop
1302 Amsterdam Ave.
New York, NY 10027

Takara Oriental Foods
2021 Cache Rd.
Lawton, OK 73501

Middle East

European Grocery Co.
321 South Spring
Los Angeles, CA 90013

Middle East Import Co.
233 Valencia St.
San Francisco, CA 94103

Cardullos Gourmet Shop
6 Brattle St.
Cambridge, MA 02138

Heidi's Round the World
1149 S. Brentwood Blvd.
St. Louis, MO 63117

Mexican/Caribbean

Del Rey Spanish Foods
Stall A-7, Central Market
317 S. Broadway
Los Angeles, CA 90013

Epicure Markets
1656 Alton Rd.
Miami Beach, FL 33139

Marshall Field & Co.
111 N. State St.
Chicago, IL 60602

El-Nopal Foods
544 N. Highland Ave.
Indianapolis, IN 46202

Central Grocery
923 Decatur St.
New Orleans, LA 70116

Pier One Imports
5403 S. Rice Avenue
Houston, TX 77036

Miscellaneous

Doreen's Wild n' Weedy
Doreen Shababy
Box 508
Clark Fork, ID 83811
202-266 1492

A journal of grass-roots herbalism. Quarterly focus on wild plants for foods, medicine, creative herbcraft, holistic health, organic gardening, seasonal celebrations, etc. Other features include book reviews, poetry, recipes and remedies. $13/year, sample issue $3.00. Member of WPPA.

Lotus Light
Box 2
Wilmot, WI 53192
414-862-2395

A terrific resource for organic herbs, spices, spice mixtures, and a variety of other earth-aware items. Great delivery times and wonderful service.

Brewers Emporium
249 River St.
Depew, NY 14043

A dependable and affordable supplier of home brewing equipment and supplies.

Angelica's
147 First Avenue
New York, NY 10003
212-677-1549

Organically grown herbs, flowers and grains. COD or money orders over $50.00 only. Minimum range for shipment arrangements is 100 miles.

Aphrodisia
282 Bleecker St.
New York, NY 10014
212-986-6440

Culinary and medicinal herbs with catalogue available on request.

Cheese of All Nations
153 Chambers St.
New York, NY 10007
212-732-0752

Credit cards are accepted and a catalogue available for a variety of cheeses.

Economy Candy
108 Rivington St.
New York, NY 10002
212-254-1531

Besides candies they also carries a good collection of dried fruits, etc. Catalogue is free. Charge cards welcome. Minimum order $25.00.

Silver Palate
274 Columbus Ave.
New York, NY 10023
212-799-6340

A collection of rare, unusual and interesting jellies, jams, preserves, sauces, and condiments. Charges accepted.

Appendix H

Measures, Conversions, and Substitutions

Our present knowledge of the universe is such as to leave
us with a very inadequate conception of the majesty of existence.

— Oliver J. Lodge

Household Measures

3 teaspoons	=	1 tablespoon
16 tablespoons	=	1 cup
2 cups	=	1 pint
2 pints	=	1 quart
4 quarts	=	1 gallon
1 stick butter	=	½ cup
1 cup	=	1 large tomato, diced
		1 large green pepper, chopped
		5 large eggs
		28 soda crackers, crushed
		2 medium ears of corn
		2 large stalks celery, chopped
		2 medium carrots, sliced

1 cup	=	16	slices bacon, cooked and crumbled
1 ounce	=	4	tablespoons flour
		2	tablespoons butter
		3	tablespoons yeast
1 pound	=	2¼	cups sugar
		5⅓	cups dry coffee
		6½	cups dry tea
		2½	cups shortening
		2¼	cups packed brown sugar
		9	eggs
		3½	cups flour
		3	cups cauliflower
		3	cups green beans

Metric Conversions

1 ounce	=	28.35	grams
1 pound	=	453.59	grams
1 gram	=	.035	ounces
1 kilogram	=	2.2	pounds
1 teaspoon	=	4.3	milliliters
1 tablespoon	=	14.8	milliliters
1 cup	=	236.6	milliliters
1 pint	=	473.2	milliliters
1 quart	=	.95	liter
1 gallon	=	3.8	liters

Common Substitutions

Buttermilk or sour milk = Yogurt; milk with 1 tablespoon vinegar or lemon juice

1 whole egg = 2 egg yolks plus 1 tablespoon water

1 teaspoon corn starch = 2 tablespoons flour

Lemon juice = Vinegar

Wine = Apple juice, cider, beef or chicken broth

Tomato juice = Equal portions tomato sauce and water

1 tablespoon fresh herb = 1 teaspoon dried herb

Bibliography

Yet if one heart throb higher at its sway, the wizard note has not been touched in vain. Be silent no more, Enchantress wake again!

— Sir Walter Scott

Ainsworth-Davis, James Richard. *Cooking through the Centuries.* Jim Dent and Sons: London, 1931.

Anderson, Diane, Managing Editor. *Cookies, Brownies and Chocolate Galore!* Ottenheimer Publications: Ontario, Canada, 1993.

Bailey, Adrian. *The Blessings of Bread.* Paddington Press: New York, 1975.

Baker, Margaret. *Folklore and Customs of Rural England.* Rowman & Littlefield: Totawa, NJ, 1974.

Bartlett, John. *Familiar Quotations.* Little Brown & Co.: Boston, 1938.

Better Homes & Gardens New Cookbook. Bantam Books: New York, 1979.

Beyerl, Paul. *Master Book of Herbalism.* Phoenix Publishing: Custer, WA, 1984.

Bishop A. and D. Simpson. *Victorian Seaside Cookbook.* Newark Historical Society: Newark, NJ 1983.

Black, William G. *Folk Medicine.* Burt Franklin Co.: New York, 1883.

Boland, Margaret. *Old Wives Lore for Gardeners.* Farrar, Straus & Giroux: New York, 1976.

357

Budge, E.A. Wallis. *Amulets & Talismans*. University Books: New Hyde Park, NY 1968.

Bullfinch's Age of Fable. Rev. Loughran Scott, Editor. David McKay Publishing: Washington Square, PA, 1898.

Chase, A.W., M.D. *Receipt Book & Household Physician*. F.B. Dickerson Company: Detroit, MI, 1908.

Cheng, Rose and Michele Morris. *Chinese Cooking*. Price Stern Sloan: Los Angeles, 1981.

Clarkson, Rosetta. *Green Enchantment*. McMillian Publishing: New York, 1940.

Clifton, C. *Edible Flowers*. McGraw Hill Publishing: New York, 1976.

Colin, Clair. *Kitchen and Table*. Abelard-Schuman: New York, 1964.

The Compleat Anachronist Guide to Brewing. Society for Creative Anachronism: Milpitas, CA 1983.

The Complete Book of Fortune. Crescent Books: New York, 1936.

Cross, Jean. *In Grandmother's Day*. Prentice Hall: Englewood Cliffs, NJ, 1980.

Culpeper, Nicholas. *The Complete Herbal*. W. Foulsham: London, 1952.

Cunningham, Scott. *Encyclopedia of Magical Herbs*. Llewellyn Publications: St. Paul, MN, 1988.

_____. *The Magic in Food*. Llewellyn Publications: St. Paul, MN, 1991.

Davison, Michael Worth, Editor. *Everyday Life Through the Ages*. Reader's Digest Association: London, 1992.

Desol, Paula. *Chinese Astrology*. Warner Books: New York, 1976.

Digbie, Sir Kenelme K. *The Closet Opened*. E.L.T. Brome: London, 1696.

Drury, Nevill. *Dictionary of Mysticism and the Occult*. Harper and Row: New York, 1985.

Dumas, Alexander. *Dictionary of Cuisine*. Simon & Schuster, Inc.: New York, 1958.

Encyclopedia Americana. Americana Corporation: Washington, D.C., 1960.

Encyclopedia of Creative Cooking. Charlotte Turgeon, Editor. Weathervane Press: New York, 1982.

Farb, Peter and George Armelagos. *Consuming Passions: The Anthropology of Eating*. Hougton Mifflin: Boston, 1980.

Farrar, Janet and Stewart. *The Witches' God*. Phoenix Publishing: Custer, WA, 1989.

_____. *The Witches' Goddess*. Phoenix Publishing: Custer, WA, 1989.

Fielding, William J. *Strange Superstitions & Magical Practices*. Paperback Library: New York, 1968.

Fitch, Ed. *The Rites of Odin*. Llewellyn Publications: St. Paul, MN, 1990.

Flower, Barbara and Elizabeth Rosenbaum, Translator. *The Roman Cookery Book*. George G. Harrap & Co.: London,. 1958.

Fox, William, M.D. *Model Botanic Guide to Health*. Sheffield Press: Fargate, 1907.

Frere, Catherine F., Editor. *A Proper Newe Booke of Cokery*. W. Heffer & Sons: Cambridge, England, 1913.

Gayre, R. *Brewing Mead*. Brewer's Publishing: Boulder, CO, 1986.

_____. *Wassail!* Philmore & Company: London, 1948.

Gordon, Leslie. *Green Magic*. Viking Press: New York, 1977.

Green, Stephanie. *Flower Power Ancient Herbal Remedy Cards*. Merrimack Publishing: New York (no date).

Haggard, Howard, M.D. *Mystery, Magic & Medicine*. Double Day and Co.: Garden City, NJ, 1933.

Hale, William. *Horizon Cookbook & Illustrated History of Eating & Drinking through the Ages*. American Heritage Publications Co.: New York, 1968.

Hartley, Dorothy. *Food in England*. MacDonald & Co., Ltd.: London, 1962.

Hechtlinger, Adelaide. *The Seasonal Hearth*. Overlook Press: New York, 1986.

Hobson, Phyllis. *Wine, Beer & Soft Drinks*. Garden Way Publishing: Charlotte, VT, 1976.

Hobson, Wendy, Editor. *The Kitchen Companion*. Tormont Publications: Montreal, Canada, 1992.

Holden, Edith. *Nature Notes of an Edwardian Lady*. Arcade Publishing: New York, 1989.

Home Preserving: Golden Hands Special #14. Marshall Cavendish Corporation: New York, 1976.

Hopping, June W. *Pioneer Lady's Country Kitchen*. Villard Books: New York, 1988.

Hunter, Beatrice. *Fermented Foods & Beverages*. Keats Publishing: New Canaan, CT, 1973.

Hutchinson, Ruth and Ruth Adams. *Every Day's a Holiday*. Harper & Brothers: New York, 1951.

Ickis, Marguerite. *Book of Festival Holidays*. Dodd, Mead & Co.: New York, 1964.

Kowalchick, Claire and William Hyloon, Editors. *Rodale's Complete Illustrated Encyclopedia of Herbs*. Emmaus, PA, 1987.

Leach, Maria, Editor. *Standard Dictionary of Folklore, Mythology and Legend*. Funk & Wagnall: New York, 1972.

Loewe, Michael, Editor. *Oracles & Divination*. Shambhala Publishing: Boulder, CO, 1981.

Lorie, Peter. *Superstition*. Labyrinth Publishing: UK, 1992.

Mangnall, Richard. *Historical and Miscellaneous Questions*. Longman, Brown, Green and Longman's: London, 1850.

McNicol, Mary. *Flower Cookery*. Fleet Press: New York, 1967.

Miller, Gloria Bley. *The Thousand Recipe Chinese Cook Book*. Fireside Books: New York, 1966.

Murray, Keith. *Ancient Rites & Ceremonies*. Tudor Press: Toronto, Canada, 1980.

Murray, Michael T. *The Healing Power of Herbs*. Prima Publishing: Rocklin, CA, 1992.

Napier, Mrs. Alexander. *Noble Boke of Cookry*. Elliot Stock: London, 1882.

Old Farmer's Almanac Hearth & Home Companion. Yankee Publishing: Des Moines, IA, 1993.

Opie, Iona and Moira Tatem, Editors. *Dictionary of Superstition*. Oxford Publishing: New York, 1989.

Riotte, Louise. *Sleeping with a Sunflower*. Garden Way Publishing: Pownal, VT, 1987.

Roden, Claudia. *A Book of Middle Eastern Foods*. Random House: New York, 1968.

Rose, Jeanee. *Jeanne Rose's Herbal Guide to Food*. North Atlantic Books: Berkeley, CA, 1989.

Rosengarten, Frederick. *Book of Spices*. Pyramid Books: New York, 1975.

Ryall, Rhiannon. *West Country Wicca*. Phoenix Publishing: Custer, WA, 1989.

Sams, Jamie and David Carson. *Medicine Cards*. Bear & Company: Santa Fe, NM 1988.

Sanecki, Kay. *History of the English Herb Garden*. Wark Lock Villiers House: London, 1992.

Silverman, Eleanor. *Trash into Treasure*. Scarecrow Press: Metuchen, NJ, 1982.

Singer, Charles. *From Magic to Science*. Dover Books: NY, 1958.

Stafford, Lord Edward. *The Form of Curry.* J. Nichols Co.: London, 1780.

Stark, Marcia. *Natural Healing.* Llewellyn Publications: St. Paul, MN, 1991.

SummerRain, Mary. *Earthway.* Pocket Books: New York, 1990.

Spayde, Jon. *Japanese Cooking.* Chartwell Books: Secaucus, NJ, 1984.

Tannahill, Reay. *Food in History.* Stein & Day: New York, 1973.

Telesco, Patricia. *Folkways.* Llewellyn Publications: St. Paul, MN, 1994.

_____. *A Victorian Flower Oracle.* Llewellyn Publications: St. Paul, MN, 1994.

_____. *A Victorian Grimoire.* Llewellyn Publications: St. Paul, MN, 1992.

Tillona, P. *Feast of Flowers.* Funk & Wagnall: New York, 1969.

Tuleja, Tad. *Curious Customs.* Harmony Books: New York, 1987.

Walker, Barbara. *Women's Dictionary of Symbols & Sacred Objects.* Harper & Row Publishing: San Francisco, CA, 1988.

Watson, Betty. *Cooks, Gluttons & Gourmets.* Doubleday & Co.: New York, 1962.

Williams, Jude. *Jude's Herbal.* Llewellyn Publications: St. Paul, MN, 1992.

Wootton, A. *Animal Folklore, Myth & Legend.* Blanford Press: New York, 1986.

Younger, William. *Gods, Men & Wine.* World Publishing: Cleveland, OH, 1966.

Index

A man who is careful with his palate
is not likely to be careless with his paragraphs.

— Clifton Fadiman

363

CELTIC FOLKLORE COOKING

Joanne Asala

Celtic cooking is simple and tasty, reflecting the quality of its ingredients: fresh meat and seafood, rich milk and cream, fruit, vegetables, and wholesome bread. Much of the folklore, proverbs, songs, and legends of the Celtic nations revolve around this wonderful variety of food and drink. Now you can feast upon these delectable stories as you sample more than 200 tempting dishes with *Celtic Folklore Cooking*.

     In her travels to Ireland, Wales, and Scotland, Joanne Asala found that many people still cook in the traditional manner, passing recipes from generation to generation. Now you can serve the same dishes discovered in hotels, bed and breakfasts, restaurants, and family kitchens. At the same time, you can relish in the colorful proverbs, songs, and stories that are still heard at pubs and local festivals and that complement each recipe.

1-56718-044-2, 264 pp., 7 x 10, illus. $19.95